ABANDONED

The true story of love, madness, murder and survival on Clipperton Island

John Watts

Author's Note

Although written as a novel, this book is based on historical fact. All of the significant events actually happened and all of the main characters were real people. Only the dialogue and some of the detail is invented for the sake of narrative flow.

CHAPTER 1

The mountains were invisible, shrouded in a mantle of swirling mist. The *chipichipi*, the persistent light drizzle of Orizaba, high in the mountains of southern México, fell from a leaden sky. The priest threw the first handful of wet earth onto the coffin. It made a terrible, hollow sound as though there were nothing at all inside. Ramón Arnaud and his sister, Adela, stood in grim silence at their father's grave. Their mother, Doña Carlota, stood between them, her body quaking with grief. The mayor of Orizaba, all the city's leading businessmen and half the population stood in the rain with the Arnaud family to honor Don Miguel.

Doña Carlota staggered slightly as they turned and walked through the clinging mud away from the open grave. Already, the coffin was sitting in a pool of water. A sudden rage came over Ramón as he stopped to look back at the two *indio* grave diggers leaning on their shovels beneath the ancient, dripping trees of the cemetery. Fill it in, you fools, he thought, he is getting wet in this rain. The idiocy of it struck him like a blow and he turned and strode after his mother.

Ramón put his arm around Doña Carlota's shoulders to steady her. He looked over her bowed head and, for a moment, his eyes met Adela's. She had the same vacant look that haunted his mother's face. It had all happened so suddenly. There had been no warning; no time to prepare themselves for the terrible emptiness and the uncertain future they now faced.

Almost twenty-five years earlier, in 1878, the French brig Sophie had rolled her way across the Gulf of México toward the setting sun. Their modest evening meal eaten, the handful of passengers lounged on deck, gossiping in low voices. The ship rose and fell with a hypnotic rhythm while, overhead, the incomprehensible tangle of sails and rigging creaked a low complaint. The flock of gulls that had been with them since daybreak had left only minutes earlier, flying low up the path of the sun.

"But what if it is all jungle? What does any of us know of México? I should never have left Lyon." Charbonneau, the fat baker, had annoyed them with his doubts almost from the moment they had left France, seven weeks before.

The tall, dangerous-looking one with the wildly hooked nose, Gaspard, spat noisily into the sea alongside, wiped his lips with the back of his hand and barked out a laugh. "It is not all jungle, René. You are forgetting the deserts." They all laughed, all except Charbonneau.

The baker wagged a sausage-shaped finger at them. "Yes, laugh at me. Perhaps you are right, Monsieur Gaspard. Perhaps it is not all jungle but will the Mexicans ever forgive us for invading their country? How will they treat us?"

Gaspard hawked overboard noisily. "You are like an old woman," he said contemptuously. "You worry about crossing the ocean. You worry about the jungle. The invasion is long forgotten. There are thousands of Frenchmen living in México now. The Mexicans want us to invest our money. We are welcome there."

The sun had gone and the deck was in darkness. Charbonneau watched the moonlight illuminating the furrow the Sophie was plowing through the still waters of the Gulf. He heard the low murmur of the captain's voice as he spoke to the helmsman. Charbonneau looked over his shoulder and saw the captain's gaunt features illuminated briefly in the glow of his pipe. The comforting smell of the tobacco was oddly familiar. It reminded him of the smell of the inn across the street from his bakery in Lyon where, every afternoon, it had been his custom to wash away the heat of the ovens with a single glass of wine. The captain knocked the dottle from his pipe and sent it hissing into the sea as he joined the passengers at the rail. "Gentlemen," he said, "if you would care to look over our bows, you will have your first glimpse of México."

They turned to look forward beneath the sails, straining their eyes against the inky blackness of sea and sky. Slowly it came into focus; a faint white triangle, apex uppermost, glowing low in the distance. "You see it now, gentlemen?" asked the captain. "That is Pico de Orizaba, the highest mountain in México, more than five thousand meters."

The passengers stared ahead intently, saying nothing. The captain looked at each in turn. This lot were much like the other Frenchmen he had deposited, most of them bewildered and uncertain, on the docks in the steaming heat of Veracruz. Each had his own reasons for leaving France for the strange land that lay over the Sophie's bows and it amused the captain to attempt to discover each passenger's story.

As far as he had been able to find out, Gaspard, for all his dangerous appearance, was simply bored with life in France and seeking adventure. A few, like Charbonneau, were escaping from failed businesses or failed marriages or oppressive families. At least one passenger had boarded the Sophie at the dock in Brest under an assumed name with forged papers. The captain smiled to himself. That one wouldn't be changing his mind and going back to France with the Sophie.

"When will we arrive in Veracruz, Captain?" asked Michel Arnaud, breaking his silence for the first time since dinner. The captain looked at him appraisingly. Arnaud never said much. While the others joked and laughed and argued, the tall, aristocratic-looking Arnaud remained aloof.

"Not for two days, Monsieur Arnaud. More if the wind dies or shifts to the west."

"But how is it possible that it could take two days?" asked Arnaud. "We can see land already."

"What you see, Monsieur Arnaud, is moonlight reflecting

from the snow on the peak of the volcano. Tomorrow, in the daylight, you will see nothing but the sea. We have a long way to sail before we are in Veracruz."

Arnaud turned again to look at the tiny glowing triangle. "Is the volcano active, Captain?"

"Not that I know of, Monsieur. There is a very fine town, Orizaba, in the valley beneath it, so perhaps not."

"I know something of Orizaba," said Arnaud. "I am from the town of Barcelonnette in the Alpes-de-Haute-Provence and many Barcelonnettes, as we are known, now live in Orizaba. I am told that the climate is agreeable and the land fertile."

Unlikely as it had seemed to Arnaud at the time, the captain had been right. Two days passed before a battered steam tug took the Sophie's lines outside the breakwaters of Veracruz and towed her to the crowded anchorage. The passengers stood on the deck, their chatter mingling with the chaotic sounds of the harbor. The heat was tremendous, almost a solid presence in the air and quite unlike anything Arnaud had experienced. He leaned back against the Sophie's deck house, trying to keep in the shade. Ships flying the flags of Great Britain, the United States, Germany and a dozen other countries lay at anchor in the harbor. Warehouses and government buildings stood shoulder to shoulder along the waterfront.

At the north end of the harbor, a great stone fortress brooded on its own island. Arnaud gestured toward it and asked the captain, "What on earth is that? It looks like something from the Dark Ages."

The Sophie's captain leaned against the deck house and nodded. "You are not so far wrong there, Monsieur Arnaud. The name in Spanish is Fuerte de San Juan de Ulúa. The Spaniards built it early in the seventeenth century to protect their treasure ships and the port from pirates. These days, of course, it has quite a different use."

Arnaud looked again at the grim structure and shuddered. "What purpose could such a place have now, except perhaps as

4

a museum?"

"Ah," said the captain. "You have much to learn about México, Monsieur Arnaud. President Díaz does not treat with kid gloves those who would dare oppose him. Any who are so foolish are condemned to live in perpetual darkness in the cells of the fort. It is said that they are so small that the prisoners can never lie down, even to sleep. When the tide comes in, they sit up to their necks in the stinking water of the harbor."

The captain saw Arnaud's look of disbelief, shrugged and went on. "You will discover that the Mexicans have colorful names for everything. Two of the dungeons in the fort are called El Purgatorio and El Infierno. I leave it to your imagination to picture what they must be like, Monsieur. I have heard it said that they are so damp that stalactites grow from their ceilings."

Arnaud frowned, shaking his head. "But who are these prisoners, Captain? What are their crimes to be imprisoned in such a place?"

"Who knows? They could be imprudent newspaper editors or overly zealous labor leaders; anyone who dares to oppose President Díaz. He has a system. The Mexicans call it *pan o palo*, bread or the club. If you support President Díaz, you will have bread, you will prosper. If you oppose him, you will feel the club or worse yet, spend the rest of your days in a cell in the Fuerte de San Juan de Ulúa."

Once settled ashore, Arnaud devoted himself to learning as much as he could about this strange new country that was to be his home. During the days, he explored the bustling streets and squares of Veracruz. He spent hours in the municipal library, learning all he could of the city and of México and its history. His Spanish improved so quickly that he surprised himself by carrying on simple conversations with merchants, waiters and passersby on the streets. Each night, Arnaud dined with one or two of the Frenchmen from the Sophie on the freshly caught seafood in which the restaurants of Veracruz gloried. Pleasantly tired from his explorations, he returned each night to his room in the imposing Hotel Imperial on the Plaza de Armas. He had scarcely thought about France since setting foot ashore.

Shortly before Arnaud's arrival in Veracruz, the rail line from the country's biggest port to the capital had been completed. The new line passed through Córdoba and Orizaba on its way to México, as the capital was universally known. Arnaud took the overnight train, arriving at dawn on a Saturday morning, well-rested and eager to explore.

Beyond doubt, the capital was impressive: a city of monumental cathedrals and public buildings, great parks and grand boulevards lined with the mansions of the wealthy, quite a few of them Barcelonnettes who had prospered in their new homeland. With the enthusiastic approval of the Francophile Porfirio Díaz, they had transformed much of the capital into a Paris of the New World. But there were also slums of the vilest kind, surpassing in squalor anything Arnaud had seen in France. The masses of humanity on the streets evoked in him a grim claustrophobia he had never before experienced. There were business opportunities in the Mexican capital, to be sure and Arnaud explored several of them with fellow Barcelonnettes, but the city was much too big and much too crowded for his taste.

On his way to the capital, Arnaud had been tempted to get off in Orizaba to explore the town in the mountains where so many Barcelonnettes had settled, perhaps because it reminded them so strongly of home. But it had been dark and he had decided to continue on to the capital. But having seen the capital, Arnaud decided that Orizaba might be more to his taste.

The air grew drier and cooler as the train climbed gradually into the heavily wooded mountains. Looking across the width of the first-class carriage, Arnaud could see the perfectly symmetrical, snow-covered peak of the volcano. The brand new British-built steam locomotive made easy work of the long grades as it climbed higher and higher, crossing deep river gorges on timber trestles and stone bridges. The train rounded a curve, the side of the mountain dropping off precipitously on Arnaud's side of the train. Suddenly, spread out far below, as though in miniature, was the city of Orizaba, nestled in its valley.

It was the most astonishingly verdant, perfect place Arnaud had seen since leaving Barcelonnette. The mountain air was clean and fresh. The icy waters of the Río Blanco rushed headlong down the mountain and past the town. Smaller streams tumbled beneath a score of bridges. Along the banks of the Rio Blanco stood rambling *haciendas* surrounded by elaborate gardens spilling over in gardenias, orchids, camellias and azaleas. The cultivated lands of the valley spread all around in a patchwork of such consummate beauty that, to Arnaud's eye, it looked like a fanciful illustration in a children's book. Over the valley, the mountains rose heavily treed toward the clouds. And, towering over everything, the majestic white cone of Pico de Orizaba.

Knowing, even before the train had hissed to a stop in the new railway station, that Orizaba was everything he had dreamed of finding, Arnaud resolved to stay. After telegraphing to Veracruz for his belongings, he moved into the hotel near the station and took a room overlooking the courtyard. During the mornings, he met with French businessmen seeking partners or capital. The evenings he spent in the elegant little Parque del Castillo, the main square in front of the parish Church of San Miguel. Sometimes he would play a game of chess or dominoes before moving to a café near the square for a glass of wine or, as the autumn wore on and the evenings grew cool, a warming cup of chocolate.

Each night, he watched with fascination as the young men and women of the town promenaded around the square in opposite directions in their ages-old mating ritual. Each Sunday, he attended Mass at the Church of San Miguel and, afterwards, strolled among the immaculately laid-out flowerbeds in the Alameda Park. It never occurred to him to leave.

"There it is, Monsieur Arnaud, what do you think?"

Arnaud looked thoughtfully at the heavyset man across the table in the hotel's dining room. Ángel Jiménez's dark brows met in the middle, giving him an almost simian quality, but his eyes were bright and intelligent. Arnaud tapped the papers in front of him. "I must confess I am impressed, Señor Jiménez."

Jiménez gestured for the waiter and smiled. "There is no time like the present, Monsieur Arnaud. Orizaba is going to be the most prosperous city in México, you mark my words. Put your money to work here."

Arnaud smiled. "I agree that the time is right for me to make an investment. I have looked at a dozen or more businesses and, to be sure, many have promise. The textile mills are bringing a fortune into Orizaba. I like your proposal, Señor Jiménez. Let us join together and make El Urbano the most profitable street railway in México."

Life in México was better than Arnaud had ever allowed himself to dream, even in his most optimistic moments before leaving France. The town hummed night and day with the sound of prosperity. Barcelonnette capital had financed the huge textile mills that drew their power from the waters of the Río Blanco. Orizaba's mills were so large and productive that the city had become known as the Manchester of México. Businesses flourished in coffee, tobacco and flower cultivation, in merchandising, transportation, printing and brewing. The street railway was an extraordinary success, carrying hundreds of thousands of passengers and tens of thousands of tonnes of freight each year. Over the years, its tracks were extended to Río Blanco, Nogales, Santa Ana, Santa Rosa and Cerritos. Arnaud found himself searching out other businesses in which to invest his profits, among them a working *hacienda* on the banks of the Río Blanco.

But such success did not come by accident. Arnaud had never forgotten the words of the captain of the Sophie and had been quick to benefit from President Díaz's policy of rewarding his supporters. Arnaud and his partners depended on the continuing goodwill of the Mexican president, of the state governor who was appointed by Díaz and of the local political boss appointed by the governor, to operate their many businesses. Arnaud went to great lengths to be recognized as a steadfast and generous supporter of Presidente Don Porfirio Díaz.

Arnaud had also taken care to avoid any hint of chauvinism. Certainly, he drank French wines and ate French food and read French books, as did those native-born Mexicans who aspired to things European and whose pockets were sufficiently deep. But Arnaud worked diligently at improving his Spanish and soon spoke the language with only a trace of a French accent. He took the Spanish spelling of his own Christian name and was known to all as Miguel Arnaud. Arnaud thought of himself as an Orizabeño and a Mexican, proud of his city and of his adopted country. México had been very good to him over the years and, he liked to think, he had been good for México. In 1901, El Urbano had retired its mules and powered its trams with gasoline engines, putting Orizaba firmly in the forefront of Mexican cities, ahead even of the capital, that still had its horse-drawn trams five years later.

Arnaud was blessed with the perfect wife, Carlota Vignon, a native Mexican of French ancestry, who was both devoted and beautiful. Their children were raised in an atmosphere of refinement and elegance. Adela, fine boned and aristocratic-looking, had excellent marriage prospects and Ramón was rapidly developing into a cultured and sophisticated young man and a talented linguist. Arnaud had high hopes for Ramón. The boy stood tall and ramrod straight, his chestnut eyes bright with a lively intelligence. Unlike most of his contemporaries, who were little more than wild-eyed rakes,

Ramón had not been spoiled by the affluence into which he had been born. While the other boys devoted themselves to interminable drinking and gambling and whoring, Ramón spent his time more profitably, learning English, French and German, studying history and acquiring a taste for music, literature, the theater and ballet.

The rain-soaked winter following Miguel Arnaud's funeral was seemingly without end but at last spring came and the flowerbeds of Orizaba once again exploded in color and scent and the mood in the Arnaud home began to lift. The night before, Ramón had made a feeble joke and Doña Carlota had laughed, timorously at first, then with gusto. Ramón had laughed with her and the two had looked at each other in surprise, then laughed all the harder until the tears rolled down their faces. And, tonight, for the first time since the funeral four long, terrible months ago, there was music in the house.

Doña Carlota was in the foyer, meeting with the lawyer to go over the details of Señor Arnaud's estate. Ramón had taken out his mandolin and played quietly while Adela sang in her clear soprano. They heard Doña Carlota in the hallway, bidding goodnight to the lawyer. There came the sound of the front door closing, followed by long silence. Ramón put down his mandolin and opened the door to the hallway. His mother was slumped against the wall, her head in her hands, crying.

"Mamá, what is it? What is wrong?" he asked, alarmed.

"Ramón," she sobbed, "we are ruined. The money is gone. All of your father's estate is gone. We have nothing."

Ramón shook his head. "No, Mamá, there has been some mistake. Papá left a fortune. You know that."

Doña Carlota took a handkerchief from her sleeve and wiped her eyes. "It is that snake Herrera. I warned your father not to make him executor. I never trusted him when he did your father's accounts. I never trusted him!" She almost screamed it. "But Papá said he was so clever with money. He has sold

10

everything and hidden all the money. Taken everything and disappeared. Señor Fuentes has alerted the *policía* but they think he has left the country. There is nothing left but the house. It is the only thing Herrera could not steal."

In the gloomy evenings, Ramón sipped coffee until well past midnight. He could never bring himself to sit in his father's chair that sat empty at his elbow. There was still a depression in the cushion where his father sat talking and laughing and singing so many long nights ago. The path of Ramón's life had always seemed to him to be as firmly fixed as the trolley tracks that ran so profitably through the streets of Orizaba. He would study literature and music and poetry and foreign languages until the time came for him to enter his father's business. He would learn everything at his father's right hand and, when Don Miguel retired, he would take over the Arnaud family businesses. But everything had changed. It was a disaster. Herrera had been seen boarding a German freighter in Veracruz. They would never find him or the money.

The terrible, humiliating specter of poverty hung over the Arnaud family. Ramón would have to earn a living, make his own way in the world, without his father's guidance and wealth. But how? What skills did he have? What could he do? Almost daily now, the creditors knocked on the door of the Arnaud house demanding payment of their bills. Ramón watched with growing alarm as Doña Carlota's proud face grew drawn and lined with worry. The cruelest moment of all came when they had to dismiss the servants. Most had been with the family for years: the gardener and cook since before Ramón and Adela were born.

But, in the midst of despair, there was good news. Adela became formally engaged to León Reyes, the son of General Bernardo Reyes, Porfirio Díaz's Minister of War and a state governor. At least, Adela would never have to worry about money. But what would happen to Ramón and to Doña Carlota? The solution came to him as he sat alone in the courtyard one afternoon reading yet another polite but firm letter from a merchant demanding payment of an outstanding debt. Only a few months before, these same merchants had groveled for the Arnaud family's business. Now, they made thinly veiled threats. How he would love to teach them a lesson they would never forget.

And then it came to him; he would teach. He would use his facility with languages to earn money as a teacher. He should have thought of it before. His French and English were faultless and his German quite passable. Surely he could make enough money as a teacher to keep the family's creditors at bay

It was absurdly easy. The wealthy families of Orizaba were eager to have their children learn French and English. To be fluent in the great European languages was a sign of refinement and success. And, in spite of his family's misfortune, Ramón was still one of them. He could be entrusted with the education of their precious children. In the days, he taught the children of the well-to-do and, in the evenings, read poetry and played the mandolin as Adela sang. But, try as he might, the money was never enough. The bills came faster than he could pay them. And, sometimes, the expression on Doña Carlota's face was more than he could bear. He knew how much it must pain her to have her only son working as the teacher of her friends' children and grandchildren. He knew only too well that she had had much higher hopes for him.

With each passing week, the meals grew smaller and meaner. The seven-course suppers of his father's day that had occupied an entire evening, sometimes going on into the small hours of the morning, were a dim memory. Sometimes, it seemed that they had never happened at all. One evening, after a particularly sparse meal, Doña Carlota took Ramón's arm and guided him into the small reception room at the front of the house. She sat him down and stood before him, nervously twining a handkerchief around her fingers. "We will have to sell the house, Ramón," she said suddenly. "We cannot keep a house of this size with only one servant girl. I know you have tried, Ramón, and may God bless you for it, but you can never earn enough with your lessons."

Ramón looked up at his mother for a moment before speaking. "But your lovely house, Mamá. Papá's house. What will you do? Where will you go?"

"I must be sensible, Ramón. I will buy a small villa. Then, I will have enough money to live out my years in dignity, something I cannot do here. I simply cannot stand this scraping about for a few *pesos* to pay the butcher or the electricity bill."

Doña Carlota's hands wrung the handkerchief into a tight ball. Ramón saw her knuckles turning white. "Soon, we will have to use oil lamps again. It is humiliating. It is too much. I cannot bear it anymore."

"I am sorry, Mamá. I have disappointed you. I should have done better. I should have worked harder," said Ramón, his throat constricting.

"No, Ramón. You have made me very proud. Your father would have been proud of you too. But you must have a career that will lead to a future for you. What prospects do you have as a teacher?"

"None, Mamá. You know that."

"Exactly. Señor and Señora Galván are among the few who will still speak to me in public. Their son, Adolfo, is at the Military College in México. He will graduate as an officer and, with the friends they have, he should do very well in the Army. Now that Adela is to marry the son of General Reyes, you could have a fine career in the Army, with his help."

"Yes, Mamá. But it costs a small fortune to go to the Military College. We could never afford it."

"Then, you must start at the bottom, Ramón. Señor Galván says that with your education, you would be made a sergeant immediately. You would become an officer in no time at all.

13

With General Reyes to help you, there is no telling how far you might go."

Ramón cringed at the thought of it. He, Ramón Arnaud Vignon, poet, linguist, mandolin player, devotee of the arts, in the Army? Had there ever been a more unlikely soldier in the whole history of the world? But, there was no point in arguing. Doña Carlota's mind was made up. He knew there would be no changing it. And, in any case, she was right. There really was no alternative. What future was there for him as a teacher? There was simply nothing else for him to do.

CHAPTER 2

At the age of twenty-two, Ramón Arnaud became a First Sergeant in the Seventh Regiment of Cavalry of the Ejército Mexicano, the Army of México. The first few weeks went surprisingly well. True, many of the officers were vicious petty tyrants and the men a gaggle of illiterate peasants but Arnaud was given the surprisingly pleasant duty of inspecting the sprawling regimental stables. For most of the day, he could escape the tedious routine of the garrison in the cool, dark stables, deliciously fragrant with straw and fresh-cut hay. He had always liked horses and spent the days affectionately slapping their gleaming flanks and examining the freshly polished tack laid out neatly for his inspection. His letters to Doña Carlota and Adela were written in a tone of pleasant surprise.

Then, without warning, his luck changed and he was assigned to one of the desert patrols. He sat shivering in the icy darkness of the nighttime desert, his knees clenched to his chest in a futile effort to keep warm, his uniform filthy, his stomach achingly empty, his hair hanging in lank, greasy strands. The sour smell of his own unwashed body filled his nostrils. He sat away from the fire, unable to bring himself to eat the disgusting mess of rancid beans and *tortillas* his men were wolfing down with animal grunts and smacking lips. To supplement their meager rations, they had speared a lizard and he could hear the obscene sound of its skin crackling and splitting as it blackened in the fire. Ramón had lost weight and often felt lightheaded but his gnawing hunger could not overcome his revulsion at the food.

Occasionally, he stole a glance at the men. Like him, they

were dirty and smelled to high heaven. About half were *mestizos*, part-Indian, part-Spanish. The rest were full-blooded *indios*, a few Yaqui, half a dozen Nahua, some Tzotzil and a random sampling of other Indian races whose ancestors had somehow survived the Spanish *conquistadors* and then the Catholic priests. They were men of sudden and startling brutality who carried out their orders to kill and maim with a strange, detached ferocity. And, God, how they hated him. He could feel it in every look they gave him and every word they spoke. He was white. The color of his skin granted him privileges they would never enjoy, could scarcely imagine.

He, at least, had joined the Army voluntarily, fool that he was. Every one of the twenty-six men in his platoon had been forced at gunpoint into the Ejército Mexicano. Every one had been torn from his home and family, from his ancestral lands, from his way of life and forced to become a *federale*. Forced to obey the orders to torture and kill or be shot on the spot by the officers. It was hardly surprising that the men despised him; they would almost certainly kill him if they got the chance and could get away with it. How could they understand that he hated the Army as much as they did? How could they know that he detested the sadistic and corrupt officers as much as they did? Officers who beat the men viciously for the slightest infraction, real or imagined. Officers who stole most of the *soldados'* ration allowance to fill their own pockets and bought food unfit for pigs with the remaining pittance. All any of the men wanted was to be back with their families, growing their beans and corn. And all Ramón wanted was to be back in Orizaba, studying his books, listening to poetry readings in the Parque del Castillo, attending concerts and operettas at the Teatro Llave and playing his mandolin.

The lizard was torn to pieces and eaten noisily. The smell of burning marijuana filled the freezing desert air. Soon, most of the men would be intoxicated with it, barely conscious. The others would be drinking the poisonous alcohol they always carried with them. The officers did nothing to stop it. If anything, they encouraged it. The marijuana and alcohol were the mental anesthetics that made the men's lives somehow endurable and, taken in such huge quantities, had the useful side-effect, from the Army's point of view, of obliterating any conscience the men possessed.

Ramón pulled his thin blanket around himself and lay shivering on the frigid sand. One of the horses stamped and whinnied. Overhead, the stars glinted like slivers of ice as they wheeled through the freezing, moonless sky. Ramón sobbed quietly. How in the name of God could he have been so reckless as to join the Army? What on Earth had he been thinking? He had already applied for a release and the notice of rejection was crumpled in his pocket. There was no way out.

Eight long, agonizing months passed before his opportunity came. With two men, he had taken a group of prisoners—runaway slaves from the plantations—into Villahermosa. It had taken five days, each prisoner a pathetic, half-starved *indio* with a noose around his neck as required by regulations, half-dragged the whole way by the horses. They had transferred the prisoners to the local *policía* in the late afternoon and, seeing his chance for freedom, Ramón had allowed his two men to go into a *pulquería*. In an hour or two, he knew, they would drink themselves insensible with *pulque*, the milky, sour cactus liquor. They would probably be unconscious until the following morning when, finding Arnaud gone, they would probably desert themselves. Whatever happened, it would be several days before anyone in the Army realized that he had deserted. By then, he would be lost in the teeming streets of the capital. The Army would never find him there. He would find work and start again; a new life with a new name.

It had been ridiculously easy. He had had two months' pay in his money belt, enough to buy civilian clothes and a train ticket to México, with ten *pesos* left over. At first, he was sure everyone in the second-class carriage must know he was a deserter but, as darkness fell and the train rattled through the night, he relaxed and finally fell into an exhausted sleep. Stepping from the train in México in the early morning, the same feelings overwhelmed him. It seemed that everyone was looking at him. They must know that he was a deserter. He must go only to places where he was not known. If anyone recognized him, he was lost. He walked quickly away from the station into the dingy side streets. Even if he had enough money to stay in a good hotel, it would be far too dangerous. Instead, he walked the streets until he stood in front of a small, run-down commercial hotel. He was about to open the door and go in when fear gripped him. They would want to know where his luggage was. They would ask for his identification papers. The *policía* might even check small hotels such as this.

He walked quickly away, the streets growing dirtier and the buildings more decrepit. Hawkers were everywhere, but they ignored him. Half-dead chickens hung by their feet in front of squalid stalls. Beggars, mutilated by disease, accident or war, squatted everywhere on the sidewalks, their filthy palms outstretched. The *pulquerías*, selling their rank liquor from wooden barrels, were open. Already, the dark taprooms were busy with ragged, dirty men searching for oblivion in the *pulque*. Ramón had drunk *pulque* once, on a bet, and the sour smell wafting out of the taprooms made his stomach heave with the memory. He knew that *pulque* had been such a popular drink of the Aztecs that they passed laws prohibiting its use by men under sixty. First offenders had their heads shaved. Second offenders had their houses burned to the ground. Third offenders were executed along with their entire families.

There were no laws in Porfirio Díaz's México against drinking *pulque. A* mental anesthetic could be as useful in the civilian population as in the military. But there were risks. The *pulquerías* were a favored hunting ground of the *engancizadores*, the men who, euphemistically known as labor agents, provided the slaves to the tobacco planters of the Valle Nacional. A man who passed out in a *pulquería* was very likely to wake up, under guard, on a train bound south for El Hule. From there, he would be marched through the jungle to the tobacco plantations. His chances of living through the first year were less than one in twenty. The biggest tobacco planters in the Valle Nacional were the Balsa Brothers, Ramón remembered. His father had been fond of their cigars. At least as good as the finest Havanas, Don Miguel had been fond of saying, and less than half the cost.

What Ramón would not give for a good cigar now. He felt for the money belt at his waist. There was no money for cigars. He must spend what he had wisely. Ten *pesos* would not last long. He wandered the streets in a haze of indecision, stopping in front of half a dozen small hotels and rooming houses. Each time, fear rose up and he walked away hurriedly. As dusk fell, he found himself deep in the worst part of the capital. He was hungry and tired and scared. His legs could barely carry him. He must find somewhere to sleep.

In desperation, he went into a *mesón,* one of the thousands of tumbledown buildings where the luckier poor of México spent their nights. Here, they would not ask for identification. He gave the proprietor ten *centavos* and found a place on the dirty floor between an old *indio* with a hacking cough and a young woman, sweating with fever, clutching two small children to her body. There were at least a hundred people sprawled on the floor: men, women, children, newborn babies. He lay down and curled into a ball, smelling the unwashed bodies around him, the *pulque* fumes, the stink of vomit. The sounds were worse: the old *indio* coughing, babies screaming and, from the far corner, the sound of retching. In minutes, he fell into an exhausted sleep.

When Ramón awoke, daylight filtered reluctantly through the grimy windows high overhead. He was so stiff, he could barely move. He sat up gingerly and rubbed the small of his back; his money belt was gone. He looked around in alarm. The building was almost empty. He got painfully to his feet and limped to the doorway. The proprietor, a fat unshaven man with pendulous jowls, sat in a broken wooden chair smoking the stub of a cigar.

"Señor, I have been robbed," said Ramón, his voice quavering.

The proprietor slowly raised red-rimmed eyes, blew out a cloud of smoke and spread his hands in resignation. "These things happen, Señor. I am not responsible."

"But you must do something. They have taken all the money I had."

"I am not responsible. What would you have me do, Señor, call the *policía*?"

"No!" Ramón knew at once that he had said it too quickly. He shook his head, again too quickly. Calm, he must remain calm. "No, Señor. No. Please do not trouble yourself. The money is gone. It will accomplish nothing to bother the *policía*."

The proprietor raised a skeptical eyebrow and looked at Ramón with growing curiosity. "You do not look like the usual guest of my humble establishment, Señor. You have the look of a gentleman about you."

Ramón took a step back. "Good day, Señor," he blurted and rushed through the door and out into the safety of the crowds on the street.

Ramón walked for hours without realizing where he was going. What could he do now? He couldn't sleep on the streets. The *policía* would get him or worse, the *engancizadores*. To escape from the Army, only to die as a slave on a tobacco plantation; it was too much. He was losing his mind. How could this be happening? The sudden rattle of a tram startled him. He quickly crossed the tracks in front of the tram and found himself on the enormous square of the Zócalo. He must be careful. Everyone who came to México sooner or later came to the Zócalo. He might be seen by someone he knew. No one must know he was here.

The heavy twin spires of the Metropolitan Cathedral towered above him. The place where the cathedral stood had, four centuries earlier, been the House of the Gods, the political and religious center of the Aztec world. Shortly before Cortés invaded, the Aztec priests had, on this spot, conducted sacrifices to dedicate a new temple. Slaves and prisoners of war were marched two abreast to the temple. Shifts of priests with flint knives cut the hearts from their living bodies. The priests threw the hearts, still beating, at the feet of the image of their supreme god, Huitzilopotchli, the god of sun and of war. After seventy thousand victims had been sacrificed, the priests had been forced to stop, too exhausted to carry on.

On the Zócalo, the first European hospital, library and church in the New World had been built. Now, the massive square was the heart of the new México—the México of Porfirio Díaz and his *científicos*. A México where science, reason and, above all, the balance sheet, were at last triumphant over religious delusion, superstition and sentiment.

Arnaud stopped and looked up at the Cathedral. In the morning light, the white marble reliefs stood out sharply against the old gray stone. The front doors were wide open and Arnaud could see the ancient sloping stone floors inside. He thought of going in. He hadn't prayed since he was a child. After all, who or what was there to pray to? But, if ever there was a time for prayer, he thought, this was it.

He was distracted by the sound of hoofbeats echoing across the Zócalo. A fine, open carriage was drawing up in front of the National Palace. Four mounted Presidential Guard were motionless behind. Ramón moved into the shadows beside the Cathedral and watched. In the carriage sat the unmistakable figure of Don Porfirio Díaz himself, white hair pushing out from beneath a gleaming top hat. Ramón watched as the liveryman opened the carriage door and helped the president alight and enter the National Palace. The old man moved slowly, using his cane. Soon, Ramón knew, Don Porfirio would be sitting in his elaborately carved throne, receiving petitioners, those who had the three thousand *pesos* El Presidente charged for an audience. Ramón waited in the shadows until the carriage pulled away, the Guard trotting behind. He looked about anxiously. He must get some money and get away from this place.

The only thing of value he possessed was his service revolver; at least they hadn't stolen that in the *mesón*. He walked quickly off the Zócalo and along the side of the Cathedral to the Monte de Piedad, the government pawn shop. The mousy little clerk examined the revolver with interest but asked no awkward questions and gave Ramón twelve *pesos*. Ramón signed the chit with the first name that came into his head. It wasn't until he was walking out the door that he remembered that Jorge Pérez was the name of the old apothecary in Orizaba.

The money in his pocket was more than he had brought to México. It would be enough to keep him until he found work but he must be careful. He couldn't afford to lose this money too. Ramón strode quickly away from the area of the Zócalo. He would be safer in the anonymous backstreets. He passed a sidewalk letter writer hunched over his portable desk. For a small fee, he would read or write a letter for those unable to do so for themselves. Perhaps, thought Ramón, he would become a letter writer. He could work anonymously. No one would ask for identification. He wondered how many letters he would have to write a day to survive.

A powerful hand gripped his upper arm. Ramón spun around to find himself facing three *policía*. The one who held his arm so fiercely growled, "You are under arrest." Ramón's heart almost stopped. His knees buckled and he sagged against one of the men. He was finished. The penalty for desertion was death by firing squad. They pulled him to his feet and marched him through the streets to the Ciudadela, the central federal army garrison. How could he have been such a fool? The clerk in the pawn shop must have a list of serial numbers of stolen or missing Army weapons. He had reported to the *policía* on the Zócalo the instant Ramón had left. If they didn't already know that he was Ramón Arnaud, the deserter, they would soon find out. Then they would execute him.

CHAPTER 3

The mornings in the Ciudadela were the worst. He lay on the thin, insect-ridden straw mattress in his cell, shivering, wide-awake, waiting, barely breathing. When it finally came, the rolling crash of rifle fire made his heart leap into his throat. Then, the gunfire reverberated around the courtyard endlessly. He buried his head beneath his arms, desperate to escape the horrible sound that seemed to go on and on. The mornings when the gunfire didn't come were no better. Then there was hour after hour of agonized anticipation as he waited for another deserter, someone like him, to die in front of the pockmarked bricks. He knew there was no mercy in the Ejército Mexicano. He knew there would be no mercy for Ramón Arnaud.

When, at last, his court-martial was convened, it was over in less than five minutes. He was permitted no lawyer, he was not allowed to make any defense but, inexplicably, miraculously, they spared his life. Perhaps it was General Reyes, the father of his sister's *fiancé*, who had saved him; there was no way to know. His head spinning, he was demoted to private and sentenced to five months in the Santiago Tlatelolco penitentiary, looming less than a kilometer north of the Zócalo. It was shameful, it was catastrophic, but it was infinitely better than standing alone, his hands tied behind his back, blindfolded, his knees like jelly, in front of that terrible brick wall in the courtyard of the Ciudadela.

Scratched in the stone above Ramón's head was a mark for every day he spent in Santiago Tlatelolco. The mattresses were thinner even than those in the Ciudadela and they writhed with vermin. In the filthy cells around him, men died noisily of yellow fever and tuberculosis. Ramón developed a painful, bubbling cough and did little more than lie on his mattress on the cold stone floor, scarcely caring whether he lived or died. His face was thin and drawn, his eyes sunk deep into their sockets. Beneath the straggly beard, his skin was shockingly pale, almost transparent. Perhaps, after all, it would have been better to die in front of the firing squad like the others. At least then his shame would be over. Now, it would last forever. Thank God his father had not lived to see this day. How could he ever go to Orizaba again? How could he face his friends? How could he face Adela? And, most terrible of all, how could he face Mamá?

In mid-December 1902, Ramón was released from the penitentiary and immediately posted to the 23rd Veracruz, a punishment battalion. Disgraced and politically untrustworthy soldiers, those who did not die in front of the firing squads in the courtyard of the Ciudadela or succumb to disease or starvation in Santiago Tlatelolco, were posted to the 23rd to fight the endless war against the Maya.

Almost four centuries after Cortés and his *conquistadors* had come to steal the land and riches of the Maya for their Catholic god and his earthly emissary, the King of Spain, the surviving remnants of their race still resisted the invaders from their final jungle stronghold of Quintana Roo on the Yucatán Peninsula. If the Maya didn't kill the soldiers who were exiled to Quintana Roo, heat, disease, starvation or their own officers would.

Ramón and a dozen others were guarded on their journey to the Yucatán by a gruff *subteniente* and a vaguely sympathetic *sargento*. They rode the overnight train to Veracruz, Ramón wide awake the whole time. The train stood in the station in Orizaba for almost twenty minutes and Ramón stared out of the window in a kind of frenzy, half-hoping to see a familiar face yet terrified that someone would see him, the son of

Miguel Arnaud, a common prisoner. In fact, he saw no one he knew and no one saw him. Anxiety turned to disappointment. In Veracruz, they boarded a ship bound for the Yucatán and their handcuffs were finally removed. Once the ship had sailed, Ramón and the others were free to walk about the decks until it docked in Progreso.

The Yucatán port was crowded with ships loading cargoes of baled sisal destined for the rope factories of the United States. Arnaud had his first sight of the Indians of the Yucatán. Mayan men, diminutive with finely chiseled features, staggered along the docks beneath bales of golden sisal twice their size. Overseers, tapping lithe canes against the sides of their polished boots, stood in the few shaded spots and watched the struggling Maya with narrowed eyes. Ramón and the others were shepherded through the docks and marched through the streets of Progreso. By the time they arrived at the tiny federal garrison, they were bathed in sweat. Without a word, they were locked into the enclosed courtyard of the garrison and left there, in the suffocating heat, without food or water.

On the journey from Veracruz, Ramón had befriended a former artillery captain who, like him, was now a common private on his way to the jungles of Quintana Roo. Arnulfo Torres was a small, dapper man with a slight limp. His crime, Ramón learned, had been to make a joke about Vicepresidente Ramón Corral and one of his Yaqui whores within the hearing of a *federale* colonel. Torres had not even had the dubious benefit of a court-martial. He had been stripped of his rank and campaign medals on the spot and posted to the 23rd Veracruz Battalion the next day.

The two men leaned against a column speaking in low voices. "You have heard of General Ignacio Bravo, Ramón?" asked Torres. Ramón shook his head. "He is the commander of the Army in Quintana Roo," said Torres. "They say he steals three-quarters of the money the government gives him to feed his soldiers."

Ramón gave a hollow laugh and patted his sides. "How much

thinner can I get? I have not eaten a proper meal for a year and a half."

"After a few months in Quintana Roo, you will look back on the meals in prison and on patrol with longing, my friend."

The next day, handcuffed to each other, they rode a boxcar as hot as an oven to the city of Mérida deep in the Yucatán. As they were marched from the rail station to the city's garrison to spend the night, they passed immaculately tended parks and extravagant public buildings. The mansions rivaled anything on the Paseo de la Reforma in México.

"Such prosperity, Arnulfo. I am amazed that a place so remote can be so rich," remarked Ramón, as they passed yet another mansion surrounded by carefully manicured gardens.

"Mérida is a city of plantation owners," Torres replied. "These houses, this city, everything in it, it was all built with the profits of the slave owners in the sisal trade. The wealthy of Mérida vacation in Europe. Their children are educated at the Sorbonne. There is more wealth here than you can imagine. Oligario Molino, he is a former governor of the state, has title to thirty million hectares of land."

Ramón shook his head in amazement. "This is nothing like I expected."

"Ramón," said Torres, reducing his voice to a whisper as the *subteniente* in charge turned and glared at them, "nothing in the Yucatán will be what you expect."

The train carried them from Mérida, through the sisal country to the southeast and into endless swamp and jungle. Hidden in the jungle, slowly vanishing beneath vines and earth and trees, were the ruins of what the Maya had built before the Spanish came: vast temples, entire cities, pyramids bigger than the Metropolitan Cathedral, pyramids bigger than those built by the Egyptians. Even after the Maya had abandoned their own gods for the god of the Spanish invaders, they were tortured and slaughtered in their tens of thousands; mutilated, enslaved or burned alive as heretics by the

Franciscans under the demonic Friar Diego de Landa. Almost the entire written history and all of the advanced astronomical and mathematical treasures of the Maya were destroyed as the works of Satan by de Landa in a massive public burning in 1562.

The survivors of the race that had built the cities now disappearing beneath jungle, the last remnants of the race that had dominated the Yucatán for a thousand years, were now little more than ragtag bands of outlaws, hiding in the jungle and hills, evading capture, slavery and death.

The train slowed to a crawl and they could feel the movement of the rails on the saturated earth below. The heat and humidity were overpowering. It was difficult to breathe. At times, the jungle grew so dense it seemed that night must have fallen. The air was filled with the screams of birds and the harsh cries of nameless wild animals. Torres sat across from Arnaud. Both men were drenched with sweat. Their escorts were halfway down the car, heads lolling on their chests in the heat. "What do you think of the Yucatán now, Ramón?" Ramón shuddered in response and bowed his head. Conversation in this heat was too difficult.

"They call this railway the Alley of Death," Torres whispered. Ramón said nothing. "Sixty kilometers of railway into Quintana Roo built on the corpses of Mexican soldiers. For every tie laid, a soldier dead."

Ramón stirred from his lethargy. "No, Arnulfo. That cannot be true. It is just one of those absurd stories you hear in the Army. It is not possible."

"It is not just possible, it is true. I was attached to the Ministry of War in México for two and a half years. I saw the reports with my own eyes. Tens of thousands of them, dead. Think, Ramón, how many soldiers have you met who came back from the Yucatán?"

Every day, there were the bodies of twenty or thirty more soldiers to dispose of: emaciated bodies, covered with sores, crawling with maggots, infested with lice and already stinking in the heat. Men who had died of malnutrition. Men who had died of malaria or yellow fever. Men who had been injured by falling trees or rock and left to die, in agony, without medical treatment of any kind. Men who had been summarily executed by the officers. In the months that Ramón had the never-ending duty of getting rid of the corpses of Mexican soldiers in Quintana Roo, he never once saw the body of a man who had died at the hands of the Maya. In fact, except for the slaves on the docks in Progreso, he had hardly seen any Maya at all.

There was supposed to be oil to help burn the bodies, but the barrels in the storehouse were always empty. The money the government paid for the oil never found its way past General Bravo's headquarters. Ramón and the others lacked the strength to dig graves in the root-gnarled, fibrous soil and so they dragged the bodies into the jungle and left them in stinking heaps. Sometimes the alligators came before they had finished and they had to run for their lives.

The officers in Quintana Roo were a breed unto themselves —practiced sadists with, as far as Ramón could discern, no human feelings of any kind. The day Arnulfo Torres died, Ramón pleaded with the *subteniente* to allow the officers' doctor to attend to his friend. The *subteniente* didn't even answer him. The man looked at Ramón in disbelief, gave a braying laugh and walked away. Torres lay in a small hut on the edge of a clearing, the life visibly draining from him. "They will not help you, Arnulfo," Ramón said. "They will do nothing."

"You are surprised?" asked Torres, shivering uncontrollably, his eyes burning with fever. He motioned Ramón to come closer. "There are only two ways out of Quintana Roo, my friend. This way," Torres gave a tortured smile, "or their way. If you ever want to see your family again, you must be the best soldier México has ever seen. You must do everything the officers tell you. You must become one of them. You must do that or you will die here, like me."

Ramón could not become one of them; he knew that. He could never be like them but, perhaps, he could appear to be. Torres' death, painful and senseless as it had been, had given him the key. He would play the role for as long as it took to get out of Quintana Roo alive. He carried out the disposal of the bodies with such efficiency that he was promoted to corporal. Driven by the memory of what Torres had said, he soon made second sergeant and the officers considered him sufficiently rehabilitated to send him, armed and with a platoon, on a mission outside Quintana Roo, chasing down runaways from the sisal plantations.

The Miranda plantation had lost a score of laborers in the preceding month. Ramón accompanied the sixteen-year-old son of the plantation owner on his rounds. His first sight of the laborers who weeded and cut the sisal had been at five o'clock in the morning. He learned later that the ragged, thin, brown women he saw had already been awake for two hours, preparing the soggy masses of half-fermented corn dough the laborers were taking into the fields for their only meal before sunset.

When he went into the fields with the planter's son, he saw the laborers, mostly Maya, but also a few Yaqui and a handful of Chinese, Koreans and Negroes. Men and women, children as young as eight, frantically stripping the leaves from the sisal plants and running to fill the mule-drawn carts at the end of each row of plants. The adults were gaunt and bowed, but the children were worse, their sunken eyes staring hopelessly from listless faces. The foreman walked among them as they worked, slashing casually at them with his heavy cane. Ramón turned to the young Miranda and asked, "Why is the foreman hitting them? What have they done?"

"Nothing. They simply need to be encouraged in their work, Sargento. Sometimes, they work too slowly. Sometimes, they take more than twelve leaves from each plant in order to fill their quota more quickly. The foreman must make sure that each plant is cut correctly."

Ramón watched a tiny Mayan boy, of perhaps ten or eleven, cutting the leaves from a towering plant in a frenzy of movement. "How many leaves must that boy cut?"

Miranda leaned back in his saddle. "Ah, he is one of the lucky ones, he has to cut only two thousand leaves a day. After his twelfth birthday, he will have to cut like a man, three thousand a day."

The Miranda plantation was not large, only two hundred and fifty square kilometers, a quarter in sisal and the rest in pasture. The main settlement was located in the middle of the plantation. The plantation store, where the laborers could receive goods up to their credit of twelve and a half *centavos* a day, was situated across the patio from the sprawling house of the *administrador*.

Ramón had left the Spanish boy in the fields and had ridden back alone to the settlement. He hoisted a bucket of water from the well that had been blasted from the solid rock and looked across the patio as he brought the ladle to his lips. Behind the store were the one-room huts where the more privileged and trusted laborers slept with their families. Beyond the huts was the roof of the dormitory where the rest spent their nights. He finished his water and, wiping his lips, walked toward the dormitory. It was surrounded by a solid stone wall four meters high topped menacingly with broken glass. There was only one opening in the wall and Ramón stood at it and looked in. The smell was choking. At night, he knew, this opening would be watched over by guards armed with pistol and sword. Inside the dormitory, fifteen hundred laborers—men, women and children—would fight for a place to lie down on the packed earthen floor measuring twenty by thirty meters.

The most attractive women and girls were taken for the use and pleasure of the plantation bosses. The rest stayed in the dormitory and became common to all the men. Ramón had heard their screams the night before, while out patrolling with his *soldados.* From behind the dormitory came the sullen whine of the stripping machine. Clouds of fine green dust rose from the machine, while half a dozen Yaqui men, their once athletic bodies reduced to skeletons, staggered under enormous loads of sisal fiber toward the drying yards. In the yards, the sisal would turn the color of gold and then be pressed into bales for shipment to Progreso and, from there, to the rope factories of the United States that made vast profits using cheap Yucatan sisal.

In the early evening, Ramón dined with the young Miranda and the *administrador* of the plantation, a grossly fat Spaniard. The beefsteak, served by a once-handsome Yaqui girl, was thick and juicy, the wine a substantial Burgundy. After the girl had left, Ramón asked the *administrador* why more of the laborers did not simply vanish into the countryside. The *administrador* laughed, his jowls wobbling. "Where can they go, my young friend? This is not the jungle. This is a barren land. There is no water for them to drink, no food for them to eat. Each laborer is photographed and must carry identification. You will find it easy to catch the runaways. Most of them will probably give themselves up to you, half-starved and dying of thirst."

"But surely this is slavery," said Ramón. "It is forbidden by the Constitution."

The face of the *administrador* darkened. "Be careful of your words, Sargento Arnaud. The laborers are not slaves, they are simply working off a debt. If a man owes you money, you may hold his body until the debt is repaid, that is the law. It is a sad but well-known fact that *indios* cannot manage money. They are offered attractive employment by a labor agent, given a small advance and they immediately spend it on food. Of course, they cannot repay the advance and what choice does the agent have but to sell the debt and therefore the debtor's body, as quickly as possible, to a planter?"

"Yes," said Ramón, "but how can they ever repay the debt if they are never paid in cash, only in credit at the plantation store?"

"My young friend," said the *administrador*, leaning back in

32

his chair and smiling indulgently, "I concede that it is a less than perfect system. But, the plantation owners must be sure of being reimbursed for the cost of feeding and housing the laborers. How else are they to make a profit?" He chuckled. "I see that you know nothing of business. The Yucatán produces more than a hundred million kilograms of sisal every year. The market is dominated by a single company. The state governor is the company's agent. Everything is controlled. The only way to produce sisal for the price the *yanquis* will pay, is the system we have."

"So the laborers work on the plantations for the rest of their lives?"

"Yes, but for most, that is not such a long time. The Maya die like flies and the Yaqui, they are strong but the climate here does not seem to agree with them. Half of them die in the first year. Happily, the father's debt is transferred to the sons and to their sons and to their sons after them, so the planter does not lose his investment."

After dinner, they stood behind the house of the *administrador*, talking and smoking as the sun went down. As darkness fell, the laborers began to troop back in from the fields, the men shuffling barefoot in light cotton trousers rolled to the knees, the women following in their flimsy cotton shifts. "Come," said the *administrador*, "you can see them have their meal. No one can say we do not feed our laborers well."

At the side of the dormitory, dozens of Maya women were making *tortillas* by torchlight. Black iron cauldrons were filled with mashed beans. The laborers were served by the women under the watchful eye of the foreman. Each laborer received two small *tortillas* and a spoonful of beans. The *administrador* motioned to the flat iron tub beside the cauldrons. "Since this is Sunday, they will get fish too." Ramón could smell the rotting fish from where he stood. A Yaqui man in the prime of life, well muscled and without the dull look of defeat in his eyes, carried his morsel of food to the wall of the dormitory and squatted down to eat. As he put the piece of fish in his mouth, he gave a roar of rage and spat it out onto the ground. Instantly, the foreman and his assistants were on the Yaqui, pinning his arms behind his back, grinding his face into the dust.

The foreman motioned to an enormous Korean who lumbered forward. The foreman drew his pistol from its holster and placed it against the Yaqui's temple. The Korean giant grasped the Yaqui's wrists and, in a single movement, hoisted the man onto his back like a child. The other laborers stopped eating and watched soundlessly. The *administrador* blew a thin wisp of smoke into the night air. "The Yaqui must learn respect," he said carelessly. "That is the *majocol*, he will administer the punishment." He gestured toward a man bending over a bucket filled with water. "He is a master, the best I have ever seen. Look at the pains he takes to select the perfect rope."

The *majocol*, a Spaniard with mountainous shoulders, was examining with exaggerated care each of the braided ropes in the bucket, taking them out one by one, measuring their length, checking the tightness of the knot in the end of each. Finally, he was satisfied and took each end of the chosen rope in his outstretched hands and pulled, the muscles in his arms rippling, until the water squeezed like drops of molten metal from between the strands. He walked to where the Yaqui hung over the Korean's back. The foreman stood beside them, his pistol aimed at the side of the Yaqui's head. "Fifty," said the *administrador*, softly.

The *majocol* drew back the rope slowly, then brought it down with full force. The Yaqui's back gleamed like old copper in the torchlight and Ramón could see scarlet pinpoints of blood appear instantly in a diagonal line from shoulder to waist. The *majocol* paused, then drew his arm back and brought the rope down again. Between each stroke, there was an eternity of apprehension, waiting for the rope to fall. With each stroke, the Yaqui grunted as the air was driven from his body, but he made no other sound. Even in the torchlight, Ramón could see that the strands of the rope were clotted with blood and flesh. The *majocol* paused to rinse the rope in the bucket to ensure that it cut with maximum efficiency. Through the blood flowing down the Yaqui's back, Ramón could see the ugly white gleam of bone. The Yaqui was unconscious but still the Korean held him as the *majocol* delivered the last of the fifty strokes at his slow, measured pace. The foreman nodded and the Korean let go. The Yaqui fell in a shapeless heap into the dust.

"Perhaps he will learn respect," said the *administrador*, examining his cigar with interest. "Perhaps not. The Yaqui men are difficult; burdened with pride. Many of them simply die of shame after a whipping. The Yaqui women are more sensible. It is not even necessary to hold them. They kneel quietly before the *majocol* and take their beating. They nurse their wounds and are soon back in the fields."

Ramón looked at the Yaqui lying unconscious, his ribs and parts of his spine clearly visible through the clotting blood. Earlier, he had seen two laborers hanging from trees by their fingers and others whose hands or feet had been hacked off with *machete*s. He had seen one Yaqui woman, hanging upside-down, spreadeagled, naked and screaming, as her body was syringed with an infusion made from hot *chiles*. He was told that she had refused to become the mistress of a foreman.

Ramón looked at the man's blood seeping into the dust. "How does it benefit the plantation to kill or cripple a worker?"

The *administrador* smiled and replied, "It has great benefit, Sargento. The other workers see the consequences of breaking the rules and so they are less likely to break them. It is, after all, only a matter of a few *pesos* to replace a worker who dies while being punished."

Ramón's leadership of his platoon had, by late spring, regained for him his old rank of first sergeant. Four months later, he was promoted to *subteniente* of infantry in the 10th Battalion of the Yucatán. Arnulfo Torres had been right. Ramón had actually surpassed the rank he held before his disgrace. Just before his discharge from the 10th, he was awarded the Medal of the State of Yucatán. His rehabilitation was complete. He was no longer Arnaud the deserter. He was Subteniente Ramón Arnaud, decorated hero of the Yucatán.

CHAPTER 4

Doña Carlota's sweet perfume filled his nostrils as she held him to her. She wiped away a tear and stood back to look at him. "You are so grown up, Ramón. And look at your mustache. You look like the Kaiser himself. But you are so thin. We must feed you properly." She burst into tears again.

Ramón patted her shoulder. "Mamá, Mamá, you must not cry. I am home and well. This is a time for happiness, not tears."

Sunday morning after Mass, dressed in his finest uniform, Ramón walked through the Alameda Park arm in arm with his sister, Adela, acknowledging the greetings of the Orizabeños among whom he had grown up. "Everyone seems very friendly, Adelita."

"Of course. You are a hero. Look Ramón," said Adela, gesturing with her parasol. "There is Señora Franco and little Eduardo. Look how big he has grown." Ramón stopped to look at the boy, dressed in his finest Sunday clothes, flying a kite between the flower beds.

"He was just a baby when I left," said Ramón.

"You were just a boy yourself, Ramón. Now you are a man, quite grown up. I am so proud of you."

"Is mother proud of me, Adelita? She has never mentioned what happened."

Adela put her fingertips to Ramón's lips. "No. And she never will. None of us will. You must not think of it. It is in the past. You are an officer now, a hero."

Later, they gathered around the piano to sing and talk, while the servants cleared away. It pleased Ramón that with the money from the sale of the big house, Doña Carlota could, at last, afford to keep a few servants and live in dignity. "Mamá," said Ramón, "I have received my orders. I must report to the 11th Battalion in Acapulco."

Doña Carlota gripped his arm. "Oh no, Ramón. You just came home."

Ramón nodded. "I know, Mamá. But I must go. I am a soldier. I have my orders."

"Of course, my dear. Of course you must. I understand."

Three weeks later, Ramón stood on the deck of the small ship that was to take him from the port of Salina Cruz to Acapulco and thought back to the life of comfort and ease he had known when his father was alive. How little he had appreciated it at the time. He staggered slightly as the gunboat Demócrata rolled to her anchor, her battered bow sheering wildly from side to side. The wind had begun to blow in earnest two days earlier, when Ramón boarded her as she lay in the crowded harbor at Salina Cruz on the Pacific coast. Ferried out to the aging Demócrata in a launch, Ramón had to pull his tunic up around his face to protect himself from the raw salt sting of the spray and the blinding needles of wind-borne sand. Seemingly oblivious to the wind and sand, the coxswain had neatly threaded his way through the fleet of brightly painted shrimp boats fighting their way back into Salina Cruz from the seething waters of the Gulf of Tehuantepec.

Ramón had watched with fascination the fishermen on their madly rolling little boats. Their hair was matted by wind and spray, their skin burned almost black by the sun. Fishing in the Gulf was always dangerous but especially so in this weather, when the strong Caribbean trade winds funneled across the Isthmus of Tehuantepec. By the time the wind reached the Pacific shore at Salina Cruz, it was often raging at fifty knots or more. The sand it carried could blind anyone foolish enough to face directly into it.

Ramón's first sight of the Demócrata had confirmed his worst suspicions. She was pitifully small, half sailing vessel, half steamship. In the relative shelter of the harbor at Salina Cruz, she rolled alarmingly. Ramón remembered reading something about the Demócrata. In July 1892, Coronel Antonio Rincón had taken two hundred Yaqui Indians aboard the Demócrata for shipment to the Yucatán sisal plantations. In retaliation for some unspecified insult, all two hundred men, women and children had been thrown into the ocean between the mouth of the Yaqui River and the seaport of Guaymas. There were no survivors.

The Demócrata's *capitán* had delayed their departure from Salina Cruz, waiting for better weather. Ramón retired to the tiny cubicle assigned to him as a cabin and read, leaving only for meals with the ship's officers. As the wind dropped, just after midnight on the second day, the Demócrata hastily weighed her anchor and steamed north for Acapulco.

At Acapulco, the mountains of western México tumble headlong into the Pacific. Jagged rock cliffs drop sheer into astonishingly blue water. Here and there, gleaming crescents of sand, as white as the finest sugar, skirt the shore. Near Acapulco, Hernán Cortés built two caravels with the vain hope of conquering the islands of the South Seas for Spain. To Acapulco, Spain's galleons had brought their fabulous treasures of silk and spices and jewelry from China to be carried over the mountains by mule train to México. From there, they went to Veracruz for shipment to Spain. Now, the path to the capital was a tortuous stagecoach route that took a week or more. In 1905, the city of Acapulco slumbered in its isolation, the red and white buildings of the town resting quietly on the bosom of the hills at the eastern end of the Bay.

Abelardo Avalos, colonel of the 11th Battalion in Acapulco, was a formidable man. He had the build of a prize fighter gone a little soft in his later years. As Ramón learned, Avalos had, at one time, been the most feared heavyweight in the Army, taking on all comers, officers and men alike, with bare knuckles, in bouts sometimes lasting forty rounds. Avalos had accumulated a modest fortune and a secure position thanks to Presidente Díaz's policy of giving gambling concessions in the smaller towns to officers who had proven their loyalty to him.

Without a word, Avalos waved Ramón to the chair standing in front of his ornately carved desk. As Ramón waited for the colonel to speak, dread rose in him. Avalos was leafing through a file. Ramón knew it must be his service record. For what seemed like an eternity, the colonel read through the sheaf of papers with a scowl, his bushy brows almost hiding his eyes. At last he looked up. "Well, Subteniente Arnaud, I see that you have had an adventurous career in the Army for a man so young." His voice was gruff, but not unkind.

Ramón was lost for words, finally managing to blurt out, "Yes, Coronel."

"I see that, since your disgrace, you have managed to redeem yourself. Any soldier who can earn promotion from private to *subteniente* under General Bravo and also win the Medal of the State of Yucatán must have some promising qualities. General Bravo is not the easiest of men to please, I have heard it said."

"I was honored to serve my country, Coronel," said Ramón cautiously.

"Of course. As are we all." Was there a slight twinkle in Avalos' eye? "Well, as far as I am concerned, Subteniente Arnaud, you begin here with a clean record." Ramón relaxed in his chair. Perhaps Avalos really meant it. His family had forgiven him. Perhaps the Army would too. Avalos wagged a thick finger. "But I warn you Subteniente, I do not tolerate disobedience, not for an instant. You will learn that very quickly."

Garrison life in Acapulco was tranquil and undemanding and Ramón quickly settled into the routine. There was little for the junior officers to do beyond inspecting and drilling the men each day and wrestling with an endless tide of paperwork, none of which seemed to have any particular purpose. Ramón's evenings and Sundays were free and he took advantage of the time to read and play his beloved mandolin and visit the surprisingly good libraries and museums of Acapulco.

Miguel Hernández led the way into the officers' *salón*. The room was full tonight, the air blue and heavy with cigar smoke. Officers crowded around the card tables, watching the high stakes games. Hernández gestured for the steward. "What will you have, Ramón?"

"Brandy, please Miguel." Hernández gave the order to the steward and turned to Ramón. Hernández was Ramón's age, with fine, dark features accentuated by the stark white slash of an old fencing scar above the left cheekbone. He was astonishingly tall, towering half a head over Ramón who was, himself, one of the tallest officers in the battalion.

"Well, Ramón, how are you finding Acapulco?"

Ramón paused, as though weighing his words. "I admit that I miss my family in Orizaba and I miss being able to get on the train for México at a moment's notice. It was nothing to go to the capital to spend a few days enjoying the opera or ballet. Acapulco is very isolated. But, I leave for Orizaba tomorrow afternoon. I have two weeks of leave coming."

"You say that Acapulco is boring and then you plan to leave and miss the ball?" Hernández chuckled.

"The senior officers' ball? Neither of us has any chance of attending, Miguel."

"Ramón, Ramón, what am I to do with you?" Hernández stretched out his arms in a gesture of feigned helplessness. "Of course, we can attend. There is plenty of excitement in Acapulco, but you must seek it out."

"But junior officers are not invited," said Ramón.

Hernández leaned forward, his eyes bright. "This is México, is it not? There is always a way. The ball is by invitation only and there is always a handful of diplomats, some prominent civilians and a few favored junior officers. Last year, the ball was the event of the year. The ballroom was a sea of gold braid and diamonds. It will be even better this year. Someone has actually arranged for a Viennese orchestra to play and rumor has it that Finance Minister Limantour is coming on the Demócrata to attend. I have some influence with the committee and I am sure that Coronel Avalos will put in a word for you. I will see that you are invited."

"I really should go to Orizaba."

"Come now, Ramón. When is the last time you danced with a pretty girl?"

Ramón thought for a moment and smiled. "It has been a long time, a very long time. In truth, Miguel, the last pretty girl I danced with was my sister, at her wedding." He shook his head and laughed. "Perhaps you are right, after all."

Hernández smiled. "Wonderful. I guarantee you a good time."

Ramón felt awkward. In the old days, he had walked into the grandest parties in Orizaba or México without thinking twice, greeting his acquaintances with a casual wave, flirting gaily with the prettiest girls. Now, he felt hopelessly ill at ease. Surely, everyone here would know that he was Arnaud, the deserter. He could see Miguel, ahead on the broad marble staircase leading up to the ballroom, elegant as always, Liliana on his arm. All around were beautiful women glittering with pearls and diamonds, smart officers in immaculate dress uniform and, the men who had the real power in México, civilians, serious men in formal dress from the best tailors in France and Great Britain.

Hernández motioned to Ramón. Ahead of them was Limantour, the finance minister, leader of the *científicos*. Someone had once unkindly called the nattily dressed Limantour a tailor's dream come true, but he had won the confidence of American and European bankers and that had made it possible for México to borrow a fortune to pay for the grand buildings and extravagant lifestyles of the *científicos*. Those who lived well under Porfirio Díaz were more than willing to forgive Limantour his obsession with attire. Ramón continued up the staircase, swept along by the river of wealth and influence.

He stood and stared. There, across the ballroom, listening as though ready to die on every word of that good-looking jackass Gabardo, was the most beautiful girl he had ever seen. She stood proud and confident. Her floor-length gown was of embroidered coral pink satin. As Gabardo jabbered on, she lifted her head and laughed. Ramón was entranced. Her hair was long and full and, with every toss of her head, it gleamed raven-black in the light spilling from the chandeliers. As she laughed, her eyes swept the room and, for a moment, met Ramón's. He felt a fool standing there, his jaw slack, his eyes fixed. And then she looked away. Ramón felt a flush rising in his cheeks. He turned to Hernández. "Miguel, who is that girl talking with Gabardo?"

Hernández assented to Liliana dancing with a handsome young captain and turned to Ramón. "That is Alicia Rovira, Ramón. The Roviras are from Orizaba. Surely you know them?"

"I know of the Roviras, but it must be ten years or more since I have seen any of the family. She would have been just a child when I last saw her. She has grown into a beautiful woman," Ramón said it quietly, all the while looking across the room.

"Señor Rovira has become very successful. The family has not lived in Orizaba for some years."

"She is so beautiful," Ramón whispered, scarcely listening.

Hernández chuckled. "Put it out of your mind, Ramón. She is very beautiful, but if Félix Rovira caught a poor *subteniente* with designs on his daughter, he would have him broken to private and, believe me, he has the influence to do it." Hernández stopped abruptly, remembering Ramón's past. "A thousand pardons, Ramón. That was thoughtless of me. Simply take it from me that Señor Rovira will want something more than a poor soldier like you or me for his daughter."

"Gabardo does not seem worried."

"You take my point exactly, my friend. Gabardo may be a soldier, but he is certainly not poor. The Gabardos own more land in the north than you can cross on horseback in two days. Rafael is the oldest son. One day, he will be one of the wealthiest men in México. A perfect match for the daughter of Félix Rovira."

Ramón wasn't listening. "I want to meet her, Miguel."

"Ramón, I warn you. Señor Rovira dotes on Alicia. He is very protective of her and he has powerful friends. For heaven's sake, Ramón, I have heard that when he is in México he rides every day in Chapultepec Park with Don Porfirio. Find another girl. There are dozens of pretty girls from good families who would faint dead away at a proposal from a man like you."

"I want to meet her now, Miguel. I have never seen anyone like her."

"Very well, if you insist, Ramón. I have an acquaintance with the Roviras. I will give you an introduction." He shook his head slowly. "But, listen to what I say, you are playing with fire. Think about what you are doing."

Ramón was already walking around the perimeter of the ballroom to where Alicia Rovira and Gabardo were standing. Hernández followed close behind.

"Señorita Rovira, how good to see you again." Hernández smiled and inclined his head briefly. To Ramón, he seemed unnaturally calm.

"Subteniente Hernández, a pleasure." Her voice was like honey. Ramón felt his heart pound and his throat constrict as she turned to him.

"Señorita Rovira," said Hernández, "may I present Subteniente Ramón Arnaud, a fellow Orizabeño?"

She smiled, "I am delighted to meet you, Subteniente Arnaud."

Ramón stood to attention and said, "Señorita, I assure you the pleasure is entirely mine." Immediately, he felt awkward, foolish. What must this beautiful, confident young woman think of him?

"Arnaud. Hernández." Gabardo nodded brusquely.

"Arnaud. I recognize the name, of course." She looked

thoughtful. Had she heard of his disgrace? If only the floor would open up and swallow him. Before he could speak, she went on, "Of course, I remember. Your father was an owner of the street railway in Orizaba. Your sister is Adela. And your name, it is French, of course." She was only being polite. It made Ramón squirm. What could she care about his name?

"Yes, Señorita, my father came to México from France many years ago."

"Do you speak French, Subteniente Arnaud?"

"Yes, Señorita. In fact, I once taught French, but I have few occasions to use the language these days."

"But still, what a wonderful thing to know French well. Even after two years of study, I am afraid my French is still not what it should be." She gave him a small, rueful smile.

"It is a beautiful language. And it has so much in common with Spanish and English." At least here was a subject on which he could converse without making a complete fool of himself.

"Say something to me in French, Subteniente Arnaud," she said with a smile.

Without thinking, Ramón blurted out, "*Voulez-vous danser avec moi, mademoiselle?*"

Smiling, she said, "*Enchantée,*" and took his arm. Ramón could scarcely believe that he had asked her to dance. As they turned to the dance floor, Ramón caught the warning look in Hernández's eye. Beside him, Gabardo glowered.

They danced most of the night together. To Ramón, everything around them was a blur of light and color. For him there was only the light in Alicia's eyes, the delicate, lingering scent of her perfume and the amazing smoothness of her satin dress beneath his hand. Several stylish officers claimed dances they had been promised and Gabardo cut in twice. Each time, Ramón stood waiting impatiently, a thoroughly unreasonable possessiveness rising in him. Once, Hernández took him aside and whispered urgently into his ear, but Ramón heard nothing.

Félix Rovira helped his daughter into the carriage and then got in himself. He was flawlessly dressed, in his early fifties. His full head of iron gray hair was brushed straight back, revealing a high forehead and eyes of the same deep brown as Alicia's. Two small medals hung below his breast pocket. He sat on the forward seat facing his daughter, top hat and cane on the seat beside him. Signaling the driver to leave, he leaned toward her, resting his elbows on his knees. "You spent a great deal of time with that young Arnaud this evening, Alicia," he said

"Subteniente Arnaud is a charming man. Did you know he is from Orizaba too? We have spent so much of our lives away from Orizaba that we scarcely know the people who live there."

"It is the price we pay for my work, my darling. I have never met Subteniente Arnaud, but I met his late father on a number of occasions. He was a very distinguished man. A great supporter of Don Porfirio and a very successful businessman. An unsurprising combination," Rovira chuckled. His tone grew serious. "Gabardo was offended by the attention you were paying to Arnaud this evening. He came to me, fuming."

"Rafael Gabardo is a fool." Alicia's eyes flashed.

"Perhaps, but a very rich fool."

"Papá, would you really want me to marry a fool, no matter how rich?" Alicia stared directly into her father's eyes.

Rovira hesitated, then said, "Licha, you are the most important thing in the world to me."

"Oh, Papá." Alicia leaned forward and put her arms around his neck. "Papá, I will always love you. You will never lose me. You know that."

Rovira moved back and held Alicia by the shoulders. "I know, Licha. I love you more than you can ever know. You must do what you think is right. I cannot hold you forever. I suppose parents never want their children to grow up, but they do so in any case. My mother used to say that children are born with little clocks in their hearts. The clock keeps time for that child alone. Each child must live its life according to its own clock, not according to what its parents want."

He held her shoulders more tightly. "When your time comes Alicia, I want you to marry a man you love and who loves you, a man who will be good to you. I have spent most of my life among the Gabardos of this world, the very rich and the very powerful. I have seen them in public and in private and I would never attempt to force you to marry for wealth or position. In any case, I know you too well. You have your grandmother's strong will. God help me or anyone else who tries to force you to do anything against your will." He smiled and leaned back against the seat and looked at her, saying nothing. The ringing of the horses' iron shoes on the cobblestones echoed sharply against the buildings they passed.

He leaned forward again and took her hands in his. "The world is a place of constant change, Licha. The only currency you can really count on is love." Alicia smiled and squeezed his hands. "Your mother and I have that love. We have been very fortunate in material ways, but we have our love for each other and that is what has given our lives meaning. Never underestimate the power of love. I want to tell you something I have never told anyone, not even your mother."

"Yes, Papá, what is it?"

Rovira lowered his voice, even though the driver couldn't possibly hear him over the clattering of the hooves. "When you were very young, I invested every *centavo* I had in a new railway to be built in the south. At that time, it seemed that a new rail line was being started every week and many men like me foolishly invested everything they had in the hope of a quick profit. The company went bankrupt before the line was even half-completed and I was ruined. I lost everything. The thought of what would happen to you and your mother nearly drove me out of my mind. México is very cruel to those without money, Licha, you know that. In desperation, I decided to take the coward's way out, to shoot myself. Do you know what changed my mind?"

Alicia's voice was barely audible. "No, Papá."

"You did, my darling. Your mother had gone to stay with a friend who had the influenza and the servants were all in bed. I had made up my mind. It was crazy but I thought that I simply could not go on. I had my pistol in my pocket. I wanted to see you one last time. I opened the door and you were lying there, asleep. You had kicked your covers off. I pulled them up and kissed you very lightly on the forehead so as not wake you." Rovira hesitated, then continued, "You opened your eyes just for an instant and said, 'I love you, Papá,' and fell back asleep. I put the pistol back in my desk and went to bed. You were three years old," his voice cracked. "You were three years old and you saved my life with those words. That is the power of love."

Tears tumbled down Alicia's cheeks. She buried her head against her father's chest. "Papá, I will never leave you. Never."

He held her to him. "No, no, my darling. Some day you must. When your heart tells you the time is right, you must go. I have been blessed with your mother's love and yours. It is more than I had any right to expect. When the time comes, I want you to follow your heart. You gave me my life. I must give you yours."

Ramón obtained consent to move from the officers' quarters into comfortable private lodgings in the home of a minor official of the municipal government. There, he spent most of his evenings alone in his room on the top floor, reading his collection of books and, when the urge struck him, playing his mandolin. Since the ball, he had been unable to get the thought of Alicia Rovira out of his mind. The dress uniform he had worn that night still held the sweet scent of her perfume. He went to where it hung and buried his face in the fabric. He wanted so badly to see her again, to feel the touch of her hand and hear the music of her laughter. How long would he have to wait until he was with her again? Already, it seemed like an eternity. It would be unthinkable to simply present himself at the Rovira villa without an invitation. He was a gentleman and gentlemen did not do such things. He took out a box of writing paper and began to write a note.

Much later, he leaned back in the chair and stretched his back. His little writing desk and the floor around it were littered with crumpled sheets of paper. His words had been either too formal or too familiar. He rubbed his eyes and made one last attempt. When it was done, he wasn't entirely satisfied, but it was the best he could do—a few lines expressing his pleasure at meeting her and hoping for the opportunity of calling on her at her convenience. He sighed, sealed the envelope and wrote 'Señorita Alicia Rovira' in his flowing copperplate on the front. He would have one of the battalion clerks deliver it in the morning.

Avalos had been in a great hurry and had ended the interview by thrusting the invitation into Ramón's hand. "I want you to represent me at this reception, Arnaud. You have excellent English, they tell me. We want to keep the British happy. Give the Consul my apologies and explain that I was called away unexpectedly to México. Arthur Brander from the Pacific Islands Company, the British company mining guano on Clipperton Island, will be there. He is a good fellow. Find out from him how things are going on the island and come and report to me when I get back from México."

It was apparent to Ramón, from the moment he was ushered into the reception room and given a glass of champagne, that the cream of Acapulco society had accepted the British Consul's invitation. They had turned out in force to drink the Consul's abundant champagne and to honor the visit of Weetman Pearson, the tweedy, dark-haired Englishman whose companies had built the port of Salina Cruz and the new railway across the Isthmus of Tehuantepec from the Gulf of México to the Pacific

The tall man with blond hair and glacier blue eyes looked more Scandinavian than English. He walked straight to Ramón and held out his hand. "Arthur Brander, Pacific Islands Company. Judging by your uniform, Subteniente, I assume you are standing in for my usual drinking companion at these things, Coronel Avalos."

Ramón smiled. "Yes, Señor Brander. I am Subteniente Ramón Arnaud. Coronel Avalos sends his regrets. He was called away to México."

"Yes, I had heard. His loss, however, is your gain," Brander grinned. "Have some caviar and some more champagne. Enjoy yourself." Brander took a sip of champagne and nodded toward Pearson. "By the way, do you know the guest of honor?"

"Only by reputation."

"Quite a fellow. I was with him at Oxford. There is talk of a peerage."

"He has certainly met with remarkable success," said Ramón.

Brander lowered his voice. "It does no harm to have friends in high places. Pearson got a fortune from your government to build his railway. I know a dozen British firms that would have been happy to do the job for half of what he was paid. But, of course, he has, shall we say, certain incidental expenses that must be allowed for. I understand that some of El Presidente's family are on Pearson's board of directors."

Ramón nodded wryly and looked up to see Alicia Rovira enter the room on her father's arm. Ramón was completely taken aback by her unexpected presence. If anything, she was more beautiful than before. Her hair was swept back, revealing a small diamond choker. The fabric of her dress was carefully cut to show her figure to best advantage. Ramón lost track of Brander's words. Had she thought about him the way he had thought about her? He felt a flush as he recalled the nights he had fallen asleep whispering her name, picturing her laughing eyes, feeling her soft touch. Only this morning, he had inhaled for the hundredth time her perfume on his dress uniform. Had his letter been too forward? Had he made a fool of himself? Would she snub him?

Ramón watched as Weetman Pearson took Félix Rovira's hand as the Consul introduced them in flawless Spanish. "You have done a great deal for México, Señor Pearson," said Rovira.

The Englishman smiled beneath his small mustache. "Thank you, Señor Rovira. We do what we can."

Rovira said, "Do not be so modest, Señor Pearson. Your canals have saved the capital from flooding and, now, you have linked our east and west coasts by rail and discovered oil into the bargain. We owe you a debt of gratitude."

"There are rewards, Señor. Believe me, there are rewards."

Alicia caught Rovira's eye and nodded across the room to where Ramón stood sipping champagne with Brander. Rovira smiled. "Go my dear. Remember, he is welcome to dine with us if you wish."

Ramón looked up to see Alicia coming toward him, her face radiant. "Subteniente Arnaud, a pleasure to see you again," she said.

Ramón bowed. "The pleasure is entirely mine, Señorita Rovira. Have you met Señor Brander?" He completed the introductions and gestured to the waiter for more champagne.

Brander excused himself graciously and Alicia said, "Thank you for your charming note."

Ramón blushed and could think of nothing to say. Alicia smiled and said, "My father has invited you to dine with us."

Ramón's heart missed a beat, then he said, "Please tell your father that it would give me the greatest pleasure."

CHAPTER 5

For once, the officers' *salón* was quiet. Ramón sat thoughtfully reading a newspaper, the smoke from his cigar twining around his fingers. A bottle of brandy stood between him and Miguel Hernández. Ramón looked up abruptly and said, "I tell you, Miguel, there is trouble coming." He dropped the paper onto the table and leaned back in his chair, lost in thought.

Hernández reached over and picked up the newspaper. *Regeneración*, it was called. He looked around the *salón* warily. "This newspaper is banned, Ramón," he said quietly. "Where on Earth did you get it?"

"It was left in the stables."

Hernández's eyes widened as he read. "Good God! They are openly promoting insurrection. Workers should strike for better pay! Mexicans should get the same pay as foreigners! These crazy ideas would lead to economic ruin. If it were not for Don Porfirio and Limantour and the foreign investment they bring in, they would not even be getting their miserable few *centavos* a day. They should count their blessings. This talk of land. When the land was in the hands of the *peones*, what did they do with it? They grew enough corn and beans to feed themselves and no one else. Half the time, they could barely feed themselves. They breed like flies. The *hacendados* and plantation owners make the land flourish. Cotton and sugar and sisal bring a fortune into this country. Don Porfirio has brought México into the modern age."

Ramón leaned back and thought. There was a very fine line in Don Porfirio's México between expressing an opinion to a friend and treason. He thought of the men in his platoon in the desert who had wanted only to go back to their homes and of the Maya and Yaqui worked to death on the sisal plantations.

Hernández carefully folded the newspaper and put it down. "Get rid of this, Ramón," he said quietly.

Félix Rovira never tired of the Capital. He had had a good ride in Chapultepec Park with Don Porfirio in the morning and had then spent a productive afternoon with the government officials best placed to advance his business interests. Dinner with the finance minister, Limantour, was the crowning touch to a very successful day. Although, like everyone else who came to the capital, he had heard the story a score of times, he sat patiently as Limantour recounted the history of the building they were in, the Casa de los Azulejos, the House of Tiles. For some reason, the story seemed to strike a particular chord in Limantour.

The exquisite eighteenth century palace had been built by one of the Counts of the Valley of Orizaba as a rebuke to his father who had told him that he was a failure who would never amount to anything. In the expression of the times, he was told that he would never be able to afford a house of tiles. Having made his fortune, the young Count built this elaborate palace in the capital, decorated with an endless variety of ornate tiles, surpassing anything in the New World or the Old. Félix wondered, half-seriously, if Limantour's father had once told him that he would never be able to afford a good suit of clothes. Perhaps that was why the clothes-obsessed finance minister loved to tell and retell the story.

The House of Tiles was the perfect place to meet. The interior was grand and imposing, the staff discreet and well-used to serving the nation's leaders with quiet grace. Félix Rovira finished his meringue and patted his lips with his napkin. Across the table, Limantour was perfectly turned out, as always. Fifteen years of successfully promoting México's great leap into the twentieth century had brought Limantour worldwide acclaim and a secret bank account in Europe reputed to contain over ten million American dollars. With his balding white hair and muttonchop whiskers and mustache, he looked every inch the successful statesman.

"This trouble in the mines and the mills, José, it worries me," Rovira said.

Limantour made a dismissive gesture. "It will amount to nothing, Félix. I have personally reassured the Americans that the troublemakers have been eliminated."

"But this unrest, where will it end?"

"It ended at the Greene-Cananea copper mine the day before yesterday. As you know, William Greene is a great friend of Vicepresidente Corral. We put a stop to it there."

The American-owned mine, a few kilometers below the United States border in the State of Sonora, had been the scene of a Mexican workers' strike, for better pay and conditions. The strike had been bloodily suppressed. The dead ranged in age from six to ninety. The surviving ringleaders of the strike and a handful of sympathetic newspapermen, were now safely under lock and key.

"José, I think there is more trouble coming."

Limantour spooned more sugar into his coffee. "Félix, there have been no more than a few dozen of these incidents around the country. Until yesterday, the workers were dealt with leniently. By failing to be firm, we only encouraged them. In Cananea, they learned that the agitation must stop. A little blood was spilled, yes, but in a good cause. We will not allow the antisocial activities of a few to destroy all our work. Do you think they have any conception how much money the Americans and the Europeans have invested in México? In return, they expect us to maintain order among the workers. It is not too much to ask. Cananea was the turning point. The trouble is over."

Ramón had had an unusually hectic day dealing with a flood of urgent demands from the Ministry of War for entirely pointless reports. Now, he was relaxing in his favorite part of the Acapulco garrison, the quiet, beautifully furnished library on the top floor. In their free time, most of Ramón's contemporaries congregated in the officers' *salón* on the ground floor, drinking, joking and endlessly gambling. Usually, he had the library to himself. But for Ramón and a handful of others, the thousands of exquisitely bound volumes on history and geography and warfare would have gone unread.

He looked through the Palladian window. It was almost three meters high and overlooked the central courtyard where, at this time on a bright mid-summer afternoon, the heat of the sun baked the cobblestones and made the air shimmer. Ramón stretched and leaned back in the overstuffed chintz armchair to the side of the fireplace. Grinning marble cherubs carried the mantel effortlessly on their shoulders. A snifter of brandy lay loosely cradled in his hands. The brandy was French and very fine. Ramón settled into his chair and smiled to himself. Life in Acapulco was a far cry from the horrors of Quintana Roo.

"Arnaud, I thought I would find you here. Sampling some of that excellent brandy, I see." Miguel Hernández grinned as he entered the library. "May I join you?"

"Please." Ramón gestured to the chair at the other side of the fireplace. "How are you, Miguel? And how is Liliana? Beautiful as ever?"

Hernández lowered his lanky frame into the chair, draping a long, gleaming boot carelessly over one arm. "We are both in excellent health. And you? I have seen very little of you since the ball. As a matter of fact, Ramón, I saw very little of you at the ball. You must have made quite an impression on Señorita Rovira."

Ramón gave Miguel a brief smile. "I am perfectly well, thank you, Miguel. I have been busy."

Hernández grinned. "Have you seen her since the ball?"

"As a matter of fact, I have. At a reception at the British Consulate. And..." Ramón smiled triumphantly, "I have been invited to dine with the Roviras."

"You are becoming quite a lady-killer, but remember what I told you. Papá Rovira is a powerful man. You must tread carefully."

Ramón nodded. "I understand, Miguel. I appreciate your concern."

"Now," said Hernández, "how are your duties? For myself, I swear this is the first time I have sat down in a week."

Ramón took a sip of his brandy. "I have no complaints, although I must confess that sometimes I grow weary of the endless paperwork. For the life of me, I cannot understand what purpose most of it serves." He shook his head.

"Of course it serves a purpose, Ramón. What would all those little gray men in the Ministry in México do if we did not give them so much paper to file away in their cabinets? In any case, there may be a remedy for your boredom. Coronel Avalos wants to see you at four o'clock this afternoon. He has an assignment for you. A real change, I believe, and something of great importance."

Ramón raised his eyebrows inquisitively. "That would be most welcome. What is it?"

"I think I know, but I will let Coronel Avalos tell you." Hernández rose, preparing to leave.

"Stay and share some of this brandy with me."

"That would give me great pleasure, Ramón, but I have some documents to be delivered by hand to the office of the Vicepresidente." Hernández patted the worn leather dispatch case under his arm. "It does not do to keep him waiting."

"Absolutely," Ramón nodded vigorously. Like all Mexicans, he understood perfectly the risks of inconveniencing Don Ramón Corral. To cause Vicepresidente Corral displeasure was to court death, even for the most powerful. Corral had earned all too well his reputation as the most feared and hated man in all of México.

Presidente Porfirio Díaz had ruled the country with an iron hand for almost thirty years, bringing unprecedented prosperity to his supporters. The *rurales*, the mounted police of the countryside, *bandidos* recruited by Díaz and given fine dove-gray uniforms and beautiful horses, kept the *peones* in their place and kidnapped new soldiers for the army and slaves for the plantations. They were authorized to perform executions on the spot. In the cities, the secret police crushed any opposition before it could begin. Presidente Díaz was ruthless but predictable, but Corral, the sadistic drunkard, the slave trader, the rapist, was a man without a soul. The two men were spoken of, in the quietest of whispers, as Díaz and Death.

As Hernández left, Ramón settled back into the comfort of his chair, turning his thoughts from Corral to the much more agreeable subject of the new job Avalos had for him.

Coronel Abelardo Avalos's lined face broke into a brief smile of welcome as Ramón pushed the door aside and entered the richly appointed office. "Good afternoon, Subteniente. I have just finished your first evaluation. I want you to know that I am very pleased with your work here."

Relief flooded through Ramón. "Thank you, Coronel."

Avalos' demeanor grew serious. "I am sure Hernández mentioned that I have a job for you, Arnaud. I will shortly be taking a party to Clipperton Island. El Presidente has decided that the flag must be raised over the island once more. We will do it with full ceremony. I want you to come with me. The damned French are rattling their sabers again." Avalos hesitated. "Excuse me, Arnaud, I did not mean to offend you. I know your family is French. I am a soldier, not a diplomat."

Ramón shook his head. "I took no offense, Coronel. I am Mexican, not French."

"Of course." Avalos smiled broadly. "Of course you are, my boy. Now, here is the point. The French ambassador has presented a note to the government pressing their claim to the island. It is ridiculous of course and very provocative. They conveniently forget that Cortés was there two centuries before them."

"Is the island so valuable that they would risk making enemies of us?" Ramón asked.

"Perhaps. Perhaps. With all their territories in the South Pacific, the French have no source of phosphate fertilizers. The British seem to have the monopoly. Clipperton has hundreds of thousands of tons of guano. Aside from that, the French would dearly love to expand their Pacific territories north of the Equator." Avalos pushed the ornately carved cigar box over to Ramón. "Here, enjoy a cigar. The finest Havanas. Signoret at El Puerto de Veracruz gets them for me."

"Thank you, Coronel," said Ramón as he selected one of the cigars. He rolled it slowly between his fingers, savoring the aroma, before reaching for the silver cutter. This was interesting, thought Ramón, no Balsa Brothers cigars for Coronel Avalos. Nothing but the very best. Business must be very good.

"Perhaps the French are simply diverting the attention of their own people from their failings in Panamá, Coronel. The *yanquis* have made more progress on the Canal in two years than de Lessops made in a decade. A confrontation with us over Clipperton Island would doubtless help the French forget their embarrassment."

Avalos let the smoke drift from his lips and watched it swirl lazily overhead. "An interesting thought, Subteniente. Certainly, no one could accuse you of not seeing things broadly." Avalos looked at Ramón. Relaxing with the cigar, the young man maintained a striking dignity. How such a promising young officer could have done the things he was said to have done was a mystery. Such was the folly of youth.

"I know the French, Coronel." Ramón smiled.

"Yes, of course you do." Avalos chuckled, his eyes almost vanishing beneath his bushy, white brows. "The Canal may be involved in another way, too. It will carry a tremendous volume of shipping, much more than the railway across the Isthmus does now. Most of the Cape Horn traffic will eventually go through the canal. The French may be thinking ahead. Clipperton could have great strategic value in the future. In any case, we leave in two weeks. I want you and a detail of four men. We will raise the flag and formally grant the British the right to mine guano under license from México."

"But Coronel, Arthur Brander's company is on the island already," said Ramón, puzzled.

"Of course they are, Subteniente. They have been there for years. We are doing this for purely diplomatic reasons. At the moment, though, there is only a maintenance and construction crew, but mining will resume within a few months. The government is taking this French note seriously. Even the Pacific Islands Company is concerned about it. Lord Stanmore and his company are British. What they want is stability. Lord Stanmore had his top man, John Arundel, travel from Australia to sign the new agreement personally, so you have some idea how seriously he takes the matter."

Avalos leaned forward and tapped the ash from his cigar. "I attended a dinner at the foreign minister's when I was in México, Arnaud. Mariscal told me that the government regards the working of the guano deposits on Clipperton under Mexican license to be the best way of asserting our sovereignty. The French must understand that we are serious about defending our territory. They must understand that there will be no backing down!" Avalos said it fiercely, his huge fist crashing into the pile of papers on his desk.

Ramón had planned his leave almost to the last minute. There would be no time to stop in Orizaba to see his mother. After traveling by ship from Acapulco to Salina Cruz, he would take the train straight through to México. Only there could he find something worthy of Alicia Rovira.

The finest department stores in México, and some of the finest in the world, stood at The Four Corners. El Puerto de Veracruz, La Francia Maritima, El Palacio de Hierro and Ambos Mundos occupied the corners of the fashionable intersection. At the Four Corners could be found the finest caviar from

Russia, vintage wines from France, beautifully made Italian furniture, delicate Belgian lace, Czech crystal—anything, in fact, that the civilized mind could conceive and European ingenuity could produce. As in other aspects of Mexican commercial life, Barcelonnettes were prominent. El Palacio de Hierro and La Francia Maritima were both owned by men from the town high in the French Alps that had been Miguel Arnaud's birthplace. The sidewalks near The Four Corners were thronged with well-dressed women bustling from store to store, followed by scurrying dark-skinned maids weighed down with their mistresses' purchases.

Ramón slipped the little package into the inside pocket of his tunic and walked back toward his hotel. The lace was exquisite, from Bruges. In the corner of the handkerchief, so delicately embroidered that they were almost invisible, were the initials "AR".

The maid took Ramón's *carte de visite* and looked at it quizzically. "She cannot read," he thought and identified himself.

She gave a brief smile and stood back to allow him to enter. She opened the door of the *salón* and announced, "Subteniente Ramón Arnaud."

Alicia sat at the piano, her hair piled extravagantly on top of her head. Félix Rovira rose from his chair and took Arnaud's hand. "Welcome to our home, Subteniente Arnaud," he said warmly.

"It is a great pleasure to meet you, Señor Rovira. I trust you are well."

"Yes, Subteniente Arnaud. Very well indeed."

"Señorita." Ramón bowed to Alicia.

Alicia inclined her head in mock gravity, her face breaking suddenly into a warm smile. "Subteniente Arnaud."

Rovira moved towards the door. "If you will excuse me, I have some work to attend to. I am sure you young people would like a chance to talk alone. I will see you at supper and we will talk then. Alicia's mother is very eager to meet you, Subteniente Arnaud."

"I am looking forward to meeting her Señor," Ramón said.

When the door had closed behind Rovira, Ramón smiled at Alicia. "No chaperone. Your father is a very modern thinker."

Alicia grinned. "Of course. He is a *científico*. You are looking very well, Subteniente Arnaud." Alicia's voice was soft. "Please sit down."

He took the chair beside the piano. "Please call me Ramón."

"I will, but you must call me Alicia."

"Yes. Alicia. It is such a beautiful name. It fits you perfectly."

She laughed. "Such flattery! It was my grandmother's name. My father's mother."

Alicia reached across the piano and picked up a daguerreotype in a heavy silver frame. She looked at it for a moment, then passed it to Ramón. The resemblance between the grandmother as a young woman and Alicia was remarkable. Even in the old-fashioned dress in the photograph, Señora Rovira would turn heads anywhere.

"She was a lovely woman, Alicia."

"Yes. I am afraid that I can remember very little about her. I was very young when she died. But Papá has told me all about her. She was very strong-willed." Alicia carefully placed the photograph back on the piano. "My father says that I am just like her." She laughed, her eyes sparkling. "Now, Ramón, tell me about your leave."

"I went to México to see my sister, Adela and her husband. I stayed on for a few days to enjoy some opera and visit the museums. I think I appreciate the city more now than ever." Ramón hesitated, then withdrew the small package from his tunic. "I bought this for you."

Alicia's face lit up. "Oh, Ramón, how kind you are." She opened the package eagerly and admired the handkerchief. "The lace is beautiful and, look, you have had it monogrammed." She held the lace to her cheek, feeling its texture. "It is a wonderful present, Ramón, I will treasure it always."

CHAPTER 6

The trip was wet and miserable: seven hundred nautical miles westward into the Pacific from Acapulco, with the little ship slamming again and again into a short, vicious head sea, her masts drawing fantastic arcs across the gloomy overcast. The Pacific came green and solid and surprisingly cold over the Demócrata's bows.

For the first twenty-four hours, Ramón lay on the cramped berth in his cabin staring listlessly at feathers of bile-green paint peeling from the iron beams of the deckhead. He lay there, his uniform sticking to his skin, anticipating with dread each sickening drop of the ship, knowing it would inevitably be followed by a stomach-turning rise up the next wave. Then, the ship would drop again. He groaned miserably and rolled over, clutching himself.

On the afternoon of the third day, the wind fell abruptly and the urgent vibration of the hull signaled an increase in speed. As the afternoon wore on, the temperature began to rise and Ramón left his stuffy cabin to join Coronel Avalos and the Demócrata's officers on the open bridge. The ship's motion had become more purposeful as the seas dropped and Ramón began to enjoy the feeling of the air rushing past his skin. Ahead of them, over the bows, the sky flushed pink, then mauve, then fiery orange as the sun dropped into the sea.

Within minutes, the *capitán* telegraphed for dead slow on the Demócrata's steam engine and turned the ship in a circle to port. All night long they circled, ten nautical miles by dead reckoning from the island. Low-lying Clipperton Island was difficult enough to sight in broad daylight. Approaching the reef-bound island in darkness was suicidal.

An hour after dawn, Ramón, lying half-asleep in his berth, heard the metallic roar of the Demócrata's cable lunging from deep inside the hull as the anchor dropped to the steeply shelving seabed just off the reef. Even here, on the island's northeast coast, the heaving legacy of the wind remained.

The foredeck crew, barefoot, trousers rolled to their knees, noisily washed down the decks. In the ship's galley, sweating cooks sang out ditties of calculated obscenity as they fired up big cast iron stoves and began making *tortillas* and scrambled eggs for the crew's breakfast. Down in the steamy forecastle, off-watch sailors lashed their hammocks and laid out their few precious belongings for the morning's inspection. Ramón swung his legs over the side of the berth and heard, transmitted through the hull, the sound of the anchor cable grinding the coral beneath the ship to powder. There was a rapid knock on the cabin door and the mess steward entered, putting Ramón's morning coffee on the small table he folded down from the bulkhead. "Good morning, Subteniente Arnaud," he said.

"Good morning. Is Coronel Avalos awake?"

"Yes, Subteniente. I have just taken his coffee to him." The steward finished arranging the coffee things and left. Ramón poured himself a cup, spooning in sugar until the black liquid had the consistency of syrup. The food on board, even the officers' food, was abominable. Sailors ate the food of *peones*: *tortillas*, beans, eggs. A little dried beef on special occasions. Not much better than the laborers on the sisal plantations. But, the coffee aboard the Demócrata was fragrant and delicious, from Córdoba, high in the mountains only a few hours from Orizaba. Ramón closed his eyes and savored the familiar aroma.

Today's ceremony demanded full dress uniform. The steward had pressed it the night before. Ramón took his time putting on a freshly starched shirt. There was no hurry. He had no stomach for food, but Coronel Avalos never missed a meal and would be at least half an hour over his breakfast. Pulling on his tunic, Ramón reflected on the chances of getting ashore dry and clean. No matter that they were about to conduct a ceremonial flag raising on top of a small ring of bird shit in the middle of nowhere, he would be properly uniformed for the occasion. He sat on the edge of the berth and sipped his coffee. In a few hours, the ceremony would be over, the supplies they carried would be landed and they would be underway for México. The thought reassured him. He rose, checked his appearance in the small, discolored mirror above the berth, brushed his hair, gave his Kaiser mustaches a last twirl, strapped on his ceremonial sword and went out on deck.

The gray morning air was cool and damp. Ramón pulled his tunic more tightly about him. He strolled forward to the break of the deck and looked down to the forward twenty pounder gun where his party of four *soldados* lounged, gossiping in low voices. Seeing them on deck, ready, he walked to the starboard rail just forward of the bridge. Gripping the rail, he looked aft. He could see the green, red and white of the Mexican ensign at the ship's stern. A kilometer off the port quarter, the jagged white tip of Clipperton Rock, *la roca*, pierced the mist. The rest of the island lay hidden, mysterious, behind a low, gray veil. The rumble of surf, breaking heavily on the beach, came muffled across the water.

Ramón turned his back to the breeze and, with difficulty, lit a cheroot. Blowing a stream of smoke into the morning air, he looked at Clipperton. Strange how it was known, even in México, as Clipperton. The island's other name, la Isla de la Pasión, had been given by the French. In French, it was Île de la Passion; named for the day the French had first landed on the island, Good Friday 1711, the day of Christ's Passion. A happy circumstance for the French that the English pirate, John Clipperton, who used the island as his base to prey on Spain's China treasure ships, had not been in residence at the time. The French would doubtless have had their throats cut and that would have been the end of their claim to the island.

Passion? Island of Passion? In the other sense of the word,

the name seemed absurd to Ramón. Judging by what he had been told about the island, it would be hard to imagine any place on earth less likely to inspire passion than Isla de la Pasión. It was a dreary circle of bird droppings a few kilometers across, lost in the vast saltwater desert of the Pacific. If it weren't for the principle involved, the absolute necessity of defending México's territory and honor, the French or the British or even the *norteamericanos* would be welcome to it. Isla de la Pasión indeed! Ramón paused, then shook his head vigorously. These were unworthy thoughts. He had a duty to perform, a duty to his country that must be carried out without question and without complaint.

Like all Mexicans, Ramón had a hatred of the kind of foreign interference that the French claim on the island represented. For most Mexicans, it was simply a matter of faith, of blind, unalterable patriotism. For Ramón, it was a rational position based on his painstaking study of the nation's tragic and bloody past. Half a century earlier, an expansionist United States had annexed vast areas of México. México's desperate attempt to drive the *yanquis* from its territory was doomed from the start. The land involved—Texas, Nevada, Utah, Arizona, California, New México and Colorado—was beyond price. It was half of the Mexican nation.

Then Napoleon III of France had invaded and installed the Hapsburg Emperor, Maximilian. Overthrown by Benito Juárez in 1867, Maximilian had been summarily executed, a signal to the world that México would no longer tolerate foreign interference. Now, the French had revived Napoleon III's contemptible claim to Clipperton. This time, México had an army worthy of the name. She would stand firm. This time, there would be no surrender, no matter what the cost.

Ramón raised his eyes towards the Demócrata's open bridge and saw the silhouette of the ship's captain. A hulking, bearded man, Capitán Diógenes Mayorga paced back and forth endlessly like one of the big brown bears in their cramped cages in the zoo in Chapultepec Park. Ramón watched Mayorga with fascination. He was a man born to be a sailor. This wet, wild world was his natural element. Coronel Avalos' gruff voice brought Ramón back with a start.

"Yes, Coronel," Ramón said, instinctively snapping to attention.

"Are your men ready?"

"Yes, Coronel."

"Good, I will be on the bridge with Capitán Mayorga until ten o'clock." Avalos' eyes swept across the gray seas towards the island. Ramón's gaze followed his.

"There is a heavy swell, Coronel. Perhaps I should go ashore alone with the party." Ramón spoke hesitantly, not wanting to offend Avalos.

"You will do no such thing, Subteniente," said Avalos firmly. "We will do this properly." In his thirty years in the Army, Avalos had never avoided danger, let alone discomfort and, although now well into his sixties, he had no intention of starting.

"Yes, sir," said Ramón. He saluted and turned to the ladder behind him. Climbing down to the main deck, he saw his men huddled, smoking. As they saw Ramón climbing down, they leaped to attention. "All of you, stand by the launch. Smartly now," he ordered. The soldiers dispersed, making their way aft to where the Demócrata's sailors were busy taking the lashings off a white-painted launch.

With each passing wave, the launch alongside the Demócrata ground noisily into the ship's side, sending showers of rust and paint chips into the boat. It looked much smaller, bobbing in the waves, than it had swinging from the side of the ship. One by one, they climbed over the Demócrata's rail, made their way down the swaying rope ladder and jumped into the launch. Ramón had been the last to make the treacherous descent. He sat in the stern of the launch rubbing his knee. He had miscalculated his leap and had landed awkwardly.

The coxswain, sitting next to Ramón, ordered the lines to the ship let go. "Push off! Pull away starboard!" he ordered. The sailors on the launch's starboard side leaned into their oars. As they passed the Demócrata's stern, the coxswain ordered, "Pull away together!"

The motion on board the Demócrata had been distinctly unpleasant. In the launch, it was diabolical. Seen from sea level, the swells looked enormous. Each time the boat plunged into a trough, both the Demócrata and the island disappeared from view. Spray swept over the sides of the boat. Ramón looked at the coxswain who was now standing beside the tiller, gazing intently ahead. He stood relaxed, moving easily with the boat's motion, paying no heed to the waves seething around them.

The roar of the breakers grew louder. Ramón swung around on his seat and looked over the bows. As the boat perched for an instant on the crest of a wave, he could see the beach growing solid through the haze. Unbroken lines of whitecaps marched toward the island. Avalos pointed toward a tangle of iron rising from the water. "That is the Kinkora," he shouted to Ramón. "A British ship that was on her way from Vancouver around Cape Horn to Britain. She ran on the reef a few years ago. Soon, there will be nothing left of her." Ramón looked at the gaunt iron remains of the huge sailing ship being lashed by the waves and shuddered.

In a trough, the coxswain ordered the boat turned around until the stern was facing the island, the men at the oars keeping the boat's bow pointed exactly into the oncoming waves. With each wave, the launch surfed, stern first, down the face, wallowed briefly in the foam at the crest and then lifted its stern skyward, as the wave passed beneath them. Ramón clung to the thwart he was sitting on. Avalos sat near the middle of the boat, quiet and dignified. Ramón wondered if anything could ruffle him. The four soldiers sat huddled in the bows, heads bowed conspiratorially together, grumbling quietly.

"Coronel, everyone, hold on tight!" The coxswain's voice rose above the roar of the surf. They were approaching the beach at tremendous speed. As each wave came up and carried the boat toward the land, the men pulled for their lives to keep the bow pointed into the oncoming surf. As each crest passed beneath the keel, they rested, slumped over their oars. Now, from the wave crests, Ramón could see the island clearly. It was nothing more than a big circle of sand enclosing a lagoon. Countless flat, yellow rocks covered the beach ahead. A few ragged palms leaned away from the wind. Beyond the beach, large patches of weed clung, here and there, to the surface of the lagoon. The only high point was Clipperton Rock at the eastern end of the island, jutting from the sand like the turret of a grotesque fairytale castle. Overhead, frigate birds rode the wind. On a slight rise of land beyond the water's edge, a group of men stood watching them.

The coxswain pulled the rudder from its gudgeons and Ramón felt the jolt as the keel rammed into the sand. A wave burst over the boat, soaking everyone and carrying them further up the beach. At the coxswain's order, the sailors leaped over the gunwales and manhandled the boat through the retreating surf. Another wave broke over them as they muscled the boat higher. The coxswain grinned and said, "It is safe to get out now, Coronel."

Avalos nodded and Ramón stood carefully and swung one leg over the boat's side. Water hissed past. He hesitated, then realizing that his carefully polished boots were already soaked, stepped quickly over the side and made his way up the beach. Behind him, Coronel Avalos eased himself out of the launch, his uniform sodden.

As Ramón walked toward the small grove of palms, he saw that the objects he had taken for rocks on the beach were moving—they were alive. He walked closer and, suddenly, the entire beach seemed to be in motion. He realized then that they were crabs, each about the size of a man's hand. Thousands, tens of thousands, hundreds of thousands of crabs, with saffron shells and big reddish-orange claws, covered the sand as far as he could see in every direction. Those nearest to Ramón froze as though listening to the sound of his footfalls. A few ventured near him and then more. Within seconds, the whole mass was in motion toward Ramón. They advanced quickly, both claws held high. They probed his boots, gingerly at first and then more forcefully. He kicked them away. More came, investigating the wet leather, searching eagerly with their clicking pincers for somewhere soft, somewhere vulnerable.

Ramón could feel the nip of their claws through the wet leather. Totally unafraid, they crowded closer and closer, their claws waving. They seemed to stare with their strange goggle eyes and Ramón felt panic rising in him. The urge to run was almost overpowering and it was only the vision of tripping and falling and being instantly covered and eaten alive by the crabs that stopped him. He rushed at the crabs ahead of him to see if they would retreat. Instead of backing away, they held their ground, standing almost upright, both claws waving menacingly, completely unafraid, their goggle eyes following him.

He kicked out hard and felt a shell crack. Immediately, the others fell on the maimed crab, their pincers clicking busily. They lost interest in Ramón and he walked quickly forward, crushing dozens underfoot. Around each injured crab, the others swarmed, reaching into the broken shell, tearing out the living flesh and carrying it to the busy, hungry mouths.

Twenty meters from the water's edge, the land rose slightly. Here, where the ground was firmer and there were just a few crabs, stood two guano workers and Arthur Brander, nattily dressed, but wearing an incongruous broad-brimmed white straw hat that he had to hold down against the wind. As Ramón and Coronel Avalos approached, Brander walked forward, his hand extended. "How good to see you again, Coronel Avalos," he said in formal Spanish.

"Señor Brander, I am delighted to see you. You look well. I

believe you have already met Subteniente Ramón Arnaud?"

Brander took Ramón's hand and smiled warmly. "Yes, of course, we met at the Consulate in Acapulco. Ramón, a pleasure to see you again. Welcome to Clipperton Island."

"Thank you, Arthur," said Ramón, unable to prevent himself looking about as he spoke.

"Señor Brander," said Avalos. "There are stores for you on board the Demócrata. Please have your men help the boat's crew begin unloading right away." Avalos turned to Ramón. "Arnaud, have your men get the flagpole from the boat and set it up as quickly as possible. Pick some high land. We will get on with the formalities as soon as you are ready."

Taking his men, Ramón selected a small rise twenty meters from the water's edge. While the men began digging a hole, Ramón strolled through the palms. He reached down and picked up a handful of sand. It seemed to be a mixture of white coral, crushed almost to powder, and reddish, gritty rock. He let it dribble slowly through his fingers. Overhead, frigate birds wheeled slowly in the wind. The air was heavy with the stink of ammonia from the guano. From the other side of the island came the endless calling of seabirds. To the south, across the eastern end of the lagoon, rose the grim face of the Rock. Beside the small coconut grove were the remains of several huts, their boards made gnarled and gray by sun and storm.

Walking slowly, Ramón made his way back to the hillock. The flagpole was in place and the *soldados* were passing the stub of a cigar around. One of the soldiers stood beside the flagpole, the halyard leading to the block dangling from his hand. "Attention!" Ramón's sudden command took the men by surprise. The cigar butt smoldering on the ground at their feet, the four stood motionless. Spinning on his heel, Ramón walked to where Avalos and Brander were conferring in low whispers. "We are ready, Coronel," he said.

"Very good, Subteniente," Coronel Avalos nodded. The three men walked to the flagpole. Ramón took the rolled Mexican flag from its place of safety inside his tunic and handed it reverently to the soldier tending the halyard. "Hank this on and be ready to hoist when I give the order. Do not let it touch the ground!"

The others stood expectantly as the *soldado* hanked the flag to the halyard. Coronel Avalos nodded to Ramón. Ramón's voice quavered slightly as he gave the order to hoist. As the flag climbed, it unfurled quickly, the bright new fabric snapping in the breeze. Coronel Avalos stood to his full height and saluted before turning to Brander. "Señor Brander, the Government of the Republic of México hereby grants the mineral rights of Clipperton Island to The Pacific Islands Company under the terms and conditions already agreed."

With a mildly amused look, Brander held out his hand to Avalos. "Thank you Coronel. I am confident that the relationship between The Pacific Islands Company and the Republic of México will be a long and mutually profitable one." Avalos took Brander's hand and shook it firmly.

Turning to Ramón, Avalos said, "This is an important moment for México, Subteniente Arnaud."

"Yes, Coronel," Ramón replied stiffly. "I am proud to be here."

"Coronel," said Brander, still smiling, "Perhaps Subteniente Arnaud would care to see the mining operation before you leave."

"Certainly, Señor Brander. Arnaud, have your men help unload the stores from the Demócrata while we have a look at what the Company is doing here."

After giving his *soldados* their instructions, Ramón strode quickly after Avalos and Brander. They made their way southward from the boat landing along the sand almost two kilometers to Clipperton Rock. The Rock stood on a small peninsula jutting into the lagoon. A hundred meters long, fifteen meters wide and twenty meters high, it looked gigantic towering over the low, narrow ring of sand that made up the rest of the island. The Rock's sides were deeply cleft, carved into a mass of crevices and caverns by thousands of years of rain and spray. Seabirds jostled noisily in every crack and cranny while others screamed in the air overhead.

They continued past the Rock. To seaward, the big Pacific swells thundered on the off-lying reef. To landward, lay the lagoon, almost oval, three kilometers in one direction, perhaps two in the other. The lagoon's surface was a jigsaw puzzle of light and dark punctuated by a few islets at the western end. They walked further, passing a large ship's capstan on a concrete base and through a sheltering grove of fifteen or twenty mature coconut palms growing in high wooden boxes to protect them from the crabs. Beyond the palms, was a group of small cabins where the guano workers lived and, beyond that, a towering dark building set well back from the sea's edge. A T-shaped iron wharf marched into the sea on rusty pilings to the outer edge of the reef. As they approached, Ramón could see a narrow gauge railway about three hundred meters long running from the front of the building, down the beach and out to the end of the wharf. Near the massive building was a smaller shed, built on the edge of the lagoon. Alongside it lay two rowboats. Beyond the buildings, pyramids of pulverized guano stood along the rim of the lagoon.

"There it is, Arnaud. What do you think?" Avalos turned to Ramón with a smile.

"Very impressive, Coronel," said Ramón, awed by the size of the main building and of the guano stockpiles. "I had no idea that your operation was on this scale, Arthur." Ramón swept his arm around indicating the enormous shed, the tracks and the wharf.

"We must prepare and stockpile sufficient guano to fill at least two ships and we must be able to load them very quickly. Every day that a ship sits idle costs the company a small fortune. This island is difficult enough as it is. There is no protected anchorage and the wharf is only usable in fine weather, usually no more than thirty or forty days a year. Sometimes, we have to load the ships from surf-boats and that is a very slow and dangerous process."

The shed, built of heavy timbers and covered in corrugated

iron, had rusted to a dark orange-brown. At the front was a cavernous opening into which the railroad tracks vanished. They walked along the front of the building and followed the tracks inside. It was dark and cool. The crushing mill and other machinery sprawled along one side. A motorized launch about twenty meters long sat on heavy wooden blocks. A line of empty wagons sat on the track. From the gloomy interior, the opening to the outside through which the track ran, seemed impossibly bright.

Brander walked forward to speak with two men near the crushing mill, leaving Avalos and Ramón free to look around. One corner of the shed was a workshop for maintaining the hopper cars, the crushing mill and the mining equipment. Huge timbers and lengths of iron in all shapes and sizes were stacked high against one wall. The two soldiers strolled through the opening facing the sea and followed the tracks across the reef to the wharf. Where the long arm of the wharf carried the tracks out over the reef, the water was hardly more than a meter deep but by the berthing face where the ships loaded, the seabed dropped suddenly, plummeting to the ocean floor, far below.

The waves were running high, surging almost to the top of the pilings. Ramón stood on the outer face of the wharf, facing seaward. He could feel the wharf moving slightly beneath him with each wave. Avalos came and stood beside him, the two men staring silently seaward. After a few moments, they walked back along the tracks toward the shed, meeting Brander. "Coronel Avalos," said Brander, "I wonder if you would care to be my guest for a few moments? I am sure you would like some refreshment before you go back to the ship."

"That would be delightful, Señor Brander. Then we must leave. Capitán Mayorga is anxious to be underway as soon as the stores are landed."

They stepped off the raised embankment carrying the tracks and retraced their steps to the coconut grove. Near the water's edge, thousands of crabs lay one atop the other against rocky outcrops, like bricks in a living wall, seeking shade from the sun as it climbed steadily overhead and burned away the haze. They turned away from the sea to avoid the crabs, passing through the coconut grove before coming to the cluster of cabins, their roofs of rusted corrugated iron, the red and white paint on their walls barely a memory.

Brander led the way to a larger building close to the water's edge that served as his home and office. He stood aside and motioned the others in. A coral stone fireplace topped by an enormous mantelpiece of solid timber dominated the room. Low, wooden chairs were arranged in front of the fire. Centered on the far wall was a battered desk almost buried beneath stacks of paper and ledgers. Brander opened the cupboard beside the fireplace and arranged three glasses on the rough timber of the mantel. He poured each of them a small drink and raised his own glass. "To Clipperton Island, gentlemen." The others raised their glasses and drank the toast.

"When will you begin shipping guano again, Arthur?" Ramón asked.

"We should have everything in full operation within two months. A company ship is scheduled to arrive within three weeks with supplies, more coal and a full work crew. The Company has recruited Italian immigrants from the United States. They can stand the heat and are very good workers."

Avalos drained his glass. "We must be going, I am afraid," he said, rising and extending his hand to Brander. "Señor Brander, I wish you every success."

"Thank you Coronel. I wish you a safe trip back."

As they made their way back along the beach toward the Rock, they stopped for a moment and surveyed the island. As Ramón had seen from the boat, it was really nothing more than a thin circle of beach enclosing the lagoon. The Rock was the only substantial thing about Clipperton. The little collection of huts near the coconut grove looked like it would be blown away by the first strong breeze.

The five-kilometer walk around the southern half of the

island past the Rock was tiring in the growing heat of the afternoon. Ramón paused and, removing his cap, wiped his forehead. Ahead, he could see several of the sailors in the Demócrata's launch leaning over the sides, hitting the sand repeatedly with their oars. As they approached, they could see that the men were striking at the few crabs that braved the burning rays of the sun to prowl the sand around the boat. The stores had all been landed and were piled on the high land near the flagpole. Crabs surrounded the pile and tentatively prodded the crates and barrels with their claws. The waves had lost much of their violence; the wash on the beach pushed the stern of the boat to and fro. The sailors jumped out at a signal from the coxswain and held the gunwales. When Avalos and Ramón and the *soldados* had climbed aboard, the sailors dragged the boat into deeper water and rowed off.

After the terror of their arrival, the ease of the trip back to the Demócrata was almost anticlimactic. They climbed the rope ladder back aboard the gunboat and, within minutes, heard the ship's windlass raising the anchor from the ocean floor.

CHAPTER 7

They were less than twelve hours from Acapulco. Ramón had been surprised by the order to go to Coronel Avalos' cabin; he had scarcely seen the colonel since they had left Clipperton two days earlier. Avalos, sitting at a small writing table, absentmindedly waved him into the cabin and Ramón stood uncomfortably, waiting for him to speak. Avalos suddenly seemed to remember where he was and looked at Ramón. "My boy, we are going to put a full garrison on that island. How would you like to be *comandante*?"

Shocked, Ramón looked up quickly. "Coronel, I am honored. But Clipperton, my God, what desolation. There is nothing there. It is the most barren place I have ever seen."

"That is its attraction, Arnaud." Avalos gripped the edge of the table with both hands and leaned forward. "Mark what I say, where there is nothing, anything is possible. Do you remember the story of what the Aztecs did long before Cortés arrived? They had been defeated by the Culhuas and driven onto a small island in Lake Texcoco. The Culhuas let them have it because it was so desolate that no one else would live there. And do you know what they made of that barren little island, Subteniente? Tenochtitlán, the most important city in the Americas. From there, Moctezuma ruled the greatest empire in the New World. When Cortés discovered Tenochtitlán, it was bigger than any city in Spain.

"And what is Tenochtitlán today, Arnaud? México. I tell you, Clipperton, for all its godforsaken appearance, is a jewel in México's crown. The phosphates are worth tens of millions of *pesos*. It occupies a strategic position. The British, the French, the *norteamericanos*, they would all love to possess it. It is vital to México that we have a military presence on that island. Señor Brander and his workers are hardly a formidable force. What is to stop the French or anyone else landing and raising their flag? Don Porfirio is absolutely firm. There will be no more surrender of Mexican territory. We will put a full garrison on that island and we will defend it to the last man."

Ramón took a deep breath and looked Avalos directly in the eyes. "Coronel, I must protest. I have no qualifications for such a posting."

Avalos gave a short laugh. "Ah, but there you are wrong, my boy. You have the perfect qualifications. In fact, you are one of very few officers in the Army who does. You speak French, English and German fluently. You will be able to deal with anyone who attempts to land. You are the ideal officer for this posting."

"But Coronel," Ramón protested, "I cannot go to so remote a place. What of my mother? She is elderly."

"There is a supply ship every three months. You will have three months leave every year. You can see her then. This is a great opportunity for you, Arnaud. You are a Mexican. You are being given the privilege of defending the land of your birth. In any case, an order is an order. We are soldiers, you and I, we have no choice but to obey. You, of all people, should know that."

"But I can appeal an order, Coronel. That is my right as an officer."

Avalos sighed and shook his head sadly. "Yes, Subteniente, it is your right as an officer but, believe me, it will do no good. I have already made a special recommendation to El Presidente, he has concurred and the decision has been made. Don Porfirio takes a personal interest in what happens on Clipperton Island and he was very impressed by your qualifications."

Of course. It all suddenly became clear to Ramón. The payments being made by the guano company were going to Don Porfirio. Don Porfirio wanted a garrison on the island to protect his own interests. The unfairness of it all overwhelmed

Ramón. Why couldn't they just leave him in peace in Acapulco? A posting to this grim, desolate place, he was sure, was just another punishment. In the Army's eyes, he still had not redeemed himself. A sudden shocking thought came to Ramón. What of Alicia? "Coronel, what if I should marry? What woman would agree to live in such a place?"

Avalos looked calmly at Ramón with his piercing eyes. Avalos was no fool. He took pains to know everything about the men under his command. "Of course, many women of education and refinement would never be able to adapt to life on a remote island like Clipperton, but," Avalos wagged his finger at Ramón, "there are some women who would make a success of it. There are some women who would see life on that island as a challenge to be met, as an opportunity to create a unique and exciting life. Perhaps that is how you should look at it."

Ramón was unconvinced. "How many men would be in the garrison, Coronel?" he asked glumly.

"You will have eleven men under your command."

"Twelve of us to defend Clipperton against the great powers of Europe or the *yanquis*? It is absurd."

Avalos' eyes flashed. "You forget yourself, Subteniente Arnaud. This decision has been made at the highest levels."

Ramón knew he had gone too far. Avalos was not a man to be trifled with. "I apologize, Coronel." Ramón wanted to say more, but could think of nothing that would not provoke Avalos and collapsed hopelessly into silence.

"This is a new age for México, Arnaud. France and Britain and the United States must learn that we will never again give up territory to a foreign power. El Presidente makes them welcome as investors and even as landowners, but he draws the line when it comes to sovereignty. And whatever may be said of Don Porfirio by his enemies, he has the support of every Mexican, rich and poor, on that account. Am I not right?" Avalos looked sternly from beneath his bushy eyebrows at Ramón.

Ramón nodded weakly. "Of course, Coronel. You are right."

"Very well. When we get back to Acapulco, file your protest if you insist and then we will see."

It took only ten days. Ramón read the letter one last time and threw it away in disgust. What a fine Christmas present. The Army had denied his appeal, as Coronel Avalos had predicted and as he, in his heart, had known they would, no reasons given.

He had been foolish to make the appeal. It was another mark against him. There was no way out. It would be almost as bad on that horrible island as it had been in the desert or in the Yucatán. No music. No books. No theater. Nothing but Army rations to eat. No one but uneducated and resentful *soldados* for company. And if, by some unimaginable, inconceivable, stroke of luck, Alicia Rovira agreed to be his wife and, if, even more inconceivably, Félix Rovira gave his consent, would she be willing to live in such a terrible, remote place? It didn't seem possible. No woman in her position would do it. Alicia was refined and cultured. She would never give up her place in society and the diversions she enjoyed in Acapulco and México.

In desperation, Ramón went to Avalos' office, hoping for a miracle. Perhaps there had been a change of plan. Avalos' clerk knew of the failed appeal and Ramón could see the barely concealed smirk on the man's face when he asked to see the colonel. Avalos admitted him immediately. He didn't give Ramón a chance to speak. "Sit down, Subteniente. You have your answer. That is the end of it. I will not hear another word on the subject. Enjoy your Christmas leave. Go to Orizaba and see your mother. I have heard that the Roviras will be in Orizaba for Christmas. Ask that pretty Rovira girl to marry you. But, by all that is holy, make sure you are back here by the fifteenth of January. Do not for one instant think of doing anything foolish. Your family may have friends in high places, but no one will be able to save you a second time. Do you understand me?"

Ramón looked at the colonel. Avalos' eyes bored right through him. What could he say? That he would disobey the order? That he would desert again? They would catch him again and they would certainly execute him this time, no matter who his sister was married to. It was no use. There was no escape. Finally, he said, "Very well, Coronel, I understand."

Avalos' face relaxed. "Come now, my boy. It is not the end of the world. Conduct yourself well on Clipperton and your youthful misadventures will be forgotten. You have a fine career ahead of you in the Army. I have my eye on you. This could be the beginning of great things."

The post office clerk slipped the stamps beneath the intricately shaped wrought iron grating. Alicia took the stamps, then bent to open her purse. Emilia García, a year or two younger than Alicia and with a plump radiance, giggled and nudged Alicia. The handsome, well-dressed young man standing at the next wicket was staring at Alicia. Alicia looked up at him and blushed outrageously. Clutching their skirts, the two young women fled, giggling, down the stairs.

The sudden spring rain had stopped; the black clouds had vanished from the sky, as though by magic, leaving the air fresh and cool. Alicia and Emilia walked along the avenue to the edge of a small park overlooking Acapulco Bay. The trees were a brilliant green, freshly washed by the rain. The wet promenade glistened in the sunshine as they walked through the park, talking and laughing. Alicia took out her handkerchief to dry the bench before they sat. She stopped when she saw it was the one Ramón had given her and looked in her handbag for another.

"That is a lovely handkerchief, Alicia," Emilia said as they sat down.

"Ramón gave it to me."

"No more secrets. Tell me all about him." Emilia's eyes had a mischievous light.

Alicia paused and said, "Well, he is very handsome and very

intelligent. He is very much a gentleman."

"There are many handsome, intelligent young gentlemen in Acapulco, Alicia."

"Yes, but Ramón is not like the rest. He is so well-read. He speaks four languages. He knows about many things."

"What sort of things?"

"Everything. He knows about art and architecture. He knows about history. He knows about music and the theater. He even knows about ballet."

"Does he know about you?"

"Yes, of course. Well, he knows some things about me. Perhaps not everything." Alicia smiled.

"Are you in love with him?"

"Yes, of course I am, Emilia. I was in love with him from the moment I saw him. That pompous ass Rafael Gabardo was going on and on about his father's land and how rich he would be some day and then I saw Ramón. He is not like Rafael. He is wonderful."

"Are there more like him? For me, perhaps."

Alicia touched her friend's arm and beamed. "I am sure there is no one else like him in the world."

Ramón and Alicia walked arm in arm through the Alameda behind her parents. Orizaba's finest park was not at its best in January, but the air was cool and delicious. The earliest flowers were just beginning to show their heads above the rich earth. "You look wonderful in your uniform, Ramón," said Alicia, warming him with one of her smiles.

Ramón hesitated then gripped her arm gently, his eyes dark and serious. "Alicia, I have been posted to Clipperton Island."

"That is the little island the French want, where Señor Brander lives?"

"Yes. Don Porfirio wants a full garrison on the island and Coronel Avalos has made me *comandante*."

"*Comandante*? That is wonderful news, Ramón. Congratulations."

Alicia was absolutely sincere. Obviously, she knew nothing of the island. "No, Alicia, it is not wonderful. It is a terrible thing. Clipperton is a horrible place, a thousand kilometers out in the ocean, covered in crabs like something from a nightmare, the waters around it infested with sharks. There is nothing there but a few palm trees and the guano miners."

Alicia sighed, "How romantic. A desert island."

Ramón ignored her. "I told the colonel I would not go and appealed the order to the Ministry of War."

Alicia's eyes widened. "Was that wise, Ramón?"

"Whether it was wise or not, I did it. They have denied my appeal. Coronel Avalos has ordered me to be back in Acapulco by January fifteenth and then I must go the island."

"But Ramón, why are you so unhappy? Surely it is a great honor for an officer so young to be given such an important posting?"

Ramón was thoughtful. "Perhaps, perhaps. I suppose it is. But my mother is growing old and I will seldom see her and..." Ramón stopped, at a loss for words.

Alicia took Ramón's arm and stopped walking, allowing her parents to go on ahead. "And what, Ramón?"

He hesitated for a moment. "What of my marriage prospects? What woman would want to live in a place such as that, cut off from society, from her friends, from her amusements."

Alicia suppressed a smile and looked down at the ground. "Oh, I see. Yes, I suppose many eligible young women would not want such a life. They would refuse to live in such a place. I understand the problem perfectly. You would spend the rest of your life as a lonely old bachelor."

She looked up at Ramón's crestfallen face and laughed. "But, silly boy, not all women would see it like that. Some women would love the romance and adventure of living on an island far away from the world they have known. I suppose you will just have to find the right kind of woman." With that, she gave his arm a playful punch and ran ahead of him, down the path toward the benches by the fountain.

CHAPTER 8

Ramón's uniform was becoming badly stained with sweat as he looked up at the Córrigan's rusty, battered side. The ship lay disconsolately at the jetty in Acapulco, a wisp of smoke curling from her blackened funnel. Ramón stood aside to let a gang of stevedores pass. Derricks hoisted barrels of nails and provisions from the mule-drawn wagons lined up along the jetty. From a porthole near the ship's stern, metal clanged as a cook dumped a bucket of rancid waste into the harbor. Ramón took out his handkerchief, sighed heavily, and wiped his face.

By nightfall, the Córrigan would carry enough building materials to construct a small village on Clipperton. Deep in her hold was sufficient food, clothing, tools, weapons, medicine and other supplies to maintain the garrison of twelve for at least six months. Part of the Córrigan's forward deck had been converted into a temporary stable for the two mules that had been lifted aboard in slings. The mules, indifferent to their novel surroundings now that they had been given fresh hay, would work on Clipperton until the hay carried for them in the Córrigan ran out. Then they would be slaughtered for meat. No grass grew on the island. To keep them in fodder would require too much valuable space in the supply ships.

The pigs were another matter. Four of them squealed relentlessly in the pen on the foredeck. They would stay on the island and form the basis of a herd that would eventually keep the garrison supplied with fresh meat and keep the numbers of crabs down. Beside the pig pen, a chicken coop was home to a small flock of hens and two roosters who were already fighting for dominance. Eight of the nine *soldados* who would man the new garrison were already on board under the watchful eye of Corporal Chávez. The last was to be aboard by midnight.

Pleased with the speed of the loading, Ramón walked up the gangway to the main deck. Mercifully, there was a slight breeze at this height above the water and the awning set over the ship's aft deck provided welcome relief from the searing sun. Beneath the awning, Sargento Irra, as solidly built as one of the pyramids his distant ancestors had built in the jungles of the Yucatan, sat at a makeshift desk. He was surrounded by stacks of manifests and bills of lading. Seeing Ramón approach, Irra stood and saluted. Ramón returned the salute. "Good afternoon, Sargento. How is the loading progressing?"

"Very well, Subteniente. We should be finished in five or six hours."

"And how are the men? What is your impression of them?"

Irra narrowed his eyes for a moment, then spoke slowly, "For the most part, they are a good bunch. I think we may have a few troublemakers. That is to be expected, I suppose." Irra avoided Ramón's gaze.

"It is not for us to worry ourselves about how a soldier comes to be in uniform, Sargento. Our job is to see to it that each man carries out his duties."

Ramón knew perfectly well what the bitterness in Irra's voice meant. The sergeant was passionately opposed to the Army's policy of forcible enlistment. "Corporal Chávez is a formidable man, Sargento. I am sure the two of you will be able to keep the men under control."

"Yes, Subteniente." Irra knew when to hold his tongue.

Leaving the sergeant to his work, Ramón walked forward onto the unshaded part of the deck. Through the open hatchways, he could see half a dozen of the *soldados* working alongside the Córrigan's sailors. As he walked by, Ramón heard the resonant boom of Corporal Chávez's voice as he cursed one of the men for working too slowly. Yes, thought Ramón, he will keep them in line.

Clipperton Rock appeared on the horizon, huge and white. From this direction, it was the perfect image of a ship under full sail. It was several hours more before the low-lying island itself became visible. The sea was calm, the encircling reef marked only by a broken, meandering ring of white foam. The trip had been so quiet as to be boring, the weather hot and humid. The calm sea was a blessing. Had the waves been too high for the Córrigan to use the wharf, they would have been forced to unload everything into surf boats, a slow and risky operation at the best of times. The ship's hold was like an oven as the men sweated, filling the cargo nets to be hoisted up and swung onto the wharf by the ship's steam-powered derricks. The two mules were on the wharf already, being harnessed to haul stores. A temporary pen had been constructed near the wharf to hold the pigs. The air above the crushing shed boiled in the heat.

The unloading was going well and the mountain of stores on the wharf was growing quickly. Ramón was pleased. He turned to Sargento Irra to speak but stopped abruptly at the rending sound of a pig's squeal. He turned to see a seaman make a grab for a pig and miss, as it ran across the deck in front of him. Two sailors had attempted to take one of the pigs from the pen, to get it down the gangway, but the scared pig, unexpectedly strong, had knocked over a wall of the pen. Now, all four animals ran squealing around the Córrigan's decks with half a dozen sailors in hot pursuit. The pigs twisted and turned around the ship's gear, the sailors slipping and cursing as they chased the squealing animals. The rest of the crew stopped work at the uproar and stood watching and laughing, urging their crewmates on. The chase went on until both sailors and pigs were winded. The three largest animals stood together in the extreme bows of the ship, their backs to the bulwarks. They panted in the heat, their flanks heaving. The sailors advanced on them in a line. The animals had nowhere to go. They were exhausted. Each, in turn, was grasped by the hind legs and walked, wheelbarrow fashion, down the gangway.

The smallest and fastest of the four animals, a young boar, remained at large. The brief respite had allowed him to get his breath. As the sailors advanced, he ran directly at them, driving for freedom between their legs. In the confusion, two of the sailors fell. They cursed elaborately. It had become a matter of honor to catch the animal. More seamen came to watch the spectacle, jeering at their crewmates. With three sailors behind it, the pig ran for the side of the ship furthest from the wharf. The sailors moved forward, hoping to trap the animal against the bulwarks. The pig, squealing with fright, nosed into one of the ship's freeing ports. A sailor clutched at its hind legs, but the pig pushed the port's door outward, slipped neatly through and splashed, squealing frantically, into the sea alongside the ship.

"Now, we will see if he can swim as well as he runs," one of the sailors said, laughing, as they looked over the rail into the turquoise water. A meter from the ship's side, the pig was swimming strongly, its snout held high.

The breath exploded from the pig's body and it shot high out of the water, locked between the jaws of a full-grown blacktip shark. The pig gave a single horrific shriek as the shark fell back into the water, spun its body and, with its rows of razor sharp teeth, scythed off half the pig's back. The pig rolled over, the sudden whiteness of ribs and spine stark against the crimson water. The shark hit again and again. More blacktips swarmed, drawn by the maddening scent of blood in the water and the irresistible vibrations of death. In the melee, one of the sharks tore the stomach from another. In an instant, the others turned on it, tearing it to pieces and thrashing the water to bloody foam. The men stood at the ship's side, shocked and silent.

"You live surprisingly well here, Arthur," Ramón said, as he took another sip of brandy

"The Pacific Islands Company looks after its managers, Ramón."

"So it would seem," said Ramón with a smile looking around the *salón* of Brander's house. Not up to the standards of the mainland, of course, but amazingly comfortable, all things considered.

"I had a look at your house today. It is almost finished," said Brander. "The men are doing a good job. They will sheathe the lower portion of all your buildings in corrugated iron. The crabs will eat their way through any exposed wood. You must be planning to open a library with all the bookshelves you have asked for."

Ramón laughed. "Reading is my weakness. I have several thousand books in Spanish, English, French and German in storage in Acapulco and Orizaba. When the house is finished, I will have them brought out."

"You will appreciate them when the weather turns bad, especially during hurricane season. Sometimes, we must keep inside for days at a time. In the meantime, you are welcome to read any of my more modest collection."

"You are too kind, Arthur. I have already imposed upon you too much."

Brander waved away Ramón's protests. "It has been a privilege having you in my home. But tell me, have you thought how to occupy your men's time? I have discovered that it is best to keep my own men busy, even if I must invent work for them. If they have too little to do, they get into trouble."

"I think there will be no danger of that. The *soldados* are basically good men. I hope to have their families brought here soon, so I will put them to work building better homes for themselves. Then I will put them to work building and planting raised gardens. They need to eat more fresh food. And they will need medical care. My cousin is a doctor. He is going to send me some more medicines and some medical books."

Brander's blue eyes twinkled. "You astonish me, Ramón."

"I refuse to let men under my command live in bad conditions. The government has placed me in command of the garrison and I intend to do my duty as I see fit and that includes taking care of my men."

Ramón wasn't due for leave for months, so the order to return with the Córrigan to Acapulco, after it had landed stores, took him by surprise. Less than twenty-four hours after stepping on the dock in Acapulco, he was being bounced and jostled in a stagecoach with Coronel Avalos. The trip over the mountains from Acapulco to México was grueling and frustrating, but there was no choice. No ship was scheduled to leave Acapulco for Salina Cruz within the next month. On the ride Coronel Avalos let down his guard and adopted an almost fatherly attitude to Ramón, but he absolutely forbade discussion of the reason for the trip. One night, in the old silver mining town of Taxco, about halfway to the capital, they stayed in an old monastery, converted to an inn. Over wine, after an early supper, Ramón and Avalos sat and smoked in companionable silence.

Avalos looked at Ramón through the haze of cigar smoke. "I must return direct to Acapulco after our business in the capital, Arnaud, but you can go by train to Salina Cruz and take the Demócrata on her next run to Acapulco. You will have time on your way back to stop in Orizaba, a week at least, to visit your family. Perhaps, when you get back to Acapulco, it will be time for you to ask that lovely Rovira girl to marry you." Ramón smiled. It was as though Coronel Avalos could read his mind. He could feel the heft of his moneybelt around his waist. There was almost half a year's pay in it and he knew exactly where he was going to spend it

Their reason for going to the Capital was incredible, stupendous. Surely, Ramón thought, it must be a dream. Four years earlier, he had been disgraced, within a hair's breadth of being executed by firing squad. Now, he was returning with

Avalos to their hotel after a secret meeting with the Secretary of War and the Foreign Minister, Mariscal. He had been entrusted with a diplomatic mission of the utmost delicacy and importance. Even more incredibly, tomorrow they would have meetings in Chapultepec Castle, including an audience with El Presidente, Don Porfirio Díaz himself.

That afternoon, Ramón walked along the Avenida San Francisco from the Zócalo toward the Alameda. Elegant stores on both sides of the street enticed shoppers with displays of exquisite European furniture, clothing and food. Ramón stopped and adjusted his pocket watch beneath the clock in front of La Esmeralda. Inside the store, the glass-fronted cases lining the walls glittered with gold and silver bracelets, emerald and ruby rings and diamond necklaces. The centerpiece was a tiara that might grace the head of a queen. As the owner took the little satin-lined box back from him, Ramón shook his head and said, "No, no, Señor, that is not right for her. What else do you have?"

The wizened old man opened a drawer beneath the display case and withdrew a flat ebony box. He opened the lid and inside were a dozen or more gold and silver rings, each tastefully set with gems. Ramón took the ring with the prettiest central stone. An emerald, suspended in a constellation of small diamonds. He held the ring up to the light flooding through the windows. How the stones would glow against her skin. "This is the one," he said.

The air of unreality was almost overwhelming. Ramón and Avalos spent more than an hour with Don Porfirio. El Presidente had confirmed everything the foreign minister, Mariscal, had told them. The Pacific Islands Company had made fabulous discoveries of guano on Nauru and Ocean Island in the South Pacific, the highest-grade guano ever tested from any deposit anywhere in the world. It was almost certain that they would abandon the much lower-grade workings on Clipperton. For diplomatic reasons, it was essential that operations on the island continue under Mexican license. As *comandante* of the garrison, Ramón was to go to Japan with the newly appointed ambassador and a translator to negotiate a long-term agreement with the Japanese for the guano on Clipperton, to take effect when the British left.

The Japanese, Díaz had told them, were intent on expanding their influence in the Pacific and, most importantly, they could be depended on to defend their interest in Clipperton with overwhelming military force if the French attempted to occupy the island. Ramón at last understood how Díaz had held on to power for over thirty years. The man was a political genius. Giving the Japanese an interest in the island was a masterstroke. The French would never dare to challenge the might of the Japanese navy in the Pacific. México's claim to Clipperton would be secure.

Ramón lay back on his bed in his mother's villa and stretched out, his fingers laced behind his head, grinning to himself. He was a celebrity. Everyone in Orizaba knew that he had had an audience with Don Porfirio and that he had been given a government mission to Japan. His mother had been almost speechless with excitement. He had been courted and wined and dined from the moment he had arrived in Orizaba. But already his mind was back in Acapulco. He would have less than a week there before taking a ship to San Francisco to begin his journey to Japan. But there was something he must do first. He would be gone for months. He wanted Alicia so badly, but the words of Miguel Hernández still haunted him. Félix Rovira would never let a poor soldier without prospects marry his daughter. México was full of smart young men like Rafael Gabardo who would one day inherit vast estates. What chance did he have?

He had seen her every time he had had leave, several times racked with guilt that he had spent almost every day of his leave in her company and had not even gone to Orizaba to see his mother. Alicia had received him warmly each time. They had seen a passable local production of La Traviata together and then walked arm-in-arm through Acapulco's parks and ornamental gardens. They had lunched with Alicia's great aunt in her decaying mansion behind the cathedral. To Ramón's relief, the formidable old lady had taken an instant liking to him. Shy at first, Ramón began playing his mandolin for Alicia. They had shopped together for Petra Rovira's birthday. They sat together beside the fountains on the waterfront, talking quietly, sometimes touching hands with a delicious daring. He would see her again and this time he would ask her, but first he must speak to Señor Rovira.

Ramón could feel the box with the ring in it tight against his chest. Alicia, he knew, was out dress shopping with her mother. Ramón almost lost his courage standing outside the door of the Rovira home. Miguel is right, he thought, Félix Rovira wants some rich *hacendado* for Alicia. He will never consent to having me as a son-in-law. Ramón took a deep breath and knocked on the door, his hand trembling. Uncharacteristically, Rovira opened the door himself, a newspaper in his hand. "Good morning, Ramón. It is a pleasure to see you again."

Ramón hesitated. He had expected one of the maids to open the door so he would have a few moments to collect his thoughts while waiting for Rovira in the *salón*. "Good morning, Señor," he stammered. "May I come in?"

Rovira moved back, motioning him in. The door slammed. Neither man spoke as Ramón followed Rovira through the foyer into the *salón*. They sat facing each other. Rovira's eyes bored through Ramón. "I think I can save you some difficulty, Ramón. I know why you are here."

Ramón took a breath. The little box felt like it was on fire against his body. "No, Señor, I do not think you do."

"Ramón, I see the way it is between you and my daughter." Rovira's face was expressionless.

Ramón began to speak but the words stuck in his throat. He sat tongue-tied, his body frozen. The worst had happened.

Miguel had been right. Rovira would tell him to get out of his house and never return. He would never be able to see Alicia again.

Then Rovira began to laugh, his quiet chuckle growing quickly into a full bellied laugh. He saw Ramón's crestfallen expression and laughed even louder. "Oh, Ramón, if only you could see yourself!" he gasped. Rovira wiped a tear from the corner of his eye. "Ramón, I am sorry. I should conduct myself with more dignity. I would be delighted to have you marry Alicia. I want only one thing for her and that is her happiness."

The weight crushing Ramón fell from his shoulders. At first, he was speechless. Then the words came, "Oh, Don Félix, thank you. Thank you so much. I will do anything to make her happy."

"I know you will Ramón. I apologize for my behavior. But sitting there, you reminded me so much of me asking for Alicia's mother's hand. I was terrified of her father. I could barely get the words out. But he gave his consent, just as I give mine. Petra and I have had a wonderful marriage and I know that you and Alicia will too." Rovira rose and clapped Ramón on the shoulder. "You must stay to lunch. Alicia and her mother are out for the afternoon. We will celebrate, you and I."

The servant girl put the *buñuelos* down and backed away, smiling slyly at Ramón. The sugar-dusted fritters steamed slightly. Rovira waved towards the platter. "Help yourself, Ramón. They are delicious." Ramón took several fritters and began to eat.

"Perhaps you do not think it, Ramón, but I am well pleased. Alicia will need someone to take care of her when I am gone. There is no one I trust more than you."

"Thank you, Señor. Rest assured that I would give my life for Alicia," he said.

"Then it is settled. When she comes back, you must ask her to marry you."

They ate in silence until Rovira spoke again. "These are

difficult times, Ramón."

"Yes, Señor, very difficult."

"This business in the mines and mills, more strikes and shootings. And take my word, there is more trouble ahead. And if there is, who knows what the *yanquis* will do if their interests are threatened? It is just as Don Porfirio says, 'Poor México, so far from God and so near the United States.'"

CHAPTER 9

Alicia sat in the formal garden of her parents' new villa in Orizaba. At the foot of the garden, a tributary of the Río Blanco flowed quietly past. Félix Rovira had bought the attractive villa, a short carriage ride from the railway station, to be closer to his expanding business interests in Orizaba. Ramón's telegram lay on the table beside her. How she ached for him. Since the announcement of their engagement, time had passed so terribly slowly. He had been gone for three months on his mysterious trip to Japan. He had sent the telegram to her from the capital saying he would be in Orizaba for Independence Day, in three days' time.

The months he had been away had been an eternity. She had lived for his letters. The first had come from San Francisco, which Ramón obviously loved. And then Hawaii. A paradise, he had written, the prettiest island in the world. And he had written to her of Japan, of the exotic customs and exquisite food. His letters had been filled with the sights and sounds and smells of far-off places but of his business in Japan he had said nothing. No matter, he would tell her now that he was back.

Ramón gave her hand a gentle squeeze. "I am sorry, my love, I can tell you nothing. I am sworn to secrecy by Don Porfirio himself."

"Oh, Ramón." She pouted for a moment and then her face brightened. "But you can tell me if it went well?" she asked, playing with the strand of pearls Ramón had brought back to her from Japan.

He smiled. "Very well indeed. The future of Clipperton is secure. And I have another surprise for you. I have been promoted to *teniente* and made *gobernador.*

Alicia threw her arms around him. "Oh, Ramón!" she cried. "What wonderful news. *Teniente* and *gobernador.* I cannot believe it."

He shrugged. "I can scarcely believe it myself. The past months have seemed like a dream. I keep expecting to wake and find it all gone."

"I am so happy for you, but why would they appoint a governor for such a small island?"

Ramón looked at her steadily. "I am sure there are foreign policy considerations. But we should not talk of that. But think, when we marry, you will be going to Clipperton Island as the wife of the *gobernador.*"

The gunboat Tampico's foredeck had been transformed into a playground. A group of brown-skinned women chattered and a small flock of children talked and laughed and chased each other around the deck. Leaning against the wheelhouse of the new supply ship, Ramón thought, we will have a community now, a real community. He was especially delighted with Juana Neri. Neri's wife was like her soldier husband in so many ways: older, solidly built, nut-brown, cheerful and utterly dependable. The other women automatically treated her with deference and respect, calling her Doña Juana. Ramón knew instinctively that she would exert a powerful influence for good on the island. And she was a midwife, something which could prove to be of great importance

Coronel Avalos had quickly approved Ramón's request to have the men's families move to Clipperton. The more Mexicans living on the island, the stronger México's claim and the better Don Porfirio would like it. Ramón looked across at Capitán Castellenes. He was leaning over the bridge railing looking toward Clipperton as it lifted above the horizon. His graying hair was blown by the wind as the Tampico steamed through the sunshine at ten knots, a hint of a smile playing around his lips.

The entire garrison was waiting when the Tampico came in. There was pandemonium on the wharf: *soldados* embracing their wives, throwing their children high in the air. Ramón watched in quiet amazement as these men who had seemed so hard, so self-reliant, revealed this unsuspected side of themselves for the first time. Work was forgotten. Just this once, thought Ramón, they can have their freedom. Let them enjoy today. Tomorrow, they can unload the Tampico. Tomorrow, they will be *soldados* again. He walked slowly up the narrow gauge track along the wharf and turned along the beach toward his house. Seeing the spontaneous outpouring of joy that the arrival of the women and children had created made him feel very alone. If only Alicia were here to share this moment with him.

Arthur Brander and Ramón stood shoulder to shoulder admiring the completed houses in the twilight. It had rained most of the day and the air was pungent with the smells of the island—birds and guano, fish and the sea. The old ramshackle cabins had been torn down. The *soldados*, with help from some of the guano workers, had labored long and hard. Now they and their families had real houses in which to live, houses that would keep out the wind and rain. The tropic night came on fast as the two men watched and light from kerosene lanterns gilded the windows of the cabins.

"It is a beautiful sight, is it not, Arthur?" asked Ramón.

Brander patted Ramón on the back. "A very beautiful sight. You are creating a real settlement on this island, Ramón. I congratulate you. How many people do you have now?"

"Twelve men, four are married and have their wives here and..." Ramón hesitated, "there are now six children. Yes, a real settlement at last. The new storehouse and the forge are almost finished. Soon, we will have to think of building a school for the children."

Brander laughed. "A school? You amaze me. Those children would never have gone to school on the mainland and yet here, in the middle of the ocean, you want a school for them. Such ambition for such a lonely place, Ramón."

"The children must be educated, Arthur. And, as you told me long ago, it does the men good to keep busy. Among the *soldados* are a carpenter, a bricklayer and a smith. Of course, most were farmers and I keep hoping that we will be able to grow fruit and vegetables here. The crabs have ruined our gardens again."

"The crabs eat the plants. They eat the soil itself. If you leave tools out long enough, they will eat the handles," Brander said. "Years ago, we brought in more than fifty tonnes of soil for raised gardens and the crabs ate all of it."

Ramón shook his head in amazement. "I am determined that we will grow our own food. Next time, we will surround the gardens with wire. We will sink it a meter into the ground so the crabs cannot dig under it."

"I finally gave up but I wish you luck, my friend."

"I have no intention of giving up, Arthur."

The windows rattled with the fury of the wind and the rain driving against the panes. Ramón pulled his dressing gown more tightly around himself. A bundle of Alicia's letters lay at the edge of his desk, in the light of the kerosene lamp, bound by a red ribbon. The letters were scented with her perfume and he closed his eyes and drank it in. He could see her now, the proud toss of her head, the light dancing in her eyes, the whiteness of her throat, the curve of her bosom. Soon, he thought. Soon, she will be here beside me.

He smiled to himself and picked up his pen. "My dearest Alicia," he wrote, "How I have missed you. I long for the day when we can be together always." He paused and thought. The Tampico would arrive any day now. He must finish this letter tonight, so it was ready to send back with Captain Castellenes. He would have no time for writing letters once the ship was in. "So much has happened since I wrote to you last. We have had wild weather for the past few days. The sea has driven right over the beach into the lagoon. The water now tastes of salt. Arthur says this happens several times a year. The men's houses are all finished and so is the forge.

"My cousin Louis, in Veracruz, has sent more medicines. I am so grateful for his help and the books he has sent. Two days ago, Doña Juana delivered the first baby to be born on our island. Cabrera's wife went into labor in the middle of the night and he came knocking on my door in a panic. It is a good thing Doña Juana was here. Otherwise I would have had to put into practice everything I have been reading in the books Cousin Louis has been sending. In any case, the Cabreras now have a healthy baby boy.

"We have had a few problems here. Our men are too busy to get into trouble, but the women are often bored and tend to argue and squabble with each other. I tried to get them to come together to start a sewing workshop, to give them something to do and perhaps earn a little money from the guano workers, but they are not interested. Perhaps you will have more luck with them. The cisterns are now completed. We have had a great deal of rain in the past few weeks and they are almost half full. We will not have to worry about drinking water any longer.

"I am afraid that the gardens were a failure, although I will try again. In the meantime, I have doubled my requisitions of fresh fruit and vegetables. The fresh food does not last long enough. In the month before the Tampico returns, we live almost entirely on beans, corn, rice, dried meat and tinned food.

"I have asked Coronel Avalos to send us a teacher. I hope he will. One of the women who can read and write has been teaching the children and a few of the men and women. She is doing her best, but she is poorly educated herself and can do only so much.

"The pigs have multiplied to eighteen now. We gave up trying to keep them penned. They run free now and live mainly on crabs which is very satisfactory since the island is overrun with them. Once a month, one of the *soldados* shoots a pig and we have a great fire and roast it on the beach. Doña Juana cooks for everyone and we have music and singing afterwards. Corporal Chávez plays the concertina extremely well. I, of course, play my mandolin.

"My darling, I cannot wait until we are married and are together forever. I think of you every waking moment and in my dreams.

"All my love, forever, Ramón."

The steady north winds of winter had ended at last, replaced by the unpredictable, uncomfortable and sometimes dangerous weather of summer. They had experienced their first *chubasco* since coming to the island. It was relatively small and short-lived but the tornado had cut a narrow swath through the newly completed buildings standing three kilometers to the west of the Rock. A storage building had vanished completely and it had taken a week to repair the others. Now the air was heavy and sticky and charged with electricity. There had been no breeze for days. A handful of terns circled lazily overhead. The Rock stood sentinel in the southeast corner of the island.

"Sargento," said Ramón craning his head back to see the jagged top of the Rock, "We are going to put a light on top of the Rock. And we are going to build a keeper's cabin and a supply cabin. I have had a letter from Coronel Avalos. The phosphate company has been lobbying the government to have a light erected. One of their captains claims to have almost run onto the reef at night."

Sargento Irra nodded his massive head. "I know, Teniente. I heard that the ship's mate miscalculated their position. It was only through luck that they saw the island in time to alter course."

Ramón walked around the base of the Rock to the seaward side. From here, the waves breaking over the submerged reef were plainly visible. "Coronel Avalos wrote that the French have been pressing their claim to this island. The government believes that erecting and maintaining an aid to navigation here will help establish our sovereignty."

"When will the light arrive, Teniente? We could build the cabin and prepare everything in advance." Irra shaded his eyes with his hand and looked up the fissured sides of the Rock.

"Yes, Sargento, that is exactly what I intend. The light has already been requisitioned by Coronel Avalos. I have the dimensions in my office. It is coming from France with the finest lenses the French can make." Ramón smiled. "I am sure they have no idea that it is to be installed on Clipperton. If all goes well, it should be in Acapulco in time to be loaded onto the next supply ship. Perhaps Lord Stanmore's captains can keep their ships off the reef until then."

"Yes, Teniente." Irra nodded.

"You will need ironwork and concrete. I will speak to Señor Brander and ask for his help. Come to my office, we will look at the plans."

Irra wasted no time and Brander was, as always, cooperative. An hour after sunrise the next day, a crew of Italian guano workers was at the Rock. While two men erected wooden scaffolding, the others drove a star drill into the side of the Rock with a sledgehammer. When each hole was deep enough, an iron pin was cemented in place. A series of pins leading to the top of the Rock would anchor flights of wooden ladders ascending to the summit. With an elevation above sea level of more than twenty meters, the light would be visible at a great distance from all directions. It would be the single most important aid to navigation off the west coast of the Americas between Panamá and San Diego.

At the storage shed beside the garrison storehouse, a team of soldiers was loading lumber onto a wagon for the two cabins to be built at the Rock. The mules that had come to the island with the first supply ship had long since been slaughtered and eaten. Now the soldiers had to manhandle the full wagon over the crushed coral and volcanic sand to the Rock. Time and again, they levered the wheels, sunk up to the axles, out of the sand, the air ringing with their curses and pungent with the sharp smell of their sweat.

Ramón sat at his desk in his modest office on a small rise overlooking both the sea and the lagoon. Through the tiny windows, he could see Brander's men and his own *soldados* hard at work. At least there was no shortage of building materials on the island. When the Kinkora had been wrecked on Clipperton's reef, she had been carrying a full cargo of sawn lumber from British Columbia, millions of board feet. Much of it had washed onto the island and been carefully stockpiled above the high water mark. The Tampico arrived every three months loaded with supplies and the storehouses were full to the rafters. Ramón wiped his brow and stood, straightened his tunic and went outside. The air was still and oppressive. By noon, the heat would be unbearable.

Ramón subscribed to half a dozen newspapers and twice as many magazines, most in Spanish but a few in English, French and German. Each time the Tampico arrived, she carried a bundle of papers for him. The latest had arrived several weeks ago and had remained unopened on the floor by his desk as he dropped exhausted into bed each night shortly after his evening meal in the communal dining hall. Tonight was different. He had deliberately taken a day of rest to refresh himself. He had strolled around the island to check on the work in progress in the morning and then taken a welcome *siesta*. He had eaten a filling meal of tinned beefsteak and then sat back with a feeling of deep contentment in his armchair with the bundle of papers and a glass of port beside him. Pulling off his long leather boots, he reached for the first paper.

It was the English-language Mexican *Herald*, published in México by *yanqui* business interests. The lead item concerned yet another wave of strikes in the Federal District. Ramón shook his head slowly. Miners, mill workers, railwaymen, they all wanted more. More pay. Better housing. Cheaper food. Ramón flipped the page. More and more of the same. There had been a time when the workers in Don Porfirio's México would never have dared to strike, but something was happening in the country, something fundamental was changing.

Ramón climbed the ladders that zigzagged to the summit of the Rock. Last night's thunderstorm had been a symphony of violence, brilliant electric flashes all around the horizon, following one after another, split seconds apart. At first, there had been no thunder but, as the storm wore on and the lightning strikes stabbed into the ocean closer and closer to the island, the ceaseless rumble of thunder reached a frightening crescendo. Lightning had even struck the lagoon with an earsplitting crack as Ramón had watched through his window. The storm had cleared the air and dropped the temperature dramatically. A cool breeze whipped at Ramón's frock coat and flattened his mustaches. At his side, still curing beneath layers of damp burlap, stood the concrete pedestal that would anchor the light. Our own *zócalo*, thought Ramón. It was the kind of irony he appreciated.

Many times he had been on the Zócalo, México's enormous main square, most memorably the day he had pawned his Army revolver. A mid-nineteenth century government had planned to erect an independence monument on what was then called the Plaza de la Constitución, but got no further than building the base. As government succeeded government, the base stood unadorned and futile in the *plaza*. Mexicans spoke derisively of going to the *zócalo*, the pedestal. It became a sarcastic reference to the failed plans of one hapless government after another. Eventually, the plaza itself became known as the Zócalo and, in time, plazas throughout the country were called *zócalos*.

Ramón smiled to himself. This wasn't quite the grand Zócalo of México with its Metropolitan Cathedral and National Palace but on Clipperton it would have to do. At least this pedestal wouldn't remain unadorned for long. The light was even now on its way across the Atlantic from its Parisian makers. A railing surrounded the top of the Rock. Already, a flagstaff was in place beside the pedestal and, overhead, a newly sewn Mexican flag snapped crisply in the wind, further proof of México's possession of the island.

Leaning against the railing, Ramón surveyed the island and the sea. It occurred to him that this was the only place from which Clipperton looked truly hospitable. From this vantage point, he could see the entire island, a low ring of sand sitting atop the crater rim of the extinct volcano thrusting up from the seabed. The lagoon filled the crater and some said that at the bottom of the lagoon was a vent leading deep into the Earth. Ramón looked with pride at his little piece of México, at the smooth curve of the beach against the deep blue of the sea, the cluster of palms near the settlement, the foaming of the waves on the sand, the line of breakers creaming over the reef. For all its shortcomings, Clipperton had a savage beauty of its own.

Even the nightmarish crabs had ceased to be much of a problem. Mainly nocturnal, they ranged the island after the sun dropped low in the sky, a moving carpet of ravenous life in a never-ending search for food. Even with the pigs crushing hundreds in their powerful jaws every day, the crabs still came. At first, the soldiers had encircled the entire settlement with wire fencing to keep the crabs out, but they had simply burrowed underneath it as the guano workers had predicted and had started eating their way into the storehouses. Then, for almost a month, the soldiers had gone out every night into the hordes of crabs swarming around the settlement, crushing and killing thousands. Over time, the crabs developed a fear of man that had been entirely absent before. The fear had somehow been communicated to all the crabs on the island, even those far distant from the settlement. Now, a crab anywhere on Clipperton would retreat from an approaching human as they had learned to scurry away from the pigs.

Ramón stood atop the Rock for almost an hour, now looking out to sea, now at the island, as though for the first time. At last, Coronel Avalos' words had meaning: Where there is nothing, anything is possible. Clipperton Island had been a burden to Ramón, an unpleasant duty to be attended to and left behind as quickly as possible. But, subtly, a change had occurred. Here, on Clipperton, anything really was possible. He was making something of this unlikely place. The governorship of Clipperton was not a temporary hell, a proving ground for an officer anxious to redeem himself and move on. Clipperton was an end in itself: a part of the Mexican nation a thousand kilometers out in the Pacific. A statement of national pride. A bastion against the old imperialism of the European powers and the new, thinly disguised and equally rapacious imperialism of the United States.

Clipperton was México and, as that realization took hold, Ramón became aware that, for the first time, he did not want the duty to end. He wanted to remain on the island as governor of México's most remote territory. He wanted to remain on the island to defend his country. With Alicia at his side, he would see the settlement grow and prosper. Soon, the light would be installed and lit, a beacon to ships of all nations. Clipperton was a living community, truly a part of modern México.

As soon as he received word from Sargento Irra that the installation of the light had been completed, Ramón once again climbed the ladders to the top of *la roca* to examine it. The light had been hoisted with elaborate care and bolted in place. The reservoir was filled with specially refined, ultra-clean petroleum oil. The beautifully fashioned brasswork and the elaborate plate with the maker's name— Société des Etablissements Henry-Lepaute Paris—gleamed. Ramón appreciated the irony in this and wondered if the French government had any idea that one of France's finest and most famous lighthouse lamp makers had provided this vital piece of equipment to México. And it was not the only thing the

French had unwittingly done to help México secure its claim to Clipperton. The narrow gauge track that carried the guano from the storage area to the pier, and made the whole guano operation economical, had been prefabricated in France by Decauville.

Ramón stood and admired the lamp's complex Fresnel lenses with hundreds of bevels carefully designed, cut and polished to amplify and focus the light produced by the burning oil. He ran his fingertips over the finely shaped glass. It was an object of surpassing beauty, a glorious piece of craftsmanship. Tonight, and every night from now on, this light would blaze proudly from Clipperton Island into the darkness of the Pacific with the power of fifty thousand candles.

The temperature of the air seemed to drop almost instantly and it grew suddenly dark. Ramón looked up to check the sun's progress across the sky. The sun had vanished behind a sickly overcast. The birds, which circled the Rock endlessly, had gone. He turned toward a sudden hissing sound behind him. The surface of the lagoon had turned a flat metallic gray. The wind blasted straight across the lagoon, the surface ripped away and blown into spume. It hit him in the chest and face like a solid object. He staggered against the railing and saw his cap fly far over the rail and disappear. The wind screamed and he could feel the railing digging painfully into the small of his back. He felt the railing move and he dropped quickly onto the top of the Rock, lying flat, gripping the corners of the pedestal. Spray torn from the lagoon and coral grit hissed past him, tearing at his face. The pitch of the wind's cry rose higher and Ramón realized that he must get off the Rock. The wind would be much stronger up here than on the ground. He must get down while it was still possible or risk being blown right off the Rock and into the sea.

He edged his way on all fours to the top of the ladder. His tunic was flung backwards over his head, blinding him. He stopped and struggled free of it. As he pulled the tunic off, it was torn from his hands and carried away. He turned his head toward the lagoon but the spray blinded him and the breath was pulled from his lungs. He faced away from the wind, his eyes almost closed, gasping for breath and inched down the ladder. Half way down, the noise of the wind rose to a maddened roar. Debris from the Rock blew into his numbed face. Ramón wrapped his arms completely around the ladder and locked his fingers together, knowing that if he let go, he would be torn from the ladder.

For a moment, the scream of the wind dropped in pitch and he scrambled down the ladder as quickly as he could. He dropped the last two meters to the ground. The wind roared again, as he crawled into one of the dark clefts in the base of the Rock, blinded by sand and grit. The cleft widened out and, inside, the air was eerily calm and stank of ammonia. Pillars of frozen lava rose all around to join high overhead, forming a roof. Passageways led off into the darkness. Ramón remained on his knees, breathing heavily. He felt wetness on his cheek and his hand came away sticky with blood. He leaned against one of the lava pillars until his eyes grew accustomed to the gloom. There were hundreds of birds perched silently in crevices all around him, watching him with mild curiosity. In the back of the cave, the herd of pigs snuffled quietly. The wind outside was a maniacal shriek. Panting, he leaned his head against the wall of the cave and waited for the sudden storm to pass.

The newly built houses had been designed with violent winds in mind and had withstood the storm well, but one of the storage sheds had lost its roof and some of their supplies had been soaked by rain and spray. Ramón, his face a mass of deep scratches, walked the full ten-kilometer circumference of the island, surveying the damage. He could see half a dozen places where the sea had been driven right over the ring of beach and spilled into the lagoon. He was thankful that he had chosen the highest land on the island's southwest side for the settlement.

No matter how strongly built, any house in the lowest parts of the island would sooner or later be washed away by the sea. Two of the old shanties near the boat landing, where the land was low, had been reduced to kindling. A palm tree had been uprooted and was lying forlornly on the sand, the crabs exploring its roots for food. Behind the guano shed, one of the rowboats lay capsized in the water beside the dock. Luckily, the guano shed itself had suffered very little damage. A few sheets of iron on the roof had peeled part way back, but that was nothing, Brander would have it repaired in no time.

Ramón was determined that nothing would stop him lighting the navigation light for the first time. After a quick supper, he went with Irra to the Rock. Ramón climbed first, enjoying the feeling of the gentle breeze against his body. He knelt beside the fuel reservoir and pumped until the tank reached its designed pressure and the relief valve began to hiss. Irra joined him and held open the top of the light as Ramón lit a taper and held it to the mantle. He opened the fuel valve and the mantle flamed and then began to glow with an intense white light. The Fresnel lenses glowed. Ramón closed the lamp, bolted it shut and stood back. To the west, the sun had just dropped below the horizon. Soon it would be night.

They walked away from the Rock in the growing darkness. The two men stopped near the new concrete cisterns to the east of the settlement and turned to look back at *la roca*. Brilliant white fingers of light, so clearly defined they seemed almost solid, fanned out from the top of the Rock. They reached across the dark sea in all directions. Ramón smiled and clapped Irra on the shoulder. "There, Sargento. Is that not a magnificent sight? Soon that light will be marked on every chart of the eastern Pacific."

That night, Ramón stood at the window of his bedroom for hours, smoking quietly and watching with satisfaction the beams of light stabbing far into the night. Of all his accomplishments on Clipperton, this was the one of which he was most proud. It was as though the island itself had been extended in all directions as far as the light could reach. He imagined himself standing at this window with Alicia at his side, the two of them silent, content and proud.

CHAPTER 10

The Pacific Islands Company's own ship, the SS Archer, visited Clipperton only once or twice a year to load guano. If the weather permitted and the seas were calm, she would make fast to the end of the pier and an endless succession of hopper cars filled with guano would be pushed by hand down the railway, out along the pier and then tipped into the Archer's hold. If the sea was not quiet, the Archer would make fast to the massive buoy a short distance offshore and wait. Sometimes, the waiting lasted for weeks. This time, the seas were calm and the loading went swiftly. The Archer's next port of call was Salina Cruz and as she pulled away from the pier, Ramón was on board, on his way to Orizaba for Christmas.

Adela's husband finished lighting his cigar and sat down across from Ramón before he spoke, "I am not sure when I have seen a finer Midnight Mass, Ramón." León Reyes was dark and heavily built and the resemblance to his father, Don Porfirio's Minister of War, grew more pronounced with each passing year

"It was a beautiful service, León. My father always said that Midnight Mass in the Church of San Miguel was better than at the Metropolitan Cathedral. Of course, the priest in those days was a great friend of his, so he may have been prejudiced."

"Not a bit of it," said Reyes. "He was right. Are your Mother and Adela going to join us?"

"They are just having a word with the servants about the Christmas *banquete*. They will be with us shortly."

Reyes blew a cloud of smoke to the ceiling. "You are looking very well these days, Ramón."

"I am sure you have heard, I have a new posting as *gobernador* of Clipperton Island. Perhaps you would convey my gratitude to your father for any influence he may have exerted on my behalf."

"I know that my father is delighted to help you in whatever way he can, Ramón, but I am sure your talents had much more to do with your appointment than anything my father may have done."

"Thank you, León, it is kind of you to say so, but please give him my thanks in any case. What is happening at the textile mill? I saw the workers swarming around when I rode past yesterday. Why are they not at work?"

"It is more of this insanity, Ramón. I honestly think the country is going mad. In Puebla, the textile workers went on strike for higher pay. The Río Blanco workers started sending them food, so the managers closed the mill. It has actually worked out quite well, since there was too much cotton on the world market and the price was depressed. If you ride up into the mountains, you will find the workers there every day gathering roots and berries for food. They must be getting very hungry by now." León Reyes tapped the ash from his cigar and leaned forward. "But enough of the mill. The problem will doubtless take care of itself. Adela has told me about your girl, Alicia. I met her father in México last year, you know."

"She is the most wonderful girl I have ever met, León. You will be able to meet Alicia and her parents on New Year's Eve. You and Adela will be staying until then?"

"Of course we will stay, Ramón. I would not miss meeting Alicia for the world."

All the public rooms of the Hotel France were awash in fresh cut flowers, their fragrance filling every corner of the hotel. In three hours, it would be 1907. It pleased Ramón that he could now afford to host his family and the Roviras at Orizaba's grandest hotel to celebrate New Year's Eve in style. Ramón and Alicia sat across the table from each other, exchanging smiles and secret glances, as course succeeded course and toast followed toast. At Alicia's throat was the simple silver locket he had given her for Christmas. Rubbing it lightly between her fingers, she looked up to see Ramón watching her and blushed. The wine steward refilled their glasses. Doña Carlota raised hers. "Ramón, you have made me proud. To 1907. May it bring you even greater success."

"Thank you, Mamá. And may I propose a toast to you? To the finest mother a man could have."

It occurred to Ramón that Orizaba, with its growing wealth and constant influx of European immigrants, had become a truly sophisticated, even a cosmopolitan, city. The cuisine at the Hotel France was every bit as good as the best restaurants in México. The wine cellar was nothing short of magnificent, abundantly stocked with the finest French, Spanish and Italian wines. Around them sat the Barcelonnette owners of the Río Blanco and other mills, the owners of the Moctezuma brewery and a generous sprinkling of the city's sleek merchants with their chattering wives, many dressed in the latest French fashions, all enjoying their New Year's Eve. There seemed to be no end to prosperity in Orizaba. As they sipped their liqueurs, Ramón steered the conversation back to the trouble at the Mill. "Have you heard what is happening, Mamá?" he asked.

"You might do better to ask those gentlemen over there," she replied, inclining her head toward a nearby table. "That is Señor Hartington. He is English, the manager of the Río Blanco Mill. Everyone says Don Porfirio will have to use the Army to get those people back to work."

"Surely there is a better way."

"Now, Ramón. You know how lazy these people can be. Some of them need a little encouragement. If it were not for the mill, most of them would starve to death." Ramón hesitated and Señora Arnaud went on, "Remember the trouble we have had with some of the servants. You know what they are like. Not much better than savages, most of them. They need a firm hand."

Ramón thought for an instant of the soldiers he had known. Savages some of them, perhaps, but made so, not born. But he could never explain that to his mother. "Yes, Mamá, of course," he said.

"In any case," said Señora Arnaud, "Let us forget about this unpleasantness and celebrate the New Year."

Ramón sat on the terrace with his sister, engrossed in a newspaper that was devoted almost exclusively to news of the trouble at the Río Blanco Mill and how it had been ended through Don Porfirio's personal intervention. The mill had been built to use the Niagara of water rushing down the Río Blanco on the outskirts of Orizaba. The rains and melting snow in the surrounding mountains provided limitless water to generate the electricity that ran the mill's hundreds of looms and other machines. The owners made much of the fact that it was the most modern and profitable cotton mill in the world, employing over six thousand people. It was an enormous complex, larger than many towns and completely surrounded by a wall six meters high.

The newspaper Ramón was reading was owned by a Liberal in México, a man transparently on the side of the workers. The paper made much of the fact that the workers lived in dirt-floored hovels or crowded barracks and were paid not in cash, but in credit at the company store where goods cost half again as much as in the market at Orizaba. Like so many businesses in the area, the store was owned by a Barcelonnette. Like the plantation laborers in the Yucatán, the mill workers could never repay the advances they had received from labor agents and so had to work in debt bondage in the Rio Blanco Mill until they died. The paper condemned the employment of young children in the mill, the thirteen-hour workday and the dangers of breathing the lint-laden air. In the poisonous fumes of the dye rooms, the writer claimed, workers usually survived less than twelve months.

Adela looked up at Ramón and sniffed, "Why do you read

that rag, Ramón? León says it is all Liberal nonsense. In any case, Don Porfirio has succeeded. León says the strike is over. The workers will go back on the same terms as they left. Life in Orizaba can go back to normal."

Ramón swept off his cap and bowed low. Alicia giggled as she stepped down from the carriage. Dismissing it, Ramón folded Alicia's hand over his arm and they walked down the sidewalk toward Orizaba's main shopping district. The streets were unusually quiet. The usual frantic hustle and bustle, the familiar sound of Orizaba's prosperity, was muted. A few riders on horseback and a handful of bicyclists went past. The cars of El Urbano, the street railway, clattered by, less than half full. At the photography studio, each tried to make the other laugh, exasperating the photographer. Finally, he was satisfied, telling them to return the next day for the miniatures that would go into Alicia's new locket.

They sat in the *café* the following day, sipping coffee and sorting repeatedly and without success through the miniatures. "This is impossible," laughed Ramón. "You select one of me and I will select one of you." Alicia smiled and shuffled them about the table. After a moment's thought, she picked one up and placed it in the locket. Ramón's image looked out from the photograph, serious, proud, a little haughty, his dark eyes gleaming with intelligence. Ramón paused, then selected a photograph and placed it in the other half. From it, Alicia, the smallest hint of a smile on her lips, the tiny trace of a dimple on her chin, her eyes lit from within, stared deep into the viewer's eyes.

Alicia snapped the locket shut and slipped it over her head, nestling it under the collar of her dress. She took Ramón's hand and squeezed it gently. "Now we will be together, always."

A thousand or more Río Blanco workers massed in front of the company store a week after New Year's Day 1907, gaunt men in soiled cotton trousers and exhausted women carrying crying babies as emaciated older children clung to their skirts. The workers' leader, Margarita Martinez, begged the clerks to open the store and extend a week's credit to the workers for corn meal and beans. "These people want to go back to work as Don Porfirio says they must, but they are starving. They have no money to buy food," she said, sweeping her arm over the silent crowd. "They do not have the strength to work. They must have food. What good are they to the Mill if they cannot work?" In answer, the clerks in the store slammed and bolted the shutters.

Low murmuring grew into an excited hubbub and then into an angry roar. The crowd surged forward and ragged, starving men reached up to the shutters of the store and began tearing at them. Gunshots rang out from the store. At one end of the building, a fire was started and the flames quickly climbed the wall and began licking at the roof. In shock, the crowd recoiled and fell silent again, watching the flames slowly engulf the building. Over the next three days, the *federales* and *rurales* hunted down the protesters, executing many on the spot and taking hundreds more to jail.

"Two hundred of the damned rabble killed. Not enough if you ask me," said Señor Galván as he rode beside Ramón along the deserted road bordering the high wall around the mill. Behind the mill, the waters of the Río Blanco rushed toward the faraway sea. Señor Galván had been a family friend for almost the whole of Ramón's life but now he seemed like a stranger. Ramón remained silent; he could think of nothing to say to this man. Señor Galván guided his mare carefully around a sprawling patch of dried blood and then reined the horse in. "And they had the courage to execute the *rurales* who disobeyed the order to shoot the vermin. That is the kind of firmness this country needs. And that woman," said Señor Galván. "What was her name? Was she shot?"

Ramón looked up. "Margarita Martinez. No. She is in Fuerte San Juan de Ulúa along with the editor of that

116

Liberal newspaper. And five hundred others have been sent to the Yucatán. They are to become laborers on the chicle plantations."

Señor Galván shook his finger at Ramón. "These people are lucky to have any work at all and they are lucky to be alive. They just will not understand that the mines and mills and plantations give them their livelihood. If they drive the foreign investors away, they will have nothing. They cannot go back to the land, they do not own it."

"That is not what they believe," said Ramón. "They believe it was stolen from them and that they will get it back. You have heard of Emiliano Zapata, organizing the *peones* on the *haciendas*?"

"I know about him, Ramón and his cry of 'Land and Liberty'. Let him try to take the *hacendados'* land and he will get what the Río Blanco rabble got, a *federale* bullet in the back. He is a zealot, a madman. He thinks that the *peones* will rise up and take back the *hacienda* lands. He will not last long, you may bank upon it."

They rode back past the mill toward Orizaba, following the railroad tracks by the river. The mountains around them darkened quickly as the sun set. On a siding half-hidden by scrub, nine flatcars sat on the rails. They were piled high with the blood-soaked bodies of men, women and children, some no more than babies. Arms and legs hung pathetically over the sides of the flatcars. There were dark puddles of blood in the gravel between the rails. Brown faces, some still frozen in soundless screams, stared at them accusingly as they rode by. Ramón nodded toward them sadly. "They will end up in Veracruz Harbor. Food for the sharks. Surely to God there must be a better way than this."

Señor Galván looked at Ramón sharply, then dug his spurs in and rode away.

CHAPTER 11

R amón sat quietly in his office reading the mail that had just been brought ashore from the Tampico. The letter from Alicia was brimming with love and excitement and plans for their wedding. Her wedding gown had been ordered from France and the bridesmaids' dresses were already being made in México. The wedding cake would have ten layers and would serve three hundred at the reception at the Hotel France. She had been furniture shopping for their house on the island. She missed Ramón terribly. Soon they would be together forever. She couldn't wait, she would burst with waiting. Ramón smiled. Even though Alicia had written the letter weeks ago, he could feel her urgency as though she were beside him. Alicia went through every detail of the wedding, asking Ramón's advice on the guest list, the flowers, the menu, the honeymoon. She sent her deepest love. He smiled again at the thought of Alicia, then another thought came to him. He must send a note to Miguel asking him to be best man and he must write to his tailor and order a new dress uniform for the wedding.

Ramón pulled the latest bundle of newspapers and magazines toward himself. More of the same. Strikes. Shootings. Hangings. More trouble in Baja, California. There seemed to be no end to it. He threw the newspapers down and reached for a cigar. He leaned back in his big leather chair, the blue smoke drifting along the rough-sawn ceiling beams. The magazines had good news, at least, of the spectacular public buildings and monuments being constructed to celebrate the Centennial of Independence in 1910. A palace of fine arts was planned for the Alameda Park in the capital. He looked at the detailed drawing of the spectacular glass curtain Tiffany would make for the theater. The two volcanoes that dominated the capital's horizon, Popocatépetl and Iztaccíhuatl, would be represented in all their majesty in the leaded glass of the curtain. Lights behind the curtain would mimic sunrise and sunset. The entire month of September was to be a public holiday.

Ramón picked up Pearson's Magazine, an English language magazine published in Britain and the United States. The lead article was an interview with El Presidente conducted by an American journalist, James Creelman. Such a thing was unheard of. El Presidente did not grant interviews to journalists under any circumstances. Ramón's brow furrowed as he read with growing disbelief. His thirty years in power had been to prepare México for democracy, Don Porfirio said. He would permit organized opposition parties to run in the presidential election scheduled for 1910. A vibrant democracy would be his legacy to the nation.

Ramón paused for a moment then shook his head in admiration. Don Porfirio was a wily old goat. He had found the perfect way to douse the flames of unrest now spreading like brushfire across the country from the mines and mills in the north to the plantations in the far south. Democracy! Ramón laughed out loud. The concept of one man, one vote, would never come to pass in México. The opposition might well form their parties and run in the election, but when the ballots were counted, Ramón knew, México would still be in the iron grip of Don Porfirio Díaz and his *científicos*.

One of the pigs had been killed and roasted on the beach near the capstan. After everyone had eaten their fill, Ramón had played his mandolin. The soldiers, their wives and children, sat on the beach, mesmerized by the music, as the sun went down. Arthur Brander walked along the beach toward them and sat down on a log and listened to Ramón play. When Ramón finished, Brander patted the log he was sitting on, motioning

Ramón to sit beside him. "I am afraid I have bad news, my friend. There was a letter for me from the Company on the Tampico. I have been recalled to London. They are sending out a German, Gustav Schultz, to replace me."

Ramón shook his head sadly, "I will be sorry to see you go, Arthur. I am indebted to you for all your help and especially for your many kindnesses to me when I first came here."

"It was my pleasure. I shall miss our talks, Ramón. I have enjoyed them a great deal."

"As have I," replied Ramón.

"But before I leave, I will make sure that your new house is properly completed. My men are almost finished."

"Once again, my thanks, Arthur. I am sure that Alicia will be grateful too." The house in which Ramón and Alicia were to live had been under construction by the Pacific Island Company's work crew, with the help of some of the soldiers, for several months. The materials needed to complete it would be unloaded from the Tampico tomorrow.

Brander stared into the darkness of the ocean. "I will come back to visit some day, Ramón. Perhaps I can persuade the Company to send me here from time to time for an inspection."

The supply ship on which Arthur Brander left brought his successor, Gustav Schultz and his wife and child. The short, stockily built German's muttonchop whiskers bracketed a smiling face. "Leutnant Arnaud, so good to see you," said Schultz in German, beaming, as he opened the door to what had been Arthur Brander's house. "Come in, come in." Ramón stepped inside.

"Herr Schultz," Ramón said, extending his hand. "I trust you are settling in well?"

"Very well, thank you. Mr. Brander's house is very comfortable."

Ramón smiled. "Arthur liked his comforts. I spent many happy evenings here with him, Herr Schultz, talking and playing cards."

"I hope that we too shall be friends. Please call me Gustav and I hope that I may call you Ramón."

Ramón nodded. "Of course."

On the way back to his new house, Ramón reflected on how desperately he wanted Alicia to share his life on Clipperton. Settling into his chair beside the driftwood fire, he lit a cheroot and opened the book Alicia had sent. The author was Francisco Ignacio Madero. His name was familiar to Ramón but, at first, he couldn't place it. Then, he remembered. Madero was a Liberal from the north who had tried and failed to mount an effective opposition to Don Porfirio at the last election. Madero's family owned vast estates and had accumulated prodigious wealth.

But Francisco Madero was not like other *hacendados*. It was said that he provided the *peones* and their families on his *haciendas* with medical care and education. That he paid them high wages and gave them clean houses in which to live. There was even a rumor that Madero had *indio* orphans living in his own home and that he fed up to a hundred children there every day. Finally, he was a vegetarian. He was regarded by the *científicos* as an absurd little man, scarcely a man at all. Not someone to be taken seriously and certainly no threat to Don Porfirio. Ramón opened the book and began to read.

It was long past midnight when he finished. The ashes of the driftwood fire lay cold on the hearth and the room was chilly. The oil lamp at Ramón's side was beginning to flicker. The book was clearly treasonous, a direct, well-articulated challenge to Don Porfirio. Madero had taken the President at his word that he would permit opposition in the election in 1910. Madero was proposing a policy of no presidential re-election; no president would be permitted to serve two consecutive terms. Such a constitutional amendment would prevent Don Porfirio from running again and would prevent any other leader from holding on to power as he had. It was scarcely conceivable that such a book could be published.

Ramón strolled slowly along the strip of beach toward the home that Alicia would soon share with him. The sun climbed high into the sky. Like the crabs lying motionless in every scrap of shade, the islanders sought refuge from the heat of the early afternoon and everyone was indoors except Ramón. The house, the only one of two stories on the island, was complete now. Ramón paused to wipe his forehead then entered the door on the lagoon side of the house. He entered the central hall that extended right through to the other side of the house where windows gave a commanding view of the sea. Bookshelves lined the *salón*, floor to ceiling.

Ramón looked at the thermometer outside the window and went to his desk to record the temperature in his journal, forty degrees centigrade. The humidity must be very nearly one hundred per cent. The weather had been settled for weeks, the sun rising and setting methodically in a cloudless sky, setting the sand alight. It burned the feet through thick leather soles and turned everything on the island into a shimmering mirage. The cisterns were only a quarter full. Fine weather was a mixed blessing; the heat was getting to be too much and they needed rain to refill the cisterns. He went to the washstand and splashed water on the back of his neck. It felt deliciously cool as it trickled down his back. He finished packing his bag and walked toward the wharf where the Tampico lay, ready to take him to Acapulco. In two weeks, he and Alicia would be man and wife.

CHAPTER 12

The rain stopped an hour before the service, leaving the pavements and cobblestones of Orizaba steaming. The white and yellow stucco of the parish church of San Miguel, freshly washed by the rain, gleamed in the sun. The strains of Ave María floated through the doorway of the church and drifted across the flowerbeds of the Parque del Castillo. Alicia walked slowly through the doors on her father's arm, her heart racing, her eyes glowing with happiness. Her Parisian dress was a spectacular confection of beadwork, lace and organza. Every pew was filled, the women in their extravagant floral hats, the men in tails or military uniform. Every head in the church turned toward Alicia. Both sides of the aisle, from the doors to the main altar, were lined with tall vases of gardenias, their scent so intoxicating, the air almost a tangible thing. The ancient walls of the church were bathed in the flickering glow of a thousand candles.

Ramón stood straight and tall at the altar, handsome in full dress uniform, Miguel Hernández at his side. The altar was buried in an avalanche of white lilies. High overhead, sunlight poured through the windows around the dome of San Miguel. She walked down the aisle toward Ramón, her heart pounding uncontrollably. As he placed Alicia's hand on Ramón's arm, Félix Rovira hesitated, then kissed her on the cheek, whispering "I love you, my darling Licha."

Ramón and Alicia walked arm in arm, man and wife, from the altar. León Reyes gave Ramón a broad wink from his pew as they passed. Doña Carlota, still in the black of mourning after all these years, clutched at Adela's arm, then wiped away a single tear. Although it scarcely seemed possible to Ramón, Alicia looked more beautiful than ever, her blue-black hair swept back beneath her headdress, her face radiant. Alicia stole a glance at Ramón and gave him a quick smile as the bells of San Miguel began to ring for them.

The *banquete* at the Hotel France had gone on hours longer than planned. The flowers, the food, the drink, the music; everything had been perfect. The only sadness had been the parting from their families at the train station as they boarded The Mexicano for the Capital. It had been Alicia's choice to spend their honeymoon in México at the Hotel Iturbide. It was a place of happy memories for her. When, as a little girl, Alicia had traveled with her parents to México for the first time, they had lived in the Iturbide for a month, just after its conversion from emperor's palace to hotel. She warmed at the memories of herself as a child running singing through the galleries of sweeping arches, always a step ahead of the lighthearted scolding of the maids

Alicia came out of the bathroom wearing a light cotton nightdress enlivened by a hint of embroidery. Her hair was loose, cascading across her shoulders. The electric light was off. The only light in the room came from a candle on the nightstand. Ramón sat on top of the bedclothes, fully dressed, smoking. He looked across the room at her and smiled shyly. "You are very beautiful, Alicia."

"And you are very gallant, Teniente," she said with a smile.

Alicia went to him and kneeled on the bed beside him. He held out his hand to her and said, "I am the luckiest man in all of México."

Alicia took his hand and placed it on the curve of her breast. She felt so soft, so round, so warm, through the thin fabric. He didn't know what to do. Once, only once, he had been with an obliging girl in Orizaba. The whole episode had been so humiliating that he had pushed the details from his mind.

His knowledge of sex, such as it was, had come entirely from the unsavory bragging of his contemporaries. He had listened, at first with envy and then with disgust, to the graphic descriptions of lurid and heartless conquests claimed by his friends and fellow soldiers. Alicia, he was sure, knew even less than he did.

He had thought of this moment so many times. But now that it was upon him, what would he do? What should he do? Avoiding her eyes, he reached tentatively for the small bow at the neck of her nightdress and slowly pulled the ribbon. It knotted and would not move. Alicia giggled. He looked up at her and she laughed again. Ramón laughed too and struggled with the ribbon. The knot came undone suddenly and Alicia gave a small gasp as the fabric fell from her shoulders. Her skin was as white as milk, her silver locket nestled between her breasts.

Ramón's throat felt constricted. He could hear Alicia's breath catching in her throat. He felt sweat trickling in rivulets down his back. He held her to him, feeling the perfect smoothness of her cheek, burying his face in her hair. It smelled faintly of roses. She shuddered as her nipples brushed against his shirt. Ramón had not shaved since the morning, since before they were married, she realized with a shock, and the tingle of his face against hers was electrifying.

Alicia and her girlhood friend, Emilia, had whiled away many happy hours imagining what this moment would be like for each of them, what it would feel like to be taken by a man. But all of the girlish imaginings had not prepared Alicia for the crazy mixture of fear and excitement that made her tremble, made her want to run away and stay at the same time.

Their two weeks in México seemed to end almost before it had begun. They went to the opera, to the theater, to concerts, to a ball at the Spanish Casino. They spent the days in the museums and art galleries and parks. Each night, they returned to the Iturbide and made love with growing ease and passion.

Miguel Hernández had been cheerfully insistent in offering them the use of his family's villa in Cuernavaca. Only fifty kilometers from México, the lush landscape of Cuernavaca seemed to wrap itself around them. The regal *haciendas* built by the Spanish still stood and, as they traveled through the countryside, they saw teams of oxen pulling wooden plows and *peones* laboring in the fields, as they had since the Conquest. The Hernández villa was much smaller than the *haciendas* but well proportioned and airy. The high wall surrounding the villa was topped by a riot of colorful flowers. The servants had taken their luggage and Alicia wandered through the villa, exploring, while Ramón leaned, smoking, against a column in the courtyard, watching what he thought must be a golden eagle spiralling effortlessly toward the sun.

The next day, at lunch in the courtyard, Ramón found that he was ravenous for meat. The tinned, salted and dried meat on the island was relieved only occasionally by fresh pork or chicken. The beef from the local *haciendas* was excellent and he sent the young *indio* girl back for more. Alicia watched him enjoying his meal. "Ramón," she said, "tell me it will always be like this."

He smiled and took her hand, saying, "How I wish it could be, my darling."

They sat on the patio of the Hotel Bella Vista, pleasantly tired from a day of riding in the hills around Cuernavaca. The young men and women of the town were promenading on the square, watching each other with bright, eager eyes. Beneath the trees, a small group of *indios* squatted on the ground. On the far side of the square, a guitarist played and sang. Ramón looked up from his dinner with satisfaction. "I must offer Miguel our deepest thanks. Cuernavaca has been wonderful."

Alicia nodded, smiling. "Yes, it has, Ramón. I have never been happier." She turned to watch a small, dirty boy enter the patio at the far end and move from table to table. On his back, he carried a bundle of rags as big as himself. As he worked his way toward them, Alicia could hear the harsh voices of the other diners sending him away. As he reached their table, a small face, contorted with pain peered out from the bundle on the boy's back. Shrunken, misshapen limbs hung motionless from the rags. The boy turned wise brown eyes on Alicia. "Alms for my brother, Señora. Alms for my brother."

Before Alicia could speak, the manager rushed onto the patio, hurling a stream of abuse and striking at the child. "My apologies, Señor and Señora. These beggars, we try to keep them away from our customers, but they are so persistent." He stood by their table, wringing his hands and clucking. Alicia, ignoring the manager, watched as the little boy struggled to carry his brother across the square.

They rode through the countryside outside Cuernavaca in silence. Ahead, passing over the trail, an old aqueduct leaped across the valley on slender arches. In the light of the setting sun, the stone of the aqueduct took on a rosy glow. Ramón stopped his horse to allow Alicia to come up beside him. The last few groups of *peones* were leaving the fields, their rough cotton clothing like patches of snow against the green of the fields. Under the arches, half a dozen of them, their faces blackened by the sun, shuffled along. They bowed deeply and murmured the obligatory "Go with God," to the young Army officer and his lady as they passed. Ramón nodded his acknowledgment and, when the *peones* had gone, he looked up at the archway carrying the aqueduct far above. High overhead, red paint had been splashed like blood on the stone. The crude writing spelled out, "*Viva la revolución*".

Alicia and Ramón stood together in the bow of the Tampico as the ship eased into the wharf where Gustav Schultz, Sargento Irra and the entire garrison stood, waving and cheering. Alicia had heard Ramón describe the island so many times that the picture of it in her mind had become very definite. Much was as she had expected: the bottomless blue of the sea, the countless birds diving and turning like scraps of white paper in the sky. But there were surprises. The land was so low, only a few meters above the level of the sea. And so much of the island was taken up by the lagoon. Coming to this island and living with Ramón had occupied her dreams for so long, but it had become very real, very suddenly. Could she stand living out here, so far from her family, from her friends? Would the people of the garrison accept her or would she be alone, isolated, having only Ramón to talk to?

As they came down the gangway, Schultz came up and welcomed them. Ramón introduced his new bride to the garrison and the women and children came forward, some bearing handmade wedding gifts. Alicia was moved almost to tears. Clearly, these people had so little to give. While the men began unloading the Tampico, Ramón and Alicia walked, hand in hand, to the settlement. "What wonderful people. How kind of them to make those presents for us," said Alicia.

Ramón squeezed her hand. "The garrison really has become a community. And now that you are here, my darling, it will be even more so."

Alicia stopped and looked up. "What a fabulous sight, those birds. I have never seen so many in my life. There must be millions of them and what a noise they make."

Ramón nodded. "Arthur once told me that a *yanqui* expedition did a survey and estimated that, depending on the time of year, there were a million birds here of eighty different kinds. And five million land crabs. You will get used to the sound. At this time of year, the birds come from all over the eastern Pacific to nest here. Those are terns. There are thousands of boobies and bigger birds too, frigate birds and albatross."

They walked on in silence beside the lagoon, Alicia looking toward the freshly painted houses of the settlement. "The children need better care, Ramón," she said suddenly. "They look dirty and their clothing is poor."

"I know, my dear but it is better than it was. They are

getting much better food now and they all have a warm and dry place to sleep but there is a limit to how much I can do. You remember, I tried to get the women interested in starting a sewing workshop. The children could have had better clothes." He shrugged. "Perhaps you can convince them. You might have more influence with them than me."

In the dining room of her new home, Alicia stood and looked around appraisingly. The furniture they had brought out from the mainland was oversized for the room, but it was of very good quality and comfortable. The new house had been almost bare when she had arrived, just a few basic, simple items of furniture from Ramón's old house and thousands of books; no drapes, no paintings, the only photograph a formal portrait of her. Poor Ramón, she had thought, living here all alone in this empty house with only his books for company. How desperately it had needed a woman's touch. Now there were drapes at every window. The main hallway was hung with an eclectic mix of paintings. Family photographs adorned the walls. A pair of canaries sang in an ornate cage. The *soldados* had wrestled the four-poster bed up the stairs and into their bedroom. A new grandfather clock, a gift from the Roviras, stood guard at the foot of the stairs. In the *salón* was Ramón's pride and joy, one of the new Victrola phonographs, with a collection of discs. Outside, Alicia, with the help of some of the women, had transplanted lianas, which grew wild all over the island in spite of the crabs, around the coral stone foundation of the house. Soon they would cover the walls, helping to keep the house cool in the blazing sun.

"Hello, my darling," Ramón called along the length of the hall as he stepped through the back door. Alicia, sitting on the floor at the far end, surrounded by the garrison's children, looked up, pushed a strand of hair from her face and smiled broadly. The hallway ran the full depth of the house and, through the window above Alicia's head, Ramón could see the deep blue of the ocean. The paintings on the walls of the hallway had been moved elsewhere in the house to make room for maps, pictures and sheets of paper with the alphabet and simple words spelled out. The children, from the tiniest mite to a twelve-year-old, sat rapt in a circle on the floor around Alicia.

These children are privileged, thought Ramón. On the mainland, if they were lucky, they would be on the streets from dawn until dusk, begging or selling matches or perhaps themselves. If they were unlucky, they would be captive on the sugar plantations or in the sisal fields. On Clipperton, they were learning to read and write. They were learning arithmetic, history, geography and simple science. Ramón clambered awkwardly over a pile of books, smiled comically at Alicia and went into the *salón*. Two of the older children were in the room, searching for books on the shelves. "Pardon us Teniente," began the oldest girl. "Doña Alicia said we could look for books to read."

Ramón smiled in resignation and sank into a chair. "Of course you may." He watched as the two girls looked systematically through the books. Who would believe it, he thought? Who in their right mind would believe that Ramón and Alicia Arnaud had turned their own home into a school and a library for the children of the garrison? Who would believe that even some of the adults were being taught to read and write by Alicia and that they too could be found in the *gobernador's* house searching for books to read? Ramón chuckled to himself. "Mother of God," he thought, "I am almost as bad as Madero. If the Ministry of War ever finds out, they will probably court-martial me again. Well, they wanted a settlement on Clipperton Island and that is exactly what I am giving them."

It was well after midnight when the last of the *soldados* and their families made their way back to their houses. Every Saturday night since midsummer, to celebrate the end of the week's work, they had had a *banquete*, each family saving a few special items of food and drink during the week to contribute to the celebration. Doña Juana cooked for everyone. Differences of rank, social standing and race were forgotten. It was a fine end to the week and, combined with the day of rest following, gave everyone something special to look forward to

Today's celebration had been different. It was Alicia's first Christmas on the island. There had been gifts and chocolate for the children. In the cool of the evening, the adults ate and drank on tables set out in the moonlight. Ramón had played records on his Victrola and then played his mandolin while Alicia sang and everyone danced.

As they made their way back into their house afterward, Alicia took hold of Ramón's arm for support. The celebration had made her more tired than usual. Ramón helped her into the house and poured her a small glass of brandy. She sat cradling it in the soft light from the oil lamps. Ramón looked at her and smiled. She had just begun to show.

The Tampico arrived on the second day of the New Year, bringing letters, newspapers, supplies for the garrison, Christmas gifts and a fresh draft of soldiers, including a new second-in-command, Subteniente Picazo and his wife. Ramón said goodbye formally to the departing soldiers and their families with Picazo, tall and thin, at his elbow. After giving Picazo his orders, Ramón turned to Alicia. "My darling, I hope you will reconsider. You must go to Acapulco with the ship to see a doctor. You cannot have the baby here."

Alicia looked at him reproachfully. "Ramón, I thought we had decided this. Doña Juana is here to help. She is a very experienced midwife. She has delivered hundreds of babies. I can have our baby here. I am perfectly healthy."

Ramón began to speak but stopped. There was no point arguing with Alicia. One way or another, she always got what she wanted. They sat up in bed in the darkness, the only light the glow of Ramón's cheroot. Through the open windows came the gentle lapping of the water on the beach. Alicia leaned sleepily against Ramón. "It was very kind of Señor Brander

131

to send us all that wine and food. It must have cost a small fortune."

Ramón stroked her hair and nodded in the darkness. "Yes, he is a very generous man. When I first came here he was extraordinarily kind to me." He could hear Alicia's breathing growing deeper as she drifted toward sleep. "There was a letter from Arthur with all those supplies," he said suddenly.

"Really?" murmured Alicia. "You did not mention it before." Ramón remained silent. Alicia was wide awake now. "Why not, Ramón?"

"He says that the Company may soon stop mining here. When the time comes, they will take all their people off with the exception of one or two men to maintain the machinery. I knew long ago that the company had discovered richer deposits in the South Pacific but I always hoped that they would remain here." Ramón lapsed into silence. Sworn to secrecy by Don Porfirio, he couldn't tell Alicia about the agreement reached with the Japanese. He had assumed that when the Pacific Islands Company eventually left the island, the Japanese would immediately take their place. But the Japanese seemed to have lost interest.

Alicia gripped his arm tightly. "What will happen when the company leaves, Ramón? What will happen to the garrison? Will we stay here?"

Ramón sighed. "I do not know, my darling. We must wait and see what is to become of us."

Alicia's time came in the middle of a hot, humid night. The baby was delivered by Doña Juana after a long but uneventful labor. Alicia lay back in bed looking tenderly at the baby slumbering in the crib beside her. The baby, tufts of dark hair sticking up at wild angles, stirred in its sleep and made a small gurgling sound. Alicia smiled. Ramón had so desperately wanted a son and she had given him one. After all the worry about having the baby on the island, the delivery had been easy, the baby strong and healthy. Doña Juana had had to do little more than hold Alicia's hand.

Ramón would be back as soon as he had given the *soldados* their orders for the day and they would talk over morning coffee. Ramoncito began to wake now, kicking his covers and whimpering quietly. Alicia pushed the bedclothes aside and stood. Before going to the baby, she went to the window facing the lagoon and looked across at *la roca*. She could just see a figure striding in the distance. It was Ramón; no one else walked with back so straight, head so high. She smiled to herself then crossed the room to pick up her son.

Capitán Castellenes patted the bundle of newspapers and magazines beside him. "There is much news, Ramón. Francisco Madero is in jail."

Ramón spoke quietly, "He had no idea who he was up against in Don Porfirio. What else could he have expected?"

"They met, Don Porfirio and Madero. Madero said he would accept Don Porfirio as President only as a step to what he calls a real democracy. Can you imagine anyone saying such a thing to Don Porfirio?"

Ramón shook his head in disbelief. "What did Don Porfirio do?"

"There were mobs in the street supporting Madero, so Don Porfirio had him arrested for inciting insurrection. He has embargoed the Madero estates. Madero has been jailed in San Luis Potosí. But, true to his word, El Presidente has let Madero's name stand for the presidential election."

Ramón shrugged. "For all the good it will do him."

Alicia took another sip of the tea her father had sent on the Tampico and turned the page of the newspaper. The tea was Darjeeling and delicious. She smiled inwardly at her father's thoughtfulness; he knew how much she enjoyed fine tea. She enjoyed reading the newspapers Capitán Castellenes brought too, especially the ones published in México and Orizaba. Madero had spoken from the balcony of the Hotel France in

Orizaba and delivered an impassioned speech to a cheering crowd of twenty thousand. Then there was the story of Madero's dramatic arrest.

Aside from the political news, there was article after article on the Centennial celebrations being planned for September. The Centennial would be a once-in-a-lifetime event, surely the greatest celebration of national pride in the history of the world. She read about the planned garden party for fifty thousand in Chapultepec Park, the state dinner for thousands to be hosted by El Presidente and the pageant of Mexican history that would take almost a full day to pass. Surely, Coronel Avalos would allow Ramón to extend his leave and stay in the capital for the month so they could see all the events and go to all the parties. Alicia almost hugged herself with excitement at the thought. She would need new dresses and hats, hers were so out of date. The minute they got to México, she would go to Ambos Mundos to shop.

Ramón shook his head sadly. "I am sorry, Subteniente, there is nothing I can do."

Subteniente Picazo, his dark brown eyes aflame, leaned across the desk toward Arnaud. "Twenty-five *pesos*, Teniente. That is what a Yaqui is worth, twenty-five *pesos*. They took him and sold him to the sisal planters in the south. He is my wife's brother, Teniente." There was desperation in his voice.

Ramón measured his words carefully. "I do not approve of slavery, whatever the plantation owners choose to call it, Subteniente. I am sorry for you and your wife, but there is absolutely nothing I can do. You know, as well as I do, that there is an order of extermination. Soon, there will be no Yaqui left in Sonora. Be grateful that you and your wife are safe here."

Picazo tensed, as though about to say something, then abruptly saluted and left without another word. Of course, he had known the Teniente could do nothing to save Tomás. No one could challenge Vicepresidente Corral and the others. For the thousands of Yaqui who had been sold into slavery or gunned down in their villages or who had had their right hands sliced off by a *federale* sword, there had been no justice. When the *federales* had murdered Chief Cajeme, there had been no justice. When General Otero had hung so many Yaqui in Navajoa that he had run out of rope and had sent out of the state for more, there had been no justice. There would be no justice for Tomás or for any Yaqui. He had known all along. But he had had to try, for Teresa's sake.

The door slammed behind Picazo and Ramón exhaled slowly and slumped in his chair. Picazo had no idea what would really happen to Teresa's brother in the Yucatán—he had only heard rumors. But Ramón knew first hand.

Subteniente Picazo held his wife that night as she cried, the letter the priest had sent a sodden ball of pulp clenched in her hand. She knew she would never see Tomás again. In a year or two, or perhaps less, he would be dead, his heart and body broken. Twenty-five *pesos* for her brother's life. And for what? To buy Don Ramón Corral another bottle of French wine or a handful of Havana cigars, while his countrymen starved to death in the streets and fields? If Corral had his way, soon there would be no Yaqui left alive anywhere in México and Don Ramón Corral and his friends would have all of their land. Since time began, the Yaqui had lived in Sonora and had grown their crops, cherishing the land.

When the Spanish came, they found an advanced civilization with schools, mines, irrigation, a system of currency. The Yaqui were admired by everyone for their peaceful and hardworking nature. But their land had been stolen from them by Corral and his cronies and now they were being kidnapped by Corral's men and sold like mules, to die of starvation, overwork and disease on plantations a thousand kilometers from the graves of their ancestors.

Ramón and Alicia walked hand in hand down the beach away from the settlement toward their log. The log was almost thirty meters long and had been washed high up onto the beach by a hurricane. They often sat on it to watch the sun go down. Behind them were thousands of booby nests made of small pieces of broken coral. The air was thick with birds returning to their nests for the night. In the low, late afternoon sun, the crabs had become active and were scuttling about, looking for food. "You know, Alicia," Ramón said, pushing one gently with the tip of his boot. "Before we were married, I spent a lot of time watching the birds and the crabs. The sea life too, as far as it was possible." Alicia nodded, watching the crab move slowly backwards.

"The first time I landed here, with Coronel Avalos, the crabs were terrifying and very aggressive. I cannot explain the fact that after we destroyed so many around the settlement, all the crabs on the island learned immediately to avoid humans. How could such primitive animals communicate with each other?"

Ramón watched as the crab seized a small dead fish in its pincer and began pulling it up the sand. "There is more to them than we understand. The boobies almost always lay two eggs and allow the crabs to take one without resisting. It is as though the birds and the crabs have an agreement. The boobies pay tribute to the crabs with one egg and, by sacrificing it, save the other one. The crabs honor the agreement. They never take the last egg. You have seen that yourself."

"Yes," said Alicia. "What I cannot stand is when the egg the crab takes does not break."

"And the crab stands guard over it and hatches the egg itself?" said Ramón.

"Yes. It waits patiently for days or weeks and, when the chick breaks out, the crab eats it alive." Alicia shuddered with horror.

Ramón sipped a small glass of cognac as Capitán Castellenes leaned forward in the chair in his cabin. "Acapulco is devastated, Ramón. There was earthquake after earthquake and then, finally, a huge tidal wave. The entire waterfront has been destroyed. Most of the ships in port were wrecked.

Fortunately, we were at sea, on our way to Baja, California. There are thousands living in the streets. There were more than seventy shocks all over the country. They say that the Metropolitan Cathedral on the Zócalo shook so much that the bells rang. And, of course, there is talk that it is an omen. The *indios* are saying that Don Porfirio and the *científicos* will be consumed by fire."

"My God, where do they get these ideas? What of Alicia's parents? Do you know if they are all right?"

"They are both fine, Ramón. There was very little damage to their house. In fact, Señor Rovira came down to the ship with another parcel for you and Alicia before we left."

Alicia unwrapped the parcel eagerly. A tin of Rodier *foie gras*. A beautiful hand-painted Japanese fan. A large bag of Córdoba coffee, the dark aroma permeating everything deliciously. Jacquin *bon bons* from the Four Corners in México. Another book for Ramón. Alicia looked at the title on the cover, *Great National Problems*. The author was a man named Enriquez. She put it to one side for Ramón. There were newspapers with horrifying photographs of the damage in Acapulco and elsewhere. Entire blocks of the city had collapsed. In other places, parts of buildings hung crazily. In most of the pictures, dazed-looking survivors wandered among the ruins. She shook her head in sadness—what a catastrophe. Thank God her parents had not been injured.

CHAPTER 13

Ramón opened his eyes slowly. His head was thick with only a few short hours of sleep. He had been up late, trying to reconcile Schultz's tonnage figures with the tally Subteniente Picazo kept and then he had read most of the very disturbing book Félix had sent. Alicia's head lay cradled against his shoulder. Her hair lay across his chest, her breathing slow and even. He felt puzzled. Something was out of place but he was unable to put his finger on it. Not wanting to disturb Alicia, Ramón reached carefully with his free hand for his pocket watch, drawing it toward him and quietly flicking it open. It was a moment before he could distinguish the hands. Seven twenty-five.

The watch could not be right. It must have stopped last night before he had gone to bed. But, he clearly remembered winding it yesterday, as he did every morning. He put the watch to his ear. It was still ticking. From habit, he wound it as he lay back and looked around the darkened room. It could be no more than a few minutes after six, at least half an hour to dawn. The ormolu clock stood across the room on Alicia's vanity. It had been their wedding gift from Miguel and Liliana Hernández. Alicia cherished it. Although Ramón would never tell her, to him, it looked garish. It did, however, keep perfect time; he checked it regularly when the supply ships arrived. Feeling confused, Ramón strained to read the clock. It was too dark. Very slowly, he slipped his arm from beneath Alicia. She rolled on to her side and cradled her head on her arm, still asleep. Ramón rose quietly from the bed and walked to the vanity. Seven twenty-six. He shook his head, puzzled.

Drawing on his dressing gown, he went to the window and

pulled aside the curtains. It was dark outside but not the darkness of a moonless night, more the kind of semi-darkness he had experienced deep in the desert with the light of the moon and stars reflecting off the sand. But, looking up, he could see there were no stars and no moon. Closing the door quietly, he left the bedroom. The hands on the grandfather clock, at the bottom of the stairs, stood at seven twenty-eight. He went to the door, opened it and stepped outside. The air was cool and damp. From inside the house, he heard the grandfather clock strike the half hour. He drew the dressing gown around himself tightly. Ramón's mind was racing. How could it possibly be so dark at seven-thirty in the morning? Something was terribly wrong.

José Cervi rubbed his brow and stared skyward into the darkness. Cervi was a Spaniard. In 1895, he had left his small uneconomic farm near Barcelona to farm in México. He had quickly learned that he couldn't make a living as a *ranchero*. He had sold his parcel of land for almost nothing to a *hacendado* and gone to work on the Cruz sugar plantation. His life in México had been two years of drought and poverty as a *ranchero* and then twelve years of driving indolent *peones*: fourteen years in a climate he detested. And now, this madness. The darkness had made them all crazy. They refused to work. No number of blows from his cane could make them see sense.

The Old Ones, they raved, it is the Old Ones. It is a sign. The Old Ones are coming to wipe away the evil. There will be war and famine and pestilence. The world of the white man is ending. Don Porfirio and Doña Carmelita will be consumed by fire. The Old Ones are coming. Even when he threatened to throw them to The Hungry, to the alligators, they would not move. He tried to reason with them, with a gang of half-crazed, superstitious *indios*. It is not the end, he told them, "It is not a sign from the Old Ones. It is a volcano. Mount Colima has erupted, darkening the sky. Tomorrow, the dust and ash will pass and the sun will return."

But, the next day, the sun did not return. Nor the day after that. Nor the day after that. For three days, Mount Colima sent hundreds of millions of tons of ash boiling into the atmosphere, blotting out the sun, the moon and the stars, plunging México and all of Central America into endless night. In the countryside, there was wholesale panic. The Old Ones who had been since the beginning of time and who still lurked in the secret corners of *indio* minds, even as they prayed to the Dark Virgin and fingered their rosaries, would return and wipe away the scourge of the white man. It would be a time of catastrophe, the country engulfed by a river of blood and consumed by a fire that would wash away the white man's evil and restore the land to its proper keepers.

"There is panic everywhere. These old superstitions die hard," Félix Rovira said as he rode slowly beside Don Porfirio. El Presidente was getting old, almost eighty now and, still, he insisted on riding every day in Chapultepec Park. To do less would be to show weakness. He had even ridden during the three days when the sun had been blotted out. Business had taken Rovira to México and, as was his custom, he had let Don Porfirio's secretary know that he was in the capital. He had done so as a sign of respect, nothing more. He had expected the President to be fully occupied with the crisis caused by the earthquakes and made infinitely worse by the eruption of Mount Colima. He was taken aback when a note was delivered to his hotel inviting him to ride in the Park.

"The trouble will pass, Félix, it will pass. When they see the ash on the ground, they will understand. They will go back to work." The President reached over and struck the branches of a shrub with his riding crop. A cloud of powdery gray ash rose from the leaves and settled onto the manicured grass. "The most ignorant *peón* must believe the evidence of his own eyes."

"Perhaps, Don Porfirio, perhaps." Rovira wasn't convinced. He was alarmed by the stories that had been filtering into

México and even more alarmed by the casual indifference of Don Porfirio. The old man was losing touch. There was real trouble. This was not an isolated incident or two. The entire country had succumbed to mass hysteria. It had begun with the earthquakes in the summer and, since the eruption of Mount Colima, it had spread with lightning speed. From the cotton fields of the north to the sugar plantations of the south came word of *peones* refusing to work, throwing themselves to the ground and proclaiming the end of the world. Some of the plantation owners had called in the *rurales* to restore order, but they had been powerless to restore order. If the stories were to be believed, some of the *rurales* had actually joined in the madness.

Don Porfirio rode on ahead at his leisurely pace. Rovira could hear the hoofbeats of the Presidential Guard as they followed behind at a discreet distance. Rovira looked at the back of the aging president. His hair, escaping from beneath his bowler hat, was now completely white, though still thick. He rode slouched forward in the saddle. It was time for him to step aside. The young Díaz would have seen the warning signs and taken action. Perhaps he had simply been in the National Palace for too long. He no longer anticipated trouble. He had clung to power so long, he thought he was invincible. Even the recent uprising in Chihuahua had not seemed to concern him much.

But who would replace him? Corral? The thought made Rovira shudder. Then, no one would be safe. Who then? Limantour? He might be the best choice, but the finance minister's father had been born in France and so he was barred from the presidency by the constitution. Still considering the possibilities, Rovira reined in his horse beside Don Porfirio's at the entrance to the stables. The wall around Chapultepec Castle rose sheer above them. Don Porfirio and Doña Carmelita lived part-time in the Castle in a splendor that surpassed that achieved even by the Emperor Maximilian.

Díaz was in residence and Rovira knew that high above,

on the checkerboard marble terrace, Doña Carmelita, having just finished her morning prayers, would be waiting for Don Porfirio to return from his ride. Less than half his age, she would be in one of her high-necked dresses, her back as straight as an arrow, sitting at an immaculately laid table, a silver coffee service by her side. Servants would be hovering at the edges of the terrace, trying to make themselves invisible.

They made an odd couple, this old man of Mixtec Indian ancestry whose veneer of sophistication scarcely concealed the rough, ruthless peasant within and the much younger Doña Carmelita, alabaster white, pious, refined and high-born. Sometimes, the peasant in Don Porfirio bubbled over in the oddest ways. As soon as he heard of the rage of bowling in the United States, Don Porfirio had had the throne room in the Castle converted into a bowling alley. Rovira had a discreet chuckle at the time. The Emperor Maximilian must have been spinning in his grave, even with all those bullets in him. But, when bowling with El Presidente, a smile never touched Rovira's lips.

A groom came out and held Don Porfirio's horse as he dismounted. "You look very serious, my friend," Díaz said as he stood beside Rovira's horse. "Do not be so gloomy. Next year is the Centennial. México will witness a celebration unlike anything the world has ever seen. A few days of darkness will be forgotten."

"I hope so, Don Porfirio."

"Of course, Félix. Now off with you. Have a good gallop, you will feel better for it." Díaz slapped the flank of Rovira's horse and, nodding his goodbyes, Rovira headed his horse into the open field below the Castle and reined it in. Sitting in his saddle and looking up at the Castle, a feeling of foreboding came over him. If Don Porfirio was wrong, and it seemed very likely that he was, anything could happen.

He drove his horse across the field and down the slope at the far end. Below, was a forest with sinuous paths leading in all directions beneath the ancient cypresses of Chapultepec Park.

Rovira rode slowly, thinking. He knew Don Porfirio wanted one more election victory. He was assured of it, of course. His people throughout the country controlled the election process. Every ballot box was watched over by fully armed *federales* and *rurales*. His people counted the ballots. It was a system that observed the constitutional niceties without threatening the continuity of power. It had worked for more than thirty years and it would work one more time, but then what? The thought continued to trouble Rovira as he guided his horse out of the trees and into the sunlight.

CHAPTER 14

They had planned to spend some of their leave in Orizaba, but when the Tampico arrived, it brought the news that Alicia's mother, Petra, had died suddenly. Ramón and Alicia decided to spend all of their time in Acapulco with Félix. The city was still struggling to recover from the devastation of the earthquakes and the tidal wave. As they made their way from the waterfront to the Rovira house, they passed families living under tarpaulins and gathered around open cooking fires amid the rubble.

Ramón was at the garrison helping Coronel Avalos with reconstruction plans for the city and would be home late. The meal was finished. Alicia and her father had talked and cried about everything: the sudden death of Petra, the horror of the earthquake and tidal wave, life on Clipperton, the new baby sound asleep upstairs, the upcoming Centennial, the eruption of Mount Colima. "What will you do now, Papá?" asked Alicia.

"Well, life is nothing if not unpredictable," said Félix. "It seems that I will be moving to Salina Cruz very shortly. Before your mother died, I began negotiations with the Moctezuma Brewery in Orizaba. Only a few days ago, they asked me to distribute their beers throughout Central and South America. I will be selling this house and the villa in Orizaba. Salina Cruz is the logical place for me to live now."

Alicia squeezed her father's hand. "Papá, that is wonderful news. Now, whenever we have leave, we can go to Salina Cruz to see you and then to Orizaba."

The table had been cleared and Félix Rovira sat with a glass of brandy, preparing to light a cigar while Alicia sipped her sherry. "You remember Rafael Gabardo, Alicia?" he asked.

"Of course, Papá," she said.

"He almost married an actress by the name of Eugenía Ricardo. He was head over heels about her. Señor Gabardo violently disapproved of Rafael marrying a common actress and arranged for her to be kidnapped by the *engancizadores*. At this very moment, she is probably planting tobacco in the Valle Nacional or worse." He paused. "That is, if she is not dead already. Rafael is now engaged to the daughter of a wealthy *hacendado*."

"That is horrible," exclaimed Alicia. "What about the girl's family? Did they do nothing?"

"There was nothing they could do, Alicia. They are people without influence and, in any case, no laborer has ever returned alive from the Valle Nacional."

Alicia remained silent. To think, if things had been different, she might have married into such a family.

Rovira watched her for a moment, then asked, "What does Ramón have to say about this Francisco Madero, Alicia?"

She looked surprised and replied, "I think he regards Madero as a well-intentioned but naive idealist."

Rovira nodded grimly. "That cursed book of his has stirred up a hornets' nest. His ideas that no president should serve more than one term and that every adult should have a vote have struck a chord. I am old enough to remember the days when Don Porfirio himself used exactly the same ideas against Presidente Juárez. Of course, for Don Porfirio, it was simply a ploy. He had no intention of carrying any of them out. Madero is a very dangerous man because he really believes in these things. He does not understand that democracy is nothing but a utopian dream. It can never exist in the real world. The powerful will always find a way to control and exploit the weak. It is the nature of existence. But some people like to dream of a more equitable world and Madero's ideas are appealing even to many who have prospered under Don Porfirio."

"But Papá, what can he possibly do against Don Porfirio?"

"Don Porfirio has given him the opportunity to do a great deal, Alicia. Madero is in jail, but, unbelievably, Don Porfirio has allowed him to remain as a candidate for the presidency. And Madero has created a party. Of course, Don Porfirio is absolutely confident that Madero presents no real threat but, I am not so sure. Just today, I must have seen 'Viva Madero' painted in half a dozen places. All this unrest is causing even Don Porfirio's greatest supporters to question his judgment and the wisdom of his remaining in office. They are growing tired of the strikes and confrontations and executions."

Rovira sat back and looked at Alicia. "And to make it worse, Vasquez Gomez has agreed to run as Madero's vice president. For God's sake, he has been personal physician to the Díaz family for years. Not that Vasquez Gomez himself presents any kind of a threat, but the idea that Don Porfirio's own doctor would back Madero is fuel to the fire. Sometimes, I wonder what this country is coming to. Fortunately, if there is trouble, you will be safely on your island. México may become a very dangerous place in the next few years."

Ramón stood behind her in their small cabin on the Tampico, brushing her hair. "The government and the French have agreed that the King of Italy will arbitrate the question of sovereignty and that his decision will be final. The government is finalizing the documentation of our claim to Clipperton to submit to the King. Coronel Avalos showed me copies of what the government has submitted to him so far."

"It is wonderful news, Ramón. Surely the King will decide in our favor," Alicia said.

"Yes. He must. It is very good news."

Alicia sighed contentedly. "Then our little world is safe. I am so happy."

Schultz spat viciously on the ground. This new assistant of Arnaud's, Subteniente Picazo, was making his life hell, pestering him about tonnages shipped down to the last particle of guano. And the damned Italians, they couldn't keep anything running. He looked at the main gearbox of the crushing mill. The big iron casting had been disassembled and was lying in pieces in the dust of the guano shed. Half of the teeth had been stripped from the pinion gear. He dipped in his finger in the thick black oil at the bottom of the gear casing. It hadn't been changed for months; he could feel iron filings gritty between the tips of his fingers. Whatever had possessed him to think he could work with the ragtag bunch they had given him? It would be months before he could get a replacement gear and the crushing mill couldn't work without it.

Against the wharf was a tired old steamer, her sides streaked with rust. Her holds were only half-full and her master was in a blind rage. The ship had been sitting idle for eight days, her pumps spewing an endless stream of rust-colored water into the sea alongside to keep her afloat. If she sat there much longer, thought Schultz, she would probably sink on the spot. He shuddered to think what the demurrage would amount to. The Company would have his head. Another ship was due in any day now and he had no guano to load. He kicked the side of the crusher and marched out of the shed toward the ship. She would have to leave half-empty.

His business concluded, Félix Rovira looked forward to his last night in México. He made a habit during his evenings in the city of taking a solitary stroll along the quiet boulevards and through the Alameda Park. He stopped and searched the skies as he had for each of the past two nights and still saw nothing. The street was quiet now, the big houses slumbering behind their stately old trees. He lit a cigar and looked up again. The night was clear and cool. Countless stars gleamed in the deep blue ocean of sky. A young maid passed by, walking her master's dog. Rovira listened to the echo of her footsteps die in the distance.

He leaned against the spiked iron fence and pulled the lapels of his coat closer together against the chill of the night. He had never had any interest in astronomy, but there would be only this one opportunity in his lifetime to see one of the great miracles of nature. He threw the stub of the cigar down, crushing it beneath his heel and looked into the sky. Perhaps they were wrong. Perhaps it wouldn't come. He was about to continue his walk when he saw it; not a star, but a searing ball of light in the icy darkness of space, tearing across the sky, leaving a long wake of luminescence tapering to infinity. He looked, fascinated. How long was the tail? Hundreds of kilometers? Thousands? Millions? There was no way to tell. He smiled to himself, pleased. He had seen it; he had seen Halley's Comet. He let out a small sigh of satisfaction and walked toward the park.

On each street corner, the red lanterns of the *policía* glowed, ready to signal each other at the first sign of trouble. He walked on toward Paseo de la Reforma and came eventually to the Alameda. The beautiful park had been the first public garden in México, built on the site of the Plaza del Quemadero, the square of the burning place, where for more than two hundred years those accused of heresy by the Catholic priests—Jews, *indios* and sundry political opponents—were burned alive in the name of God during the Inquisition.

The park underwent an eerie transformation late at night when the day's fashionably dressed promenaders were safely in their beds between crisp, clean sheets. Unarmed, Félix walked along the pathways without fear. No one would dare confront him, a gentleman, even in the middle of the night. Groups of the ragged homeless huddled in the pools of light thrown by the lamps. Others lay on the benches, swathed in scraps of clothing and layers of newspaper. A beggar, horribly disfigured by burns, squatted in the shadows at the side of the path, murmuring to himself. Soon the *policía* would come and chase them away into the night but, when the officers had gone, they would be back. Then, the Alameda would be theirs until dawn when they would vanish into the crowded, dirty alleyways and begin sifting through the night's rubbish for food. Much like the crabs on Clipperton Island that Alicia had told him about, thought Félix, always searching for food.

The Alameda at night had a surreal quality. The lights, in clusters of globes, cast a soft golden glow over the trees and grass and pathways. A few years ago, the Alameda had been lit with hydrogen gas lamps. Now, the lamps were electric. Félix looked at the lights with satisfaction. The electrification of the capital was another achievement of Don Porfirio. El Presidente had truly brought México into the twentieth century.

Félix couldn't help but feel a sense of disgust as he walked among the lost souls in the Alameda. These were the people who had failed to take advantage of the opportunities available to them in Don Porfirio's modern México. They complained endlessly about their lot in life and drank *pulque* until they lapsed into unconsciousness whenever they had a few *centavos*. Some of them looked at Félix with barely disguised hatred for his good looks and fine clothes. Others watched with ravaged, expressionless faces, their eyes devoid of emotion. Ahead on the path, a group rose from the ground almost as one and pointed excitedly into the night sky. Their frenzied cries and pointing alerted the others and soon they were all on their feet, yammering in half a dozen languages and hopping with excitement. They must be looking at the comet.

An ancient *indio*, his face fissured like a dried river bed, glared at Félix brazenly and hissed in Spanish, "Look well upon it, Señor. It is an omen. It is the end for you and your kind." Félix ignored the crazy old man and pushed his way quickly through the growing mob and away from the Park.

Pedro Alquini sat on the small dock on the lagoon behind the crushing shed. The crushing mill was silent, the only sound was the voices of the guano workers calling across the shed to each other in Italian. Pedro didn't have much to do with the guano workers. None of the *soldados* did. The workers lived in a big weather-beaten hut beside the guano shed and kept to themselves. Since the women and children had arrived, the soldiers had had even less inclination to mix with the workers. Pedro's wife had come to the island, a jolly, laughing woman and a fine cook. Soon she would have their first child. Pedro wanted a boy. It was better that she should be here. Life on the mainland had been hard for her. Even with the few *pesos* Pedro had sent to her and the little she could earn by selling *tortillas* in the street, there had never been enough. At least here, there would always be a roof over their heads and enough food to eat. In another week or so, they would even have a little house to themselves.

Clipperton was the best posting he had had in his eight years in the Army. The *federales* had taken him one evening as he was bringing his master's oxen back from the fields. His master, a small *ranchero*, had protested to the local authorities but it was no good. The next day, he was sent to Sonora as a *soldado*. In Sonora, the Army food had been poor, what little there was of it, and he had only seen his family once in seven years.

Clipperton was paradise by comparison. The duty was good too. For the past two weeks, all Pedro had to do was count the number of wagons of guano pushed into the shed for crushing. At the end of each day, he gave Subteniente Picazo the tally. It was the kind of duty that gave a man a lot of time to think. Pedro looked across the lagoon. The sky was a deep blue and the water very clear. He could see the layer of rotting weed lying suspended just below the surface. It looked like the bottom of the lagoon, but that was an illusion. The layer of weed was like soggy paper; a stone would fall right through. In some places, the real bottom was more than twenty meters down. To Pedro's left, the four diminutive Egg Islands lay in a straight line across the corner of the lagoon. Two kilometers directly across the lagoon stood *la roca*, white with the droppings of the birds. The sun twinkled on the Fresnel lenses of the navigation light on the Rock's summit.

At the water's edge, two crabs scavenged in a patch of shade cast by the boat dock. Pedro watched quietly. The crabs were so wary now, they were scared away by the slightest movement. One crab found a fragment of vegetation and dragged it away from the lagoon. The other seized the opposite end and began a tug of war. The larger of the two abandoned the piece of weed and attacked. They rolled and scuffled, pincers clicking, the weed forgotten. The bigger crab seized one of the other's claws and crushed it. The injured crab crawled away, the useless claw dragging in the sand alongside. Pedro watched as the victor returned to the weed, tearing pieces off and carrying them to its mouth. The injured crab raised its good claw and, with a single motion, amputated its damaged limb where it joined the body. The crab scurried away. Its amputated claw lay on the sand, slowly opening and closing.

CHAPTER 15

The Centennial celebrations had brought hundreds of thousands of people from throughout México and from around the world to the capital. Everywhere, flags and banners fluttered in the breeze. Floral archways leaped across avenues and boulevards. There was always the sound of a band somewhere in the distance. Ramoncito was between Alicia and Ramón, holding their hands tightly as they walked slowly through the happy crowd thronging the Alameda. Looking toward the east end of the Park, they could see the skeleton of the Palace of Fine Arts, the iron girders forming its filial dome a promise of glories to come.

"Look, Ramón. It looks just like a giant spider's web," said Alicia.

Ramón laughed, "Yes, it does. That is exactly what it looks like."

Alicia shielded her eyes and looked again at the Palace. "It will be so beautiful," she said. "What a pity that it could not be finished for the Centennial."

Ramón gazed at the building. Work had stopped for the holiday and the building site stood deserted. Gigantic blocks of white Carrera marble lay brilliant in the sunlight. The finely worked columns of the massive semi-circular portico stood naked like an Art Nouveau Stonehenge. "Yes, it is a pity. But so much has been done for the Centennial, we can wait for this," said Ramón. "We will be able to go to the art galleries and attend concerts when it is finished. It will be something for us to look forward to."

They continued to walk through the Alameda, passing the massive new monument to Benito Juárez that Don Porfirio would soon dedicate. The seventy tons of bronze, honoring the man who had defeated Maximilian, still lay tightly cocooned in tarpaulins. As they walked past the fountain, toward the corner of the Alameda, where it fronted on Paseo de la Reforma, the crowds grew thicker, the air charged with excitement. They came out of the poplars and worked their way to the edge of the broad avenue. In the distance, the new Monument of National Independence towered over the boulevard leading to Chapultepec Park and, coming from the direction of the monument, a long line of carriages and automobiles snaked its way toward them.

Ramón hoisted his son to his shoulders and peered down Paseo de la Reforma. Young girls dressed in gaily patterned dresses skipped along the avenue strewing flowers across the pavement. Behind them, dragoons on coal black mounts rode with perfect precision, their plumed helmets glinting gold in the sun. After the dragoons came the big black Mercedes that had become such a familiar sight during the month of the Centennial. Don Porfirio, his nut-brown face split into a continuous smile beneath the shock of white hair, waved from the automobile to the cheering crowds surging along both sides of the avenue. Beside him, Doña Carmelita waved demurely with a gloved hand. As the Mercedes passed close by, Ramón and Alicia could clearly see El Presidente beaming in triumph. Behind Don Porfirio's car, carriages and automobiles carried Mexican and foreign dignitaries. Alicia pointed excitedly to an open black carriage with flamboyant gold tracery carrying a middle-aged man in a top hat and satin sash and a much younger woman. A murmur of delight came from the crowd as the carriage passed by.

"Oh, Ramón, look at the hat," Alicia gasped. In the carriage, a beautiful young woman with rich olive skin smiled and waved from beneath a spectacular hat topped by an enormous ostrich feather. Alicia waved madly to her. "I know her, Ramón. She is the daughter of the Marqués de Polavieja, the Spanish ambassador. Her hat is miraculous."

The young girl spat on the rag and tried to wipe the semen from her body. She smoothed the grimy cotton dress down over her hips and got to her feet. The man had been another one of the foreigners attending the Centennial. As soon as he was done, he had fled the dirty little room. At least it was better than the alleys, she thought. When they had first brought her to the capital a year ago they had forced her to prostitute herself in the alleyways on her back or stomach or knees in the rotting garbage. She took the little leather bag from its hiding place and counted out the money. One *peso* and twenty *centavos*. It was almost enough. Perhaps, tonight, she would not be beaten

She could hear the racking sobs of the new girl through the paper-thin walls. Belinda had seen the girl, almost paralyzed with fear, before she had been taken to the Señor. She was about twelve, the same age as Belinda had been when she had been kidnapped from her village near Oaxaca. She knew exactly what the Señor had done to the new girl. He did it to all of them the first night. Belinda knew who he really was and the knowledge was very dangerous. She couldn't read, but once she had seen a newspaper with a photograph of him standing beside El Presidente, waving and smiling. She had recognized at once the closely cropped white hair, the dark bushy mustache and, behind the wire-rimmed spectacles, the mad, burning eyes of Vicepresidente Don Ramón Corral. She had never told anyone the name of the man who had had her kidnapped, who owned her, who had tortured and then raped her, who forced her to give her body to a score of strangers every night. To whisper his name would, she knew, mean certain death.

Chapultepec Castle rose magnificent above the Park. The Castle was decked from top to bottom in flags and banners. The velvety lawns of the Park, where Aztec rulers had once had their pleasure gardens, were speckled with brightly colored marquee tents. On every patch of open grass were people; people laughing, people eating and drinking, people clapping, people listening to music and singing. The biggest garden party in history had drawn even more than the planned fifty thousand people.

Ramón and Alicia were both bone weary. They had been on their feet since early morning, going from one spectacle to another. They strolled along the path around the lake, walking against the tide of revelers still sweeping into the Park, to the café on the lake's edge. Ramoncito, exhausted, was asleep in his mother's arms. Alicia was glad to be out of the sun, sitting peacefully at a shaded table overlooking the lake. Ramoncito had wakened long enough to eat a mouthful of ice cream and had fallen asleep again. He lay on her lap, dead to the world, occasionally giving his thumb a lazy suck. The sound of a brass band, playing martial music, wafted disjointedly across the lake.

Ramón made a sweeping gesture over the lake toward the crowds turning the Park's lawns into vast swirls of color. "I am so proud to be alive at this moment, Alicia," he said. "I am so proud to be Mexican."

The *policía* had their orders. The Kaiser and the Mikado must never see a beggar on the streets of Don Porfirio's México. The international press, who were in the capital in their hundreds, must never see a cripple or a starving child. Barricades were set up around the parade routes and monuments and only the well-dressed were permitted to pass. The vistas of gleaming monuments and fabulous public buildings were not to be spoiled by the sight of society's dregs. The more serious troublemakers had long since been identified by the secret police and were safely under lock and key in Belem Penitentiary where they were already dying from dysentery. The homeless were gone from the Alameda and from the forests of Chapultepec. They had been driven with canes and pistol butts from the fine boulevards. They swarmed like starving rats in the filthy backstreets and alleyways of the capital where the visitors would never go. They huddled together, shuffling aimlessly, sometimes stopping to sift through rotting heaps of garbage. Nothing would be allowed to mar the celebration of the Centennial of Mexican Independence—certainly not the people of México.

Don Porfirio presided over the pageant from a reviewing stand resplendent with the national colors. At his left sat Doña Carmelita looking bored and cooling herself with an exotic silk fan. At his right was Vicepresidente Don Ramón Corral. The man who was depicted in the underground press as a death's head was younger than Díaz and taller. Behind his spectacles, his dark eyes burned like live coals. Even the *científicos* who sat on the reviewing stand with Corral readily believed the rumors that the man who stole the land of the Yaqui and then sold them into slavery on the sisal plantations and into prostitution in the putrid brothels of México was dying of syphilis. A world without Don Ramón Corral would be a safer world for everyone.

Each element of the pageant recreated with infinite detail the sweeping drama of Mexican history from the mighty Indian civilizations of the time before the Spanish came, through the fateful meeting of Cortés and Moctezuma, to the bitter struggle for independence from Spain. Alicia had taken Ramoncito back to the hotel and Ramón had stayed on alone, watching the thousands of performers in their wonderfully detailed costumes. He recognized the events portrayed in almost every part of the pageant and was glad he had stayed, weary and emotionally drained though he was. When the last float had passed, Ramón walked slowly through the crowds along Paseo de la Reforma, past the grand houses covered in flags and banners, their window boxes overflowing with flowers, back to the hotel, sharing the sidewalks with more than half a million people.

The young maid stood back to hold the mirror. Alicia looked at her hair piled high in extravagant swirls. "Very nice," she said. She stood up as the girl gathered the brushes and combs together. "Take good care of Ramoncito tonight. We will be gone all evening. Tomorrow, you will be able to see some of the celebrations. Now away you go."

"Yes, Señora." The girl gave a small bow and closed the door quietly behind her.

Alicia looked down at her figure, running her hands down over her hips. She was only two months pregnant and barely showing. With her new green satin dress from Ambos Mundos, she knew she would feel beautiful tonight. In the adjoining room, Alicia could hear Ramón talking to the valet who came up to the suite to shave him. Since they had arrived, Ramón had had himself shaved twice a day. She knew that he missed his little luxuries on Clipperton. Perhaps when they went home, she would learn to shave him.

Alicia held the skirts of her dress carefully as the driver helped her into the hired carriage. With Ramón looking especially dashing in his finest dress uniform beside her, she sat proudly, looking with pleasure at the magnificent houses along Paseo de la Reforma. The street was crowded with carriages and, here and there, an automobile drove among them, making the horses whinny and shy. Sitting beside a radiant Alicia, Ramón was as happy and as proud as he had ever been. This was the day of a lifetime. Exactly one hundred years ago today, a town priest, Miguel Hidalgo, had called on his parishioners to rise up against the Spanish and take their independence. Six bloody years later, Agustín de Iturbide was crowned Emperor of the newly independent México in the Metropolitan Cathedral. But the battle had not ended there. Civil war and invasions by the Americans and French had kept the new nation in a state of continual turmoil.

Stability had finally come, sixty years after the War

of Independence, with Porfirio Díaz. The hero of the war against the French had been president longer than most of the population had been alive. His works were everywhere: spectacular public buildings, the equal of anything in Paris or London, and proud monuments trumpeting México's new place in the modern world. On this glorious day, México stood at the pinnacle of her achievements. Ramón and Alicia sat glowing with pride and contentment in the back of their carriage.

Ramón helped Alicia down from the carriage in front of the National Palace. The Zócalo swarmed with the curious who hoped to catch a glimpse of leaders and dignitaries from around the world. They had been invited to a state dinner with Don Porfirio in the specially constructed ballroom in the National Palace. Alicia and Ramón walked arm in arm among the throng. Here and there, they saw a face they recognized and waved gaily. Alicia knew her father was on the Zócalo somewhere but had no hope of seeing him in the crush of people. There was a hush as Don Porfirio's Mercedes edged slowly along and stopped in front of the National Palace. As the President alighted, he waved his top hat to the crowd and a huge roar went up for the man who had brought México into the modern age.

Ramón laid his cutlery down carefully across his plate. Every piece of the place setting was made of solid gold. He turned to Alicia and shook his head in amazement. "Twenty boxcars of Dom Perignon," said Félix Rovira, ringing his fork against his champagne glass. "El Presidente knows how to celebrate in style."

"But Papá, the cost!" exclaimed Alicia, an argumentative look in her eye.

José Limantour put down his knife and fork and wagged a perfectly manicured finger at Alicia. "The celebrations cost twenty million *pesos*, Señora Arnaud. But, never mind the cost. Do you see who is sitting over there next to Don Porfirio?"

Limantour nodded his head toward the heavily mustachioed figure with the withered arm whispering in the President's ear.

"Of course, Don José," said Alicia. "It is the Kaiser."

Limantour nodded. "Yes, the Kaiser. And do you see who else is here?" He swept his arm around the room, glittering with gold and crystal. "The Mikado. The Guggenheims. William Randolph Hearst. Lord Cowdray. French and Spanish bankers. Newspaper and magazine editors. Thousands of them, from all over the world. Madero said we could have fed and housed the poor of México for a year on what this meal cost. He was wrong. More like five years, if he only knew the truth. But Señora, what sense would that make? Mindless charity. We could feed them for a year or five, but they would be just as hungry the year after. The poor will always be poor. That is their destiny. But spend the money bringing the leaders of the world here to see what we have accomplished and we lay the foundation for an even better future for those of us whose destiny it is to prosper."

The tinkling of gold cutlery on crystal grew to a deafening crescendo as Don Porfirio rose to his feet. The crowd broke spontaneously into applause as El Presidente stood in his broad satin sash, his chest covered with medals, nodding his acknowledgment to the crowd, his old eyes crinkling with pleasure. The applause grew louder and louder until, finally, he held up his hands for silence.

"My friends," he said as the applause gradually faded, the familiar voice still strong and resonant. "I thank you from the bottom of my heart for your kindness." He looked slowly around the room. "I have lived an eventful life." A wave of applause swept the room. He held his hands up again for silence and continued. "But this day is the greatest day of my life. One hundred years ago, our people began their struggle for independence. One hundred years ago, they set out on the difficult path that led to the creation of a nation that has now taken its rightful place among the nations of the world. It has been my privilege to have played my own small part."

The room broke into tumultuous applause. Don Porfirio paused for a moment and cast his gaze briefly to the ceiling, where thirty thousand electric stars twinkled. Looking grave, he said, "My friends, it is my duty to report to you on the outcome of the Presidential election. The votes of the people of México have been counted and I have great pleasure in telling you that the people have once again elected me unanimously." Díaz paused for a moment, staring at his audience, as though challenging someone to contradict him. There was absolute silence. He went on, "I am humbled by the faith of the people in my abilities and honored to have been chosen to serve another term as president, at the will of the people of México."

There was pandemonium in the room as four thousand people rose as one. Cheers and hurrahs punctuated the thunderous applause. At the back of the room, prominent members of the Mexican and international press, in full evening dress, engaged in a brief shoving match to be first through the doors to file with their papers and wire services the wonderful news of the unanimous reelection of Porfirio Díaz.

Ramón and Alicia stood with Félix Rovira on the balcony near the top of the Monument of National Independence, sixty meters above Paseo de la Reforma. They were still slightly breathless after climbing the stairs. By a miracle, the monument had been completed in time for the Centennial. At first, like the Palace of Fine Arts, the enormous weight of the monument had caused it to sink into the spongy earth that lays beneath most of México, until it leaned at a frightening angle. It had been painstakingly disassembled, new foundations laid and then rebuilt. Of the many monuments dedicated during the month of the Centennial, the Monument of National Independence, towering over the route from Chapultepec Park to the National Palace, was the crowning glory.

Félix Rovira had arranged for them to climb the dizzying

circular stairs inside the column before the viewing areas were opened to the public for the first time. Looking down from the balcony, they could see the crowds far below admiring the statues of México's greatest heroes. Traffic surged around the base of the monument: riders on horseback, sleek black automobiles, electric trolleys, horse-drawn carriages and bicycles. And, all around, thousands of Mexicans and visitors walking. México lay spread out before them in all its Centennial finery. In the distance, the twin volcanoes reared toward the sky. Overhead, El Ángel, the symbol of México's triumph over foreign domination, soared on her golden wings.

Holding his bowler hat firmly on his head, Rovira leaned over the railing of the balcony and looked pensively down at the traffic and the crowds. He raised his gaze toward the spires of the Metropolitan Cathedral looming over the Zócalo. Hundreds of thousands of people were crowding the square in front of the National Palace from which Porfirio Díaz ruled the nation. "I am very much afraid that Don Porfirio has misjudged the mood of the people," he said quietly.

Ramón moved along the railing toward him. "But, Don Félix, what can happen? The election is over. Madero is in jail. All México is celebrating the Centennial."

"Rebellion, Ramón. There could be open rebellion. Who will believe that every single vote among millions was cast for Don Porfirio? It is too much. Everyone knows someone who voted for Madero, even with a *federale* or *rurale* standing with a rifle over the ballot box. Whatever we may think of him, Madero's appeal to the people is unquestionable." Rovira watched the crowd for some time before speaking again. "You know, Ramón, in the old days Don Porfirio listened to his friends and advisors. Today, he does what he pleases and damn the consequences. He seems to think that the Centennial will make everyone forget the election. That is why he announced the result last night at the *banquete*. And to make matters worse, the *peones* are convinced that the earthquakes, the eruption of Mount Colima and Halley's Comet are all omens that Don Porfirio will fall."

Alicia put her hand gently on his arm and said, "Oh, Papá, you worry too much."

Rovira tenderly patted her hand and looked again toward the Zócalo. "Not a bit of it, my dear. In these times, one can scarcely worry enough."

As they had been talking, the sky had been steadily darkening. With an earsplitting crash, the first bolt of lightning struck somewhere in the Alameda. The sky opened and rain fell in torrents. On the crowded sidewalks below, pedestrians ran for shelter.

CHAPTER 16

Alicia shielded her eyes from the sun and watched as the *soldado* climbed the palm. He took his machete and hacked half a dozen coconuts from the tree. They fell heavily to the sand. Ramoncito went forward to pick up one of the nuts in its green husk. It was big and heavy and he tottered beneath its weight as he carried it back to Alicia. She took it from him and they walked away from the grove, hand in hand.

On the sand behind the houses of the *soldados*, the women were doing their laundry, laughing and gossiping, the drying laundry fluttering around them in the gentle breeze. Beyond the settlement, Alicia could see the masts of a ship lying at anchor off the guano wharf. She put down Ramoncito' s coconut and sat down near the water. The little boy took off his shoes and paddled out into the waves. Alicia put her arms around her knees and watched him. He looked so much like his father. He even behaved like his father, always neat and tidy, always responsible. A short way down the beach, a young booby strutted on skinny legs just above the waterline. The boy picked up a small piece of driftwood and scurried after it. The bird ran ahead, keeping just out of reach.

Directly in front of Ramoncito, the water exploded and a full-grown moray eel, its gray sides shining in the sun, its jaws wide open, shot from the water and seized the booby. The bird's wild squawk of surprise ended abruptly as the moray crushed it in its jaws and wriggled back across the sand to the sea. Alicia sat shocked for a moment, then rushed to her son and swept him into her arms and away from the water.

Ramón met the Tampico's captain on the beach as the launch brought him in. He was eager to speak to Castellenes. They had had no news from the mainland since returning to Clipperton, weary from celebrating the Centennial. Castellenes had dark circles under his eyes and his hair was unkempt. Ramón had seen the Tampico on and off for three days, hove to in the sweeping gray seas to the northwest of the island. He had watched the ship through his telescope, the spray blowing along her deck as she rolled heavily. He had thought of Castellenes out there enduring God alone knew what miseries to deliver the garrison's supplies. A lesser man might have run back to Acapulco, but Castellenes kept his ship within sight of Clipperton the whole time, waiting for a change in the weather. Finally, on the morning of the third day, the seas began to drop and, by late afternoon, the Tampico was able to creep close enough to drop its anchor and launch a boat.

The two men shook hands warmly and Castellenes handed Ramón a leather dispatch case. "I have newspapers for you on board," Castellenes said. "I will have them sent to your house. Have you heard the latest news?"

Ramón laughed mirthlessly. "The only news we get on this island comes from you, my friend. Do not keep me in suspense, what is it?"

"Madero is in the United States and calling for a revolution."

"How did he get to the United States? I thought he was awaiting trial in San Luis Potosí."

"He escaped. After the election, Don Porfirio allowed him to leave the jail each day to go riding. That is probably the only thing Madero and Don Porfirio have in common." Castellenes gave a hollow laugh. "Some railway workers spirited him away and he was across the border in disguise before anyone could stop him."

"Incredible. Perhaps it is best that he is out of the country."

"Perhaps not. He issued a statement calling the election a fraud and declaring himself president. He has called for a general uprising against Don Porfirio."

"The people would never dare rise against Don Porfirio."

"As you say. There was only minor trouble here and there, except in Chihuahua. Some armed horsemen attacked the garrison and cut the telegraph wires. Madero himself crossed the border, but the Army chased him back into the United States. The rest of the Madero family is backing him and have called for a revolution. They are afraid Don Porfirio will seize all their estates. They see it as their only choice."

Ramón shook his head. "The Maderos will be lucky to be *rancheros* when Don Porfirio is finished with them."

The growing unrest on the mainland had convinced Ramón and Alicia to remain on the island to celebrate Christmas. A huge parcel arrived on the Tampico in November from Doña Carlota, filled with presents for Ramón and Alicia and Ramoncito. Alicia spent hours working with the garrison women making *piñatas* for the children. In the week before Christmas, the children took turns enacting the journey of Mary and Joséph to Bethlehem, parading around the settlement wrapped in sheets, half laughing, half serious. At midnight on Christmas Eve, Ramón had read briefly from the Bible on the rise of land at the lagoon's edge. As she listened to his deep, precise voice, Alicia thought of her family and of Doña Carlota. Her father had been only too right. México was becoming a dangerous place. She looked out of the window and up into the sky, brilliant with stars. Everyone they loved in México would just now be returning from Midnight Mass, looking up at the same stars.

As February drew to a close, the Tampico returned with startling news. There had been full-scale revolt in Baja, California. Francisco Madero had crossed back into México and taken control of the revolution that was now spreading like wildfire throughout the country. Emiliano Zapata, the peasant leader, had assembled an army in the south and was threatening to take the *peones'* lands back from the *hacendados.* Presidente Díaz, it seemed, was powerless to stop the unrest. "I must go on the Tampico my dear," Ramón told Alicia. "I must speak to Coronel Avalos and I will telegraph your father in Salina Cruz. If one is to believe what is in the newspapers, the situation is very serious."

The Acapulco garrison was in chaos. Coronel Avalos had been called to the capital for emergency meetings and no one seemed to be in charge. Ramón, unable to get clear instructions from anyone in Acapulco, cabled to Avalos in the capital and then to Félix Rovira in Salina Cruz. Rovira responded first with an urgent request that Ramón travel to Salina Cruz immediately. With no possibility of a ship back to the island for at least a month and no word from Avalos, Ramón took the nightmarish stagecoach ride south. Félix Rovira's villa, on the outskirts of Salina Cruz, perched neatly on a low hill overlooking the waters of the Gulf of Tehuantepec. The distant blue hills rolling into the ocean were obscured by a soft mist. To the north, the lagoons that dotted the coastline lay placid. Ramón approached the villa slowly, fearful of the news he would hear. It had actually come to revolution and, of all people, Alicia's father would know how bad the situation really was.

Félix Rovira welcomed Ramón warmly. "What a pleasure to see you Ramón. I am glad that you were able to come. Alicia must be near her time. Is she in good health?"

"Yes, Don Félix, she is in perfect health."

"And Ramoncito?"

"As healthy as an ox."

"Good, good."

Ramón waited for Rovira to speak.

"I am afraid things are as bad as they can be, Ramón. Everything is confusion. Don Porfirio seems to have no idea how to handle the situation and Corral, of course, is worse than useless. His answer to almost any problem is simply to slaughter everyone. I have heard that Limantour will attempt to negotiate with the Maderos but I do not hold out much hope. The situation grows more serious every day: trains stopped and robbed, telegraph wires cut, Army patrols attacked. And this Emiliano Zapata, I fear him even more than Madero. Madero was born a *hacendado*, there must be a limit to how far he will go. And Pancho Villa is only an opportunist, a cunning *bandido*. But, Zapata, now there is a true believer. He is totally committed to taking the *haciendas* and giving the land back to the *peones*. He spent years using the legal system trying to get the lands restored. But, of course, even though he has the actual deeds to the land going back centuries, that did him no good. He will not stop until he has succeeded or until someone kills him. He is the rarest and most dangerous kind of leader, one who intends to do exactly what he says he will do."

"But what can Zapata and the rest of them do against the Army, Don Félix?"

"Ramón, do not underestimate these people. That is exactly the mistake Don Porfirio made. To the people, Madero is their savior. He is almost a god to them. They call him the Apostle of Democracy. And Zapata, never, never underestimate him. He has raised a formidable army. They have horses, they are heavily armed and they grow stronger each day. Zapata has already taken half a dozen *haciendas* and divided the land up among the *peones*. The *hacendados* are terrified of him.

"In the north, Villa and Madero have thousands of armed men. It seems that every peasant has left the fields and joined the revolution. Even the women are fighting. Madero and Villa are fighting the kind of war that is every military man's nightmare. A feint here, a larger attack there, endless sabotage. They are completely unpredictable and totally fearless and, when they do engage the Army, many times they outnumber the *federales*. The Army is a fraud, Ramón, as you must know. In reality, there are only half as many *soldados* as there are supposed to be. For years, the generals have been collecting pay and ration allowance for tens of thousands of *federales* who do not exist. And most of the ones who do exist have been forced into the Army at gunpoint and will desert to the rebels at the first opportunity.

"I would say this to no one else in this country, Ramón, but I say it to you, in confidence, as a father would to his son. One way or another, Don Porfirio will have to go. He will not stop this revolution. Unfortunately, we have no one we can offer to the people to take his place. We are in a very grave predicament. Limantour is barred by the Constitution. And, can you imagine Corral as president? My blood runs cold at the thought."

Alicia eased herself carefully into her chair. The baby gave a little kick. Alicia sat still for a moment, feeling the baby move, then leaned forward and unwrapped the parcel her father had sent with Ramón. It was about the size of big loaf of bread, but very heavy. She removed layer after layer of stiff brown paper before reaching a dark wooden box. She opened the brass hasp and drew a sudden breath. The box was filled to the brim with loose gems and silver and gold jewelry. Beneath the jewelry was a thick bundle of banknotes. A fortune. Slipped down one side of the box was a piece of heavy blue paper. Alicia pulled it out and unfolded it. She smoothed it flat and read, "My darling Alicia, I hope you will not think this the craziness of an old man. Most of the jewelry in this box belonged to your mother and is the greater part of your inheritance. I want you to have it now. It will be safer with you on your island. My love forever, Papá."

Coronel Avalos had telegraphed orders to Ramón in Salina Cruz and Alicia waited for Ramón to tell her what what they were. When he remained silent, she grew worried. Finally, she could stand it no longer. "Ramón," she said, "you know I do not wish to interfere in military matters but I must know what is happening. What did Coronel Avalos say to you?"

Ramón touched her cheek. "In so many words, Alicia, he said what your father said. My orders from him are to maintain the garrison exactly as it is until further orders. As to what will happen when Don Porfirio goes, and clearly the Coronel thinks he will go, I do not know. He said the position of anyone in the Army, especially officers, will be very dangerous in the coming months. It seems that Clipperton is the safest place in all México for us."

Alicia lay in bed in the darkness quietly waiting for the next contraction. When it came, she let out a little moan. Ramón was awake instantly. "My darling," he whispered. "Are you alright?" Alicia took a deep breath and sighed. "I think it is time. Perhaps you should get Doña Juana." Ramón gave her a gentle hug and swung out of bed, dressed quickly and was gone in moments.

Alicia was on the edge of sleep, half dreaming when she saw Doña Juana lighting the oil lamp on the table beside the bed. Doña Juana looked toward Alicia, her calm brown face crinkling, and spoke gently, "Be calm, my child, all will be well." She moved to the bed and stroked Alicia's forehead and hair."

On the morning of the twenty third of May, Abelardo Avalos heard of the humiliating agreement Limantour had been forced to make with Francisco Madero. Díaz was finished. Since Madero's forces had captured the city of Juárez early in May, the situation of the government had grown increasingly desperate. The entire country was in rebellion. Federal garrisons had been wiped out in the north. Towns across México had fallen to the rebels. Train service had all but stopped under the relentless attacks by Pancho Villa and his men. The *haciendas* were falling one after another to Zapata. Communications were in a shambles. Authority was openly defied everywhere. And Porfirio Díaz, old and tired, confused by the public mood and disoriented by narcotics prescribed for a lingering toothache, had been unable to stop any of it.

Limantour's attempt to negotiate with Madero had been a fiasco. He had had nothing with which to bargain. With the mills and *haciendas* on the outskirts of the capital in flames and Díaz in a state of drugged stupor, there had been no alternative but to agree to a new presidential election. Díaz would have to resign. Madero had agreed that México's ambassador to the United States should serve as interim president until the election. Corral would be dismissed immediately. But, in spite of the agreement with Madero, Díaz hung on grimly, hiding in the National Palace behind a line of heavily armed Presidential Guard. Vicepresidente Ramón Corral had vanished.

Avalos had heard the cries of the immense crowd surging on the Zócalo as he made his way to his temporary office in the Ministry of War that morning. "Down with Díaz!", "Death to Corral!", "Death to the *científicos!*" Occasionally, the crowd caught a glimpse of Díaz himself, bewildered and frightened, looking out onto the Zócalo from an upper window, and the cries of "Resign!" reached a fever pitch.

Later, as Avalos sat at a desk in the Ministry, vainly trying to concentrate, he heard the sudden thunder of Maxim machine guns followed by piercing screams and knew at once what had happened. The Maxims roared again and he ran from the Ministry to find pandemonium on the streets. Crowds were running in blind panic away from the Zócalo. People lay trampled and bleeding on the pavement. Avalos shouldered his way with other *federales* through the hysterical mob to the edge of the square. The Presidential Guard was still in formation behind the Maxims, their backs against the long front wall of the Palace. Beneath the spires of the Metropolitan Cathedral, hundreds of bodies lay heaped and sprawled. Most were still, some cut almost in half by the machine gun fire, their life spilling wetly across the warm stones of the Zócalo. Others lay moaning pitifully, writhing in the sea of blood washing over México's heart.

More than two hundred men, women and children lay dead. Hundreds more, many horribly wounded, screamed in agony while, among them, others roared with rage. A curtain on the upper floor of the National Palace moved slightly and Avalos saw, for the last time, the man who had given the order to fire.

Félix Rovira sat on the terrace, looking out across the waters of the Gulf. Fifteen hundred kilometers away, across the curve of ocean, lay Clipperton Island and Alicia. Thank God Ramón had been posted there. Had he stayed on the mainland, he would have been sent after Villa or Zapata and Alicia could so easily have been made a widow. The Revolution seemed far from Salina Cruz, tucked away in the remote southwest of the country. They had heard of the slaughter on the Zócalo, of course, and of the flight of Díaz first to Veracruz and then to exile and his secret bank accounts in Paris. But, life in Salina Cruz had continued on its sleepy way, unchanged. It was an oasis of tranquility in a land ravaged by war and, most recently, epidemic, as cholera, typhoid and the other diseases of chaos spread across the country.

With Díaz gone, train service had been restored and Rovira had traveled with some trepidation to México to sign several business agreements. He had been there the day Francisco Madero had triumphantly entered the capital to a hero's welcome. Work and business had come to a standstill and the sidewalks were blocked with humanity as the man upon whom the future of México now depended drove through the city on a white horse, waving to the wildly cheering crowds. The train that had carried him to the throng of well-wishers at the railway station had taken thirty hours to make what was normally a five-hour trip to the capital, as crowds of ragged peasants repeatedly blocked the tracks to welcome their liberator. There had been wild celebrations and an almost hysterical optimism for the just and democratic México that would now be built under the idealistic guidance of Francisco Madero. Even the minor earthquake that shook the city on the morning of Madero's arrival, normally a bad omen, had been seen as a sign of a break with the old, for the new and brighter future that lay ahead.

Coronel Avalos stood rigidly at attention, shoulder to shoulder with the other Army officers. He looked at the man who had just been sworn in as president of México. Madero was tiny and his diminutive stature made him look frail and ineffectual among the heavyset, mustachioed men witnessing the ceremony in the National Palace. His high-pitched voice sounded absurd. And, of all things, he was a vegetarian. How could such a man hope to hold power when all those around him, the Army officers, the civil servants, despised and mocked him?

But, six months after his triumphant entry into México, Madero still held the imagination of the public. He had won the only legitimate democratic election in Mexican history with a staggering ninety percent of the popular vote. And he had done it, in spite of the relentless attacks, lies, fearmongering and cruel caricatures of the nation's conservative press. But to lead the country, Madero needed the genuine cooperation of the Army and the civil service and that, Avalos knew, he would never have.

Avalos gazed out of the Ministry of War window across the city streets. He was in a foul temper after his meeting with the War Ministry staff. "I am not pleased, Hernández, you know that. But we are soldiers, we must follow the orders of the government."

"Of course, Coronel," Miguel Hernández replied.

"For the time being, Madero is president. We must live with that fact. Of course, he may not be president for long. Villa and Zapata will press Madero to redistribute the *hacienda* lands immediately and, when he hesitates, they will turn on him like a pack of wolves." He turned to face Hernández. "And there is bad news about Clipperton Island. I learned this morning that Lord Stanmore has given formal notice to the government that his company will remove its workers from the island within the year. He has finalized the lease for Nauru. He has a thousand-year lease at fifty pounds sterling a year. Can you imagine? All the best quality guano they could ever ship, for nothing. The German, Schultz, will remain on Clipperton to maintain their option. I am afraid the Japanese seem to have lost interest."

Hernández shook his head slowly. "What will happen to Ramón and the garrison, Coronel?"

Avalos shrugged. "I do not know if Madero will stand up to the French. He may just withdraw the garrison. I will do my best to see that it is maintained, but my influence with these people is limited."

Ramón sat on a low wooden bench in front of the fire, quietly playing his mandolin. Alicia, sleepy, sat across from him in the big leather armchair, nursing baby Alicia, Ali as they called her. Behind the sweet sound of the mandolin, the wind growled outside, rain hammered the windows and the sea thudded heavily on the beach. Ramón stopped playing and looked at Alicia and the baby, a smile playing at the corners of his mouth. They were both sound asleep. For the past four days, they had remained in the house as a succession of gales of increasing fury had battered the island. All work had come to a standstill. It had been a wonderful opportunity to relax and read and be with his new daughter. The storehouse was filled with food brought by the Tampico. The cisterns were overflowing with fresh water. The gales had brought ashore massive amounts of driftwood for the fires. Whatever the future held, they were safe and secure here.

Ramón had made one trip to the Rock early in the storm to be sure that the light was being properly tended by the new lightkeeper, Victoriano Álvarez. Ramón got up and glanced out of the window facing the Rock. The light was just visible across the lagoon through the driving rain. It was kept burning day and night in this kind of weather. But on a night like this, with such poor visibility, the light might not be enough to keep ships off the reefs surrounding the island

When the light was lit, Álvarez had to climb the ladder to the top of the Rock every eight hours in all weathers to pump up the pressure tank to keep the mantle burning brightly, an unpleasant and sometimes dangerous job. It was lonely duty at the light, cut off from contact with the rest of the settlement. Before Álvarez arrived, the *soldados* had taken the job in rotation, a week at a time. The married men disliked the duty and there had been several occasions when the light had been allowed to go out or the complex lenses allowed to become dirty. Ramón looked at the light again. Now that they had an unmarried, full-time lightkeeper, things should be better. Certainly the *soldados* would be happier. Ramón picked up his mandolin and sat back on the bench and played a lullaby for his sleeping baby and wife.

García and Vélez sat with their backs against the palms, looking out to sea. The two *soldados* had become inseparable friends since traveling to Clipperton together on the Tampico. Vélez passed García the handmade cigarette they were sharing and asked, "Armando, do you believe what Subteniente Picazo says about this Madero?"

García took a thoughtful puff and replied, "Picazo is learned. He was taught to read by the priests at the mission in Jalpan. He reads the Teniente's newspapers. He knows what the newspapers say."

"But will our lands be returned to us? Will they stop stealing our sons and daughters? Will they let us leave the Army and go back to our land?"

"Picazo says the newspapers hate Madero. He says they are afraid of him. But the newspapers say that Madero promises to give the land back and end slavery. Picazo says Zapata will force him do it. And Zapata is one of us."

Ramón finished climbing down the ladder from *la roca* and

waited for the lightkeeper, Victoriano Álvarez, to descend. "The light is in perfect condition, Álvarez," said Ramón. "You are doing a good job."

The powerfully built Negro smiled. "Thank you, Teniente." The two men walked toward the two stout cabins at the base of the Rock. Álvarez undid the heavy lock on the door of the first cabin and Ramón looked inside. Drums of specially refined petroleum oil for the light, spare mantles, cleaning supplies and food were neatly stacked inside. Ramón nodded approvingly. At the second cabin, the one in which he lived, Álvarez opened the door for Ramón.

"Here is the log, Teniente," he said. Unusually, Alvarez was literate. He had grown up in Colima as part of the household of the governor of the state and was rumored to be his illegitimate son. Ramón sat at the small table and leafed through the book, noting that the times of lighting and extinguishing the light were carefully entered every day, the times of pumping up the pressure tank, the dates of refilling the reservoir and cleaning the lamp, the amount of petroleum oil remaining in the storage cabin, all neatly and properly entered. There was a record of ships sighted by Álvarez through his telescope. Ramón nodded approvingly.

The cabins had been very strongly built and anchored to the ground due to their exposed position near the Rock. The one that served as Álvarez's home was small and contained only a bed, a table and a chair, several oil lamps and a small iron cook stove. Everything was neat and tidy. Ramón led the way outside. "And, now, the siren test," he said. Álvarez reached for the crank of the siren bolted to the side of the storage cabin and swung it around. A loud wail filled the air. Ramón smiled. "Another perfect inspection, Victoriano."

Álvarez grinned. "Thank you, Teniente."

"Do you get lonely here?" asked Ramón. "When the men tended the light in rotation, they always complained about the duty."

Álvarez shook his head. "It is not so bad, Teniente. I like

being alone here. It gives me much time to think."

CHAPTER 17

Miguel Hernández sat in the library of the Ciudadela looking glumly at the shelves. He had never taken a book down. He leaned forward now and picked one at random. A history of the Yucatán. He opened it and looked at the engravings of elaborate Mayan temples. He grimaced and pushed the book back into its place. Ramón had been a voracious reader. In the old days, in Acapulco, if he could be found nowhere else, it was a safe bet that he would be here, his nose buried in an obscure military history. Miguel missed Ramón. He missed Coronel Avalos too, the crusty, short-tempered old goat.

He had seen the Coronel take the bullet that had killed him. Avalos had been riding just in front and to the right, as they galloped up the hill. Somewhere ahead was the party of Villa's men they had almost caught in the act of destroying a bridge. But the rebels had stopped running and had prepared an ambush among the rocks. The *federales* had ridden right into it.

The Coronel had been the first of fifteen men to die, falling headfirst in front of Miguel's horse. Miguel had dragged him out of the line of fire and into shelter behind a rock, but Avalos was already dying, gasping for breath, blood frothing pink from a wound deep in his chest. His breathing had suddenly grown rapid and shallow and he was dead in less than a minute. For all Miguel knew, the Coronel's bones lay bleaching there now, picked clean by the vultures, in territory no *federale* would dare enter.

But life went on. Since he had been assigned to General Victoriano Huerta's staff, Miguel had seen firsthand the running battle with Zapata. When Francisco Madero had refused to immediately seize the hundreds of millions of hectares of *hacienda* lands and divide them up among the *peones*, Villa and Zapata had turned on their former ally as a betrayer of the Revolution. They now fought Madero with the same grim determination and peasant cunning with which they had once fought Díaz. And what strange bedfellows war made. General Huerta, the man Madero had chosen to preserve his presidency against the attacks of Villa and Zapata, made the dreaded Ramón Corral seem like a choir boy. Unwittingly, Madero had made a pact with the devil.

In the Díaz days, Miguel had often seen General Huerta at the Ciudadela while on business in the capital. With his reputation as an Indian killer and soldier of ruthless efficiency already well established, Huerta had a commanding presence. He was of pure Huichol Indian descent, heavily built, and his thinning white hair and wire-rimmed glasses served, somehow, to make him more intimidating rather than less. His drink was cognac and he could be found in the Café Colón, near the Ciudadela, every night, expounding loudly and with crushing finality on any and every subject. The terrified waiter didn't refill General Huerta's glass, but brought new bottles. Hour after hour, Huerta sat at his table, one hand on his glass, the other on the bottle. It was said that the general had only two friends on Earth and their names were Hennessy and Martel.

In the National Palace, Francisco Madero, so well meaning, so full of hope for a new México, was bewildered. "Why do they persecute me so? How can I build a democratic nation when I must constantly fight simply to remain alive?" His brother and closest advisor, Gustavo, plump and mustachioed, perched on the edge of the Presidente's desk peering through his one good eye and said, "We are trapped between Zapata and his *peones* wanting justice overnight on the one side and the *hacendados*, the foreign investors and the Church, who have taken everything and will give up nothing, on the other."

"Zapata and Villa cannot expect me to reverse four centuries of injustice in a few months. More than half of the people of this country, over nine million of them, are in slavery or peonage. A few thousand people, a hundred foreign companies and the Church own almost all the land. If I could free all the slaves and *peones* tomorrow, they would have nowhere to grow corn, they would starve. Do you know what the *hacendado* who stole the land of Zapata's village said when Zapata told him that the people had nowhere to grow food?" Gustavo shook his head. "He said, 'Let them grow it in flowerpots.' What can I do with people like this? William Randolph Hearst alone has possession of over sixteen million hectares of land stolen from the *peones*. He already calls in his newspapers for my overthrow and the invasion and annexation of México by the United States. What do you think the *yanquis* would do if I tried to take the land back from Hearst and return it to the *peones*? What is the answer?"

"The answer, my dear brother, is that there is no answer."

Miguel Hernández sat at a desk in General Huerta's field headquarters. The general was in a murderous mood. The bodies of the thirty-five peasants who had seized and occupied the *hacienda* lay outside, their blood seeping into the dust. Huerta had reserved the executions for himself and, as always, performed them with his revolver to the victim's temple, children first, for maximum effect, then the women and, finally, the men.

For six weeks now, they had pursued Zapata through the south. He had led them a wild chase across rivers and through mountain passes where the horses grew lame, never letting the *federales* get close enough to engage him in battle. For the first time, Miguel was sure he had caught a glimpse of Zapata himself, standing on the edge of a canyon, looking down on them as they rode nervously through.

By the time a *federale* had raised his rifle to fire, Zapata was gone. Miguel had seen photographs of the rebel leader, in his early thirties but his eyes smoldering with four hundred years of rage. It had almost seemed that he could feel the intensity of the man half a kilometer away. Now, Zapata and his army were entrenched in impregnable positions in the mountains. Every pass was guarded, every canyon a potential deathtrap. The *federales* would never dislodge him.

Since they could do nothing with Zapata, perhaps it was as well that they had been recalled. Miguel rose and went outside the *hacienda*. The bodies lying in the dust were buzzing with flies. He thought of getting a burial party to dispose of them but changed his mind. What was the point? They would be leaving in the morning. A week in México to re-equip and then Huerta's army would be off to the north to fight the latest challenger to Madero's struggling government—Pascual Orozco, who had the backing of the most powerful *hacendados* of them all, the Terrazas family, with twenty thousand square kilometers of what had once been *indio* land at stake.

Francisco and Gustavo Madero worked far into the night. Strollers on the Zócalo could see the glow of light in the Presidente's office until long past midnight. Vicepresidente Pino Suárez had left for his apartments several hours earlier, leaving the Madero brothers to decide what to do with Félix Díaz. He was Porfirio Díaz's nephew and his abortive rebellion in Veracruz had been put down in short order. He had been tried and sentenced to death for treason. "We cannot allow him to be executed," said Francisco Madero. "Our purpose is to bring humanity to México. I will not have his blood on my hands."

Gustavo blew a long stream of smoke and watched it drift slowly away and disappear before giving a hollow laugh. "He would kill you without a moment's hesitation."

"Perhaps, Gustavo. But should I reduce myself to his level? I am not Félix Díaz or Porfirio Díaz or, God be praised, Ramón Corral."

"As always, Francisco, you will follow your principles. Grant the reprieve at your peril."

"Very well. Then there is the matter of Bernardo Reyes."

"You will grant him a reprieve too, in spite of the fact that he also tried to overthrow your government."

"There is nothing wrong with mercy and forgiveness, Gustavo. I will grant reprieves to them both. They will have to stay in jail for the time being, but we will not treat them like common criminals. Have Guzmán prepare the stays of execution and arrange to put them in the same cell. They can keep each other company. They will be permitted to have books and visitors. We are not barbarians."

Gustavo Madero's expression was grim. "There is a total of more than a million *pesos* unaccounted for, Francisco."

"I know, I know. I have seen the figures. How could General Huerta do this? He is no better than a common thief. Surely, the glory of his victories should be enough for him. He and his troops were welcomed back into México as conquering heroes. He is the man of the hour."

"Men like Huerta take it for granted that they will enrich themselves at the public expense. The leopard does not change his spots. Huerta could never have resisted the temptation of millions of *pesos* in his war chest."

"I have no choice, Gustavo, I will have to dismiss him from the Army. And we must look into laying charges against him."

"He is a dangerous man, Francisco."

"He is a thief, Gustavo. There is no alternative. I cannot permit a general of the Army to steal public funds. We fought the Revolution to end corruption, not to perpetuate it. He will have to be dismissed."

CHAPTER 18

Ramón leaned against the iron railing of the balcony in the Hotel San Agustín smoking and watched through the French doors as Alicia spoke to the hotel chambermaid, Altagracia. Alta, as the children called her, was eighteen with skin the color of *café con leche*. Gleaming black hair, made up into a thick braid, fell to her waist. The children adored her and Alta had eagerly accepted Ramón and Alicia's offer to become their maid. She would leave with them for Orizaba as soon as Ramón had seen his superiors at the Ministry of War and then travel with the Arnauds to Clipperton.

"Now remember, Alta, the children must be in bed by eight o'clock," Alicia said for the second or third time.

"Yes, Doña Alicia, eight o'clock. I understand," Altagracia replied with the hint of a smile.

Ramón entered the room, buttoning his tunic. "Alta has taken care of half a dozen brothers and sisters, Alicia. She will take good care of Ramoncito and Ali. Now we must get going or we shall be late."

They walked arm in arm through the busy streets to the little French restaurant where they were to meet Ramón's sister, Adela and her husband. Adela and León Reyes were already seated. Reyes could barely contain himself, impatiently waving the waiter away before he could even offer them an aperitif. "Madero has my father in jail. By God, he will pay for this."

The *federales* came in the night to free Bernardo Reyes and Félix Díaz from the comfortable cell they shared. The long-planned coup against the government of Francisco Madero had begun. Madero and his brother watched in horror from the presidential office the next morning as hundreds of cavalry, with Bernardo Reyes at their head, charged madly across the Zócalo toward the National Palace. The thunder of the horses' hooves was lost beneath screams as the mounted soldiers cut a swath with their horses and swords directly through a throng of worshipers crossing the Zócalo on their way to Mass at the Cathedral. Homeless children, who came to the Zócalo every Sunday to beg from the churchgoers, lay trampled and bleeding on the stones.

Madero saw the Commander-in-Chief of the Presidential Guard, defying the cavalry charge, fall wounded in front of the Palace. Then he saw Reyes, riding like a madman, brandishing his sword, leading his cavalry against the massed ranks of the Guard. He watched in horrified fascination as, less thirty meters from the Palace, Reyes crumpled and fell heavily from his horse, his chest pierced by a Guard's bullet.

The cavalry withdrew and regrouped, but their charges against the Presidential Guard became increasingly disorganized under withering gunfire. Finally, they retreated to the Ciudadela, leaving the bodies of Bernardo Reyes and his soldiers and of hundreds of churchgoers lying on the stones of the Zócalo. Through the closed window, Madero heard the high-pitched screaming of a wounded horse. He clapped his hands over his ears, trying to keep out the terrible sound. There was a single shot and the screaming stopped.

"We must recall General Huerta, Gustavo," said Francisco Madero, perched on the edge of his desk and nervously drumming his fingers. "The Commander-in-Chief is too badly wounded to go on. We need a real soldier to get Félix Díaz out of the Ciudadela."

"What about your principles, Francisco?"

"I am no more pleased about this than you are, Gustavo, but there is a greater principle at stake here. A coup by the Army must be crushed without delay. If we leave Díaz and his men in the Ciudadela, who knows what the rest of the Army will do? We have to get them out immediately and arrest Díaz. For the sake of the Revolution, Gustavo, we must recall General Huerta."

General Huerta's face creased into a satisfied smile as he stood behind the sandbagged artillery emplacement on the Zócalo and watched a shell arc high through the air before dropping lazily and harmlessly into the wide courtyard of the Ciudadela. Of the thousands of shells fired in six days of almost continuous bombardment since he had been reinstated, only one shell had scored a hit on anything of significance in the Ciudadela. Most landed harmlessly in the courtyard or had hit houses in the neighborhood around the garrison. Huerta was pleased with his men. With that one exception, it had been a masterful display of gunnery.

Huerta and Díaz had met in the office of the United States Ambassador to México, Henry Lane Wilson, to sign a pact to overthrow Francisco Madero and to install Huerta as president. A democratically elected president who vowed to return the land stolen from the peones was a serious danger to American interests. Wilson had done his utmost to destabilize Madero's presidency, publicly referred to him as a madman and now orchestrated the coup by Huerta and Díaz.

Huerta's troops formed a tight square around the Ciudadela. On every street corner, a Maxim machine gun lurked ominously on its tripod behind sandbags. Hundreds of bodies lay sprawled in the streets, civilians too slow or too stupid to get out of the line of fire. And, around the Ciudadela's walls, lay hundreds more bodies, the bodies of troops loyal to Francisco Madero. They had been singled out by Huerta and ordered to make suicidal frontal assaults on the Ciudadela, across open ground, where they had been systematically shot to pieces by Félix Díaz's machine guns.

Francisco Madero and his brother remained isolated in the National Palace, surrounded by the Presidential Guard under their new leader, General Blanquet. Huerta chuckled at the thought of the ridiculous little Madero brothers in their supposed place of safety. He had appointed General Blanquet personally. When the time came, El Presidente would receive a nasty surprise from the commander of his Presidential Guard. As the days passed and the shooting continued, the death toll mounted into the thousands. No one dared remove the bodies in the streets. Some were doused with gasoline and burned where they lay, sending clouds of black, greasy smoke into the skies. The remaining bodies heaved with maggots and, as they hatched, the air filled with swarms of flies and the sickly sweet smell of rotting human flesh. Dogs and rats grew fat and sleek on the corpses.

Terrified civilians, their mouths and noses tightly covered with bandanas and handkerchiefs, ran through the streets with white rags tied to sticks, desperately trying to get to safety with their few precious possessions. Electricity and water were shut off and food grew scarce. The trains had stopped running and there was no way Ramón could get Alicia and the children out of the capital. He made them stay in their hotel rooms, well away from the windows, not even permitting them to go downstairs to take their increasingly meager meals. The staccato rattle of machine gun fire and the deep boom of artillery were so frequent that Alicia didn't argue.

From the office he had commandeered near the Ciudadela, General Huerta watched the carnage in the square with satisfaction. He returned to the desk so abruptly vacated by its previous inhabitant and leaned back in the chair, his feet on the desk. He leaned forward lazily and picked up one of the leaflets that had been circulating throughout México, supporting the Díaz coup and urging the overthrow of Madero. The printing presses in the basement of the United States

Embassy on Paseo de la Reforma had been working overtime. Henry Lane Wilson hadn't been a public relations man for nothing

There were dark circles beneath Francisco Madero's eyes and his shoulders had begun to sag, making him look more diminutive than ever. He had barely slept for eight days. He had had a cot brought into his office but, every time he closed his eyes, another burst of machine gun fire or boom of artillery brought him to full wakefulness. He looked down on the Zócalo. The bodies had at last been removed and the massive square was empty. The Presidential Guard formed a stalwart line in front of the National Palace. He said quietly, "We must accept the American Ambassador's offer, Gustavo."

Gustavo Madero, his face drawn with exhaustion, turned to face his brother, "I know, Francisco, we must have an end to the killing. There are almost five thousand dead. This cannot go on. Ambassador Wilson has offered to arrange a ceasefire so General Huerta can go into the Ciudadela and negotiate a truce with Díaz. We will give Díaz safe conduct out of México and be rid of him once and for all."

"Then we agree. Telephone Ambassador Wilson immediately and tell him that we accept his proposal."

Gustavo Madero carried the small briefcase himself. General Huerta's messenger had been insistent that he come alone to the Hotel Gambrinus to work out the finer points of the negotiations he was to hold with the rebels. With any luck, Díaz would be out of the Ciudadela and on his way to Europe in twenty-four hours. Madero made himself comfortable and raised a small glass of wine as he waited for Huerta. As he took a sip, General Huerta entered. Madero rose and shook the general's hand, saying, "My brother has asked me to thank you for your loyal service, General Huerta."

Huerta gave Madero an expansive smile through his wire rimmed glasses. "It is my duty and my pleasure, Don Gustavo. I trust El Presidente is bearing up well?"

"As well as can be expected, General." Madero sat and gestured to the seat opposite. "Let us get on with the details you are to discuss with Díaz." Gustavo Madero bent to open his briefcase and, as he did, four *federales* burst through the doors of the dining room and seized him, pinning his arms to his sides.

"General, what is this? What are you doing?" he gasped.

Huerta ignored Madero's protests and said coldly to the *federales*, "Take him to the Ciudadela."

Almost at the same moment, General Blanquet with members of the Presidential Guard burst through the door of Francisco Madero's office in the National Palace. Blanquet strode across the room pistol in hand and stood before Madero. The diminutive President looked at the much larger man for a moment, realized that he had been betrayed and then slapped Blanquet hard across the face. "Traitor," Madero said quietly.

The carriages and cars drew up in front of the American Embassy on Paseo de la Reforma in an unbroken stream. Ambassador Henry Lane Wilson was hosting a reception and black tie dinner in honor of the birthday of George Washington. The champagne flowed like water beneath red, white and blue bunting and Wilson moved skillfully through the crowd, with just the right word or phrase for everyone. Generals Félix Díaz and Victoriano Huerta were there, side by side, champagne glasses in hand. Big men, imposing in full dress uniform complete with ceremonial swords, bristling with medals. Ambassador Wilson raised his glass and waited for the murmur of conversation to die. "Long live Generals Díaz and Huerta," he said, "the saviors of México." The glasses were raised and the toast drunk.

The Cuban ambassador, Manuel Marqués Sterling, waited anxiously for the right moment. Sara Madero had visited him late that afternoon, devastated by the kidnapping of her husband. In tears, she had begged him to ask the American ambassador to save the President's life. The time came and Sterling asked Wilson in a confidential tone, "Ambassador Wilson, what are you going to do with Madero?" Wilson took a sip of his scotch and raised an eyebrow quizzically. "You cannot let them kill him," said Sterling. "Please spare his life."

Wilson smiled wistfully and directed a thin stream of cigarette smoke across Sterling's shoulder. "Come now, Your Excellency, I can do no such thing. México is a sovereign state. It would be improper for me to interfere in her internal affairs."

The celebration of democracy at the Embassy rollicked on gaily while outside the skies darkened as clouds piled up overhead and a hard cold rain began to fall. In the deserted courtyard of the Ciudadela lay the tortured and dismembered body of Gustavo Madero. His one good eye had been gouged out with a bayonet. Behind the Lecumberri Penitentiary, at the foot of a grim stone wall, the gunshot-riddled body of Vicepresidente Pino Suárez was sprawled on the sodden earth. A few meters away lay another body. Blood soaked the back of the neat pinstripe suit and was being washed into the ground in rust-colored rivulets. The body of Francisco Madero, the only democratically elected president in the history of México, lay face down in the mud.

Those who really mattered; the Army officers, the Church, the oil companies, the wealthy, the foreign owners of the mills, mines and factories, the *norteamericanos*, they were all delighted with Presidente Victoriano Huerta. At the urging of Henry Lane Wilson, the new government was quickly recognized by Great Britain, Germany, Spain and the other sources of foreign capital. The Archbishop of México celebrated a Te Deum, a Mass of praise and thanksgiving, for General Huerta in the Metropolitan Cathedral. The Catholic Church and the Embassy of the United States provided cash to finance General Huerta's new government. The General's likeness was to be seen everywhere, even gracing the package of the most popular brand of cigarettes.

Every night, as México's new president drank his cognac in the Café Colón, his death squads roamed the capital. Opposition disappeared suddenly, silently. Only a single senator had the courage to question the illegal ratification of Huerta's presidency. Belisario Dominguez died of his wounds later that night. In the final convulsion of Francisco Madero's short-lived democracy, Congress met to hold formal inquiries into the disappearance of thousands of people who had questioned Huerta's installation as president. Within an hour, the building was surrounded by *federales* and *policía* and the hundred and ten deputies were marched off to the Belem Penitentiary.

CHAPTER 19

With each arrival of the Tampico at Clipperton, the news grew worse. Villa and Zapata would not tolerate Huerta and were once again raging across the country. Villa had re-entered México from his hideout in the United States and was wreaking havoc in the north. Zapata's army had come down from the mountains and was once again seizing *haciendas* in the south. As the months went by, the armies of enraged *peones* drew ever closer to the capital. Ramón had agonized over his decision until, one night as he and Alicia sat quietly at the dining table after dinner, he said quietly, "I must go to the Ministry of War for orders, my darling, and I want to see Adela and Miguel."

Alicia knew that he was afraid that he might never see his sister and his best friend again, although he would never admit it. "I will go with you, Ramón. We can leave Altagracia and the children with your mother in Orizaba and then spend Christmas there on the way back." Ramón was about to speak, to tell her that it was too dangerous for her to travel in México with him, especially now that she was pregnant again but he lapsed into silence. Who knew when either of them might see México again?

The train sighed into the station in the capital as Ramón and Alicia followed the conductor down the almost empty first-class carriage. With three quarters of the country in the hands of the rebels, most trains were carrying only a handful of people. Any train, anywhere, was liable to be stopped and its passengers robbed or worse. The locomotive had pulled only one passenger car from Orizaba. Behind it were fourteen boxcars from Veracruz, filled to their roofs with German arms and ammunition for General Huerta's besieged *federales*.

Pancho Villa and his peasant army routinely hijacked such trains and fought from town to town on the railroads, eating, sleeping and copulating in the boxcars of a score of commandeered trains. Horses, children and goats traveled with them. At each town, the ragtag army swelled until there was no room left in the boxcars and new recruits climbed onto the roofs of the cars to follow Villa into battle.

The women, the *soldaderas*, were armed and fought alongside the men. Twelve-year-olds wore bandoliers and carried Mausers taken from the bodies of dead *federales* in a hundred towns. Among the ranks of Villa's army were more fortunate *federales* who had deserted and joined the Revolution. On Villa's personal train were foreign journalists who found in the wild Mexican *bandido* the perfect romantic hero for the sensational copy they sent back to New York and Berlin and London. And there were Villa's two lieutenants, men whose names struck terror into the heart of every *federalista*: Rodolfo Fierro and Tomás Urbina. They were sadists who raped and burned and shot prisoners wantonly, who used tortures learned from the desert Indians, staking *federales* and suspected collaborators to anthills to be eaten alive.

The Arnauds' train was one of the lucky ones and pulled into the station in the capital unmolested in spite of the tempting shipment of arms it carried. Ramón straightened his uniform as he stepped down. The only sound was the gentle hiss of escaping steam. They walked quickly from the eerily deserted station and hailed a carriage.

Miguel Hernández held the door of his new automobile open for the two women. Alicia and Liliana settled themselves into the leather seats, looking bright and sunny in their new dresses and flowered hats. Neither Alicia nor Ramón had been in an automobile before and both found the experience slightly unnerving. Miguel closed the door behind Ramón and then took the seat beside the driver. He opened the sliding window and said, "Do not be nervous. Automobiles are all the rage, or at least they were. Just sit back and enjoy it." He motioned to the driver and the car rattled away in a cloud of blue smoke. As they drove away from the station, they were struck by how few people were on the streets. They turned onto Paseo de la Reforma and into the area of grand homes.

Alicia leaned forward and said, "Please have the driver slow down, Miguel." The car slowed to a walking pace and Alicia leaned out of the window. These were the houses in which she had attended gay parties and talked in giggles and whispers about dashing young men and the mysteries of love. It all seemed so long ago. So much had changed. The houses still slumbered behind their centuries-old trees but many looked deserted and the paint on the facades was peeling and the window boxes that had once spilled over in riots of multicolored blooms were barren. The México of the Porfiriata had existed only four years before but it seemed a lifetime ago.

They came to the corner of the Alameda where the skeleton of the Palace of Fine Arts stood, still unfinished. Miguel gestured toward the rusting ironwork. "There has been no work on it since Don Porfirio fell," he said. They passed the Columbus statue and followed the sweep of Paseo de la Reforma around the base of the Cuauhtémoc Monument. Atop the monument, the proud Indian leader shot an arrow into the air while, around the base, reliefs depicted the horrific tortures inflicted on him by the Spaniards.

Opposite the American Embassy, El Ángel soared above them. Ramón shielded his eyes and looked up at the golden-winged figure, brilliant in the sunshine. He thought of the day, at the height of the Centennial celebrations, when he and Alicia had stood together with Don Félix on the balcony just below El Ángel and Don Félix's prophetic words. He had been right. Don Porfirio had misjudged the mood of the people and he had fallen. At this very moment, Ramón knew, he was dying a very rich but broken man in Paris.

Chapultepec Park was quiet. Normally, after Mass on a sunny Sunday, the Park would be brimming with people. The wealthy would be riding their horses on the winding paths. There would be kites and balloons in the air and parents playing with immaculately dressed children. There would be model boats sailing on the lake and food vendors everywhere. But a mood of apprehension seemed to strangle the capital and had reduced the Park's inhabitants to a few solitary walkers. These days, only the churches were full.

They left the Park and the car turned in the direction of San Ángel. Liliana patted Alicia on the knee and gave a thin smile, "Miguel has a wonderful surprise for you two." Alicia returned the smile and clung tightly to the hand strap as the driver flung the car around a curve toward the elegant suburb.

They hadn't been to the San Ángel Inn for years and the flood of warm memories Alicia felt mingled with a painful feeling of emptiness. México had lost its life, its zest. The streets were almost deserted. The vendors and musicians and shoeshine boys were gone. The vibrant ebb and flow of humanity that had made this one of the most exciting places on Earth had been supplanted by a desultory trickle of unsmiling people, looking down at their feet as they went grimly about their business. They walked into the Inn and Ramón greeted Madame Roux, the imposing Frenchwoman who had converted the old pulque *hacienda* into México's most fashionable restaurant. "Ramón, look at you, so handsome," she cried in delight. Her face broke into a warm smile and she kissed Ramón on both cheeks, then stood back to look at Alicia.

"And you, my darling," she said, "So beautiful. All grown up into a lovely woman. It is years since I have seen the two of you. Come, you must have the finest table in my restaurant." She led the way to a window table where they would have a view over the flower-filled courtyard.

As Madame Roux bustled away, they settled at their table.

Ramón clapped Miguel on the shoulder. "This is a great treat for us, Miguel. Thank you."

Alicia touched the back of Liliana's hand gently. "A wonderful surprise. Ramón and I have often talked about coming back here."

"Excellent," said Miguel. "We are here to enjoy ourselves and to celebrate your promotion. Congratulations, Ramón. It was long overdue, Capitán Arnaud."

"Thank you, my friend. A promotion was the last thing I expected when I went to the Ministry this morning."

"And what orders did they give you? Will they maintain the garrison?"

Ramón offered Miguel a cigar and, lighting his own, said, "The government is convinced that the King of Italy will decide in our favor and they want to get the guano mining underway again as quickly as possible. I have been instructed to return and carry on as before. Almost all the men in the garrison are to be replaced. But now, of course, there is a shortage of shipping. The Tampico will not be available to take us back until January at the earliest."

Liliana leaned forward. "But that is wonderful. You can spend more time with your families and, Alicia, you can have the baby in Orizaba instead of on the island."

Alicia waited for the wine steward to finish pouring and said, "I would be perfectly happy to have the baby on Clipperton, Liliana. Doña Juana is an excellent midwife. But since there is no ship, our baby will be born in Orizaba."

Liliana looked around the almost deserted restaurant. "The city is so sad now, isn't it?"

"It breaks my heart," said Alicia. "México was so full of life and color. And now, now it is dying. Are people so scared they stay home?"

"They do," said Miguel. "And no one travels. No one laughs or smiles. Look around." Only two other tables were occupied. At one time, it had been necessary to reserve days or weeks in advance to dine at the Inn. "The restaurants are empty and so are the theaters. Everyone is terrified. This is a city under siege. Even the *yanquis* have abandoned General Huerta. They have embargoed arms shipments to the government."

Ramón drained his wine and asked, "But why do they now oppose General Huerta? Do the *yanquis* really want Villa and Zapata giving the land back to the *peones*?"

Miguel laughed, "Of course not. Huerta is proposing to nationalize the oil industry so they have abandoned him to his fate."

Alicia could hear Ramón playing the piano in the *salón*. She knew Doña Carlota would be sitting close by him on the bench as he played, a look of frank adoration on her face. Ramoncito and Ali were safely tucked in bed. Altagracia had drawn Alicia's bath for her. What luxury it was to have endless hot water and a bathtub she could stretch out in. The fragrance of the bath oil rose from the water in a delicious steamy cloud. She chased Altagracia away and dipped her foot into the water. A little too hot.

She wiped the steam from the full-length mirror and looked at her reflection. Her hair was piled on top of her head, her eyes framed by escaping wisps of hair. She undressed languidly, allowing her robe to slip to the marble floor. Alicia ran her hands down her sides, over her hips and across her growing belly. It was full and round and hard with Ramón's baby. A faint brown line ran down from her navel. Was that a little kick? She smiled at her reflection and hugged her belly before easing herself over the edge of the tub and into the steaming, soothing water. Her belly was so big it rose out of the water like an island. She heaped bubbles on her baby and felt another kick.

The Arnauds occupied the first pew on the left-hand side of the altar in the parish church of San Miguel. They sat close together, Doña Carlota, Ramón with his son quiet beside him, Ali squirming and pointing delightedly at the statues of the saints, and Alicia, cradling the sleeping Lydia, now almost four months old and always called Olga. All the pews were full for Midnight Mass this Christmas Eve in Orizaba. Ramón watched the priest as he delivered the Mass. He was a young man, dark and intense. This new priest had brought progressive ideas to the seventeenth century church the Arnaud family had attended for as long as Ramón could remember. Ramón's mother often returned from Mass these days fuming over the young priest's thinly veiled references to Mexican politics in his sermons. Ramón could see Doña Carlota growing uncomfortable as the priest launched into a Biblical parable clearly referring to the cruelty of the Huerta regime. Ramón crossed his arms and listened in quiet amusement.

After the service, they walked back across the Parque del Castillo and through the quiet nighttime streets of Orizaba. The *chipichipi* fell gently. The mountains above the town were white with a dusting of fine snow. Ramón carried Olga, while behind them they could hear the two older children singing and splashing through the puddles with Altagracia. In the distance, the Río Blanco gurgled down the mountainside toward the sea. The moon broke through the clouds suddenly, bathing the glistening street in soft white light. Alicia took Ramón's arm tightly in hers and leaned against him as they walked.

Their time with Félix was almost at an end. The Tampico lay against the pier in Salina Cruz and tomorrow, shortly after dawn, would take them to Acapulco where they would load supplies and a new draft of *soldados* before steaming to Clipperton. Altagracia was settling Ramoncito and Ali into bed. Olga lay slumped over Alicia's shoulder. "Papá," Alicia said. "I am so happy to be going back to our little island. It breaks my heart to see our country torn apart like this. But I worry about what will happen to you here all alone."

Félix moved over and sat beside her, holding and patting her hand. "You must not worry about me, Alicia. Salina Cruz is as far from trouble as it is possible to get in México."

"Perhaps General Huerta will stop Villa and Zapata. The government still controls the ports and gets plenty of arms from Germany," said Ramón.

Félix shrugged. "Yes, of course, but as soon as the government gets the Mausers, the rebels steal them. Zapata is running wild; there seems to be no stopping him. His army grows more powerful day by day. And Villa, the boxcar *bandido*, now there is a clever scoundrel for you. So audacious. Did you hear how he captured Juárez? Drove a train filled with men and horses straight into the town in the middle of the night. He took the garrison completely by surprise and seized the town. They say he looted three hundred thousand *pesos* from the brothels and gambling halls. A very profitable attack. And then there is Obregón."

"I know about Villa," said Alicia. "They say he became an outlaw after he killed a *hacendado* who was trying to violate his sister. And Zapata, he has never forgiven the *hacendados* for taking the *peones'* land. I read that the *hacendados* even took the streets of his village and plowed them up for sugar cane. But I have not heard of Obregón. Who is he?"

"A brilliant campaigner," said Ramón. "He is the most disciplined soldier of them all and a strategist to be reckoned with. The Yaqui follow Obregón like a god, even though he is not one of them. If he orders them to advance directly into machine-gun fire, they obey without question. He has taken all of Sonora and is now threatening Sinaloa and Jalisco."

Félix looked with concern at Alicia. "My darling, I believe we are frightening you with all this talk of fighting. Let us speak of happier things."

"Another year, Ramón, can you believe it?" Alicia murmured it into his ear, as they stood on the foredeck of the Tampico in Acapulco Bay, watching the last of the stores being loaded aboard before the ship steamed for Clipperton.

"I hope 1914 is a better year for México than 1913, Alicia.

My God, but it must end. There has been too much death." Ramón leaned over to watch a group of soldiers coming up the gangway.

They had met the new members of the garrison the night before. Ramón had liked his new second-in-command, Teniente Secundino Cardona, immediately. Slightly built, with a wispy mustache and a serious demeanor, Cardona stopped at the head of the gangway, his wife, Tirza, beside him, and saluted Ramón crisply. Ramón smiled and returned the salute.

"He loves music," Ramón said, turning to Alicia. "And he says he can sing. I hope so. He will be a good addition to our *banquetes*."

Ramón returned the salutes of the other members of the garrison as they came aboard: a corporal and nine new *soldados*, some with wives and children. Ramón shook his head in disbelief. "Do you realize, Alicia, that once these troops replace the men on the island, our population will be thirty-one? What a pity that Coronel Avalos could not live to see this day."

It was a pleasantly warm, windless night. The children were sound asleep. Doña Juana tended the pig crackling on a spit near the old capstan. They were all dressed in fresh, clean clothes for the weekly *banquete*. The flickering light from the fire and torches cast long shadows across the sand. Standing by the trunk of a fallen coconut palm, Pedro Carbajal and Mauro Salina played their guitars quietly. The new *teniente*, Secundino Cardona, sang the love song in a clear tenor, the others joining in on the choruses.

Overhead, the moonless sky was white with stars. Alicia, holding Ramón's hand, closed her eyes and allowed the music to transport her. Very faintly, she could hear the waves lapping on the beach as though in accompaniment. Scarcely aware of what she was doing, she began to sing with Cardona in her sweet, high voice. As she began to sing more clearly, Cardona and the others stopped to listen. There was nothing but the dark tropic air, the rustling of the sea, the gentle plucking of the guitars and Alicia's voice like silk in the night.

CHAPTER 20

"**I** love this time, Ramón." Alicia sat at his feet, her head lightly on his knee. Before them, flames from the burning driftwood crackled orange and red up the flue. Outside, the gusts of a three-day-old storm hammered against the walls of the house. In the distance, the surf rumbled on the beach. "The children are safe in bed. We are warm and snug in our little home. It is not the life I expected when I was a girl in Orizaba, but I love it. I used to dream of living in a grand house, even grander than Papá's house, with servants and a beautiful courtyard and of going to parties every week, but I am so happy here."

Ramón smiled down at her and stroked her hair. "It is not the life I expected either, Alicia, not at all what I pictured myself doing. But I am perfectly content. Coronel Avalos, God rest his soul, once said to me that the best thing about Clipperton was the fact that there was nothing here. For a long time, I had no idea what he meant, but he was right. We have taken a place that was nothing and built a community. I am proud of what we have done here." Ramón pulled Alicia more tightly against him. "And, more than anything, I am glad that we are safely here with our children in these dangerous times." They sat together in the warmth, staring into the flames without speaking, as the rain drove hard against the windows.

Almost asleep in the warm glow of the fire, their reverie was broken by an urgent knocking at the door. Altagracia's feet beat a rapid tattoo down the hallway, then the howl of the wind grew sharply as she opened the door. It was Álvarez, the lightkeeper, breathless with exertion. "The Capitán," he gasped. "I must speak to Capitán Arnaud."

"Altagracia, bring Victoriano in," Ramón called out, rising from his chair.

"Capitán, a ship." Álvarez gasped for air. "A ship has run onto the reef near the boat landing." Water streamed down the lightkeeper's coat and soaked into the Persian rug.

"What kind of ship is it, Victoriano?" Ramón grunted as he pulled on his long leather boots.

"A schooner, four masts, perhaps eighty meters long, Capitán. She is breaking up. There have been two flares so far. I sounded the siren but no one could hear over the storm. I had to run all the way here," Álvarez gasped.

Ramón finished pulling on his boots and stood. "Good work, Álvarez. Get Teniente Cardona. Tell him to get all the *soldados* and to get the biggest surf boat ready. You go with him and get ropes and lanterns from the store. I will meet you at the boat landing."

The lightkeeper turned on his heel and strode quickly from the room. Ramón turned to Alicia. "You stay here, my love. We will do all we can."

"Ramón." Alicia clutched Ramón's arm, "Please be careful."

"Yes, my dear." With that, he pulled on his oilskins and was gone, the door slamming with the storm behind him.

Below the Rock, the sea seethed angrily across the beach and into the lagoon beyond. When the moon broke through ragged gaps torn in the racing clouds, it was possible to see waves breaking with methodical fury on the reef. As Ramón ran breathless to the beach, a fiery red glow burned for a few seconds then disappeared as quickly as it had come. Cardona was on the beach already. "Capitán, a flare," he said, pointing. His voice, torn away by the wind, was barely audible.

"Yes, Secundino, I saw it. Is the boat prepared?"

"Yes, Capitán."

"Good, I want the four strongest men. You stay here and keep the lanterns burning."

"I will go, Capitán."

"No, Secundino, I will go. It is my responsibility." Ramón

could not let Cardona do it. The thought of taking the boat out into the raging darkness terrified him, but no one must suspect, least of all his second-in-command, that he was afraid. He must go himself.

"Yes, Capitán." Cardona nodded and turned to the group of men holding the boat as it surged back and forth in the surf. "Almazan, Neri, Nava, Salina, into the boat," he ordered. The four clambered aboard. Ramón leaped in after them. Cardona and the men on the beach manhandled the boat out into the surging waves until the oars could get a grip on the water. Ramón sat at the tiller, urging the men on. Fifty meters from shore, the waves curled menacingly, breaking heavily over the boat's bow.

"Pull, pull!" Ramón screamed to make himself heard through the tumult. He knew he needed more manpower on the oars but he had to leave room in the boat for survivors from the wrecked schooner. As they got further from the shore, the waves were less steep, the boat more responsive to the rudder. Again, there was a red glow from the end of the reef. He steered the tossing boat directly for it. "Pull, men! Pull!"

Already their floorboards were awash. Keeping one hand on the tiller, Ramón leaned forward and bailed as quickly as he could. He looked back toward the beach. There were half a dozen pinpoints of light. Cardona must have gotten more lanterns. The light on *la roca* was burning strong and bright. Now, the schooner was beginning to take definite shape. She was heeled over at a crazy angle, her two remaining masts at least fifty degrees from the vertical. She was solidly on the reef, held fast in the ragged grip of the coral as the waves washed over her. "Pull, men, we're almost there!" Ramón was growing hoarse with shouting.

With great care, he maneuvered the boat almost within touching distance of the stricken schooner's side. They could see the ship's crew clinging to the rigging as waves washed right across the deck. The spray was torn away horizontally across the sea and through it Ramón could just see a woman clutching a small child and another child standing beside her at the shrouds, its arms wrapped around the woman's legs. The ship gave a sudden lurch and the woman and children fell to the deck. Ramón could see that the sea was filled with broken spars and tangled rigging. The boat pitched heavily and crashed down onto the spars.

"Back water!" Ramón's voice rose against the wind's roar. They had to get the boat away from the heavy spars before its planking was stove in. They drew astern, the wind and surge pushing them back. They fought their way around toward the schooner's stern, away from the chaos of rigging and spars in the water. The stern of the schooner was pitched unnaturally high and, at times, the surf boat's bow went right beneath her counter. It was just possible to see the ship's name and port of hail picked out in gilt on the transom, Nokomis, San Francisco. One of the schooner's crew peered over the stern.

"Jump! Jump!" Ramón had to scream to be heard. The man on the ship shook his head uncomprehendingly. "Jump, jump!" Ramón shouted, this time in English. More heads appeared over the ship's taffrail. With each wave, the small boat was pushed in toward the schooner's stern. The soldados had to time their strokes perfectly to keep the boat from being smashed against the heavy planking of the ship. The schooner gave a tremendous lurch and with the sound of splintering timber settled further over onto her side. "Quickly, she is breaking up!" Ramón shouted. He knew his men didn't have the strength to keep the boat in position much longer. The woman had worked her way back to the stern. One of the men there took the small child she handed him and, locking his legs around the mooring bitts on the schooner's deck, leaned out over the rail, the child in his arms. They would have only one chance. If they dropped the child into the sea, there would be no possibility of finding it in this wild night.

"Neri, get a rope around yourself and get as far up into the bow as you can to take the child!" Ramón shouted. He took the boat in as close as he dared. Neri, the rope under his arms kept taut by Almazan and Salina, leaned over the surf boat's bow and raised his arms to take the child. Just as he grasped the child, the boat plummeted into a trough. Neri fell heavily over the bows of the boat and into the surging water, the child still in his arms. "Pull him alongside. Get the child," yelled Ramón. Neri was kicking and spluttering, holding the little girl almost out of the water. Almazan and Salina pulled him alongside the boat and Ramón leaned over and took the child from his outstretched arms.

The line held by the men in the boat went bar taut and pulled through their hands, burning their palms. Jesús Neri gave a single, short, high-pitched scream. The line went slack. "Pull him in! Pull him in!" ordered Ramón, holding the child across his lap. Almazan and Salina heaved the rope in, hand over hand. Neri's head slammed into the side of the boat. "Careful, men! Get him in, quickly!" yelled Ramón.

The two men leaned out and grabbed Neri by the arms, heaving him into the boat. His light weight surprised them and he almost flew over the gunwale as the men fell backwards with Neri on top of them. He was alive. Ramón could see his eyes, huge and white, swiveling in panic, his mouth gaping in a soundless scream. Below his rib cage, his body was completely gone, taken in a single bite.

With the schooner's crew on board the tossing surf boat, it was dangerously overloaded. Once out of the shelter of the stricken ship, the full fury of the storm hit them. Each sea, running up astern of the boat as the *soldados* pulled for the beach, pushed them forward, driving the bows down. The water was halfway to their knees. The sailors from the Nokomis bailed frantically while Ramón struggled to keep the stern directly into the onrushing waves. For the first time in his life, he asked for God's help as he steered for the pinpoints of light far away on the beach. They ran through the ragged seas, almost blinded by the spray. Ramón could see the woman, sitting in the water in the bottom of the boat clutching her children, shivering violently. The grossly overloaded boat was sluggish and unresponsive. The men at the oars were exhausted, missing strokes, gasping for breath, their eyes glazed.

Ramón knew he didn't have the skill to bring the boat in neatly, stern first, like the sailors did. He just wanted to get them all onto dry land before the boat sank beneath them. They were only two or three wavelengths away now. Riding the face of a wave, they rushed towards the beach. There was a resounding crack as the boat's bow hit the sand with a terrific blow. Carried forward again by the force of the sea, the boat was driven bodily sideways onto the shelving beach. The tiller was wrenched from Ramón's hands as the rudder hit the bottom and was torn from the boat. They sat slumped in the boat, too exhausted to move, the waves bursting over them. Cardona and the others rushed forward to help.

Outside, the storm still raged. There were eight of them, Americans and Norwegians. The two little Norwegian girls were sharing the Arnaud children's rooms. The crew had been taken in by the *soldados*. Ramón and Alicia sat with Captain Jensen and his wife in front of the fire. Ramón's right hand was wrapped in bandages where the tiller had slammed it against the gunwale of the boat. He looked up at Mary Jensen. She was Alicia's age and size and Alicia's dress fit her perfectly. Jens Jensen was about the same height as Ramón but much more heavily built. The clothes that Ramón had given him scarcely fit, the shirt pulled tight across his chest. He sat with his legs stretched toward the fire. "Captain Arnaud," he said in Norwegian-accented English, "we will always be grateful to you. If your man hadn't held on to Emma, we would have lost her. And we would all be dead if you hadn't had the courage to bring that boat out to us."

"It was our duty, Capitán Jensen, nothing more." Ramón looked into the fire.

"Don't be so modest, Captain. It was a very brave thing to do," he said.

Ramón continued to stare into the fire. It wasn't brave, he thought, it was madness. The night had taken on a surreal quality. His hand throbbed miserably. It was almost impossible to believe that, only two hours earlier, he had taken a small boat out through the surf in the middle of a raging gale. And, no matter what happened during the rest of his life, nothing could ever equal the horror of Jesús Neri flying over the gunwale into the boat, half his body taken by a shark but still alive. Ramón closed his eyes and sank instantly into a deep, dreamless sleep.

Ramón sat behind his desk, tapping his pen sharply against the paperweight. He looked down at the paperweight. Alicia had given the beautifully cut piece of Czech crystal to him before they were married. He struck it more forcefully, then realized what he was doing and lay the pen down carefully on the desk. Captain Jensen stood in front of him, his arms folded across his chest. Ramón was tired of Jensen's endless pestering.

"As I have told you before, Capitán Jensen, the Tampico is only a few weeks overdue. Sometimes, the ship is delayed due to bad weather or other causes. The government has other uses for the Tampico. Be patient, I expect her to arrive any day now."

"I'm very grateful to you for everything you've done, but I am very anxious to get my family back to San Francisco."

"Of course, Capitán Jensen. I understand."

"I am also worried about how much food you have. You now have eight more mouths to feed."

Ramón nodded. "That is my concern too. I have had Corporal Lara do a complete inventory of our stores. There is sufficient for all of us for three months on three-quarter rations. Certainly, the Tampico will be here before then."

Alicia and Mary Jensen strolled beside each other along the beach. Alicia was delighted to have a woman of her own age and education to talk to, even in broken English and Spanish, laughingly punctuated by endless gesturing. The children were playing together near the house and had overcome the language problem the same way. Their screams of pleasure echoed behind the two women as they walked away from the house.

Ahead of them stood the Rock, its angular sides sharply outlined against the cobalt blue of the sea. As they walked toward the Rock, they could see the cairn and the iron cross marking the grave of Jesús Neri. Out on the reef, lay the wreck of the Nokomis. A boat, heavily laden, was returning from the broken schooner. She lay on her side, her remaining masts in the water, her decks draped in fallen rigging. Her bow was now underwater and they could see birds jockeying for position on her uplifted stern. They reached the water's edge just as the boat came in. Up on the beach stood a jumbled pile of casks and chests retrieved from the schooner. One of the sailors jumped out of the boat and approached the women. He was short and gnarled and walked with a rolling gait. "Good morning, Mrs. Jensen, Señora," he said.

"Good morning, Henriksen. Why on earth are you taking food? We'll be home in a few weeks." Mary Jensen looked in amazement at the boat, filled almost to the gunwales with casks of salt beef and ship's biscuit and bottles of liquor and wine.

"Captain's orders, Mrs Jensen. He told us to take off anything of value. He says there is no way to know how long we'll be here. But look," he pointed towards the pile further up the beach, "we've got the Captain's sea chest and yours."

"That's wonderful, Henriksen."

"Excuse me now, Mrs. Jensen. We've got to get back to work. If the sea gets up again, there won't be much left of the ship. We want to get everything useful off her by nightfall." Henriksen tugged the peak of his cap and turned to the boat.

Alicia and Mary stood watching the men unload the heavy casks and roll them up the beach. "Alicia, do you think the supply ship will come soon?"

Alicia smiled. "The Tampico is often late. At this time of

year, the weather is very changeable. Once, Ramón and I had to wait in Acapulco for almost three weeks before the *capitán* would leave the harbor. Do not worry, Mary. You will be home soon."

Sargento Irra entered Ramón's office behind Teniente Cardona. The shoulder of Irra's tunic was spattered with blood. "Capitán," Cardona said, clicking his heels in front of the desk.

"Yes, Secundino?" Looking up, Ramón saw the blood on Irra's uniform. He shook his head sadly. "What is going on here?"

"It is the *yanquis*, Capitán. Sargento Irra tried to stop a fight between two of them and they both attacked him."

Ramón looked appraisingly at Irra. He was a powerfully built man. His head seemed to be planted directly on his broad shoulders. "It would take a brave pair of men to take you on, Sargento Irra."

Irra smiled ruefully. "It was that short one, Capitán, the one who is built like an ox. The two of them had been drinking and were fighting. I pulled them apart and the short one hit me from behind with the butt of his knife."

"Well, we cannot have this sort of thing going on. I will speak to Capitán Jensen. In the meantime, Sargento, if they want to kill each other, let them. We don't want any more Mexican blood spilled. Is that clear? Now come over by the window and I will look at that cut."

Ramón pulled strongly at the boat's oars. The boat surged out into the lagoon. Ali and Ramoncito sat side by side on one of the boat's seats, each trying to row with one of the long oars. Alicia sat behind them with Olga, smiling at Ramón as the children splashed the oars against the mirror-smooth surface of the lagoon.

"A beautiful day, my darling," she said. Ramón smiled and pulled toward the Egg Islands at the westernmost end of the lagoon. Because there was protection from the crabs, the four little islands were favored nesting grounds. In breeding season, there were so many birds nesting that it was impossible to walk across any of the islands. Ramón tipped his oars into the boat and lay back with his hands behind his head. He closed his eyes and felt the sun warm his face. Alicia opened the bag at her feet and passed the *tortas* to the children and Ramón. They were made with the wonderful rolls Doña Juana baked for everyone. Alicia had made her special mayonnaise. Ramón had speared the lobster.

Ramón looked up at Alicia and smiled. "Delicious, my love," he said, between bites. When they had finished eating, Ramón rowed them toward the middle of the lagoon, gave one last mighty pull and then lay his oars inside the boat and lay back again. The two children hung over the side of the boat, peering into the depths of the lagoon and splashing each other. "I told the men the story about the treasure left by the English pirate," said Ramón.

Alicia laughed. "Silly. Now, they will dig up the whole island."

"They are bored. We have built everything we can build. They need something to keep them occupied. It does no harm."

"Imagine if there really were a treasure and they found it," said Alicia running her fingers through the water. "But there is no treasure really, is there, Ramón?"

He opened his eyes and thought for a moment. "No one really knows. It is possible. The English pirate Clipperton used this island as his base for twenty years. He must have attacked many Spanish galleons in that time and taken a fortune in treasure. Perhaps he buried some of it here. People have searched before. If you look just north of *la roca*, you can see depressions in the sand made by people digging."

Alicia sat up straight and looked around. The lagoon was completely enclosed. There was no opening to the sea. "Perhaps it is all a myth. How could he have used this island as a base? He could not keep his ship here safely."

Ramón picked up his oars and began to row slowly toward the dock. "It was different then, Alicia. In those days, he could anchor his ship in the lagoon. In Clipperton's time, there were two channels leading from the sea into the lagoon. In the documentation prepared by the government for the arbitration, there is a chart that shows where the openings used to be. Unfortunately, they were closed by a hurricane half a century ago."

"Papá, I want to dig for the treasure too!" cried Ramoncito.

Ramón laughed. "Very well, but you must let your sister help."

CHAPTER 21

Clipperton's supply ship Tampico lay at anchor at Topolobampo in the Gulf of California. Captain Castellenes sat in his cabin, writing in his personal journal. General Huerta's government had ordered him to take the ship into the Gulf as a show of government resolve; the states all around the Gulf were in ferment. Soon, Castellenes hoped, he could take the Tampico south to Acapulco to pick up stores for the garrison on Clipperton. Ramón and Alicia must be wondering where he was. The door of his cabin slammed open and five officers burst in, one holding a pistol to the Captain's head while others tied him up. Castellenes was shocked to see the ship's first officer, Teniente Palacio, among them. "What are you doing, Palacio? This is mutiny. Have you gone mad?"

Palacio shook his head sadly. "No, Capitán, we have not gone mad. We are seizing this ship in the name of the people. The Tampico will now fight for the freedom of the Mexican people against General Huerta."

The children had been upstairs for an hour. The Jensens were eating with Gustav Schultz and his family. Altagracia rattled the ladle carelessly against Ramón's bowl as she served the soup. Alicia spoke sharply. "That is Royal Doulton, Alta. Be more careful." Altagracia lowered her head and stood beside the table, wringing her hands in her apron. Alicia looked up at her and asked. "What is it Alta?"

"When will the ship come, Señora? We are running out of everything. There is no sugar, no coffee, almost no cornmeal. There are no onions for the soup. The soap and candles are almost gone."

Alicia looked across the table at Ramón. He thought for a moment and said, "It is nothing to concern yourself about Altagracia, the Tampico will come soon."

"But Capitán Arnaud, Capitán Jensen says it may never come. He says we may be stranded here."

"Be calm, Altagracia. He has no patience. Now stop worrying and do your chores." Ramón turned back to his meal. Altagracia cast a worried glance at Alicia and, picking up the tureen, hurried from the room. Ramón took his spoon and began to drink his soup

Alicia watched him for a moment before speaking. "Ramón, it is not just Altagracia. Everyone is worried. The Tampico is almost eight weeks overdue. It could not be the weather. The weather has been perfect for two weeks now."

"Perhaps the government has need of the Tampico elsewhere for the time being, my dear. Remember that General Huerta is fighting a rebellion. We both knew there would be inconveniences living here. It is our duty to suffer them without complaint. Besides, look around you, this is scarcely hardship." He waved his hand across the table. In the center, candles flickered in the two gold candlesticks Alicia had brought back from the capital. Fine china and elaborately engraved silverware gleamed in the candlelight. Ramón stirred his soup. "This is not quite the bouillabaisse of Madame Roux, but I have had worse." He smiled. "Much worse. Do not concern yourself, my dear. Capitán Jensen is an alarmist. Now that he and his family have moved in with Gustav, you will no longer have to listen to his complaining. We will do our duty, the Tampico will come, Capitán Jensen and his people will leave and life will go on as before." Alicia gave him a little smile and picked up her spoon.

The crew of the seized Tampico were tired of hiding in deserted bays around the Gulf of California. Teniente Palacio and the other officers who had mutinied knew the time had come to run the blockade of government ships lying in wait outside the south end of the Gulf and make for a Constitutionalist port. Just before dawn on June 16, 1914, they felt the surge of the Pacific beneath them as the ship passed Cabo San Lucas. Unknown to Palacio and the other mutineers, the government gunboat Guerrero, faster and more heavily armed than Tampico, had seen her in the dawn light. The Guerrero gave chase and, by noon, Tampico lay on the bottom of the sea. The American destroyers Perry and Prebble watched the uneven battle, as did the American cruiser New Orleans. They picked up what survivors they could. Neither Captain Castellenes nor Teniente Palacio were among them.

Secundino Cardona stood on the beach looking out onto the wreck of the Nokomis. There was very little left of the American schooner. The aft half of her keel stuck out of the water with only a line of frames clinging to it. Along the water's edge, bits of planking washed back and forth against the sand. Above the high water mark lay a pile of salvaged rigging and sailcloth. Cardona walked over to the pile and sat on a bundle of sailcloth, making himself comfortable. Time passed so slowly these days. They had long since repaired the last of the storm damage and Capitán Arnaud seemed to have lost interest in finding jobs for the *soldados*. So they spent the days restlessly, hoping each minute to hear the siren sound or the cry that the Tampico had been sighted. Cardona was growing tired of the salt beef and endless greasy seabirds and fish. Tirza could work miracles with a bird or fish if she had some onions and garlic and a few herbs, but those had been used up long ago. Please God, he thought, let me look up and see the Tampico. He waited for a minute then raised his eyes and scanned the horizon. There was nothing but endless ocean.

Jensen stood in front of Ramón's desk. Ramón finished writing in his day book and closed the cover with a snap. "Yes, Capitán.

What can I do for you?"

"We've been here for two and a half months. My men are tired of eating rice and beans and fish and I'll tell you something, if that ship doesn't come soon, there is going to be trouble."

Ramón shook his head slowly. "Capitán, Capitán, calm yourself. The supply ship will come. We have learned to live with these little delays. In the meantime, please keep your men under control. I will not tolerate lawlessness. If there is any more trouble, I will have no choice but to put the guilty parties under arrest."

Jensen stood to his full height. "I wouldn't do that, Captain Arnaud."

Ramón bristled. "I remind you Capitán that you are on Mexican soil. I am governor of this island. My word is law here. Keep your men under control."

Jensen glared at Ramón and, without a word, spun on his heel and stormed from the office. Heaving a long sigh, Ramón leaned back in his chair and gazed through the side window toward the open ocean.

The weather had turned foul. The wind picked up coral and guano dust and flung it into their faces as they strode toward the settlement. The rain was light but, driven hard, it soon soaked them to the skin. Cardona almost broke into a run trying to keep up with Ramón. Without waiting for the *teniente*, Ramón flung open the door to Sargento Irra's office and went inside. Irra jumped to his feet, saluting. "Capitán."

"Well, Agustín, what is it?"

"I had to put them in the cell, Capitán."

Ramón nodded abruptly and strode down the dark passageway behind the Sargento's desk. At the end was a heavy door with a small barred opening up high. Ramón looked through the bars. The cell was scarcely two meters square and completely bare. Two of the Nokomis' sailors sat on the rough planking with their backs against the far wall looking up at him with hatred. The short one, the second mate, Hansen, had a jagged gash across his forehead. Ramón turned and walked back down the passage.

"Tell me what happened, Agustín."

"We were playing cards with them, Capitán."

"And drinking, I suppose," interjected Ramón.

"They had a little wine, Capitán. For no reason, the short one threw his cards at Carbajal and attacked him. He was yelling something but I do not know what he was saying. We tried to hold him back and then the other one pulled out a knife. He kept screaming something about México. Carbajal tried to stop him. He has a bad cut on his hand. I hit him with this." Irra patted the pistol in his holster. "And Carbajal held the short one."

"A very pretty mess, Sargento. Keep the two of them in the cell until I tell you otherwise. If Jensen comes around, tell him to see me."

Jensen marched furiously up the path towards Ramón's office, his face grim. Ramón stood leaning in the doorway, his arms crossed. "Arnaud, let my men out of your damned jail."

Ramón regarded Jensen coolly. "Captain, I told you that I would not tolerate lawlessness. Your men cannot behave themselves so they will remain under arrest."

"Look Arnaud, the only reason we're still here is because you people can't run your supply ships properly."

Ramón's eyes darkened. "Be careful, Capitán Jensen."

Jensen paused for a moment, then said, "I have a proposition. Halvorsen has offered to take a boat to México to get help. Let those men out of your jail and I'll have them off this island in twenty-four hours."

"They would be throwing away their lives. What chance would they have on such a voyage in a small open boat? Be patient, the supply ship will come. Your men will come to no harm where they are."

"I'm afraid I don't have as much faith as you, Captain

Arnaud. I don't think that damned ship is ever coming. If someone doesn't go for help, we'll all rot here. And I'll tell you something else, those men are not staying in jail. Either you release them and give us a boat or you're going to have a revolution on your hands right here."

Ramón glowered. "I do not like being threatened, Captain. I remind you that you and your men are guests on Mexican territory. However, it is your own men's lives you wish to risk and I would be happy to have them off this island. I will release your sailors from jail into your custody and they may take one of the boats, provided they leave within twenty-four hours. But remember, this is your decision and you are entirely responsible for their conduct until they leave and for their safety afterwards. I will instruct Corporal Lara to issue stores to them for the boat."

Jensen nodded, "Very good. They will be gone in twenty-four hours."

They stood together on the beach and watched the tan-colored sail grow smaller. There was a good breeze from the northwest, a fair wind for Acapulco. The surf was breaking lightly on the beach. Ramoncito struggled to hold the big brass telescope. "I cannot see them, Papá." Ramón steadied the telescope for him. "There they are!" he cried, "I see them! Will they bring us a ship, Papá?" Ramón put his hands in his pockets and looked at the speck of sail diminishing in the distance. The telescope, too heavy for Ramoncito to hold any longer, sagged.

"Perhaps, Ramoncito, perhaps."

Ramón was aware of the presence of Jensen and his wife just behind him. They stood with Alicia watching the boat draw away from the island. The fools are committing suicide, Ramón thought. They would have to travel at least a thousand kilometers before reaching land. With the currents and the storms and the sharks, they had no chance. They had taken plenty of food and water and a small compass but it was a small boat and completely open to the sea. If a storm came up, they would certainly capsize and drown, if the sharks didn't get them first. Ramón took his son's hand and led him away from the beach.

CHAPTER 22

Ramón put his book on the bedside table and turned down the oil lamp. He felt Alicia beside him, wide awake. "These people have no respect for us, Alicia. They have no faith in us. I told them again and again the Tampico would come. I am glad those men are gone, but I think it is a mistake. They will never reach Acapulco."

Alicia rolled towards him and put her head on his chest. He stroked her hair as she spoke. "Mary is very frightened, Ramón. She was crying when they left."

"She has every reason to be scared, my dear. You have seen the kind of storms that can spring up out of nowhere between here and the mainland. Imagine if a *chubasco* came up. That boat would be gone in minutes."

"Yes, Ramón. I am frightened for them too."

María and Tirza were Yaqui. Both women were strong and broad-shouldered, their hair a gleaming coal-black, their skin the color of burnished bronze. Each morning, they went to where the birds nested on the beach and collected eggs. After the birds stopped nesting, they would have eggs from the hens. The older woman, María was about thirty. She carried the eggs in her basket, speaking rapidly in Yaqui. "I remember when Rosalía loved these eggs," she said. "Now she hates them."

"They taste like fish," said Tirza, pulling a face. "But we must eat them."

"What I would give for some dried beef or some meal to make *tortillas*."

"Ah, *tortillas*! Secundino loves my *tortillas*," said Tirza. "But what can I give him now? Doña Alicia gave me some hard biscuits from the wreck. They were like solid rock. I ground them and made *tortillas*. Even that was better than nothing. But now, the biscuit is gone. There is nothing left."

"Perhaps the boat will reach México and help will come."

"No. It has been more than a month. Secundino says they are dead. They could never sail that little boat all the way to México."

María walked in silence beside Maria for a moment then said, "Álvarez has food hidden at the Rock."

Tirza stopped. "How do you know that?"

"Rosalía told me she saw him carrying a cask away from the storehouse."

"It could have been anything."

"She was sure he was stealing food."

"Well, go to him and demand your share."

María shuddered. "Never! He frightens me. The way he looks at you. It is as though he looks right through you."

"Then forget about these tales of hidden food."

Schultz was raving. Ramón crossed his arms and watched the German gesturing wildly, his thinning hair plastered against his scalp, the pitch of his voice rising steadily. "Your ship will never come, Kapitan!" he screamed. "Never! Do you understand? *Mein Gott*, I should have left on the last guano ship. A man cannot live on seagulls forever." He slumped down into his chair, his head in his hands, his chest heaving.

Ramón continued to stand with his arms crossed, looking coolly down at the exhausted Schultz. "Are you quite finished, Gustav?" he asked quietly.

For a moment, Schultz's eyes flared and then he sagged back and started to sob. "Go. Go. Please leave me in peace." He waved Ramón away. Ramón stood straight and turned to go. Hysterical, he thought. The sooner Capitán Castellenes gets here the better for everyone.

The sea was quiet. The surf had stopped its pounding on the

reef. A slight swell sucked idly at the pilings of the wharf. From further up the beach, came the calling of the birds. Teniente Cardona had ordered Mauro Salina to make an inventory of the timber and iron remaining in the guano shed. What possible use the Teniente could make of such an inventory Salina had no idea. It could wait. He sat facing seaward, his back resting against the capstan. He flung the tiny, sodden stub of his last cigar toward the water and looked slowly around the horizon. The dorsal fins of three reef sharks circled lazily just off the end of the wharf. He watched them, fascinated. Each of the sharks circled independently but remained linked in some indefinable way with the others, never straying too far, never breaking the rhythm. Fifty meters beyond the sharks, a tern sat high on the water, preening. Salina turned his attention to the bird. Probably a male bettered in his quest for a mate on the beach, out there to repair his wounded pride. The bird cleaned busily under its wing, turning the glassy surface into an endless series of ever-widening concentric circles.

Without struggle, without sound, the bird was gone. Ten seconds later, the shark was back with the others, circling.

CHAPTER 23

It was less than half an hour to sunset. The fishing boats were returning home. It had been a good day, hot and bright with a gentle onshore breeze. Pedro looked with satisfaction at the mound of silvery bodies lying in the bottom of his boat. He shielded his eyes with his hand and looked seaward. The sun had acquired an almost supernatural redness and looked huge, suspended, shimmering, just above the horizon. He knew, from countless days fishing, that within minutes of the sun setting the wind would drop. Half an hour later, the offshore breeze would come up, as the land that had baked all day in the sun sent its heat out to sea. Tomorrow would be another good day for fishing.

Anchored well out, away from the small boats clustered in the sheltered eastern end of the Bay, was a gray painted warship. Pedro knew very little of the world beyond Acapulco, but he recognized the *yanqui* flag drooping motionless over the ship's stern. A canvas awning shaded most of the after part of the ship. Her guns were trained primly fore and aft, neat white canvas covers concealing the menace of the muzzles.

Pedro rested on his oars and looked again. Just below where the sun was about to kiss the sea, a tan-colored sail bobbed. It wasn't a local boat, he could tell by the color and shape of the sail. It was headed toward the entrance of the Bay. Pedro had learned infinite patience tossing alone in his boat far offshore. He waited and watched. The sun touched the horizon directly behind the strange boat and began to sink below the curvature of the earth, sending an undulating ribbon of fire across the sea toward him. He pulled slowly towards the beach, keeping his eye on the other boat until his bows nestled into the sand.

The boat was now in line with the gap. Soon it would pass the island just outside the Bay.

Pedro called to the fishermen who were gutting their catch on the beach and pointed at the stranger. They stopped their work and gathered together near Pedro's boat as it touched the sand, talking quietly and watching the strange boat come in through the gap, running before the light breeze. They could see now that the sail was torn in several places and badly weather stained. Two, perhaps three people were in the boat. As it came in through the gap, it altered course slightly and ghosted towards the American warship. It was none of their concern after all. Pedro stepped from his boat and tended to his fish.

Captain George Williams sat at his desk on board the cruiser USS Cleveland. It was stifling down below and his shirt clung wetly to his back. As soon as he had finished drafting his report to Admiral Fullam about the survivors of the Nokomis and the steps he was taking he would go for a turn up on deck to get some air. Until four hours ago, their visit to Acapulco had been uneventful, the port captain mildly confused by their presence, but perfectly accommodating all the same. Williams looked up to see Ensign Rivers about to rap on the open cabin door.

Rivers was feeling the heat too. Drops of sweat beaded on a face too smooth to have seen a razor. His hand stopped in mid-air. "Captain, Sir, the executive officer said to tell you that the stores are all aboard."

"Okay, Rivers. Tell the navigating officer to plot a course for Clipperton Island. How are Halvorsen and the other two doing?"

"The doctor says they'll be fine, Sir. He says they're dehydrated and sunburned but in pretty good shape, all things considered."

"A nice little piece of seamanship, Rivers. Shades of Captain Bligh's voyage in an open boat. Pray you'll never have to do something like that."

A worried expression crossed Rivers' face. "No, Sir. I mean yes, Sir."

"You're damn right, 'Yes, Sir.' I wouldn't want to have to do it either. Now, go check with the doctor. If he says it's okay, get those men ashore. The British Consul will take care of them. I don't imagine they'll want to go back out to that island if they can help it."

Corporal Lara stood breathless in front of Ramón. "The German has gone crazy, Ramón. He is trying to swim to México."

"Mother of God," Ramón sighed. "Let us see what we can do."

Near the water's edge, two *soldados* were trying to hold Schultz down. He was stark naked and writhing convulsively. He was screaming in German, covered in sand, his eyes wild. Ramón stood over him and asked, "What is the meaning of this?"

Schultz screamed incoherently.

"We dragged him from the water, Capitán. He was trying to swim away," said Lara. Schultz began to struggle again. Lara sat astride the German and pinned his arms to the sand.

Suddenly, Schultz saw Ramón. "You!" he screamed, "What are you doing here? I am leaving! Tell them to let me go!"

"Calm yourself, Gustav. What are you trying to do?"

"I want to go to México. I cannot stay another minute in this hell. We will all die. You will see. We will all die." He began to struggle beneath the *soldados*, then his eyes rolled back and his body went slack.

Ramón shook his head sadly. "Carry him to his house. I will bring some medicine."

Sargento Irra sat on the log beside Carbajal, dozing, when he heard the siren at *la roca* sound. He looked up and, just at the edge of visibility, a shape grew. Irra rubbed his eyes and looked again. Getting slowly to his feet, he waited a moment and then called, "Get Capitán Arnaud. Now!" Carbajal raised his eyes wearily to Irra, then saw past the *sargento* to the bows of a ship appearing from the mist beyond the reef. Without acknowledging Irra's order, Carbajal was on his feet and running, casting a glance over his shoulder before disappearing over a rise of sand.

As Irra watched, the mist parted and the rest of the ship came into view. Just aft of her bows, a sailor cast a lead line, calling the marks to the bridge as the ship felt her way gingerly forward. Ramón, still buttoning his tunic, came up and stood stiffly beside Irra.

"Do you recognize the ship, Agustín?"

"No, Capitán but it is a *yanqui* warship."

"Get the surf boat ready. I will go out to her immediately."

Water boiled along the ship's sides as her engines were thrown astern. The churning of the propellers stopped and she stood motionless, smoke rising in thin, dark wisps from her stack. Across the still water came the roar of the anchor cable running out.

Ramón climbed the boarding ladder to the deck of the USS Cleveland with Captain Jensen right behind him. "Welcome aboard, sir," a young lieutenant greeted them in English. "I'll show you to the Captain's cabin."

"Captain George Williams, commander of the USS Cleveland," Williams introduced himself. He was about forty with a ruddy complexion and a ready smile.

"Capitán Ramón Arnaud, governor of Clipperton Island. A pleasure to meet you, sir." Standing aside to allow Captain Jensen to enter the cabin, he said, "This is Captain Jensen of the American schooner Nokomis that was wrecked here some months ago."

Jensen was glowing. "They made it didn't they? They made it! I knew they would. That Halvorsen is a fine seaman."

"Yes," said Williams, "they made it. They had no water for the last two days, but they sailed right into Acapulco Bay and, by great good luck, we were anchored there."

"And they are all well?"

"Sure. A little sunburned and thirsty but fine. Please take a seat gentlemen. I'll have someone rustle us up a cup of coffee. Captain Arnaud, we have some supplies for you from the garrison commander in Acapulco. A hundred and thirty seven cases of stores. I understand that your supply ships have not been arriving and I want you to know that I am prepared to give passage to Acapulco to everyone on the island, if that is what you want."

Ramón leaned back in his chair, thought for a moment, then addressed Williams,

"Your offer is very kind, Captain Williams, but there is really no need for you to inconvenience yourself on our account. We still have some food and with what you have brought, we should have sufficient for five months or so. Our supply ship will certainly arrive long before then. Our duty is to remain at our post."

"As you wish, Captain Arnaud."

"But there is one thing you could do, Captain Williams. I would greatly appreciate it if you would give passage to Gustav Schultz, the representative of the Pacific Islands Company and his wife and daughter. He is behaving erratically. I am concerned that his sanity is in question."

Williams raised his eyebrows. "Of course, Captain Arnaud. I will give passage to anyone who wishes to leave."

Ramón extended his hand. "Capitán Jensen, please remember to contact the garrison in Acapulco and tell them of our situation."

Jensen took his hand and shook it warmly. "Of course, Captain Arnaud. I will take care of it. I know we've had our differences but I can never thank you enough for what you and your soldiers have done for us. We owe you our lives."

Most of the *soldados* and their families stood on the beach near the boat landing, watching as the surf boat carried the

Nokomis's crew to the Cleveland and returned with a load of supplies. After the boat was unloaded, it made one more trip out to the ship with the Jensens and the Schultz family before returning heavily laden with crates and barrels. Alicia and the children stood slightly apart, waving to Mary Jensen and her two girls, who stood at the ship's rail. Before the boat reached the shore, the Cleveland's anchor was being weighed. Soon, she began to turn in a long arc and moved slowly away from the island. A single blast from her horn sounded and then echoed faintly from *la roca.*

Alicia and Tirza walked back along the beach as the ship grew smaller in the distance. The children, splashing along the lagoon's edge, paid no heed to the Cleveland. She was of another world.

Altagracia beamed as she put the serving dishes on the table. At last, there was food to make a real meal. Ramón picked listlessly at his food, saying scarcely a word. Alicia looked at him with concern. "What is it, my dear?"

"I wonder if we are doing the right thing."

"The right thing? Do you mean by staying at our posts? You offered all the women the chance to go with the Cleveland. No one would leave. Not even Tirza and she is pregnant."

"For the men, there is no choice. It is our duty to remain. But, perhaps I should have ordered the women and children to leave. You could have stayed with Don Félix until the Tampico is running normally again."

Alicia paused before she spoke. "And leave you here? The children and I will be fine, Ramón. I would not leave without you."

"What if there are no more ships?"

"You know the Tampico will come. Capitán Castellenes may be late, but he will come. He has always come. Clipperton is of great importance to México. We will not be forgotten. You told me yourself that with the stores Capitán Williams landed, we have enough food for five months at least. The Tampico must come before then."

The day after the Cleveland left Clipperton Island, half a world away in Sarajevo, a bomb exploded beneath one of the parading cars, slightly injuring an army officer. The target of the assassination attempt was not hurt. Beside him, his wife screamed. As they sped from the scene of the attack, he leaned forward in the open car and told the driver to make for the hospital. There would be no more parades today. He would visit the injured officer in hospital. His driver stopped the heavy car to turn around.

Gavrilo Princip sat quietly in the tiny street side café drinking a cup of coffee, watching the car turn. He gasped in surprise and a spasm of consumptive coughing racked his thin body. He had recognized the ostentatiously uniformed man in the back of the turning car and, when the fit of coughing ended, he walked calmly forward. Princip drew his revolver and shot the Archduke Franz Ferdinand cleanly through the neck. The Great War, the war to end all wars, had begun.

CHAPTER 24

A light breeze blew through the open-sided dining hall. Corporal Lara bowed low to the women. "Thank you, ladies. The food was superb." Maria and Doña Juana giggled. It had been a feast. The men had caught fish and lobster and the women had outdone themselves preparing food that had come with the Cleveland. There was good coffee to be drunk, even some tobacco and cigars. Already, some of the *soldados* had their cards and dominoes out on the tables.

Rosalía Nava walked past Alicia holding the Irra boys' hands and with the Arnaud children trailing behind. "We are going to dig for treasure, Doña Alicia."

Alicia laughed. "Very well, Rosalía. Just be back by dark. If you find the pirate's treasure, will you share it with me?"

The girl grinned widely. "Of course, Doña Alicia."

Carbajal and Salina began tuning their guitars and Ramón picked up his mandolin. Alicia closed her eyes as they began to play. There was something magical about these nights spent together, cooking and eating, listening to music and dancing. Secundino began to sing. Alicia rose slowly and walked from the dining hall. She saw the children on their treasure hunt, scraping away sand near the small wooden dock on the lagoon. She smiled and turned the other way, walking along the beach. The waves lapped the shore gently. She walked as far as the cisterns, stopped and turned. The sun had just dropped below the horizon. Someone had lit the oil lamps in the dining hall. Alicia stood and watched for a few moments, then sighed with contentment and began walking back to the others.

The two *soldados* perched precariously on the coral outcrops, their fishing poles extended toward the main body of the reef. Pédro Carbajal let out a whoop as the tip of his pole bent suddenly under the weight of a fish. He pulled back and a long silvery-blue body flew through the air. Pérez clambered through the shallow water to help land the fish. Already, a reef shark, sensing the panic of the hooked fish, was rushing into the shallows near the two men. Pérez turned quickly and jumped from the water. The other man flicked his catch out, losing only the tail to the shark. When the fish lay dead on the beach, Carbajal carefully removed the hook from its mouth. He hefted their catch then took out his knife and began to gut the fish, throwing the offal far out into the water. Almost before it hit the surface, the shark was there and it was gone

They stood and watched the birds fighting and squawking. "We should have gone with the *norteamericanos*," said Carbajal. "What if the Tampico never comes?"

Pérez wiped the blood from his knife and sheathed it. He made a gesture of resignation. "Then it is very simple, my friend. We will all die here."

Carbajal looked closely at the surf boat drawn far up from the water's edge. Pérez seemed to read his thoughts. "We are not sailors like those men from the Nokomis. We don't know how to sail or find our way across the ocean, Pédro. Besides, look at this." He leaned into the boat's bow and rapped the handle of his knife against the cracked stem. It gave a hollow sound. "It is no good. And look all along here." He waved his hand along the forward half of the keelson. It was splintered in a dozen places, the planking beginning to pull away. "You would not get five kilometers in that boat. Even if you could keep the water out, it would fall apart in the first storm."

Félix Rovira had spent many contented hours in the little *café* on the edge of the *plaza*. Even in the tropical heat of Salina Cruz, the *plaza* with its palm trees and tinkling fountain was always cool and breezy. Across the *plaza* was the old city hall and cathedral. Away to the east, through the whispering fronds of the palm trees, he could see the glint of the ocean. His favorite time of day was in the late afternoon as the sun dropped and the terrace of the *café* was thrown into full shade. Most afternoons, a few musicians played for coins on the *plaza*. Rovira listened to them as he watched the sun twinkling on the waters of the harbor. He had spent most of the day working on his memoirs.

Sometimes, he wondered if anyone would be interested in reading them. The three decades of the Porfiriata had been eclipsed by the savage drama of revolution and counterrevolution that had gripped the country for the past five years. He settled his bill and strolled toward his villa. The day was warm and the road out of town dusty. Rovira stopped to take off his straw hat and wipe his brow. The Gulf was pleasant today with, scattered here and there, an embryonic whitecap tumbling down the face of a wave.

He looked across the Pacific to the northwest. He had not heard from his daughter for more than six months. Alicia's last letter had been carried to Acapulco on a *yanqui* warship and mailed from there. It had taken almost a month for the letter to get from Acapulco to Salina Cruz. Alicia had written to him of the wreck of the *yanqui* schooner and of the supplies the Cleveland had landed. Given the chaotic state of the country, who knew when he would get her next letter? The Tampico hadn't been in Salina Cruz harbor for months now. When the ship returned, he would make sure he got a parcel on board for Alicia and the children.

A light rain began to fall as Rovira came to the flower-topped wall surrounding William Wiseman's home. The British Consul's villa stood on the hill beside his own. He enjoyed Wiseman's company enormously. There was a lack of intellectual stimulation in Salina Cruz that the consul did much to remedy. His Spanish was flawless and, in private conversation, his comments on political developments in México and the world were pointed and wry. Rovira walked through the iron gate and knocked on the front door.

The two men lit their cigars and sat beneath the awning as the rain danced on the gaily striped canvas above their heads. "You are fortunate to be out of Acapulco and México, Félix," said Wiseman. "I hear that many of the well-to-do are in hiding and have been forced to sell their belongings for food. They are calling these times the day of the *peón*."

"Yes," said Rovira, "I am happy to be in Salina Cruz. Villa and Zapata would not have been too kindly disposed toward me, I think. How did General Huerta manage to escape with the rebels in control of the capital?"

"He was safely on board a ship, with a fortune stolen from the Treasury, before Obregón even entered the city. As soon as the Americans invaded and occupied Veracruz, Huerta knew he was finished. He must have made his escape plans then. The general was not about to let himself be taken prisoner by Obregón."

"What else have you heard about life in México?"

"I hear occasionally from the Embassy when the telegraph is working, Félix. Obregón rode in with thousands of half-naked Yaqui with their blowguns and bows and arrows. Then Villa and Zapata entered with their armies, firing their rifles in the air and shouting revolutionary slogans. Imagine that sight on Paseo de la Reforma! Of course, everyone expected the worst, but they were all surprisingly well-behaved. Villa and Zapata met at the San Ángel Inn. According to reports, they watered their horses at the fountain in the courtyard. What else could you expect of them?" Rovira chuckled.

"Obregón made it his business to find out which businessmen had been hoarding food to drive up the price. He put them all to work sweeping the streets. But, the best story is what Zapata did at the Country Club. He took it over, dug trenches in the sand traps on the golf course and turned the first floor of the clubhouse into stables for the horses. His men slept on the floor of the ballroom with their women. They cut the leather sofas apart to make ammunition bags and belts. Do you know the club president, Eugene Bailey?"

"I met him at the club once, when I was there as a guest. I could not join, of course, since three-quarters of the membership was required to be American or British and the Mexican quota was perpetually full."

Wiseman smiled. "Well then, Félix, perhaps you will find something to admire in Zapata after all. Bailey went to the club to protest about what Zapata was doing. Bailey thought he was lowering the tone of the place. Zapata listened carefully to him and then, without a word, had him stripped naked and gave him a whiskey barrel to wear through the streets on his way home."

"That would have been a sight to see," Félix said, laughing.

"To be sure. Instead of wild mayhem, as so many expected, there has been a slow decay. The civil servants have more or less disappeared and the city's services are collapsing—no electricity, no water, no trams. Apparently, Villa and Zapata know how to manage a war, but not how to manage a peace."

"And they have fallen out with Carranza."

"Of course. The only thing Carranza had in common with Villa and Zapata was a desire to overthrow General Huerta and take power. He has no interest in taking the *hacienda* lands or interfering with the *yanqui* oil companies. In the final analysis, he is Porfirio Díaz reincarnated. I have heard that he is being financed by Standard Oil and the Texas Oil Company. And, of course, President Wilson is supplying him with arms and money. Carranza has established a parallel government in Veracruz and controls more of México than Villa and Zapata do now. I think most of the major powers will recognize his government. I think that, for all practical purposes, the Revolution will be over when Carranza takes power."

Rovira frowned. "No, William. Zapata and Villa will not allow it. They are still committed to putting this country into the hands of the *peones*."

"Yes. I have no doubt that they will continue to fight, but the Americans have embargoed arms sales to them and have made sure that, in the end, Carranza will prevail." The two men sat side by side, listening to the rain, smoking quietly

Rovira hesitated, then said, "And the war in Europe, William, how is it going?" He deliberately avoided asking after Wiseman's younger brother, a major in the British Expeditionary Force who had been reported missing in action in Belgium.

Wiseman turned toward Rovira. "It is a nightmare, Félix. They are calling it the war to end all wars and pray God they are right. The casualties are in the millions." He stopped and sighed. "There is no word of Gerald yet."

Rovira patted him on the arm. "Do not give up hope, my friend. He is probably being held prisoner by the Germans."

"I hope so, Félix. That is the best I can hope for."

The soldiers had gone out early Christmas morning, catching dozens of lobster on the inner edge of the reef. Some paddled in the shallow water and speared the lobster while the others, Mausers ready, kept watch for sharks. At midnight, Ramón read the story from Luke of the birth of Jesus and then they had the Christmas *banquete*, the highlight of the year. Rosalía Nava sat with the other children at one of the big tables, bouncing Olga on her knee. On the table was their Christmas chocolate, saved from the stores brought by the Cleveland. Outside, over an open fire, María and Altagracia grilled the lobster. Alicia whisked the last of the olive oil into the eggs the children had collected on the beach. Ramón leaned over her shoulder and kissed her on the cheek and whispered, "Your delicious mayonnaise. Mmmm."

The *soldados* and Sargento Irra sat together at one of the tables, playing cards. Álvarez and Corporal Lara sat at the next table, playing dominoes and laughing uproariously. Doña Juana and Tirza, hugely pregnant, came through the door of the dining hall, carrying between them a platter heaped with fancy rolls. The children watched eagerly as the platter was placed on the table next to them.

"Ah, smell that bread Ramón," Alicia murmured.

Ramón smiled. "Now, you must be glad that I saved the last of our flour until now. We can have a proper Christmas *banquete*." Afterward, the children huddled over their chocolate in the glow of the oil lamps while the adults sat contentedly sipping their wine, the men smoking. Doña Juana and María gossiped happily. Ramón picked up his mandolin and played a few fast opening bars. After a moment, Secundino stood and sang, his voice clear and powerful. Álvarez, Carbajal and several other men got to their feet and began to clap in time to the music, soon joined by the women. Then, the dancing began. Alicia rose smiling and began to whirl around the dining hall with the others.

Tirza lay down and Doña Juana put the baby to her breast, then covered them both with the sheet. The baby started to suckle immediately. "A fine, healthy girl, Tirza," said Doña Juana. Tirza closed her eyes and let her head fall to the side

Secundino Cardona rose from his chair and moved to the bed. "Thank you, Doña Juana."

She laughed. "You had more to do with this little one than me, Secundino."

Bending over, he ran the tip of his finger around the baby's head, then kissed Tirza on the forehead. Suddenly, he felt dizzy and sat quickly on the edge of the bed. Tirza looked up at him. "Secundino, are you alright?" she asked.

Cardona closed his eyes for a moment. "Dizzy. I will be fine." He waited a moment then reached for Tirza's hand. "She is beautiful, Tirza. A beautiful girl."

Ramón heard the second knock and called out, "Enter." Evita Irra, tiny and slim, walked shyly into the office. Her son, three-year-old Antonio clutched her hand, fussing and fidgeting. Ramón looked up from his work and said, "Yes, Evita, what is it?

"It is Antonio, Capitán. There is something wrong with him.

He is not himself and his mouth bleeds. And look at his legs."
Ramón looked down to the boy's sturdy brown legs and raised
an eyebrow. "They look like perfectly healthy legs to me, Evita."

Evita shook her head vehemently. "No, Capitán. The color,
look at the color. Please, Capitán."

Ramón sighed. Being doctor to a garrison of thirty people
had its frustrations. He knelt by the boy and looked closely.
It was hard to see anything through the boy's naturally dark
skin. "Here, Antonio, come into the light," he said. The boy
gave his mother a nervous glance and followed Ramón to the
window. Ramón lifted him up onto the table and examined
his legs closely. Faintly perceptible, beneath the brown skin of
each leg, were dozens of purplish spots extending from ankle
to thigh. And the ankles and knees seemed puffy. Ramón
furrowed his brow and asked, "When did you first notice this,
Evita?"

"Perhaps a week ago, Capitán. There were just a few spots,
but they have spread."

Ramón nodded. "We will have a look in the mouth now,
Antonio," he said. The little boy looked toward his mother
nervously then opened his mouth. The gums were badly
swollen. Ramón took hold of a tooth and applied a slight
pressure. The tooth moved in its socket and blood began to
ooze from the gums. He pressed against another. It was loose
too and more blood ran down the gums.

A cold shiver ran down Ramón's spine. He had no idea
what was wrong with the boy. If it was a serious, contagious
disease, perhaps something brought to the island by the
Cleveland, they were all in great danger. He must identify it
as quickly as possible. He looked across at the wooden chest
that contained all their medicines. It was almost empty now:
a bit of laudanum, some valerian root, a small bottle of oil
of clove, some sutures and dressings; nothing he could use to
treat a serious illness. He turned to Evita. "I must look in my
books, Evita. In the meantime, take Antonio home and keep
him there. He is to be near no one but you. No one. Not even his

father or Francisco. Do you understand?"

Evita's eyes flashed bright with fear. "Yes, Capitán."

"And you are to feed him from his own bowl and spoon. No one else is to use them. This is very important."

Tears were welling up in Evita's eyes. "Yes, Capitán, but what is it?" She lowered her voice to an almost imperceptible whisper. "Will he die?"

"I cannot tell you what it is yet, Evita but be brave. I must learn more. As soon as I know, I will tell you. Until then, you must do exactly as I say, for the safety of your family and everyone else on this island. Do you understand?"

"Yes, Capitán," Evita whispered.

Ramón watched the door close behind them and then reached for the first of his medical books. He noticed that his hand was shaking as he reached out for the book. Over the years, he had become quite expert at suturing minor wounds, splinting broken fingers and diagnosing common ailments. But the residents of Clipperton were remarkably healthy and he had never had to deal with a serious illness. He had never seen anything like little Antonio Irra's symptoms. By evening, he had been unable to find anything useful in his books. Bleeding gums weren't that uncommon but the purple patches on the boy's legs troubled him. As the night wore on, Ramón grew increasingly desperate. There was nothing in any of the books. All he could do was isolate the boy and hope that no one else had been infected with whatever it was.

Altagracia had roasted booby for dinner yet again. How sick Ramón was of the greasy, fishy-tasting birds. Tomorrow, he would get the men out fishing again. Carbajal had brought a full load of driftwood to the house just before dinner and Ramón sat with his feet stretched toward the fire. They might lack fresh food and medicines, but the supply of firewood washing across the Pacific was endless. On the floor beside him, a dozen books lay stacked. He had found nothing in any them. He leaned to pick up his last medical reference and smiled. The Ship Captain's Medical Guide, first published in London in 1868 for ship's captains so they could provide medical attention to their crews. He had not opened it since Capitán Castellenes had given it to him, several years ago. It was the 1904 edition and the Tampico's captain had made Ramón a present of it when he had acquired a new edition. The calfskin binding was salt stained.

Where in God's name was Castellenes? What was keeping him? Ramón began to read, searching for a clue to what was wrong with the Irra boy. The pages grew blurred and Ramón's head kept falling forward but, each time, he jerked himself back to wakefulness. He could hear, from the far corner of the room, the low murmur of voices as Alicia and Altagracia went through the dwindling list of supplies in the house. There was really nothing left but salt, vinegar and spices. Just as he was about to close the book and go to bed, he found it: damage to the capillaries, purple patches on the skin, bleeding gums. He went over the paragraph again and then read on. A wave of relief swept through him. He sagged back into the chair, the book lying open in his lap. It wasn't contagious. They were safe. "Alicia," he called out. "I have it! I have it! Scurvy, the boy has scurvy like sailors get! He has all the symptoms. It is not contagious."

Ramón finished reading the page as Alicia came and stood by him. He snapped the book closed. "It is our food. There is no goodness in it. What Antonio needs is fresh fruit and vegetables, especially lemons and limes and oranges, even onions or potatoes. All we have are the coconuts." He thought for a moment. "First, we must make sure he eats fresh coconut. Then, I will examine everyone to see if anyone else has developed symptoms. We will have to ration the coconuts to make sure everyone gets their share."

Everyone on the island gathered as ordered on the square of hard-trodden coral dust between the settlement and the ocean. The sun had not yet reached its zenith and the air was still agreeably cool. The soldiers and their wives talked in muted tones and the children played quietly. Ramón raised his hand for silence. A hush fell. Even the children were silent. Ramón looked around. They had all grown thin, cheekbones prominent. The men were unshaven and unwashed. The women's long, dark hair hung in lank strands.

"You want to know why I examined every one of you yesterday," Ramón said. There was a murmur of assent. He told them about Antonio Irra's symptoms and about the disease called scurvy. How it had killed thousands of sailors through the centuries before the British discovered the miraculous properties of fresh vegetables and fruits, especially lemons and limes. Seven islanders had the early stages of the disease, he told them, and it was likely that they would all get it if nothing was done.

"We have no lemons or limes left. No onions. We only received a small quantity of fresh fruit and vegetables from the Cleveland. But, we do have coconuts. Those who have been eating coconuts have the fewest symptoms. From this moment, coconuts will be strictly rationed. Teniente Cardona and I have calculated that the trees produce enough coconuts so that we can share three each week. I will divide the coconut water and flesh equally in front of everyone, each Sunday morning. The shells will also be divided and shared for boiling to make a tea that may have value. Every person must eat their share and no one is to touch a coconut except for the share they are given by me. Is that understood?" There was a murmur of assent

The thought of giving birth on the island in her weakened condition frequently kept Alicia awake at night. She had known for months that she was pregnant but had said nothing to Ramón. He had been so preoccupied and she had put on so little weight, that he hadn't noticed. It was her secret. She stood in the shade of the coconut grove and ran her hands across her belly. There was a very slight rounding, nothing more. When she undressed at night, she saw the thickening of her ankles. But the swelling could be the scurvy. Everyone's joints were swollen. The coconuts didn't seem to be helping much. Alicia sat down with her back against a palm. What was happening to her baby? Did it have scurvy already? So far, she had been one of the lucky ones, her teeth and gums were still good. She had only a few purplish spots on her legs, none of the massive blotches that some of the others, especially the men, had. But she felt weak and drained and her body ached. What would happen to her baby if she grew still weaker?

She shaded her eyes and looked up into the palms. Ripening coconuts hung plump beneath the fronds. If only there were enough nuts to keep them all alive. The women and children might survive, little Antonio Irra was much better already, but the men would surely die. They got the same share as the women and children but their bodies were bigger and the ration was not enough for them. Alicia picked up a handful of the granular island soil and let the mixture of powdered coral, volcanic sand and guano sift through her fingers. It was a bitter irony. All around them lay a fortune in fertilizer; fertilizer that had the power to transform barren land into endless fields of crops. Yet here the guano worked no magic, produced no bounty.

Ramón and Secundino Cardona walked with extravagant care. The pain in their joints grew worse daily. Ramón looked across the lagoon toward the Rock. He knew that he should walk over to check on Álvarez. But there was no oil for the light so what was the point? And Álvarez came to the settlement every Sunday for his ration of coconut. It was so far to the Rock and Ramón's knees hurt so badly. What Álvarez did now was his own business. Ramón heard himself give a short, silly laugh.

He stumbled and put his hand on Cardona's shoulder to steady himself. "My earnest apologies, Teniente," he said and giggled. His head started to swim and he sat down suddenly on the sand, exhausted and disoriented and began to sob.

The regular hiss of the sea on the beach measured the time. The harsh grating of the shovels came as an assault to the ears. Ramón stood beside the grave holding the Bible in front of him. Alicia stood beside him, clutching his arm. The rest of the garrison stood around the grave as it was filled, heads bowed. Almazan and Carbajal shoveled slowly and deliberately, the dust carrying away in the wind. María Nava stood silent, her chin quivering, her arm around Rosalía. The girl's eyes were bright with tears. Ramón looked around their little cemetery. A cross for what was left of Jesús Neri and, now, one for Luis Nava. Luis's death had been a shock. Ramón had gone to see him only last night. He had been weak and his gums were bleeding profusely, but he had been perfectly lucid. He had even joked with Ramón. María had woken up in the morning to find her husband dead beside her.

Corporal Lara tapped Ramón insistently on the shoulder. Ramón heard Lara's words through a haze. "Capitán, Capitán," Lara called again.

Ramón forced his eyes open. He was so tired. He just wanted to remain sitting on the sand, leaning against the trunk of the coconut palm and never have to move again, but he knew he had to answer. He forced himself to say, "Yes, Felipe, what is it?"

"It is Constancio, Capitán, he is asking to see you."

Ramón took a deep breath and stood up slowly, arrows of pain shooting though his knees and hips. Lara walked ahead, leading the way to Constancio Mejía's cabin. Ramón saw that Lara was having trouble walking, too. The corporal slowly shuffled his feet through the sand. What was the point of him looking at Mejía? He couldn't save the man. He couldn't save any of them.

Mejía lay in his bed, shivering, a blanket pulled up to his chin. Like the others, the whites of his eyes were bright red with broken blood vessels. His mouth hung slack and Ramón could see the man's diseased gums and missing teeth. "How are you Constancio?" asked Ramón, his voice hoarse.

Without speaking, Mejía slowly pushed the blanket down to his waist. Ramón's eyes widened. A deep gash ran from Mejía's breastbone to his left hip. Blood oozed from the edges of the wound. Ramón's fatigue vanished. This was the final straw, the men trying to kill each other. "Who did this to you Constancio?" he demanded.

Mejía raised his eyes to Ramón and spoke for the first time. His voice was weak. "One of Villa's men in Chihuahua, Capitán," he croaked.

Ramón bent over and examined the wound carefully. The skin around the gash was red and hot. The man was losing his mind. "What are you talking about, Constancio? That was five years ago. This wound was made within the last two or three days."

"I swear, Capitán. I was cut by a saber, five years ago. It just opened up again. By itself."

"Mother of God," said Ramón. "It must be the scurvy. I read that it breaks down old scars, but this? I would never have thought it possible. Does it hurt?"

Mejía nodded through clenched teeth. Ramón carefully pulled the blanket back up to Mejía's chin. "Constancio, you will have to be brave. I will have to suture it closed."

CHAPTER 25

L ooking across the end of the lagoon from his cabin by the Rock, Álvarez could see the settlement. Two ant-like figures moved around the buildings. He only went to the settlement on Sundays to get his ration of coconut. Not that he needed it. What a fine joke that was, the little piece of coconut flesh and the sip of coconut water measured out so carefully to each of them. If the Capitán only knew that several times a week he climbed one of the coconut palms and took a nut, careful to leave no trace. Let the weaklings starve. He would not.

None of them were real men, not like him. Álvarez clenched his fist and felt the muscles in his arm tighten and swell. He knew what they really thought of him, that he was little better than an animal. But, each morning, he lifted rocks to keep his strength alive: rocks the others could barely move. And these days even the Capitán left him alone. The damned *indios* and *mestizos* with their idiotic superstitions and the precious Capitán and his fine lady, so white, so proper. Now, they were all dying.

He laughed out loud and felt the power surge through his body. While they clung together in fear like little children, he lived alone, the King of the Rock. They whined about eating seabirds and eggs but he ate them with relish and grew stronger with every passing day. And, of course, he ate the seaweed that washed up on the beach every day, a gift of the waves that they were too proud or too stupid to eat. Why should he tell them that it made him strong?

He saw a flash of white near the settlement and knew it would be Doña Alicia taking one of her walks. He often watched her through his telescope. She had skin as smooth as silk, hair black as night and, even now, her breasts were still full and moved beneath her shift as she walked. What could that little dandy of a *capitán* do with such a woman? Could he make her cry out? Could he make her writhe beneath him, her legs forced wide apart, the sweat pouring from her body like a river? Such a woman should belong to a real man, a man who would take her like a wild animal and give nothing back in the taking. Álvarez closed his eyes and felt his heart racing. He ran his tongue slowly around his lips.

The soldiers began to die like flies. Constancio Mejía. Arnulfo Pérez. Faustian Almazan. Pedro Carbajal. Even the seemingly indestructible Sargento Irra who, at the end, had been reduced to a pitiful husk of a man. Each grave was more shallow than the one before it. They were so weak and their limbs so painful, they just could not dig any deeper. And, in the end, did it matter?

The face looking at Ramón from the mirror was unrecognizable. The Kaiser mustaches had long since disappeared into a scraggly black beard, smeared with gray. The thinning hair hung lank and greasy. The cheekbones were hollow and gaunt. Ramón drew back his lips. There were only a few teeth left now. He grasped one to test its firmness and it came out in his fingers, leaving a black, bleeding hole in his gum. He shifted his weight and spat the blood into the porcelain basin. He dropped the tooth and it rattled into the basin.

He changed his position. His knees hurt so much. He couldn't stand in one place for more than a few seconds at a time. He looked in the mirror again. The most intriguing thing about this stranger in the mirror was his eyes. They were sunk deep into their sockets, surrounded by dark circles. The whites were a mass of broken blood vessels. But they radiated a peacefulness, as though the figure in the mirror knew that everything would be alright. Reassured, Ramón limped back to his window and looked out to sea again.

Alicia had gone to see Evita Irra herself. Ramón, sitting blankly staring in his chair by the window, had ignored her pleas for him to go with her. Finally, she had given up and walked to the little house at the edge of the settlement. She knew she would be able to do nothing for the dying woman but, perhaps, she could reassure her about her boys. Antonio and Francisco sat propped against the shady side of the house watching her. They were dirty and thin but they looked healthy, especially Antonio, who had been the first to show the symptoms of scurvy. Alicia's legs felt thick and heavy and her ankles ached terribly as she walked. Her time had almost come and the little weight she had put on with the baby was increasing the strain on her legs. My God, she thought, what will I do if Ramón cannot help me after I have the baby?

Evita seemed unconcerned, unaware that she was dying. She lay on the bed in a grimy cotton shift, her bloated limbs looking for all the world like gigantic *moronga*, the dark blood sausage from the Valley of México. She smiled weakly at Alicia. "Thank you for coming, Doña Alicia," she whispered. "Where is the Capitán?"

"He is very busy, Evita. He asked me to come in his place," Alicia lied. How could she explain to the islanders that while their families were dying, hers was slipping into madness? How could she tell them that Ramón spent almost every waking minute sitting rigidly on the hard wooden chair by the window in their bedroom, looking out to sea, refusing to speak, refusing to eat. How could she tell them that she took him a piece of roasted bobo or some scrambled egg each day and that, when he finally left his chair as night fell, the plate of food would be sitting untouched on the floor?

Alicia sat on the edge of the bed, took Evita's hand and felt for her pulse. It was very fast and faint. The woman's skin was raging hot to the touch. Alicia looked down at her. Evita was twenty-eight years old. With her ravaged, toothless face and thinning hair, she looked sixty. This had happened even with the coconuts.

"How are my boys, Doña Alicia?"

Alicia forced herself to smile and patted the dying woman's hand. "They are fine, Evita. Little Antonio grows stronger each day."

Evita sagged back into the pillow with the ghost of a smile. "Then what the Capitán said is true."

For a moment Alicia was puzzled, then she understood everything; Evita had been giving her share of the coconuts to her two boys.

Alicia lay her hand on Evita's forehead. "Yes, Evita, it is true. Go to sleep now. I will come and see you again tomorrow," she said, realizing that she would probably never see Evita alive again.

They had huddled in the cellar for two days as the hurricane had battered the island. Ramón was consumed with impotent rage when he saw that the storm had torn the crown completely off one of the coconut trees. Now, there would be even fewer nuts for them. The crown was floating in the middle of the lagoon, probably with some coconuts clinging to it. It took the combined strength of Corporal Lara, Teniente Cardona and the two surviving *soldados* to drag the boat to the edge of the lagoon and launch it. Ramón watched as the two *soldados* slowly rowed out toward the clump of palm fronds.

Ramón bent down painfully and dipped his fingers into the lagoon and tasted them. Salt. Waves must have been driving over the beach into the lagoon. He looked over to the guano shed. More corrugated iron had peeled off and, just outside the shed, one of the wagons had blown off the track and was lying on its side in the sand. Ramón turned to Teniente Cardona. "Secundino, how are your legs? Can you walk to *la roca*?"

Cardona closed his eyes and hesitated, then said quietly, "Yes, Ramón."

"We must make sure that Álvarez is alive and the light is undamaged," said Ramón.

They walked slowly, side by side, both limping. Ramón gestured to the damaged cabins of the *soldados*. "We cannot repair them again, Secundino. Have the families whose cabins are damaged move into the storehouse."

Cardona nodded and pointed ahead. "Look, Lara's house is gone." Where the corporal's cabin had been, a few posts stuck out of the sand. There was no other sign that it had existed.

Ramón sighed. "Lara can move into Irra's house."

The two men continued to walk along the beach toward the Rock. They stopped to examine the two concrete rainwater cisterns. The end of one had been partly undermined by the waves. They had closed the inlets of the cisterns before the storm struck so the thousands of liters of water they contained were uncontaminated by the salt spray driven by the hurricane.

"I am sorry, Secundino, I must rest," said Ramón, lying face down on top the cistern. Without saying anything, Cardona lay beside him and closed his eyes. The regular pounding of the waves on the sand seemed to be synchronized to Ramón's breathing. He drifted into oblivion.

Cardona touched his back gently, calling, "Ramón, Ramón." He stirred and, lifting his head, remembered where he was. The two men slowly slid off the cistern and trudged toward the Rock. Ahead, several dark objects were lying on the rise of land near the cemetery. Perhaps trees washed ashore by the storm. Perhaps something useful. Both men's vision was blurred and neither could make sense of the shapes until they were no more than a few meters away.

Ramón stood frozen to the spot, unable to speak. Cardona made the sign of the cross and muttered, "Mother of God." In front of them was the cemetery, what was left of it. Bodies had been washed from their shallow graves by the storm. Some were partially decomposed. Strips of flesh and clumps of hair clung to grinning skulls. Several bodies were intact and recognizable. The body of Evita Irra lay across the body of Arnulfo Perez, their limbs grotesquely intertwined.

Ramón observed with coolly detached interest as his vision ebbed away. He stood, utterly blind, until the earth began to sway slowly beneath him and he fell unconscious to the sand.

Ramón stood on the slight rise behind the house. Inside, Alicia lay on their bed, her head buried in her arms, sobbing, devastated by her inability to console her husband. Ramón had not cried since he had been a little boy. But now, as he stood looking out over the gray ocean, he felt the tears welling up. They came up from the pit of his stomach, his throat constricted so tightly he couldn't draw breath. At last, came a wrenching, heart tearing sob.

He fell to his knees, his body shaking uncontrollably. He had killed them all. He had killed every one of them as surely as if he had put his pistol to their heads and pulled the trigger. He had killed them with his arrogance, his conceit. An avalanche of self-disgust buried him. He was the Capitán who had killed them all. The Capitán who was too proud to send them to safety on the Cleveland. The Capitán who watched them die hour by hour, minute by minute and did nothing. The Capitán who mouthed meaningless words from the Bible over their corpses.

Toward evening, Alicia came out of the house, her eyes dark with crying. She saw Ramón lying face down on the ground, his arms and legs outstretched. The thought came instantly, he has killed himself, he is dead. She ran to him and, kneeling beside him, shook his shoulders, crying, "Ramón, Ramón!" He rolled over slowly, eyes unseeing. Alicia could see the marks of tears in the dust on his face. Both his hands were bloody. "Ramón, it is all right, I am here."

"Alicia," his voice was barely audible, "Alicia, help me. God, help me. What have I done?"

"You did everything you could, Ramón," she whispered.

"Everything I could?" His voice broke. "I killed them all. I kept them here. They should have gone with Capitán Williams. I kept them here and I killed them. And I will probably kill you and our children and everyone else on this island."

"No Ramón, you did not kill them. No one could have known what would happen. You were only doing your duty."

"Duty? What is the greater duty? Guarding this godforsaken pile of birdshit or protecting my own people? If there really was a God, what would He say is the greater duty?" He gave a maniacal laugh. "If there really was a God, would He let these people die?"

"Come with me Ramón. We must go inside now." Alicia took Ramón's elbow and helped him to stand up. She had to guide him to the house and through the door. She helped him upstairs to their bedroom and undressed him. He sat, unprotesting on the edge of the bed, as she removed his clothes. She was shocked at the pallor of his skin, the purple blotches on his legs and arms, his swollen knees and ankles, his skeleton so clearly, so painfully, visible. When she was done, she pulled the covers over him and, kissing him gently on the forehead, left.

Alicia went to the *salón* and sat on the floor in front of the embers dying in the fireplace. She was alone. Altagracia was in her room. The children had fallen asleep hours ago. Alicia pulled the blanket closer around her as the room grew cool. She could feel the baby moving; this poor baby who would be born into a world of suffering and death. Finally, the fire went out altogether. She made no move to rekindle it or to go to bed. She sat hunched on the floor, staring at the ashes. She was still sitting there, wide awake, when the sun rose.

Ramón stumbled breathlessly down the stairs, his eyes wild with excitement. "Alicia, Alicia, a ship!

"Where Ramón? Are you sure?"

"Yes, my love," he gasped. "Just on the horizon. Come. You must come and look." He ran up the stairs and into the bedroom with Alicia close behind. He pointed through the window, his voice almost hysterical. "There, there!"

"Where, Ramón? Where?"

"There!" He pointed frantically and his voice rose. "It is right there in front of you! Are you blind, woman?"

"Ramón, I can see nothing."

"I will get the men. Get the women and children to the beach. Light the signal fire." Ramón threw on his tunic and cap and strapped on his holster before rushing down the stairs. Alicia remained for a few seconds at the window, carefully scanning the horizon. Shaking her head, she went back to the kitchen, calling for Altagracia and the children.

"Where is Álvarez? We need every man," Ramón shouted at Cardona as he hurried onto the beach.

"He is at the Rock, Ramón. He is always at the Rock."

"There is no time to get him. Secundino, all of you, get the boat down to the water. There is a ship out there."

"Where, Ramón? I cannot see a ship," said Cardona, staring intently seaward.

Ramón pointed directly offshore. "There, right on the horizon, scarcely moving."

Cardona shaded his eyes and looked again, gently shaking his head. "It is a cloud, Ramón. It is only a cloud."

"It is a ship, Teniente Cardona. Do not dare question what I say. Now get that boat into the water."

"But Capitán, the boat is damaged. It will sink."

"It will get us to that ship. Now get moving!" Ramón stood to his full height, his eyes blazing.

Cardona spread his hands in a conciliatory gesture. "Capitán, there is no ship."

With great deliberation, Ramón took his pistol from its holster and trained it on Cardona's chest. "I order you to get that boat to the water," shouted Ramón.

"Capitán, what are you doing? There is no ship," said Cardona, pleading.

"Now!" Ramón screamed, raising the pistol until it was

pointed directly at Cardona's heart.

Resignation passed over Cardona's face. "Yes, Capitán. Men, get the boat down to the water."

Ramón watched intently, the pistol at his side, as the men struggled with the boat. The weight of it was almost too much for them to handle. "Hurry, hurry," he screamed. "The ship will be gone."

When, at last, the boat was in the water, he ordered them into it. They climbed slowly aboard, nursing their painful limbs. When they were all seated, Ramón edged carefully over the gunwale into the boat, keeping his pistol trained on Cardona the whole time. Cardona looked at the wild-eyed figure brandishing the revolver in the stern, the long greasy black hair and the gray-flecked beard blowing in the wind. They would have to get the gun away from him before he killed them all.

Ramón sat at the tiller, the boat surging back and forth in the waves, and ordered the men to row.

"Capitán! Please, Capitán! It is only a cloud. The surf is too dangerous." In spite of his racing heart, Cardona spoke slowly and calmly as though to a distressed child.

Ramón's voice was icy. "Cardona, if I hear one more word of disobedience from you, I will shoot. We are going to row out to that ship and we are going to save our families. Now all of you, row!"

The women and children gathered on the beach. They had seen Ramón climbing into the boat with his revolver drawn and had watched the men row out through the surf. The boat was a few hundred meters offshore, above the outer edge of the reef where the waves grew short and steep and were breaking with malevolent fury. They could see the boat moving slowly seaward, tossing violently. In the bows, a man stood suddenly. There was the faint sound of a gunshot. They watched as the man crumpled, then lurched sideways and fell overboard. Two of the men in the boat stood and lunged at the figure in the stern. The boat slewed around sideways in the waves. The women and children watched in horror as a wave caught the boat broadside and threw it high into the air, flipping it over as though it weighed nothing at all.

They waited on the beach, stunned and silent, until well past sunset. The signal fire had long since gone out, leaving only the bitter smell of burned wood. In the moonlit night, they saw nothing. In the ink-black waters above the reef, the hammerheads swarmed, the scent of blood strong in the water.

CHAPTER 26

Alicia and Tirza sat silently together before the fire. The bone-dry driftwood burned furiously; white hot sparks trembled, hung suspended for a moment, then raced up the chimney into the swirling darkness. The words had seized Alicia's throat, choking her, as she had told Ramoncito, Ali and Olga that Papá was gone, that he would never come back, that he was dead. It had taken all her strength of mind to explain something to the children she could scarcely believe herself.

The others were in bed now, asleep at last. Only Alicia and Tirza remained awake, Tirza with Lupita asleep on her shoulder, staring fixedly at the flames with reddened eyes. The two women said not a word, hearing only the harsh crackle of the fire and, above it, the wind rising in the night.

The wind had grown steadily over the hours, becoming a full gale, battering the house and blowing the smoke from the fire back into the room. Tirza sat silent, her shoulders trembling. Alicia, tormented by her own loss, could say nothing to comfort her. Finally, exhausted, Tirza fell into a restless sleep, curled on the floor around Lupita, leaving Alicia alone with the night, cradling her unborn child, her fatherless child. The storm continued to increase in strength until, just after midnight, it reached hurricane force.

Outside, the ocean began to cover the low-lying parts of the island. The remaining surf boat, drawn up far from the beach and tied to one of the coconut palms, was seized by the waves and smashed into matchwood against the trees. With each blast, the house shifted slightly. In the gusts, the walls and roof creaked ominously and, at times, it seemed that the roof might blow off. Most frightening of all was the incessant shrieking. The fire had long since burned out and Alicia had blocked the chimney with paper and rags to stop its howling. She sat on the floor, Tirza and Lupita lying asleep beside her. Alicia cupped her hands around her belly. It felt hard as rock. The new life within her was quiet. The baby had scarcely moved or kicked for two days.

Ramón was dead. Their baby would never know its father. How could she make their child understand what kind of man he had been? She stopped. Their child might die. She might die. They might all die here. She drove the thought from her mind. They would find a way. Somehow, they would survive. The wind shrieked louder and Alicia shuddered. Tirza stirred and moaned in her sleep. Another gust and the heavy casement window blew open. Its catch broken, it was flung inward by the wind, smashing back against the wall and sending shards of glass skittering across the floor. The heavy damask curtains, torn from their rings, flew across the room sending chairs and the bird cage crashing. Through the opening, the wind was a maddened roar. In the distance, the furious pounding of the waves on the beach came like an ominous drumbeat. Another buffeting gust came and the house groaned with the force of the wind. Tirza was awake now, pulling the blanket tight around Lupita.

"Tirza, get the children and the others quickly! We have to get everyone down into the cellar!" Alicia had to shout to be heard, "Now, we must do it now!" They ran through the house shaking everyone awake. "Get up, the roof may be blown away! We have to get into the cellar! Quickly now!"

Alicia pulled at the black iron ring of the trapdoor. She felt so weak. It was too heavy for her to move by herself. Altagracia grasped the ring with her and slowly they raised it, their fingers jammed painfully together. "Hold it there, Altagracia." Alicia ushered Tirza and Lupita down into the darkness of the cellar. "Just go down and wait. We will light lamps when the trapdoor is closed."

Ramoncito ran into the *salón*. Behind him was Doña Juana with Olga on her hip and Ali clutching her nightdress with one hand and Rosalía's hand with the other. "Quickly children, down into the cellar. Hurry. There isn't much time." Alicia urged Doña Juana and the children down the ladder and followed, balancing the weight of the trapdoor above her. "María, get down here with me. Alta, help me to lower this. Carefully, just lower it as we go down."

They went down the ladder, step by step, until the trapdoor dropped solidly into place above them. The thick coral stone walls of the cellar and the heavy planking of the floor above muffled the sounds of the wind's fury, leaving only an eerie, distant moan. But, transmitted through the ground, the pounding of the waves on the shore was louder than ever. Alicia took the last step onto the dank, damp floor of the cellar. The air was cold and smelled of decay. Some of the children were crying in the dark. She felt her way along the wall, running her hand slowly along the rough wooden shelves. She found what she was looking for and struck one of the matches on the stone of the wall. As it flared into life, she saw the fear in the eyes of the women and children as they stood, shivering. "Everything will be alright. Here Alta, take one of these." She handed Altagracia one of the half dozen lanterns that stood on the shelf. "Quickly, girl, before the match goes out." Altagracia fumbled with the glass chimney of the lantern. The match died, plunging the cellar into darkness. Alicia struck another. This time, Altagracia had the lantern ready, the wick caught and they had light. The women and children huddled together near the glowing lantern.

Rosalía stood to one side, holding her mother's hand, her eyes cast down. She looked up and asked in a small voice, "Doña Alicia, will we be safe here?"

Alicia paused, "Yes, Rosalía. The storm will be gone by tomorrow. We will be safe." She had no doubt that the cellar could survive the wind, but wondered to herself whether the seas driven up the beach by the hurricane might reach high enough to flood it, drowning them all. The ground around them was trembling with the fury of the sea. The sand of the floor felt even damper than usual. Perhaps it was best not to think too much about it. There was nowhere else to go. They huddled together, shivering, speaking in low voices. As the night wore on, the moaning of the wind dropped note by note until it stopped altogether. All they could hear was the surf.

"Doña Alicia, the wind has dropped," María touched Alicia's arm. "Listen."

"It is the eye of the hurricane, María. Soon the wind will come again. We must stay here."

Outside there was an eerie stillness. The air crackled with electricity. Everywhere was ruin. Roofs on four of the houses had been carried away. The flag pole on the point had been snapped off just above the ground. The pole itself and the flag had disappeared. The wharf was submerged in the surf, its pilings leaning crazily landward. Great sheets of corrugated iron had been torn from the heavy timber frame of the guano shed and been sent knifing through the air. Almost two hundred meters from the shed, a coconut palm stood decapitated, its thick trunk neatly sheared five meters above the ground by a flying sheet of iron.

Alicia arranged her blanket beside her children and lowered herself onto it. As she did, she felt a sharp pain in her belly. It was gone in a moment and she lay on the blanket, on her side, pulling a corner of it over her. She felt numb and cold and utterly drained. There was nothing left to do. Oblivious now to the presence of the others, she heard only the pounding of the sea through the ground next to her ear.

Ramón held her close. She could feel the beating of his heart. She could smell his cologne and feel the strength of his body. He gently gripped her hair and tilted her head back. He kissed her, tenderly at first, then with mounting passion. She felt her blood rise and returned his kisses, her tongue seeking his, her arms pulling his body into hers. "Alicia, my love." He whispered it softly through her hair. She sighed. He turned and fell into the sea. She looked everywhere, crying out his name. He was gone, vanished. She looked towards the horizon and saw a black ship. It flew no flag. Desperately, she looked for Ramón. She looked back to the horizon and it was empty. A terrible, overwhelming panic grew in her stomach. It twisted and turned and hurt, as though someone were pushing a long, jagged knife deep into her body. She screamed.

"Señora, Señora, wake up." Tirza was holding Alicia's shoulders and shaking her. Alicia felt the pain again and she groaned. "Doña Alicia!" Tirza's voice was urgent.

Olga was awake now. In the glow of the lantern, her eyes were wide with fright. The pain subsided and Alicia came half-awake, her face streaming with sweat. Between her legs, her clothing was soaked. "Tirza, my waters have broken. I am going to have the baby."

Tirza knelt at Alicia's side. "Everything will be alright, Señora, Doña Juana is here."

In the light of the hurricane lanterns, Alicia could see the reassuring warmth of Doña Juana's smile. She stroked Alicia's face gently with the back of her hand. "We have done this together before. I will take care of you. You have nothing to fear." Turning to the others, she said, "Get our blankets and help me get the Señora onto them. Children, you must move. Mamá will be fine. Ramoncito, help your sisters." They rolled Alicia onto the blankets, covering her body with her own blanket. Again the pain came but, this time, she didn't cry out. Tirza and Altagracia sat beside her as the contractions came in waves.

The eye of the hurricane had passed over and the winds had returned, more fiercely than before. It was as though the sea had come to reclaim the island. Torn from the surface by the hurricane, it filled the air, reducing visibility to nothing. There was no longer any boundary between sea and land and air. Piled up by the wind, the sea buried the strip of beach beneath its fury and drove directly into the lagoon. The waves flooding up the beach washed at the rise of land just below the house.

For hundreds of miles around Clipperton, the ocean seethed. Alone on the mountainous seas, a battered ship fought for her life. A tough little steamer, built on the Clyde thirty years earlier, she had a good, strong Scottish engine and a lifetime tramping the world's oceans behind her. On a good night, the men clinging to the handholds in her wheelhouse would have been easily able to see the light on Clipperton Rock. In the driving rain and spray and fury of this endless night, even if the light had been lit, they would have seen nothing.

Hours of fighting the hurricane had strained the old ship badly. As she perched atop mountainous waves, her bow and stern unsupported, then plunged headlong into the troughs, hundreds of the rivets holding her iron plates together snapped off cleanly. Below the waterline, in her boiler room, the firemen staggered and lurched with shovels full of coal to keep up steam. No one had to tell them that without steam the old ship would fall off the wind, go broadside to the waves and be rolled over. As they worked, oily water swirled over the floor plates around their legs. The pumps could not keep up with the sea coming through the strained hull plating. The water in the bilges rose steadily throughout the night, greedily licking at the bottoms of the fireboxes.

In his cabin, Arthur Brander lay wide awake in his berth, his muscles exhausted by the constant need to brace himself against the ship's wild motion. Diverting the ship to Clipperton on its supply run from Panamá to Ocean Island was seeming like less and less of a good idea, but he had promised Ramón that he would visit. Lashed in a corner of his cabin were boxes of delicacies for Ramón and Alicia; tea, brandy, olive oil, Italian cheeses and chocolate for the children. There were even books and newspapers and some records for Ramón's Victrola. Brander sighed with frustration. With this weather, it might be days before they were able to approach Clipperton.

Two hours before dawn, the water reached the fire doors.

The chief engineer ordered his men out. As they climbed the greasy ladders, hanging on grimly through each roll of the ship, the sea flooded into the fireboxes. The dials on the steam pressure gauges began to fall. The beat of the engine slowed. As the last fireman scrambled up the ladder onto the main deck, the ship fell off to port and lay broadside in the trough.

Unable to rise quickly enough to the onrushing wall of water, she rolled her lee deck under, the sea tearing the lifeboat from the port side. In the wheelhouse, the helmsman was thrown from the wheel and fell headfirst into the engine room telegraph with a sickening crack. The ship had just started to recover when another wave smashed into her, rolling her completely over. The next wave broke over her upturned bottom. Within two minutes, the ship and the men trapped inside her were gone.

The baby's head had crowned an hour earlier and the contractions were urgent and forceful but still the baby would not come. The blankets were soaked with sweat and blood. Tirza was at Alicia's side, stroking her hair and soothing her. Doña Juana knelt between Alicia's legs, willing the baby to be born. Alicia strained and pushed with all her might, then fell back. "I am too weak. I cannot do this any longer," she moaned. The contractions were so strong, surely her body must tear from the strain.

"Just one more time, Señora. The baby is almost here." Doña Juana wiped the blood and mucus from Alicia's body and from the top of the baby's head. She saw with alarm that the head was darkening. She had seen many babies stillborn; time was short. Another contraction came and Alicia pushed with it, digging her nails so deeply into Tirza's palm that she drew blood. The baby hadn't moved. "Señora, your muscles are too weak. You must squat like the *indio*. The baby will come then." Doña Juana wiped the sweat from her own forehead and sat back on her haunches.

Alicia raised her head to look at Doña Juana and shook her

head slowly. "I am not an *indio*. I will not squat."

"Señora, if you do not, the baby will die and you may die."

"No, Doña Juana." In the glow of the oil lamps, Alicia's face was gray, her eyes dark and sunken, an exhausted mask. She grimaced as another contraction came. She pushed with all her power, screaming with frustration. It was no good and she sagged back, beaten. It wasn't possible. She couldn't do it. She let her head drop onto the blankets. She lay there, panting, the sweat running down her face. After a moment, she opened her eyes and reached out for Tirza's hands. "It is the only way. Tirza, help me up."

Alicia's knees shook uncontrollably as she squatted on the blanket. Tirza kneeled in front, steadying her, Alicia's hands on her shoulders. Doña Juana knelt behind. When the next contraction came, Doña Juana urged her, "Push, Señora. Push hard." The contraction seemed to last forever. Alicia held her breath and pushed and pushed until she thought she would faint. "It is coming Señora, the baby is coming. Push."

The contraction ended and Alicia let her breath out with a rush and drew new air hungrily into her lungs. Within seconds, another contraction came, even more powerful. "Push! The head is out, push now!" Doña Juana had her hands beneath Alicia and caught the baby in a warm rush of blood and fluid. "It is a boy, Señora, a son." Doña Juana held the infant in her arms, running her finger inside his mouth to remove the mucus. He gave a small cry. He was breathing regularly and the bluish pallor of his skin was turning to pink.

Alicia lay back on the blanket, exhausted. She gave a weak smile. "Please, Doña Juana, can I have my son?" she whispered in a cracked voice. Doña Juana placed the child on Alicia's chest and drew the blanket over them both. Alicia raised her head to see her son. "He is my little angel. I will call him Ángel in honor of his grandfather." Alicia held the baby close to her body. In seconds, she was asleep.

CHAPTER 27

The sun climbed slowly into the pallid sky. Most of the houses in the settlement had been reduced to kindling, their contents smashed or soaked or simply gone. Of the guano shed, there was little left but the frame and a few tattered remnants of corrugated iron. The island was littered with debris. Near the settlement, only five coconut palms remained standing.

Alicia lay on the divan in her *salón*, her newborn son suckling vainly. She had no milk. For the others, there had been so much and for this one, this little boy who would need it most, none at all. He cried in frustration and hunger. She wanted to cry too. How could she make milk when she ate nothing but gulls, fish, eggs and part of a coconut each week? She stroked his little tuft of shocking red hair to quiet him. Where had he got that hair? None of the Roviras or Arnauds had red hair. Perhaps it was because of the food.

Outside, there was little wind. The day had dawned bright and serene. The only sound from outside the house was that of the surf pounding on the beach. Alicia could hear Altagracia and Rosalía cleaning up the broken glass strewn across every room. Doña Juana and María were nailing sailcloth over the window openings. The children were with Tirza, searching the ruins of the buildings for food, clothing, for anything of value. Alicia looked down at Ángel, asleep at last, and closed her eyes.

She could see Ramón, as the little boat pitched in the surf. She could see the boat thrown high in the air, rolling over. Taking forever, an eternity. She could see the men dropping out and falling into the waves, one after another as though in some crazy game. And then the fins of the sharks, circling and lunging. Hundreds of them. She must stop. She would drive herself mad. Upstairs, Altagracia and Rosalía chattered as they worked. Didn't they feel the pain? Didn't they feel the emptiness? Alicia drifted into sleep.

She woke in mid-morning to the sound of Tirza and the children coming back. Tirza's eyes were heavy and underscored by dark lines but the children laughed and pushed each other as though they had just returned from a picnic. They carried small treasures they had found in the wreckage of the buildings.

"Did you find anything worth saving, Tirza?" Alicia leaned on one elbow, careful not to wake Ángel.

"A little, Señora. There are tools, some clothes and some furniture. But the damage, it is terrible. This is the only house with a full roof."

"Then everyone will stay here until we are rescued."

"Do you really think we will be rescued, Señora?"

"Of course. But if not, we will sail for help, like the crew of the Nokomis."

"There is no boat, Señora. It is smashed to pieces."

Alicia paused. "We can build another, Tirza. There is a lot of wood. Álvarez is good with tools and as strong as an ox. He will build us a boat."

"Yes, Señora," Tirza said.

"By the way, did you see Álvarez?"

"No, Señora. Perhaps his cabin was blown away during the night."

"No. It is built like a fortress. But we need him now more than ever. Someone will have to go to the other side to fetch him."

They had no bodies to bury but Victoriano Álvarez had made wooden crosses for Ramón, Secundino and the others. He had driven them into the ground at the cemetery and Alicia had read from the Bible. Then, they had all stood without speaking, unsure what to do next. Alicia had raised her head and looked about her. There were now nineteen crosses. Nineteen dead. Fourteen still alive. One man, five women and eight children. Alicia's head dropped to her chest and she sobbed. How many more would die? How much more would they have to suffer?

Later, she sat in the chair where Ramón had spent so many days looking out to sea. Now she too faced the sea, but saw nothing. Ángel lay cradled in her arms, sound asleep. Finally, in desperation, she had asked Altagracia to beat birds' eggs with milk made from coconut flesh to see if he would take it. He had sucked a cloth dipped in it eagerly and now lay contentedly asleep, his hunger pains gone for the moment.

The sea was empty. Great combers swept across the reef and thundered against the island's flank. Bits of wreckage were scattered high up the beach. Alicia walked gingerly, conscious of a burning pain between her legs. She folded her arms in front of her chest and stared at the spot out over the reef where the boat had capsized, where Ramón had disappeared. A piece of timber washed toward her. She recognized it as part of the boat's mahogany gunwale cap. She picked it up and, clutching it, walked farther along the beach. Small fragments of the boat littered the sand. She walked along slowly, head down. All her life, she had had someone to depend on. First her mother, then her father and then Ramón. Her mother was dead and now so was Ramón. In the chaos in México, her father might very well be dead too. Alicia had never felt so alone. She turned back, and clutching the splintered piece of mahogany, walked up the beach toward the house.

Altagracia almost knocked her over as she came running headlong down the path. "Señora, it is Álvarez. He has taken the *capitán's* guns," Altagracia blurted it out breathlessly.

"What do you mean Altagracia?"

She stood for a moment, her breath coming in gasps. "He came to the house. He has gone crazy. He made me give him Capitán Arnaud's old revolver and the Mauser. He said he was in charge now." Altagracia's voice was panicky and she wrung her hands in her apron as she spoke.

"We will soon put a stop to this. Where is he now?"

"I do not know Señora. He is probably back at *la roca*."

"Alta, be calm. I will speak to him." Alicia put her arm around Altagracia's shoulders and led her back to house. They could hear Tirza and María talking excitedly inside. As they walked toward the door, Álvarez came around the corner of the house. He was filthy and unshaven. Two revolvers were jammed carelessly into his belt and Ramón's Mauser lay cradled in his arms.

"What are you doing with my husband's rifle, Álvarez? Give it to me at once."

Alicia's voice had the unmistakable ring of authority, acquired over a lifetime of dealing with servants and people like Álvarez. He was taken aback for a second but his eyes burned. He raised the rifle across his chest. His voice was thick. "It is a different world now, Señora. I am in command. You do not tell me what to do."

"Remember your station, Álvarez. Now give me that rifle." Alicia's voice grew harder.

"I know my station, Señora. I am the only man on this island, the only *soldado*. I am in command. You will do as I say." Álvarez sneered and fingered the trigger of the Mauser.

Alicia stood with her hands on her hips and stared. "You will pay for your insolence."

"I pay for nothing, Señora. I take what I want."

"We will see about that," Alicia said it calmly and, turning quickly on her heel, entered the house. Altagracia followed close behind her. Álvarez watched them appraisingly, then turned slowly toward the Rock.

Inside, Tirza and María were talking heatedly in Yaqui. Lupita lay asleep in Tirza's arms while María held Ángel. When they saw Alicia enter, they reverted to Spanish. "Señora, you must stop Álvarez, he is acting like a madman," Tirza spoke rapidly, her voice pitched an octave higher than usual.

"Be calm, Tirza. I know he has taken Capitán Arnaud's guns.

He is an insolent dog. He thinks that because he is the only man on the island, he will do as he pleases. He will learn. When you searched the houses, did you find any of the *soldados'* guns?"

"No, Señora. They were gone. I thought they must have been blown away or buried in the wreckage but perhaps Álvarez took them."

Alicia looked thoughtful. "María, Tirza, run down to the storehouse and see if the *soldados'* rifles and pistols are in the racks. Quickly now. Do not let Álvarez see you. If they are still there, bring them back and all the ammunition you can carry." The two women rushed from the house.

Altagracia pulled at Alicia's sleeve. "Señora, what will he do?"

"Nothing, Altagracia." Alicia patted her hand.

"But Señora, I am afraid of him."

"Do not worry, Altagracia. Do nothing to provoke him. If Tirza and María find the *soldados'* rifles, we will be on equal terms with him."

"But what if he has taken all of the rifles?"

"We will deal with that when the time comes. In the meantime, we must get this house cleaned up. We will be safe living here together."

They spent the rest of the day cleaning the house and repairing as much of the damage as they could. Tirza and María had returned without the rifles. Álvarez had taken them and all of the ammunition. All of the bayonets and even the gun rack itself were gone. Alicia began to feel alarmed. She was unsure how strong her influence over Álvarez really was. True, he still seemed awed by her social standing and the whiteness of her skin but she had no idea how far he might go now. Maintaining control over people like Álvarez has been ridiculously easy in the world Alicia had known all her life. But this was a new world, a world full of terrifying unknowns. The forces that had maintained the gulf between people like Álvarez and Alicia had vanished in the surf with Ramón.

The house was tidied by nightfall. They had brought everything of value from the ruined houses into the shelter of Alicia's home. For supper, they had all shared a coconut and gulls that María had clubbed on the beach and roasted. The older children were upstairs. Ángel lay asleep in his crib, his hunger satisfied for the moment with coconut milk and beaten gulls' eggs. Alicia felt utterly drained. More than anything, she needed sleep. Sitting by the fire with Tirza, María, Doña Juana and Altagracia, she thought of Ramón. The desperation in him must have been overwhelming to make him imagine a ship, a ship that would rescue them all. Poor Ramón. She looked through her lashes at Tirza. Ramón had forced Secundino Cardona and the others into the boat. Tirza had lost her husband and Lupita had lost her father. Francisco and Antonio were now orphans. What would happen to them all? Even if Álvarez could be controlled, they couldn't live on seabirds and fish and the occasional coconut forever. She couldn't think. It was too much. Picking Ángel up from his crib, she carried him upstairs, leaving the other women murmuring quietly in front of the fire.

The temperature had dropped dramatically and it was cold in their bedroom. Her bedroom. It was just her bedroom now. She had never spent a night in this bed without Ramón. Never a single night without his arms to hold her and his words to comfort her and his strength to draw on. She looked out of the window into the darkness across the lagoon. The light on *la roca* was not lit. A shudder ran down her spine. Álvarez was dangerous, she knew that now. But what could they possibly do against him? He had all the weapons. She cradled Ángel to her body and, shivering, pulled the heavy blankets over them both.

The day dawned brilliantly. The sky was cloudless and the air felt dry and fresh. Tirza had taken the children to the beach to collect eggs for breakfast. They were boiling now on the wood stove. At least there would never be a shortage of eggs to gather or driftwood with which to cook them. Alicia sat at the kitchen table feeding Ángel with the coconut milk and egg mixture. María and Tirza laid the table while Doña Juana tried to open an under-ripe coconut with a heavy cleaver. The storm had scattered coconuts across the island. Some would keep. The damaged ones would have to be eaten quickly. None must be allowed to go to waste.

Even the sharp edge of the cleaver made little impression on the tough shell. Doña Juana hacked away at it in growing frustration until it cannoned across the room, hit the floor and split open neatly. Her look of utter disbelief made the other women laugh. Then they realized that the coconut water was lost and became suddenly quiet. As María leaned over to pick up the halves of the coconut, the kitchen door crashed back against the wall and Álvarez lunged into the room, bandoliers criss-crossing his chest, a bayonet hanging from his belt. Cradled in his arms lay the Mauser rifle.

"I must have a wife! A man needs a wife!" he roared. Álvarez paused and looked around the room. "I will have her, the fat one with the big tits!" Álvarez poked Doña Juana's breast with the muzzle of the rifle, his rough voice booming in the small kitchen. "She will be my wife." Doña Juana stood, her eyes wide with fright, her back against the sink and raised the cleaver in front of her like a shield.

"What are you talking about, Álvarez? Are you mad? You will have no one. Get out of here and get back to your cabin." Alicia spoke slowly and deliberately, hoping that only she could hear the fear hiding behind her words.

Without speaking, Álvarez lowered the Mauser towards Alicia. As he did, Doña Juana flung the cleaver at him. It was too heavy for her and it clattered harmlessly to the floor at his feet. Enraged, he advanced on her, flinging the table aside. The children cowered back against the wall. Alicia stood to one side, clutching Ángel to her body. Doña Juana dropped to her knees, covering her head with her hands, whimpering, "Oh Señora, help me. Please God, help me."

Álvarez grabbed her long braid and pulled her head back savagely. With his free hand, he rammed the muzzle of the Mauser into her exposed throat. He looked directly at Alicia. "She will come with me, Señora," he spat the words out, "or she will die."

Doña Juana was gulping for air, her eyes rolling back in her head, hysterical with fear. Alicia looked at Álvarez. His eyes were bright with madness. She knew now that she could never control him. "Now, Señora!" he rasped as he jammed the rifle barrel harder into Doña Juana's neck, making her cry out in pain.

"Go with him, Doña Juana," Alicia spoke quietly, looking directly at her, imploring her to see reason.

"Señora, no!" Doña Juana half screamed, half sobbed. "No!"

"He will kill you unless you go, Doña Juana. Go with him."

"You are very wise, Señora," Álvarez sneered.

"Señora, no!" It was the cry of a small child.

"God will protect you Doña Juana," whispered Alicia.

Álvarez dragged Doña Juana to her feet by her braid and pulled her from the room, laughing.

"Your white God is not here, Señora. There is only me. I am God now."

CHAPTER 28

The boobies were easy to kill. The clumsy birds made no attempt to escape. It was a simple matter to club them as they sat on their nests on the beach. The two women squatted on the sand in their blood-stained dresses made of old flour sacks and curtains. In ropes at their waists were long, sharp knives from the kitchen. In front of them were a dozen dead birds. Alicia, her long hair matted and tangled, picked one up and began plucking it.

"Poor Doña Juana. It makes me sick to think of what he has been doing to her all this time. He is an animal," said Tirza.

Alicia paused, a bird in her hand. "We have to find a way to stop him."

"If he tried to take me, I would kill him."

"How would you kill him? He has all the guns," said Alicia.

Tirza took her club and smashed it down on a crab that had begun to probe one of the birds. Immediately, other crabs scuttled toward it. "Like that, Señora. If I had the chance, I would kill him like that. Or I would stab him. Or strangle him."

"He is a big man, Tirza, and very strong. Perhaps we could poison him."

"With what?"

"I do not know. Perhaps there is something left in Ramón's medicine chest. I will look tonight."

"Then we would have to get him to take the poison."

Alicia sighed with frustration. "I know, I know. We have to think of something."

They scrubbed their clothes with sand and washed their bodies with the second-last bar of Ivory soap. The last bar was to be saved for the day they were rescued. Their clothes, now little more than rags, were laid to dry over rocks along the edge of the lagoon. The water in the lagoon was almost as warm as a bath. There was no longer any place in their lives for modesty; they all sat together, naked, in the water, the children splashing and playing, the women speaking together in low tones. They had all grown thinner but the purple patches on their legs and the swelling in their knees had almost disappeared now that there were fewer people to share the coconuts. Alicia sat behind Altagracia, cutting her hair. Altagracia sobbed quietly. "You can grow it back silly girl," Alicia laughed as she cut. "Look, it is all snarled. We all have to have our hair cut off. When I am done, you can cut mine."

Rosalía chased the two Irra boys behind the women, splashing them. "Take care!" yelled María. Rosalía threw a glance over her shoulder and, laughing, continued to chase the boys through the shallows. Tirza, gently washing a struggling Lupita, smiled. "It is good to see the children laugh and play."

"Doña Alicia! Doña Alicia!" called out Rosalía, with the two Irra boys at her side, staring into the lagoon.

"What is it, Rosalía?" cried María. "Don't bother the Señora, she is busy."

"Doña Alicia, come, come!" Rosalía's voice had an edge of panic in it.

Alicia gave a rueful smile and got up, handing Altagracia the scissors. She saw the look on Rosalía's face and strode quickly up the sand to where the girl stood, her arms folded tightly across her chest, staring and shivering. In front of her, floating just below the surface of the lagoon, lay the body of Doña Juana, her eye sockets empty, her face bleached white, her long braid waving slowly in the water beside her.

They could hear the children over the rise, stealing birds' eggs under Rosalía's direction. Collecting eggs had become the children's job and Rosalía had turned it into a game for the little ones. Alicia, Tirza, María and Altagracia sat side by side on a log. On the sand in front of them were scores of fish they had caught from the wharf. Each woman had her knife and they were systematically gutting and splitting the fish to be hung up and dried. "Once these are dry, we will take them into the house. Then we will have food if we are trapped indoors by another hurricane," said Alicia, throwing another split fish on the pile

The sudden crack of a rifle shot shocked the women into silence. It echoed back from the Rock and then there was another shot. They saw a small pig crumple several hundred meters up the beach. Álvarez walked toward the pig, the rifle in his hands. "Mother of God, he is coming," cried María.

Alicia stood up, putting her knife into the rope around her waist. "All of you, get Rosalía and the children and take everyone into the house. I am going to talk to him."

"No Señora, he will kill you," pleaded Altagracia.

"He will not dare kill me. Now go, all of you." Alicia began to walk across the sand toward Álvarez.

Álvarez walked up to where the pig lay twitching on the sand. He could see Doña Alicia walking toward him and the other women running away. He smirked and laughed to himself. There was nowhere to run on this island. There was no escape. He knelt down by the pig and, taking his bayonet, slit open its belly in a single motion. The animal's intestines spilled across the sand. From the corner of his eye he watched Alicia approach, noting the knife at her waist.

She stopped and watched. He seemed to have suffered not at all from the lack of food. His shoulders and arms rippled with power as he finished gutting the pig. The Mauser lay on the sand at his side but she couldn't possibly get to it quickly enough. She thought of the knife at her waist, but Álvarez had his bayonet in his hand. He would gut her like the pig. "Álvarez," she said, struggling to keep her voice steady.

He looked up slowly, his face gleaming with sweat. "Good afternoon, Doña Alicia." He smiled. "Would you like some of this pig?"

Alicia hesitated, then spoke, "You have murdered Doña Juana. How could you do such a thing? Have you gone mad?"

Picking up his rifle, Álvarez rose to his full height, towering over Alicia. "She would not be as a wife should be."

"She was not your wife," hissed Alicia.

"She would have made a good wife. It is a pity."

"You are mad."

Álvarez looked Alicia directly in the eye. "I am not mad. I am king of this island. I take what I want. If I want a woman to be my wife, I take her."

Alicia's breath was coming faster. "Leave us alone. If you come near us again, we will kill you."

Álvarez snorted contemptuously and knelt down beside the pig again, deliberately turning his back on Alicia. Her fingertips were on the handle of her knife but she knew he was waiting for her. She could see him, tensed, ready. Alicia turned and slowly walked back around the lagoon to her house.

The iron cauldron bubbled as the driftwood fire burned furiously. Tirza skimmed off the oil on the surface, ladling it into an old ten liter can. The children had found the dead shark washed up on the beach before the crabs and gulls had eaten it. It was a hammerhead, at least four meters long. The liver had weighed well over fifty kilos and they were rendering it for oil for the lamps. They would have light for months. Tirza ducked and gasped as a breeze blew the stink of the boiling liver into her face.

María came out of the house carrying two cups. Giving one to Tirza, she sat on the log. Tirza sat beside her. "Coconut shell tea," sighed Tirza. "I would give the world for a cup of coffee."

"Yes, but Doña Alicia says this is good for us."

"Perhaps it is. I don't know María, I am just so tired of all this. Do you have any shoes or sandals left?"

María laughed. "No. And Rosalía's wore out months ago. I tried to cut down a pair of Luis' boots but they don't fit. Do you want them?"

Tirza shook her head and lifted one foot, wide and heavily callused. "My feet are like leather. I cannot feel the heat of the sand. I left my last pair of boots outside months ago. The crabs ate them. In the morning, there was nothing left but the buckles."

The two women sat quietly for a moment, drinking their tea. María leaned toward Tirza. "What do you think Álvarez will do now? Will he kill us all?"

"I think he will try. He knows that if any of us leave here alive, he will surely be executed."

"What are we going to do, Tirza?"

"We must kill him. We have to kill him."

Alicia came running back up the stairs, breathless. "Has anyone seen Altagracia?" she panted. "No Doña Alicia," came the half-awake replies. Alicia opened the doors and looked into each of the bedrooms on the upper floor and then went back downstairs. The canvas on the window of Altagracia's room had been torn from the nails holding it in place. The mattress was pushed halfway off her bed and her one sheet, her only remaining item of bedding, was gone. The main door that had been bolted on the inside was unlocked. Alicia sank down on Altagracia's bed and put her head into her hands and wept. Álvarez. The bastard.

He had taken her from her bed with a knife at her throat and dragged her half-naked, clutching her sheet, the two kilometers to his cabin at the base of the Rock. He had hit her repeatedly when she pulled back or fell. Both her eyes were swollen and drops of blood flecked the sheet. The more she cried, the more he hit her. She lay in a corner on the floor of the cabin, her body drawn into itself, trying to hide under the sheet, making no sound, wildly hoping that if she made herself small enough he would forget she was there. The cabin was small, no more than four meters in each direction. Álvarez sat at a rough wooden table near the door, drinking the vinegary red wine from the Nokomis.

She looked around. The walls were solid, heavy timber. The cabin had been built to survive any storm. There were two tiny windows, high up. She knew that both had heavy wooden shutters outside that could be drawn closed and locked from the inside. The place was filthy and stank like Álvarez. Against one wall was a low bed; grimy bedclothes lying half on the rough wooden floor. She shuddered. The door was made of heavy planks with a big, old fashioned iron lock. Next to the door was the gun rack. The *soldados'* Mausers were in it, an iron bar drawn through their trigger guards and locked. Of the pistols and bayonets, she could see nothing; they must be in the other cabin, where the oil for the light was kept.

Álvarez slouched at the table, one hand on the wine bottle. In front of him, on the table, lay two big iron keys tied to a leather thong. They must be the keys to the doors of the two cabins. If only he would fall asleep. She slowly sat up, her heart beating fast, trying to make no sound. The light gleaming through the windows gradually turned orange and Altagracia knew it would soon be dark. If only she could escape, he would never find her in the darkness. She would rather face the crabs than him. Perhaps, if she had the keys, she could get a pistol from the other cabin.

His head fell forward onto the table but he didn't wake. He lay there snoring, his outstretched hand clutching the wine bottle. Altagracia stayed still for what seemed like hours. It was getting darker. She must move now. Soon, she would be unable to see anything in the dark cabin. She stood slowly, wrapped the sheet tightly around herself, and made her way toward the table, treading carefully, wary of making the floorboards squeak. In the growing darkness, she could barely make out the key in front of him. With excruciating slowness, she reached out and picked it up. She held it in her hand. But the thong ran under Álvarez's arm and hand. She pulled at it carefully. He moved slightly and grunted. She held perfectly still, her heart pounding, her breathing tortured. Surely, he could hear her heart. She pulled again, slowly and gently.

Álvarez was awake and on his feet at astonishing speed for so big a man. The thong had been wrapped around his hand. He yanked the keys from Altagracia. "So, you would leave your Victoriano!" he sneered. Altagracia could barely see him now in the deepening gloom, but she could smell the wine on his breath and the sour animal stink of his body. He reached out and held her arm. His breath rasped. "There is no escape. I am the master of this island."

"No!" Altagracia screamed, fighting off his grip. She felt his enormous power as he tightened his grip on her arm. He laughed at the blows she rained on his face and chest. They had no effect at all. He crushed her to him. She struggled, but he simply held her all the tighter.

"How about a kiss for Victoriano?" He forced his face against hers, prying her mouth open. His breath reeked of wine. The heavy bristles on his face cut into Altagracia's skin. She thought for a second that she would bite his tongue off, but she knew that then he would certainly kill her. It writhed around inside her mouth and all she could think of was a foul, disgusting snake. He flung her backwards onto the floor and stood over her in the darkness. She heard his belt fall onto the floor and heard the rustle as he dropped his heavy sailcloth trousers. The rank smell of his body came even more strongly. He squatted down on her hips and grasping her sheet, tore it aside.

Altagracia lay there, paralyzed, feeling his weight crushing her hips into the hard floor and his rough hands mauling her, pulling painfully at her nipples. She was beyond crying out. She was a rabbit frozen with terror. She was long past resistance. He got to his knees and ripped the remnants of the sheet away. She was twenty years old. She had never had a man. She had never kissed a man, unless you counted the quick kisses on the cheek the braver *soldados* stole. One day, she wanted to give herself to her husband. In her daydreams, it was someone like Capitán Arnaud, someone elegant, refined, distinguished.

Álvarez's thick, dirty fingers were deep inside her now, probing. Strangled whimpers escaped from her. Her chest was so tight, she had almost stopped breathing. She could barely feel the roughness of his hands or smell him or hear his animal grunting.

Someone like Capitán Arnaud. Someone who would brush the back of her hand with kisses and bring her chocolates and beautiful presents from the French stores in México, like the Capitán had brought for Doña Alicia.

He forced himself into her. Even though her mind was past resistance, her body was not. Her muscles tightened to keep him out. It seemed to excite him all the more. He rammed into her, tearing her, the rough planking of the floor gouging her back. She couldn't feel the pain. His face was directly over hers, his saliva dripping onto her face, his breath coming in rapid grunts. He held her wrists down hard against the planking, forcing himself all the way into her.

Someone who would hold her with tenderness and touch her gently and lovingly. Someone who would love her and protect her. Her hands had gone numb. He drove into her, his flesh making an obscene slapping sound against her body. It was a dream. She was sitting somewhere high, looking down, watching it happen to a stranger and not caring.

His thrusts grew faster and more powerful until, suddenly, he went rigid, squeezing Altagracia's wrists so tightly she thought they might break. His back arched and he let out a series of small grunts then suddenly collapsed on her. He stank. He was heavy and his weight was crushing her. She could scarcely breathe. Perhaps it would be best to stop breathing. Perhaps it would be best never to breathe again. Then, he rolled off her and onto the floor beside her. Altagracia lay still.

Álvarez's breathing became heavy and regular and he began to snore. She rolled away and brought her knees up under her chin, locking her arms around them. She felt nothing but a terrifying emptiness. Whoever this nightmare was happening to, it could not be her.

CHAPTER 29

Félix Rovira slouched in his seat in a state of misery that seemed to crush his very heart. The other occupant of the first-class compartment, a smartly dressed young woman traveling alone, looked at Rovira and quickly averted her eyes. Her disgust at the sight of the unshaven and obviously drunken old man was tempered somewhat by a tinge of pity. Judging by his clothes, he had probably once been a man of substance.

The rhythmic clicking of the train's wheels was like a cruel metronome counting off every agonizing second of time in a world without Alicia. At least before, there had been hope. Now, there was none. Since the defeat of Villa and Zapata, he had written letter after letter to Carranza's government, asking about the fate of the garrison on Clipperton Island. Eight letters, ten, twelve, what did it matter? They had all gone unanswered. Finally, in desperation, he had taken the train to México to find out for himself. He had left his hotel early every morning for more than a week to arrive at the Ministry of War before the offices opened. Finally, he had been able to persuade a surly clerk to make an appointment for him with a low level functionary who could answer his questions about the garrison.

He had had to wait two days until the appointment. Both mornings he walked from his modest hotel to spend the day in quiet anguish beneath the trees in the Alameda. Each day, he stopped and sat in the park trying to remember what it had been like before the Revolution. It was a blur. It was too long ago. Too much had happened. The second morning, he had met Liliana Hernández, dressed in black and walking a small tan-colored dog in the Park. He recognized her immediately, in spite of her widow's weeds. They sat together on a bench and she had blurted out that Miguel had been absorbed into Obregón's army for the final fight against Villa, along with the other remnants of the *federales*. He had died at Ceyala, only hours before Villa's defeat. In her grief, she hadn't even asked after Ramón and Alicia. Rovira, fearing the worst, couldn't bring himself to tell her that he had heard nothing from his daughter for almost a year.

As Rovira walked along the dreary hallway to the office deep within what was now Presidente Carranza's Ministry of War, he wiped his hands on his trousers. He stopped and took a deep breath before continuing. Surely, they knew who he was. He had been a friend to Porfirio Díaz for almost two decades. They must know. No matter. If they were going to do anything to him, they would have done it before now. He had already been in México for ten days.

He looked at the brass nameplate and entered the anteroom. There was an empty desk, half-buried beneath an avalanche of paper, in front of the door leading to the inner office. Through the frosted glass in the door, Rovira could see a silhouette moving back and forth. On the dirty floor of the anteroom, a dented brass spittoon leaned drunkenly against an old umbrella stand. Rovira took one of the two leather seats against the wall. He was about to consult his pocket watch when the inner door opened and a small ferret-like man with hair slicked back peered out.

"Señor Rovira?" he asked, raising an eyebrow.

"Yes. And you are Señor Vega?"

"At your service, Señor. Please come in."

Rovira entered the inner office. A green-shaded electric lamp glowed on the dark, cluttered desk. Along one wall were files stacked like bricks, bound with green and red ribbon. Vega gestured toward the chair in front of the desk. "Please have a seat, Señor Rovira. I understand you are interested in Clipperton Island."

Rovira leaned forward in his chair. "Yes, Señor. My daughter is the wife of the *gobernador*, Capitán Ramón Arnaud."

Vega made a tent of his fingers and studied Rovira through them. "Ah, yes, I have been making some inquiries. I believe Capitán Arnaud's father was well known for his support of Porfirio Díaz and, of course, Capitán Arnaud was promoted from *teniente* by General Huerta. I have been informed that Capitán Arnaud was a great favorite of Abelardo Avalos, another well-known supporter of Presidente Díaz." He clucked his disapproval. "And you, Señor Rovira, I understand that you too were a supporter of our former president. Is that not correct?"

Rovira hesitated. There was no point lying. This man obviously knew everything. He said, "Yes, Señor Vega. That is correct."

Vega gave Rovira an ingratiating smile. "Of course, these things do not concern us now. Presidente Carranza is, as you know, devoted to building a strong, democratic nation, based upon sound constitutional principles, not with stirring up the animosities of the past."

"Most commendable," remarked Rovira shortly. "Now about my daughter, Señor."

Vega assumed a distressed expression. "Brace yourself for a terrible shock, Señor Rovira. It is my unhappy duty to inform you that the entire garrison on Clipperton Island perished many months ago."

Rovira felt the blood drain from his face. His heart hammered wildly in his chest. It was a full minute before he could trust himself to speak. "But when did you learn this? Why were my letters to the Ministry never answered?"

"Ah, but these are difficult times, Señor Rovira," said Vega. "We have had a number of reports from ships passing the island over the past six months. The navigation light is extinguished. There is no sign of life. As you can appreciate, there has been some confusion within the government in recent times. My clerk was able to find your letters only yesterday. But, there can be no doubt of the situation. All members of the garrison are dead." Vega patted a thick manila folder. "Please accept my heartfelt sympathy."

Rovira had watched Vega mouthing the words as though behind a window. The ferret-like face dissolved into a blur and Rovira rushed from the office. Oblivion had come much later that night in the back of the carriage he had hired to take him from the grimy little *cantina* to his hotel. As he lay across the seat of the carriage, stinking of drink, he remembered the night that he and Alicia had ridden home from the ball where she had met Ramón. He had told her then that one day she must leave him. But not like this, he thought, please God, not like this.

CHAPTER 30

Tirza spooned the last of the scrambled booby eggs onto a plate and gave it to Rosalía. The girl nodded her thanks and went to sit with the other children at the table. Alicia sat beside them, feeding Ángel. Ramoncito stopped eating and looked at Alicia. "Mamá, when is Alta coming back?" he asked.

Alicia closed her eyes and paused before answering. "I hope she will be back soon, Ramoncito."

"I miss her, Mamá. Why did she go?"

Alicia reached over the table and stroked his hair. "I know you miss her, little one. We all do. Alta had work to do at *la roca*. She will come back as soon as she has finished." Alicia met Tirza's eyes and looked away. "Now all you children, out of the house. See how much driftwood you can collect by lunch time."

As Rosalía herded the last of the children out of the door, María said, "The children's clothes are falling apart. That is Rosalía's last dress. I made it from the curtain you gave me, Doña Alicia. Everything wears out so quickly on the sand."

Tirza plucked at the front of her tattered shift, made from an old tablecloth. "I have only this and one more I made from canvas."

Alicia nodded. "All our clothes are falling apart. I have this one," she said stretching the coarse sailcloth from the Nokomis between her hands, "and one good dress left. I have cut the others down for the children. We each must save one dress and something for each of the children to wear when a ship comes."

"Señora, we will have to go naked if we are going to save

281

anything at all. Everything is wearing out. The meal sacks are all gone," said Tirza.

Alicia nodded, "Yes, I know. Does it really matter, now? We all bathe together."

"Not to us, Señora," said María. "But what about Álvarez?"

"There is nothing we can do about it, María," replied Alicia. "And Álvarez only comes over here once every few months. We will just have to watch for him. And each of us should always carry a knife."

"Doña Alicia, do you really think Álvarez will let Altagracia go? He will kill her just like he killed Doña Juana," said Tirza.

Alicia paused before replying. "I do not know, Tirza. Perhaps if she does not resist him, she will live." The three women sat silently, finishing their food.

"Today," said Alicia when she had finished eating, "I want you two to move upstairs. You can share my room. I will sleep downstairs in Altagracia's room."

"But why, Doña Alicia?" asked Tirza. "We would all be safer upstairs together. He will come through the window for you just as he did for Altagracia."

"No, he will not dare to touch me. If I am downstairs and he comes, I may be able to stop him taking one of you."

As Tirza and María moved their few possessions upstairs into her bedroom, Alicia opened the door of the wardrobe. There was Ramón's dress uniform, his helmet with the golden eagle, his high leather boots, his belt. It was all growing dull with mold. Beside Ramón's things was her last remaining dress. These were to have been the clothes they would wear when the Tampico finally arrived. She reached out and touched Ramón's tunic, feeling the weight of the fine fabric. She had cut up all of their other clothes to make things for the children but she couldn't bring herself to desecrate Ramón's dress uniform.

The children walked along the beach, small bundles of driftwood under their arms. The three older Arnaud children were tanned brown from head to foot, their hair bleached almost blond by the sun. The two Irra boys and Rosalía had turned almost black. Ahead, a moray shot from the water and seized a crab. Unconcerned, the children stood still and watched until the moray slithered back into the water with the crab in its jaws. They knew enough to keep their distance from the water's edge. They continued to walk, stooping from time to time to pick up wood. They stopped near the cisterns, opened the tap near the bottom of one and took turns drinking. Antonio Irra climbed onto the top of a cistern. Beside the light on top of *la roca,* Álvarez lay stretched out, watching the children through his telescope.

The constant calling of the seabirds faded away and the air suddenly felt cool against their bare skin. A light rain began to fall. There was no wind and the rain fell more and more heavily on the mirror-smooth surface of the lagoon, bouncing high, as though hitting a hot griddle. The rain fell more heavily still. The children could feel the pressure of it on their shoulders and on the tops of their heads, almost pushing their feet into the sand. Rosalía lifted Antonio off the top of the cistern.

The rain became a deluge. They could see nothing. Rosalía pulled the smaller children toward herself and they crouched, huddled together, in the sand beside the cistern, shivering. The tumult of the rain eased and the wind began to blow. Rosalía stood and looked over the top of the cistern, seaward. On the other side of the reef, two waterspouts were writhing, as though dancing together. Rosalía dropped quickly and pushed the other children flat onto the sand. The wind rose and began to scream. Behind the cistern, the children were protected from its full fury and from the spray being blown across the beach from the sea. Down the beach from them, the heads of the palm trees streamed horizontally in the wind.

As suddenly as it had begun, the wind dropped. A last few drops of rain fell. Rosalía got to her knees and looked over the edge of the cistern. The waterspouts had disappeared. A rainbow arched over the sea. She picked up some of the driftwood and got up, laughing. She pulled the other children to their feet and cried, "Quick. Pick up your wood. I will race you to the house. Then, we will dig for treasure."

The three women sat together at the end of the wharf, the sea surging gently around the pilings below them, their fishing poles extended out over the water. From the ruins of the guano shed behind them came the sound of the children playing. The sky was cloudless, the air pleasantly warm and the sun felt good on their bare bodies. The fish they had caught lay on the wharf beside them. They had run out of fish hooks long ago, taken by barracuda and other fish too large to land. Now, they fashioned strong hooks from the wire handles of old oil cans.

Three kilometers away, near the base of the Rock, Altagracia squatted by a fire in the sand, roasting a booby skewered on a stick. The fat dripping into the fire smelled like burning fish. She was filthy, covered in an amalgam of sweat, soot and coral dust. There were bruises on her face and around her upper arms. Both of her breasts were covered in bite marks. Her eyes were listless and vacant.

Twice, she had tried to escape and twice he had brought her back. The second time, he had padlocked a chain around her ankle and chained her to an iron ring in the side of the cabin. He had kept her there for two days and nights. He had raped her repeatedly in the sand, still chained, and then left her each night for the crabs. She had had to stay awake all night to keep them off her body in the dark. She had begged to be allowed back into the cabin with him.

On top of *la roca*, Álvarez lay beside the light with his telescope trained toward the wharf. He could see the backs of the women sitting on the end of the wharf. They stood and picked something up. It must be fish. They walked down the wharf toward the guano shed. Álvarez could see clearly that they were naked. They reached the end of the wharf and a group of children came out of the shed. They took the fish from the women and went toward the houses. The Señora and the others turned and walked along the beach toward the cisterns, coming toward *la roca*.

Since the women and children had stopped wearing clothing, Álvarez spent hours at the top of the Rock watching them through his telescope. Today was the best he had seen, all three women were walking along the beach, facing him. He moved the telescope over them as they walked. Looked at their unsuspecting faces as they talked. Stared at their breasts, their thighs, at the dark triangles between their legs. He saw that each woman had a rope around her waist with a knife hanging from it. He laughed out loud.

By the feeble glow of the single oil lamp, Alicia made a mark through the day on her homemade calendar; December 25, 1915. Christmas. She hadn't even bothered to tell the others it was Christmas. There were no presents, no chocolate, nothing for a *banquete*. Why get the children excited for nothing? Dates meant nothing to them. She gently closed the book she had made into a calendar. It was Ramón's day book. Beautiful, bound in morocco leather, given to him by his sister. Alicia had counted the days. Seven hundred and thirty-four days since they had left Acapulco for the last time. Five hundred and forty-nine days since the Cleveland had left. Two hundred and seventeen days since Ramón had died. Two hundred and seventeen days and interminable nights. Alicia shivered and wrapped the curtain around herself more tightly.

She jumped at a sudden pounding on the door. Alicia's heart turned cold. He must have killed Altagracia. Who would he take this time? Trying to hold the curtain around herself, she took her knife from the rope around her waist and walked cautiously through the house. Peering through a gap in the sailcloth covering a window, Alicia saw Altagracia standing at the door. Álvarez was nowhere in sight.

She unlocked the door. Altagracia stood naked and filthy on the step. "Doña Alicia, he told me to leave. He would not let me stay in the cabin any more. He made me leave." Her voice was piteous, her eyes pathetic and blank.

Alicia's heart sank. "Mother of God. Poor Alta. Here," said Alicia, taking the curtain from her shoulders and wrapping it around Altagracia. She put her arm around Altagracia and led her into the house.

"She barely speaks," said María, stooping to pick up a piece of driftwood. "What did that bastard do to her?"

"I do not know," replied Tirza.

"Why does he do this to us?"

"He is a madman, María." Tirza dropped her load of wood near the pile for the signal fire.

María dropped hers and turned back along the beach for more. "I could not stand to have him touch me. I would rather die than let that animal touch me."

Tirza said nothing and kept walking beside María, stopping occasionally to pick up driftwood.

"Look," cried María, "What is that?"

The two women walked up to the object washing back and forth at the water's edge. It was a glass ball of cobalt blue, the size of a big coconut, wrapped in coarse netting. "A Japanese fishing float," Tirza said.

"How could it have come all the way from Japan?" asked María. "It would have been smashed by the sea."

Putting down her wood, Tirza picked the float up, turning it around and around in her hands. She knew that Japan was almost on the other side of the world. This fragile ball of glass, that would shatter if she dropped it onto the coral debris of the beach, had traveled across the full width of the Pacific, thrown about for years by towering waves, blasted by hurricanes. And yet, it had survived and found its way here.

"It survives," she said, "because it yields to the sea." The dark glass gleamed in her hands.

They roamed the beach through the nesting boobies. Thousands of rough nests made of palm fronds, bits of wood and pebbles littered the beach. Overhead, the frigate birds rode the wind, dropping to steal fish from unlucky boobies as they returned from beyond the reef to feed their chicks. Many of the nests still contained a single unhatched egg, diligently watched over by a booby parent. They had already collected several dozen eggs. Rosalía's hand bore the marks of the boobies' bills. Tirza and María carried the eggs in wire baskets. Alicia stooped over, pushing an enraged bird off its nest with a stick so Rosalía could take its eggs. The smaller children gathered driftwood out of sight, around the curve of the beach.

"You, María Nava, you will come with me!" Álvarez's voice boomed out from the rise of land behind them. She raised her eyes toward him. The others stood absolutely still. Álvarez advanced on María. "Come with me! Now!"

"You pig!" María spat the words at him. "Never!" She pulled her knife from the rope around her waist and held it in front of herself uncertainly. Álvarez moved towards her. In the silence, they could hear the broken coral on the beach being ground beneath his boots. He drew closer and she made a weak slash at him with her knife. He avoided it easily and grabbed her wrist, crushing it, shaking the knife loose.

"Come!" Álvarez squeezed María's arm until she cried out in pain.

"No!" Her eyes bright with fear, she screamed and frantically kicked at his legs.

It had no effect. Still holding her wrist, Álvarez struck her across the face viciously. She sagged toward the ground and he struck her again before letting her fall. Rosalía ran to her mother, hammering Álvarez's back with her fists, screaming, "Leave her alone! Leave my mother alone!" Álvarez turned and flung Rosalía away as though she weighed nothing, sending her rolling across the sand.

Álvarez stood over María, menacing her. The pistol hung carelessly at his hip, the bandoliers crisscrossing his chest. He looked gigantic towering over her. María sat in the dust at his feet. Blood seeped from the split skin over her cheekbone and dribbled down her chin. She sat in the sand, trembling, pitiful, naked. Álvarez reached down slowly and took hold of her shorn hair, forcing her head backwards. He leaned over until his face was almost touching hers. "You will come with me," he hissed. She spat full in his face. For a moment he stopped, stunned. Then he loosened his grip. María fell backwards onto the ground, leaning on her elbows, staring up at him. Wordlessly, he drew his pistol from its holster. Raising the gun, he sighted carefully along the barrel and pulled the trigger. When the report came, it sounded too muted to be real. A crimson stain mushroomed across María's left breast. She fell backwards into the coral dust, her eyes wide in surprise.

Rosalía fell to her knees beside her mother's body. "Mamá, Mamá," she screamed, burying her head against her mother's face, her arm across the growing stain on María's body.

"What have you done? Bastard! You will die for this. Bastard! Bastard!" Alicia's voice shook with rage, her body trembling.

Álvarez pointed the pistol at Alicia and smiled, slowly looking her up and down. "If a ship comes, I will kill you all. Who will there be to tell the tale?"

Rosalía continued to sob uncontrollably, pulling frantically at her mother's body, as though she could shake her back to life. Tirza stood nearby, staring in disbelief, then began to scream obscenities at Álvarez. He calmly raised the gun, pushing the muzzle hard into Tirza's face until she stopped. He looked down at Rosalía clinging to her mother's bloodied body, nudging her with his toe. "You, girl, you will come in place of your mother."

"Álvarez, no!" Alicia screamed hysterically, moving towards him. "Mother of God, she is a child. Take one of us."

Álvarez spoke slowly and menacingly. "I am the king of this island. I take whatever woman I want."

"She is not a woman. She is a child. Look at her," Alicia almost sobbed.

Álvarez looked appreciatively at Rosalía, lying across her mother's body, her eyes wide with terror. She was the size of a ten-year-old. Her slim, boyish body was just beginning to bud. He licked his lips and smiled. "She will make me a fine little wife." He reached down and, taking hold of Rosalía's upper arm, pulled her away from María's body, lifting her completely off the ground with one hand. Instinctively, Alicia moved forward, her hand on her knife. Álvarez put the gun to the side of Rosalía's head. "Stay back Señora or I will kill her."

Rosalía began to kick and struggle, screaming incoherently. Álvarez shook her like a terrier with a rat. He gestured to Maria's body with the gun. "Bury that one, before the crabs eat her." Then he dragged Rosalía off the beach, walking backwards, keeping the gun trained on Alicia. They could hear Rosalía's screams until Álvarez had dragged her halfway to the Rock.

Tirza seemed dazed. "Mother of God, he will kill us all."

Alicia stood trembling with rage. "We will make him pay. We will make him pay for this. We will make him pay for everything. Now help me, we must bury María before nightfall. We cannot get her to the graveyard, we must bury her among the coconut palms." They dragged María's body off the beach and into the coconut grove. The air was very still. The birds had finished their feeding and neither woman could trust herself to speak. The silence was broken only by the sound of the shovel grating in the rough coral debris. They took turns until the hole was deep enough to discourage the crabs from digging for María's body. Digging in the coarse, rocky sand exhausted them. Their sweat ran down through the coral dust caking their faces. They sat together and rested at the edge of the grave, María's body lay behind them. Her blood had turned a dark brown. The sun had just gone down. They would have to hurry, soon it would be dark and the crabs would begin to move.

A long, thin, high pitched scream came across the lagoon on the dead stillness of the air. A few seconds later, it came again. Then, there was silence.

CHAPTER 31

Alicia sat at the dining room table with Ramoncito and Ali and Francisco Irra. She watched them as they bent over their papers, writing. Soon, they would be out of ink. Perhaps gulls' blood would work or soot from the lamps, mixed with fish oil. She would think of something. The children were completely unselfconscious, sitting together naked at the table, doing their lessons, as through it were the most natural thing in the world. They had become almost like savages; their skin dark, their feet like leather, running around the island clubbing birds for food, stealing their eggs, walking for kilometers along the beach, picking up driftwood.

Alicia smiled to herself. That description fit her too. It fit all of them. Imagine if anyone from her old life could see her now; a naked savage, her hair cut to nothing, her skin dark from the sun, a knife at her waist. It was unbelievable. She smiled again and ran the tips of her fingers down her throat to play with her locket. A moment of fright as her fingers missed it. It was gone. Alicia looked around in panic. It was not in her lap, not on the table, not on the floor.

Tears welled up, choking her. She couldn't lose her locket. It was a part of Ramón she had with her every minute. She thought frantically of the last time she remembered touching it. Yesterday, at the capstan. She had carried Ángel along the beach looking for a shark or dolphin washed ashore to render for lamp oil. She had stopped to rest at the capstan, putting Ángel down in the sand to play. She had leaned against the capstan and opened the locket, looking at the miniatures of Ramón and herself; the two of them so young, so full of love and hope. Then she had closed the locket and picked Ángel up to carry him home. She remembered ignoring a little tug around her neck as she had picked him up. She must have broken the chain.

Telling the children to finish their lesson, she ran from the house, slamming the door behind herself. Tirza and Altagracia were splitting and hanging fish to dry in front of the house. Tirza called out, but Alicia waved her off and ran down the beach toward the capstan. Starting on the seaward side, where she remembered standing, she got on her hands and knees and began sifting the coral sand through her fingers. She couldn't find it. She grew frantic and began digging with her hands, tears of frustration welling up.

From *la roca*, Álvarez watched Alicia through his telescope as she crawled back and forth for hours scrabbling desperately in the sand.

"Look, the birds are leaving," said Tirza as they walked back from the coconut grove. Ahead of them, to the west, the sky was almost black with boobies and terns.

"There must be a hurricane coming," said Alicia. "We must get everything ready. Is there plenty of dried fish in the cellar?"

Tirza nodded. "Yes, Señora."

"Alta, get the children and collect some eggs, boil them and put them in the cellar. Do we have enough oil for the lamps?"

"Yes, Señora."

"We probably have until tomorrow before the hurricane is here. The birds usually leave at least a day before the storm, but we will get everything ready by nightfall."

They had laid planks on the earthen floor of the cellar so they would remain dry as the waves began to drive up the beach and saturate the sand. They had passed four storms in the cellar and, with each storm, they had made improvements. Now they were dry, had food to last for days, bottles of water from the cisterns, a few blankets to share and plenty of light. The children had come to see the times in the cellar as an adventure. In the glow of the oil lamps, they read to each other and talked as the wind and rain buffeted the house above them.

Alicia and Altagracia lay side-by-side on the planks, facing each other, sharing a blanket. "Doña Alicia?" whispered Altagracia.

"Yes, Alta," Alicia replied.

"He hurt me."

Alicia reached out and smoothed Altagracia's hair. "I know, Alta."

"He hurt me so much."

Alicia could think of nothing to say. She continued to stroke Altagracia's hair.

"Rosalía is so small. What will happen to her?" Altagracia whispered.

Alicia closed her eyes. The question had tormented her since Álvarez had taken Rosalía. What he had done to Altagracia was terrible, but what would happen to Rosalía was unimaginable. She was just a child, small for her age, her body not developed.

Álvarez was a massively built, powerful man. A man without feelings. A man without a soul.

Tirza walked slowly along the beach carrying a basket in one hand and holding Lupita's hand with the other. Like the others, Tirza had lost weight, but her body was still strong and lithe. She moved with the natural, athletic grace of the Yaqui. Her leg muscles rippled as she walked. The little girl jumped and squealed with delight as the waves washed up around her ankles. Out over the reef, Tirza could see a school of small sharks thrashing the water in a feeding frenzy. Near the capstan, she turned away from the sea toward the lagoon. Little snails lived along the lagoon's waterline and she would fill her basket with them to be steamed for lunch.

Looking across the lagoon, she saw Rosalía. Even though it was almost a kilometer and a half across the lagoon, Tirza knew it had to be her. The air was crystal clear. She was at least two kilometers away from the Rock and going the long way around to the settlement. Álvarez must have thrown her out, just as he had thrown out Altagracia. At least she was alive. She was moving very, very slowly. Soon it would be noon and the heat in the open would be unbearable.

Picking up Lupita, Tirza strode back along the beach to the house. Seeing the children doing their lessons at the table, she said, "Rosalía is on the other side of the lagoon, coming here. I am going to get her. Watch Lupita." Without waiting for an answer, she ran from the house and along the beach toward the guano shed. Near the track leading to the wharf, she stopped and looked across the lagoon. There was Rosalía, directly across the lagoon, standing still. Tirza began to run again, with a long, easy stride. Past the Egg Islands at the western end of the lagoon. Around the corner of the lagoon, with the surf booming on the reef a hundred meters offshore. Past the foundations of two old cabins on the north side of the island. Tirza's breath came easily, her body feeling strong and alive with the running. Ahead, along the strip of beach, she could see Rosalía, standing motionless, halfway between the sea and the lagoon.

Tirza stopped an arm's length away from the girl. She was naked and filthy, her face and body covered in coral dust and soot, streaked with grease from roasting birds. Rosalía's eyes were directed toward Tirza but they were lifeless. Tirza said softly, "Rosalía?" The girl continued to stare at her blankly. Tirza spoke again, "Rosalía? It is me, Tirza." Still, the girl didn't answer.

Tirza put her arm around Rosalía's shoulders and guided her toward the lagoon. "Here, Rosalía, we will sit down together in the water for a while and get clean." The girl offered no resistance as Tirza led her to the water. The two sat quietly in the warm water, side by side, Tirza holding Rosalía's hand in her lap. Tirza was almost afraid to look at Rosalía, imagining the horrors she must have endured, not knowing what to do or what to say. Suddenly, Rosalía began to cry. Huge, racking sobs that left her breathless. Tirza held Rosalía against her, feeling the girl's anguish. Rosalía cried desperately, gasping for air.

Tirza could feel the girl's tears falling on her skin and her own tears falling down her cheeks. She held Rosalía, whispering words of reassurance. When Rosalía was finally exhausted, her sobs subsided and the tension drained from her body. She sagged against Tirza and fell instantly asleep. Tirza held her until the sun began to go down. "Little one, wake up," said Tirza softly, stroking Rosalía's matted hair. Rosalía stirred. "We will make you clean and then go to the house." Rosalía stared dumbly at Tirza. "Lean back, little one," said Tirza, putting her arm behind Rosalía's neck. "I will wash your hair." She washed the coral dust out as well as she could, then washed Rosalía's face and forehead. "You are such a pretty girl with that dirt gone," said Tirza.

Tirza rubbed the grime from Rosalía's shoulders and chest. The girl screamed suddenly, piercingly. Tirza hesitated, then gently splashed water to rinse off the dirt. Bile rose in her throat. She swallowed it back, choking. "Mother of God," she gasped, "what has he done to you?" Where Rosalía's nipples had been, were livid craters of burned flesh.

Alicia and Altagracia sat beside each other, crying. Tirza stood in front of them, her body quaking with rage. "We must kill the bastard now!" she screamed. Alicia reached out to touch Tirza, but she backed away. "No! We must kill him now!" she screamed.

"Quiet, Tirza. You will wake her," Alicia pleaded.

Tirza glared at Alicia, then fell into a chair, her face distorted with rage.

Altagracia's voice was tiny. "How can we kill him? He has all the guns. He is so strong."

"I will find a way, Alta," said Tirza grimly. "I swear by all the Saints in Heaven, I will kill the bastard for this."

Rosalía began to cry. Tirza got up and climbed the stairs. They had put Rosalía in the big four poster bed that had been Alicia's. The girl lay on her side, crying forlornly. Tirza leaned over her. "It hurts, little one?" Rosalía nodded, sobbing. Tirza felt her own tears welling up. "Lie on your back, I will make it better," she said.

Tirza took a cut green coconut from the floor and scooped out cool jelly with her fingertips. With infinite care, she applied it to the burned flesh. Rosalía flinched, took a deep, shuddering breath and closed her eyes. The sight and smell of the burns made Tirza's stomach turn. When she was done, she lay down carefully beside Rosalía and held her, stroking her hair, until they both fell asleep

CHAPTER 32

The heat was stifling. Álvarez carefully eased the sailcloth away from the window frame with the tip of his bayonet and looked into the room, bathed in the white light of the full moon. Near the door, Angel slept in his crib, an arm dangling pinkly from between the bars. On the bed, Alicia lay asleep on her side. She stirred restlessly beneath the thin sheet, almost transparent with her sweat. Beads of sweat ran down her face and neck. Her breathing grew rapid, uneven. She shifted and breathed rhythmically again.

With infinite slowness, Álvarez lifted one leg over the windowsill, slowly putting his weight on it and then hoisted his body carefully through the opening. His chest was streaked with the blood of the gulls. His right arm hung at his side, the bayonet dangling from his fingertips.

He moved to the side of the bed and stood there, looking down. Alicia stirred in her sleep, rolling onto her back. Álvarez watched as the thin sheet covering her rose and fell with each breath. His own breath came more quickly as he traced the outline of her breast beneath the sheet with the tip of the bayonet. The sweat rolled down the back of his hand, dropping onto the sheet. Slowly, he lifted the edge of the sheet with the tip of the bayonet and very carefully pulled it back. Alicia's body glistened with sweat in the moonlight. She made a sound and stirred.

In a sudden move, Álvarez pushed the edge of the bayonet against her throat. Her eyes flew open and met his. She lay absolutely still. "Señora," Álvarez's voice was harsh and guttural, "you will never leave this island alive. If a ship comes, you will die. Like this." Making a horrible, gurgling sound,

Álvarez drew the bayonet in a light, rapid stroke across her throat and was gone.

Alicia lay on the bed, shaking, a thin red welt growing across her throat. Beside her, Ángel slept peacefully.

With the lightest possible touch, Tirza finished applying the coconut jelly to Rosalía's burns. They were healing, bright pink skin growing over the ravaged flesh. Against Rosalía's brown skin, the scar tissue stood out grotesquely. Rosalía watched every move Tirza made. Tirza looked up and saw a single tear welling at the corner of Rosalía's eye. Tirza knew it wasn't just the pain. Rosalía would carry the horror of what the monster had done to her for the rest of her life.

Alicia drove her spear down and pulled it up with a good-sized lobster wriggling on the end. Tirza stood in shallower water, watching carefully for sharks and morays. "That is enough, Señora, we have six," she called out. Alicia walked out of the water, using two hands to hold the spear. "A pity we have no olive oil for mayonnaise, Tirza."

Tirza walked out of the water and stood beside Alicia. She nodded her head toward the cisterns. "There is the bastard. He is coming this way."

As Álvarez approached, they could see he had the bandoliers crisscrossing his chest and the Mauser in his hands. "Mother of God, he is coming for one of us," said Alicia. She could feel her heart pounding wildly.

"Better one of us, than one of the children."

"Will this never end, Tirza?"

"We have to find a way to kill him, Señora."

"I know. If a ship comes, we will not be saved. He will kill us all as soon as he sees it. If he takes you, I will come to the Rock, to see if there is a way we can do it. If he takes me, you come."

"Señora, if he takes you, I will take care of your children. If he takes me, promise me that you will take care of Lupita and Rosalía."

Alicia squeezed Tirza's hand. "I promise it, Tirza."

Álvarez stopped in front of the two women, looking them up and down, in turn. He raised the rifle slightly in Tirza's direction. "You will come with me," he said, quietly.

Tirza stared at him for a moment. "I will come with you, but one day," she paused and spoke evenly, "I will kill you."

Álvarez threw his head back and laughed. Then, without a glance at either woman, he turned back to the Rock. Tirza looked at Alicia in resignation and followed behind him.

Alicia sat alone listening to the rain beating against the sailcloth stretched across the window openings. From time to time, the wind howled in the chimney, sucking sparks from the driftwood fire. Wrapped in an old green and gold curtain, she sat at the writing table, by the light of a single oil lamp. In front of her was her calendar. It was Christmas 1916 but, again, she had told no one. They had forgotten about Christmas. Methodically, she added up the days. A thousand and sixty-nine days since they had left Acapulco. Nine hundred and fourteen days since the *yanqui* ship Cleveland had left. Five hundred and eighty-two days since Ramón, Secundino and the others had died.

Alicia groaned and let her head sag. How much more could they endure? Little Ángel was almost two and he still couldn't walk. His little legs were terribly bowed and unable to take his weight. The other children seemed healthy enough but they were all small for their age. And poor Rosalía. Her scars had healed, but she was damaged in ways they could not imagine and she could not tell them. And now he had Tirza.

The longer they were trapped here with him, the older the children grew. He had taken Rosalía when she was only twelve. Who knew what he would do next? It was even possible that he might take one of the boys. On the rare occasions when Álvarez had come near the settlement, Alicia had thought she had seen him leering at the naked children, especially Francisco and Ali. Francisco was almost twelve now, small but attractive and wiry. His brother Antonio was six. Ramoncito was seven and a half. Ali was already six and a half. Olga was three and a half. Poor little Lupita, who couldn't understand where her mother had gone, would be two in a few weeks and Ángel was twenty months. They were all growing up.

Álvarez was the Devil incarnate. There was no limit to what he might do. There was absolutely no doubt that, if they remained trapped on this island long enough, at the very least, he would take the girls, all of them, one after the other, Ali, Olga, Lupita. It was unthinkable. They had to kill him.

There was no sign of Álvarez. The bastard was probably up on *la roca*, again, spying on the others with his telescope. Tirza pulled the half-roasted piglet off the fire. She straddled it and, aiming carefully, pissed on it noisily, making sure that she covered it all. The steam rose up, warm and satisfying against her legs. She bent down, turned the piglet over and pissed on the other side. She put it back over the fire, wrinkling her nose at the smell.

Álvarez, sitting on the step of his cabin, tore the last scrap of meat from the bone and chewed. He looked at the bone quizzically for a moment, then threw it away and sucked the grease from his fingers.

"Water," grunted Álvarez. Tirza looked at him for a moment, then got slowly to her feet. Picking up the enamel mug from the step, she walked around the side of the cabin to the Rock. She went directly into a deep crevice in the side with the oak cask Álvarez had arranged to catch water running off the steep east side of the Rock. Filling the mug, she spat in it, stirred it with her finger, then walked back out into the sunlight and handed the mug to Álvarez.

He took a deep drink, then shifted his weight and pulled at the stiff canvas bunched uncomfortably in his crotch. He was wearing the new sailcloth trousers he had made Tirza sew for him. Even though the rest of them had gone naked and barefoot for more than a year now, he always wore trousers and boots. The stupid, useless *puta* had made the most uncomfortable pair of trousers a man had ever worn. She had probably done it deliberately. He should whip the filthy bitch.

Tirza had seen, when he had taken the sailcloth for the trousers from the supply cabin, that it was filled with casks, crates and weapons. If only there were a way to get at the *soldados'* pistols. But the door was heavily built and he always kept the key with him. Tirza sighed and squatted down beside the fire.

"Tirza!" Alicia called out. Tirza turned and saw her striding along the beach.

"Doña Alicia," replied Tirza, standing up.

Álvarez stood, fingering the butt of his revolver. "What do you want?"

"I came to see how Tirza was, Álvarez," she said firmly.

Álvarez looked pointedly at Alicia's body for a moment and then turned quickly and went into his cabin, slamming the door behind him. Alicia looked around. The ground around the fire was littered with old bones. Against the side of the cabin, leaned a large hammer on top of a pile of coconut shells. Around the corner, was a pile of feathers with a rusty ax lying on top. Alicia gestured with her head. The two women walked away from the cabin around the end of the Rock.

"We have to kill him," said Alicia.

"I know, Señora, but how?"

"He lets you keep your knife?" asked Alicia.

"Yes. I need it for work. He knows I could not overpower him."

"What about the hammer and ax by the cabin?"

"For coconuts and birds. They are always there. He is not afraid of me. He is not afraid of any of us."

"What about the two of us, Tirza? What if the two of us attacked him with our knives?"

"No, Señora. You cannot imagine how strong he is. He would kill both of us."

CHAPTER 33

The news ran like wildfire through México's diplomatic corps. By the next morning, it was on the front page of newspapers all over the world. In a secret cable, the Germans, embattled in their trenches by the British and the French, had invited México to become their ally. In return, they would give whatever financial and military support it took to recover from the United States the territories she had taken from México. Foreseeing an eventual American entry into the war, Berlin wanted to keep the Americans occupied with their own troubles along the Río Grande. The Germans also revealed their intention of beginning unrestricted submarine warfare on February 1.

Presidente Carranza was mortified. He had always been friendly with the Germans, but war with the United States was unthinkable. This time they would steal the rest of the country and México would cease to exist as a nation. The note had been sent from Berlin to the German ambassador in México. Inexplicably, the Germans had borrowed the American diplomatic cable to send the coded message via their embassy in New York. British Intelligence had the American cable tapped and the German code long since broken. They were reading the message within minutes of it arriving in the German Embassy in México. Given how the British had obtained the message, Whitehall couldn't pass the bombshell directly to Washington. On the other hand, American reaction to the note might well set the stage for the entry of the United States into the war. The solution was elegantly simple, a well-placed leak in México. In México, Carranza hastily distanced himself from the Germans. In Washington, there was predictable outrage. In April, the United States declared war on Germany.

Alicia sat in the warm water at the edge of the lagoon, washing Ángel with a small square of sailcloth. There was no soap and the little boy squirmed as Alicia rubbed the harsh fabric against his skin. Altagracia and Rosalía sat nearby, scrubbing the other children in turn. There was someone in the distance, walking toward them. They realized, as soon as the figure passed the capstan, that it was Tirza. She strode directly toward them. The women got to their feet and embraced her.

"Have you killed him?" Altagracia blurted out.

"No, more is the pity," replied Tirza. They all looked at her body surreptitiously, searching for burns and bruises; the marks of Álvarez. They could see none.

"Lupita! Rosalía!" she called out.

"Mamá! Mamá!" squealed Lupita, struggling in Rosalía's arms.

"My babies," said Tirza putting her arms around both of them. She kissed Rosalía tenderly on the cheek, took Lupita from her and held the little girl tight. "You have grown, Lupita. What a beautiful little girl. Has Rosalía been taking good care of you?" Lupita snuggled against her mother, cooing with delight. Tirza sat down in the water, holding Lupita. Rosalía sat in the water beside Tirza, leaning against her. Tirza put her arm around her.

"Are you alright, Tirza?" asked Alicia, laying Ángel over her shoulder.

"Yes. The bastard could not break me. I made myself too much trouble for him. That is why I am here. He told me to stay away from him." Tirza gave a harsh laugh.

Alicia nodded. "But, you are all right?"

Tirza closed her eyes and drew a deep breath. "Yes, Doña Alicia. I am alright."

Alicia lowered her voice. "Are you pregnant?"

"No."

"Why has he made no one pregnant?"

Tirza pursed her lips and thought. "Rosalía was too young, she is not ready. But Alta and I, perhaps we cannot have babies because our food is so bad." She laughed again. "But I think the real reason is that he is not the man he thinks he is."

USS Yorktown rose sluggishly to the long swell as she left San Diego astern. The sun had barely begun to burn off the patches of haze that clung to the sea. On the gunboat's open bridge, Captain Harlan Page Perrill stood erect, his hands in his pockets, feeling the air grow cooler as the ship picked up speed. He removed his wire-rimmed glasses and wiped the droplets of mist from them with the soft cloth Charlotte had found for him in her sewing basket. Thin, of medium height, with brown hair and eyes and a vaguely benevolent appearance, Perrill scarcely looked his forty-three years. A lifetime of devotion to the Navy had given him command of USS Yorktown, while the pounding of the Navy's guns had cost him the hearing in one ear. Twenty minutes earlier, they had passed under Point Loma. Somewhere up on the Point, unseen, Charlotte and the children stood watching Yorktown head into the Pacific. The sadness of being unable to see them through the haze still lingered.

"Ten degrees left rudder." Perrill's voice was quiet and controlled.

"Ten degrees left rudder, Sir." Lieutenant Raymond Kerr repeated the order, then leaned to the speaking tube and transmitted it to the quartermaster in the wheelhouse below. The ship's bow began to swing slowly to port. The wake arced astern.

Perrill continued to stare ahead, lost in thought. "Amidships."

"Amidships, Sir." Once again Kerr bent to the speaking tube.

"What's your heading, Lieutenant?"

Kerr leaned over the bridge compass. "Two two oh, Sir."

"Okay, steady on that Mister Kerr. If you need me, I'll be in my day cabin."

"Aye, aye, Sir. Two two oh."

Perrill scanned the horizon one last time. They had the sea to themselves today. He slid down the ladder and, stepping over the coaming, entered the accommodation. His day cabin was cramped but had the great virtue of having a settee long enough to nap on. Hanging his cap carefully on the hook behind the door, Perrill stretched out on the settee with a heavy sigh. Another Mexican cruise. He shook his head slowly. Everyone on board had had their fill of them. There was a war to be fought and poking around in Mexican backwaters wasn't much of a contribution.

But maybe Admiral Fullam was right. Now that the Germans had declared unrestricted warfare in the Pacific, they might use some of the more remote bays of Baja California as bases for U-boats or surface raiders. They could easily harass shipping on the U.S. west coast from Baja. As commander of the United States Navy's fleet in the North Pacific, Fullam was the man responsible for the safety of that shipping. Perrill chuckled, thinking back to the day in Fullam's office when he had been briefed. Fullam, a big, ruddy-faced man, had stood over a chart of the Pacific in his shirtsleeves, slapping a set of parallel rulers gently against the palm of his hand. He gestured towards Baja. "You know the drill, Perrill. Get in, have a look for signs of the Germans using the place, get out. Don't upset the Mexicans. Better still, don't let 'em know you're there."

"Yes, sir."

"But be thorough. I don't want you skipping past some cozy little bay just because the soda pop's running low. The one you miss might just be the one the Boche are holed up in."

"Yes, sir."

Fullam laid the parallel rulers across the chart from Honolulu to Panamá.

"Perrill, everything north of these rulers is in my area of operations." Fullam looked steadily into Perrill's eyes as he spoke.

Perrill's tone was quizzical. "Yes, Admiral?"

"There's an interesting island right here, about seven hundred nautical miles off Acapulco; Clipperton, named after some Limey pirate." Fullam tapped his finger on the transparent ruler where it lay over the minuscule dot representing the island. "It's remote and perfectly located. If I were a German admiral, it might be the kind of spot I'd choose as a base if I wanted to go after shipping coming up from Panama. They'd have to blast a new opening into the lagoon but that isn't such a big deal. There were openings into the lagoon at one time."

Perrill nodded, "Yes, sir."

"The problem is that I have to be sure that the island is in my area of operations before I can send you to have a look."

"I understand, sir."

Fullam leaned over the chart and deliberately pushed the parallel rulers a touch southward. Clipperton now lay above the edge of the rulers. "Well, what is your considered opinion Perrill? Would you say that island is north of the line?"

Perrill looked at the chart and then squarely at Fullam, hesitating only for a moment. "Definitely north of the line, sir."

Fullam clapped Perrill warmly on the shoulder. "I've always said you were a fine navigator, Perrill. Glad to see you haven't lost the touch."

"Slow ahead." Perrill's voice was almost a whisper as he peered ahead of the ship. The seaman down in the wheelhouse repeated the order and moved the brass lever on the telegraph. The answering signal came immediately from the engine room. Through the deck, Perrill could feel the beat of the propellers slow. Off to starboard, the sun hung suspended. In a few minutes, it would be below the horizon and the sea would be dark. Perrill had hoped to sight Clipperton today, but it was too late now; much too risky a place to approach in failing light. The Sailing Directions had been explicit about the reefs encircling Clipperton and the difficulty of sighting the island in anything but perfect weather. To top it off, the light on the island had been reported as being extinguished. Better to slow down and arrive in broad daylight tomorrow morning.

This was the end of the cruise. Yorktown had been at sea for six weeks. They had found nothing in the remote bays of Baja California beyond a few shrimp boats. There had been no incidents with the Mexicans and Admiral Fullam would be pleased to know that no German subs or raiders were lurking in his area. After a quick look around Clipperton Island, it would be full ahead for San Diego and a week's leave for all hands. Perrill hoped to get a little gardening in at the house on Point Loma before going to sea again.

Perrill woke to the sound of rain thundering on the deck overhead. From up forward came the sound of sailors stumbling into shelter. They'd slept on deck to avoid the oppressive heat of the mess deck and been caught by the sudden squall. The ship had an uneasy motion. Perrill uncapped the speaking tube and called, "Bridge, everything alright up there?"

Lieutenant Kerr's voice came back right away, "Yes, sir. Just a squall."

"Stay well off the island and call me if there's any problem."

"Yes, Sir. Goodnight, Sir."

Perrill capped the speaking tube and rolled over. The air was heavy with humidity. He knew he wouldn't be able to get back to sleep in the sticky heat of his cabin. He lay in the darkness listening to a succession of brief squalls pass over the ship. He was just beginning to drift off when the Filipino steward knocked on his cabin door with his oh six hundred wake-up call.

On the bridge, the wind bit into Perrill's face. A brisk southwesterly had sprung up overnight, raising a short, jagged chop. Yorktown's progress had slowed almost to a crawl in the head sea. On the port wing, the navigator stood cradling his sextant, hoping to get a quick sun shot though a break in the pus colored cloud. "No sight yet, Mister Kerr?" Perrill asked.

"No, Sir. The overcast is too heavy. It doesn't look like it's going to clear up for a while yet."

"Right. Take special care with your dead reckoning. We don't want to end up on the reef." Perrill ordered half ahead then peered forward across the empty gray sea.

CHAPTER 34

The hands of the grandfather clock had been stopped at ten minutes after ten for almost two years. There had seemed to be little point in keeping it going. Time no longer had any meaning. Alicia stopped as she walked past it. It probably is about ten o'clock, she thought. Ramón would have been having his mid-morning coffee with one of Altagracia's pastries now. Alicia felt her body grow heavy and slow. He had been dead for over two years, but the sadness could rise in her so quickly, almost paralyzing her, causing her to gasp for breath. No, she thought, not again, not today, I want to be happy today. She opened the door and went out. The day was overcast and cool. A boisterous but inconsistent breeze annoyed the tops of the palm trees.

She walked toward the beach to gather eggs. It was amazing how the children had adjusted to a diet of roasted gulls and boobies, eggs, the occasional fish and coconuts. Of course, the younger children had never known anything else. To them, those were the only kinds of food people ate. But how long would it keep them alive? Poor little Ángel's legs were so bowed, his bones so soft, they could not support his weight. He had to be carried everywhere. Would he ever walk?

She straightened slowly, holding the egg and rubbing the small of her back. She had fourteen eggs in the basket. It was enough for now. She took her time walking back toward the rise of land beside her home. Walking across the rise, from long habit, she quickly scanned the horizon. She stopped abruptly and looked again. She stood motionless, staring far out to sea, her only movement to brush the short wisps of hair from her eyes as they were blown about by the breeze. Mother of God, could it be happening to her too? She looked again. No. It was real

With a last glance seaward, she turned towards the house. The children were at the cisterns, filling buckets with water. Altagracia was upstairs. Tirza sat at the table, her head in her hands. Alicia entered the house in silence and went up to her and said, "Tirza..."

Before she could complete her sentence, the door was thrown open. Álvarez, towering, bearded and filthy, stepped onto the threshold and leaned against the doorway. Slowly, his eyes roved the room, seeing the two women naked, taking in everything. Tirza remained still. He fixed his eyes on Alicia. He examined her slowly from head to foot. He was silent for a moment, smiling. Their eyes met. He spoke quietly, "Now, it is your turn to be my wife."

"Pig!" Tirza spat the word at Álvarez.

"Tirza, remain calm." Alicia grasped Tirza by both shoulders and looked squarely into her eyes. "I will do as he asks. I will go with him. It is for the good of us all."

"You are very wise, Señora," Álvarez sneered, running his fingertips over the butt of the pistol at his hip. "It is good that a woman knows how to obey."

He could scarcely believe it. If he had known it would be this easy, he would have come for her long ago. He had never had a white woman. The *indio* women were nothing to him; sluts, whores, animals. But Doña Alicia, she was something special. The thought excited him. He could feel himself growing hard against the coarse sailcloth trousers. The smooth, white flesh. The Capitán's wife. One of the whites who had ordered him about like a dog since he was old enough to walk. One of the whites who lived in luxury, with their fine food and clothes and servants, while he had spent his whole life with nothing.

He would make her pay for all of it. He would rip and tear her delicate, pampered body. He would whip her and burn her as he had that little slut, Rosalía. He would take her in every way a man could take a woman. He would take her until she cried and screamed and begged and was nothing better than an animal. And, when he had had enough of her, he would kill her. He would kill them all. When a ship finally came, he would be the only one left alive.

Alicia spoke calmly, "Just give me time to pack my things, Victoriano. I will come to you soon." Álvarez, having no doubt that she would come, smiled and said, "I will be at my cabin. Do not keep me waiting." He turned and swaggered from the house, leaving the door open.

Alicia smiled grimly and patted Tirza's shoulder. "I want you to come with me."

Álvarez sat on a driftwood log in front of his cabin. The rusty hammer lay on the ground at the side of the cabin atop a heap of coconut shells. The ax, crusted with the dried blood and feathers of seabirds, leaned against the wall. A booby, skewered on a stick, roasted over a pile of glowing coals. Álvarez was growing impatient. In a few more minutes, he would take the Mauser and fetch the white *puta*. Looking up, he saw Alicia and, beside her, Tirza. The two women were speaking rapidly in low voices. "Why is that slut here?" he hissed

"Tirza helped me carry my things," Alicia replied quietly.

"Put that bag inside and go. Stay away from here," he growled at Tirza. She moved forward without saying a word, walked carefully around Álvarez and, pushing the door to the cabin open, put the bag down inside.

Álvarez, leering at Alicia, had lost interest in Tirza. Slowly, he looked Alicia up and down. With her hair shorn and disheveled, her face sunburned, her eyes haunted, her body thin and hard, she was still beautiful. It was a dream come true. "You will make me a good wife. Tonight, you will cook me a fine meal and then you shall warm my bed. You can start by taking off my boots and rubbing them with oil." Alicia stood motionless.

"Now!" Álvarez roared. Alicia went up to Álvarez and stood before him. "Take off my boots, woman!" Alicia, naked, knelt in the dust at his feet.

Álvarez stretched his leg lazily toward her. His face slowly broke into a crooked leer. "I think you will be the best wife of all."

As Alicia leaned forward, Álvarez watched her breasts move. She lifted his foot and began to pull slowly on the boot. Álvarez stared, entranced. Alicia raised her eyes from the boot and looked up at Álvarez. He sat there, triumphant. He was enjoying this more than in his wildest imaginings. This was a woman, a real woman, with a real woman's body. Not like that stupid little whore Rosalía with her tiny pointed tits and endless sobbing after her slut of a mother. And not like that whining Altagracia or, thank God, that hellcat Tirza.

Behind Álvarez, Tirza stood, both arms raised, holding the ax overhead. Her expression was vacant, as though she were in a trance. Alicia pulled at Álvarez's boot, imploring Tirza with her eyes. Álvarez looked at Alicia questioningly. "What is it woman?" In his triumph, he had completely forgotten Tirza. Behind him, she stood frozen, unable to move. Alicia knew it was only a matter of seconds before Álvarez realized that Tirza was behind him and turned around and saw her holding the ax. Then he would kill them both.

She screamed, "Now, Tirza!"

Instantly, Tirza brought the ax down in an awkward, glancing blow. Álvarez slumped forward onto Alicia, knocking her over, then rolled onto the ground beside her. With infinite slowness, he raised himself on an elbow and turned to Tirza, blood streaming down the side of his head. "Mother of God! You filthy whore! I will tear you apart!" His voice was low, shaking with menace. Tirza stood paralyzed. The ax hung limply from her hands. Alicia lay on the ground, dazed, Álvarez's blood splattered across her face and chest.

With a roar of rage, Álvarez wiped the blood from his eyes and slowly raised himself to his knees. His gaze swung to the hammer leaning against the wall of the cabin. With blood running into his eyes, he crawled to the cabin, groped along the wall of the cabin and seized the hammer. Alicia fell on him, pinning his arms to his sides, barely able to get her arms around him. With the bellow of a wounded animal, he struggled to break Alicia's grip. Even badly hurt, he was still powerful. She was at the limit of her strength. He shook her violently, but she clung on. She felt her grip weakening, her strength going. Everything was slippery with blood. One of his arms was almost free, trying to raise the hammer.

"Tirza, again! Again, Tirza! Again!" Alicia screamed.

Tirza stood shocked, paralyzed, the ax still in her hands. The last of Alicia's strength was ebbing as Álvarez struggled to get up, the blood streaming down his face, blinding him and covering her. Alicia's vision began to darken and she felt as though she were going to faint. "For Rosalía, Tirza. For Rosalía," Alicia half-screamed, half-sobbed. With a roar, Álvarez broke free and she collapsed onto the sand.

Tirza screamed and, in a single motion, using all the force in her body, she raised the ax over Álvarez and brought it down squarely on the top of his head. There was a sickening crack as his skull split and the blade of the ax plunged deep into his brain. Álvarez sank to the ground, twitching. His bladder and bowels emptied, filling their air with a fetid stink. His head was a bulging mass of blood and bone and oozing soft pink tissue. Alicia lay motionless. Tirza fell on her knees beside Álvarez and pulled the ax free from the ruin of his head. She struck him again and again. "You pig!" she screamed. "You pig! You pig! I will kill you!" She continued to rain blows on Álvarez's lifeless body, screaming obscenities at him.

"Tirza, Tirza. Enough, enough. He is dead," whispered Alicia, getting to her hands and knees. "He is gone, Tirza. He is dead. It is over."

Tirza let the ax fall beside Álvarez's body. She seemed stunned. "Señora, we are free," she gasped and began to sob, dropping to her knees in front of Alicia. "We are free."

Alicia held her as she cried. "Yes, Tirza, we are free."

"Mamá, Mamá, a ship!" Ramoncito ran headlong toward

them, yelling with excitement. He stopped suddenly, his eyes wide open in shock. His mother and Tirza knelt in the sand in front of him holding each other, their naked bodies covered with blood. Beside them, the lightkeeper lay motionless. The boy saw the blood, the hair, the bone. He raised his eyes to Alicia but she said nothing.

"Mamá, there is a ship!" He pointed out to sea. "Look, Mamá! Look! A ship!"

Alicia turned slowly in the direction he was pointing. A gray-painted warship was steaming very slowly, less than a kilometer offshore, leaving an ever-expanding vee in the still water behind her. Alicia nodded slowly. "Yes, Ramoncito, I see it," she said quietly. "Run now. Find the others. Tell everyone to get dressed."

CHAPTER 35

Perrill was lost in thought when the call from the masthead lookout came. The sailor must have had the eyes of an eagle; no one on the bridge sighted land until fifteen minutes later, when Clipperton Rock appeared through the haze. As they drew near, he could distinguish the ring of heavy breakers almost encircling the island through his binoculars. He turned to Lieutenant Kerr, who was also examining the island through binoculars, and said, "Pretty heavy surf. No good anchorages and I don't see an entry into the lagoon, Lieutenant. I can't imagine a U-boat or a surface raider using this place."

Kerr let his binoculars fall on their strap. "No, sir."

"Alright, let's make a circuit half a mile outside the surf line. If we see anywhere to land, we'll put a boat ashore to check on the navigation light."

The Yorktown's sailors lined the rail as the ship slowly circled the island. Beside Perrill on the bridge, Kerr looked through his binoculars at the Rock. "The light's still there, Sir."

Perrill raised his binoculars and looked. "Right, Mister Kerr. The surf's not too bad just ahead there, let's send a boat away and find out. Have a boat's crew get early dinner and see who wants to go with you for a look."

Yorktown inched ahead at dead slow before finally coming to a standstill just off the northeastern side of the island. She rolled gently in the slight swell. From the bridge, Perrill could hear the sounds of the bluejackets clearing the boat for launching. Ross, the Yorktown's assistant surgeon, came out onto the bridge. "Captain, I'd like to go ashore with Lieutenant

Kerr, with your permission."

"Certainly, Mister Ross. Go and stretch your legs. You've got two hours to have a look around. Mister Kerr will check out the light and then we're on our way home."

Ross pointed towards the shore. "Look, Sir, there are people on the beach."

From his place on the bridge, Perrill watched the launch lowered from the davits and row towards the island. As it got closer in, he could see it tossing in the surf and the people on the beach gesturing wildly. "They're not going to make it, Sir. The surf is too high." Ensign Felix Stump passed his binoculars to Perrill.

Perrill held the binoculars to his eyes and watched the boat twisting in the surf. "You're right, Stump. Have a blank six pounder fired and hoist the recall."

Alicia, Tirza and Altagracia stood in a group on the beach wearing the clothes they had saved for the day they were rescued. Alicia and Tirza had washed most of Álvarez's blood from their bodies and hair. The children had been sent to the house to get dressed and wait with Rosalía until they discovered who the men in the ship were. In silence, the women watched as the boat came toward them. Directly ahead of the boat, a line of hissing surf marked the reef. "Look where they are going!" Altagracia's voice was half shout, half sob. "They will capsize!" The boat was in almost exactly the same place over the edge of the reef where Ramón's boat had been lost.

The women shouted and waved frantically, pointing to the east, where there was a break in the reef and the water was calmer. The men in the boat didn't seem to understand. Tossed about by the waves, the boat kept coming. The women shouted until they were hoarse, gesturing wildly. The sound of a shot crashed across the water. The women looked up in alarm. Without a glance at the island, the men turned the boat around and began rowing back to the ship.

"No! No! What is happening? Where are they are going?" The tears were streaming down Tirza's face. She clutched at Alicia's arm. "Señora, they are going. They are leaving us here."

The two women stood silent, watching the boat draw slowly away. Alicia felt the misery strangling her. She wanted to fall on the harsh coral dust of the beach and go to sleep forever. How could the men in the boat turn around and leave them? The women watched as the boat was hoisted up the ship's side and it began to move ahead. They turned and walked slowly away from the sea.

It was too much. They could take no more. In three years, this was the only ship to come near the island. The pain, the suffering, the death, the horror of Álvarez, they had survived it all for nothing. They couldn't last another three years, waiting for a ship that might never come. This had been their only hope. Soon this ship would be gone and they would be alone, abandoned again. She turned to the others, her voice breaking. "This was our only chance. We must end it. We cannot allow the children to suffer any more. If we die first, they will be left alone here to starve. We must take them and walk out over the reef."

They walked back to the house with leaden feet, not speaking. They knew Alicia was right. Somehow, each had known that one day it would come to this, that they would have to end it themselves. The ship had been their only chance. Now, they would die slowly of scurvy or starvation, until only one of them remained, perhaps one of the children, to die alone, without so much as a hand to hold. They would never be rescued. Better to take their own lives quickly, together.

Alicia went to the pantry and took an empty brandy bottle from the shelf. She wiped the dust from the label and looked at it for a moment before clutching it to herself, sobbing quietly. Ramón had ordered half a dozen bottles of his favorite French brandy once a year through the wine merchant in Acapulco. It always arrived on the first ship after Easter. The evening it arrived, Ramón would get their best glasses and pour them each a small measure. She could hear his words now, urging her to be patient, to let the brandy warm in her hands before sipping it. She could see the smile on his face as he took the first sip, his eyes closed. She could smell his cigar. She could feel the brandy's fire as it trickled down her throat; the warmth of their companionship wrapped around them like a blanket.

Alicia took the piece of paper she had written on and folded it carefully over and over again and then slipped it into the bottle. She pushed the cork home with the heel of her hand and stood the bottle in the center of the table. This message would be their only memorial. Perhaps no one would ever read it. Perhaps no one else would stand where she stood now.

She gave their names and ages: Altagracia Quiroz, twenty-two years; Rosalía Nava, fourteen years; Tirza Randon, twenty-two years; Guadalupe Cardona, two years; Francisco Irra, twelve years; Antonio Irra, six years; Ramón Arnaud, eight years; Alicia Arnaud, six years; Olga Arnaud, four years; Ángel Arnaud, two years; Alicia Rovira de Arnaud, twenty-nine years. In a few short sentences, she told of the deaths from scurvy, of Ramón and the other men dying in the surf and of their decision to end their agony. There was no mention of Álvarez. At the bottom was the date they had walked into the sea, July 18, 1917.

They went back to the beach with the children. The tightness in Alicia's chest was unbearable. She could barely breathe. Francisco Irra carried Ángel all the way, the little boy's useless legs dangling. Alicia held Olga's hand so tightly she cried out. Rosalía, Altagracia and Tirza, carrying Lupita, were with the others, their voices somber as they shepherded the children along. Ahead, the surf hammered its relentless rhythm on the reef. They walked slowly toward the sea, the children uncomprehending but quietly obedient.

Perrill ordered the ship stopped and the boat lowered again.

This time, the sailors avoided the line of surf and approached the island through the smoother water to the east. The Yorktown waited for a few minutes, steam hissing from the relief valve. Perrill could see that this time the boat could reach the shore without trouble and gave the order for half ahead. Yorktown picked up speed slowly and steamed off to the west, parallel to the shore to complete a circuit of the island.

As the sailors in the boat looked shoreward, the ragtag group appeared on the beach again, their heads bowed, shuffling slowly towards the water's edge. This time, some of the women carried children on their hips and there were other, older, children dressed in what looked like flour sacks. As the launch approached the shore, one of the women looked up and saw them. She let out an inarticulate cry that drifted faintly across the water to the boat's crew. The others on the beach looked up and stood motionless. Then they all began to wave and shout.

The keel of the boat grated sharply against the sand and a sailor leaped over the bows with a painter to hold the boat in. Lieutenant Kerr, gleaming in his tropical whites, stepped ashore. He took his cap off and, holding it beneath his arm, approached the women, smiling. "Who are you?" Alicia demanded in Spanish. The other women and children stood behind her.

Kerr spoke slowly in English, "Americans. United States."

The tension flooded from Alicia's body and her shoulders sagged. She turned to the others. "They are *norteamericanos*. We are saved." Alicia turned towards the American and spoke in her halting English. "I am Alicia Rovira de Arnaud. My husband was the Governor of this island. Please, you must take us from this place."

CHAPTER 36

"**M**y God, what a story," thought Kerr as he walked toward Clipperton Rock with two bluejackets in his wake. With Alicia's basic English and his smattering of Spanish, he had begun to understand what the women and children had lived through, cut off from the mainland, the scurvy, the deaths. Kerr saw the crude crosses clustered in the cemetery. He shook his head slowly and kept walking. Ross had taken the rest of the bluejackets and gone with the women to the settlement to get their belongings. As soon as he had checked the light, Kerr would meet them at the settlement and then get them to the ship.

Kerr approached the Rock and, shading his eyes, looked toward the top. Hundreds of birds circled the Rock and darted in and out of its fissured sides. It took less than a minute to climb the wooden ladders to the top and examine the light which seemed to be in good condition. The wind was stronger on top of the Rock and he had to remove his cap and hold it beneath his arm. He could see the entire island from up here. He knelt to examine the light. The Fresnel lenses were intact. He undid the brass butterfly nuts holding down the chimney, tilted it back and looked at the mantle. Everything looked fine. All the light needed to work was oil. He lowered the chimney and tightened the nuts.

Kerr stepped from the bottom rung of the ladder and walked around the Rock to the light keeper's cabin. He saw feathers strewn on the ground and the ax and noticed what seemed to be a large area of blood soaked into the sand. Then he saw the body and heard the clicking. There was a jagged whiteness where the head should have been. The body lay downwards, the remnants of the skull turned to one side. The top and back of it were completely gone. The limbs were thrown out grotesquely. Fragments of bone, dark clumps of hair and pieces of brain littered the sand.

The crabs were busy. They fought with each other for the privilege of probing the gaping skull with their greedy pincers. Kerr lashed out at them, kicking them away from the body. For a moment, they retreated backwards, pincers waving in threat. Kerr knelt beside the head. The empty eye sockets stared back at him. What was left of the skull was almost empty. He forced himself to touch some of the skin-covered flesh still adhering to the vertebrae of the neck. It was slightly warm. Kerr felt the bile rise in him. He ran blindly away from the horrible thing and fell to his knees retching. The crabs went back to their work

Kerr found the others coming back from the settlement. A bluejacket pushed a loaded wheelbarrow. The older of the two Indian boys carried the Arnaud baby. The younger carried a scrawny hen under each arm. Doctor Ross and Señora Arnaud were deep in conversation. Kerr motioned Ross aside and whispered breathlessly. Ross stood still for a moment then nodded, "Okay, I'd better go and look. The Captain will want to know everything."

As Ross hurried towards the Rock, Kerr asked Alicia who the man at the Rock was and how he had died. Alicia looked at him blankly. "I know you understand some English, Señora. What happened here?"

Alicia paused before saying slowly, "It is Álvarez, the lightkeeper. He died of scurvy."

Of course she was lying, the man's skull had been battered into fragments. And he could see smears of blood on the woman's face and neck. He was about to ask her again, then thought better of it. He'd leave it to the skipper to sort out. "Are those chickens going too?" he asked Alicia, pointing to two bedraggled hens.

"Yes, Lieutenant, they are Tirza's hens. We cannot leave them here to die."

"No, I suppose we can't. Well, let's get moving. The Captain will be anxious to get underway."

Kerr walked behind, watching. He had offered to carry the Arnaud baby to the boat but the Indian boy had refused to give him up. Alicia told him that the baby was over two years old but couldn't walk. His legs were badly bowed. "What's the matter with the baby, Señora?"

"Doctor Ross said it is from bad food, *teniente*. His legs are too weak to support his weight. Ángel is the worst, but all the children have suffered. Francisco, the boy who is carrying Ángel, is twelve but look, he is no bigger than an eight-year-old."

The Yorktown's sailors stared at the children and women as they climbed down to the deck from the boat swinging in its davits. They were gaunt and stank of fish and sweat and dirt. They stood in a group, clutching each other, eyeing the sailors warily. The children seemed terrified, trying to hide behind the women's legs. Perrill shook his head in disbelief. "Get these people down to the sick bay, on the double. Mister Ross, after you've done what you can for them, report to me."

The door was open and Lieutenant Kerr knocked and walked in without waiting for an answer. He started speaking rapidly. "It's unbelievable, Captain. They've been cut off on that island for years, no food, no medicines. More than twenty people have died. There's a body by the light keeper's cabin. A black man. The body was still warm when I got there. The white woman is the widow of the garrison commander. She says the lightkeeper died of scurvy, but his skull was cracked wide open. They were in terrible shape, I couldn't leave them there," he finished breathlessly.

Perrill paused for a moment and then spoke. "Alright,

alright, slow down Mister Kerr. Now take me through this again, slowly." Kerr took a deep breath and related everything in detail. Perrill leaned back and thought for a moment, "You did the right thing, but this is a little more than we bargained for. Is there anyone else on the island?"

"No, sir. We searched all the buildings and brought everyone off."

"So, those women killed him."

"It seems that way, Sir."

"What did you do with the body?"

"I just left it there, Sir. The crabs had already half-eaten it. There'll be nothing left but bones by nightfall."

"Jesus. How many crabs are there?"

"Thousands, millions. They're everywhere," replied Kerr.

"I don't suppose they've seen any Germans?"

"No, Sir, I asked them. They didn't even know there was a war on. The last newspaper they had was four years old."

"Well, they'll be going back to a different world to the one they left. We can't do any good here, Lieutenant. We'll get under way. I want to be well away from here before dark. We'll have to take these people to a Mexican port. Plot a course for Salina Cruz."

* *

Yorktown steamed slowly through the darkness across a gently rolling sea. Ross sat at the wardroom table, a mug of coffee cupped in his hands. Perrill leaned back in his chair at the head of the table, the smoke curling lazily from his corncob pipe. Beneath them, the ship had a purposeful feeling as she plowed her course for Salina Cruz. "Well, Mister Ross, got everyone bedded down?"

"Yes, Sir. I've turned the sick bay over to them. They can use the head and sink there and the motion isn't too bad. All of them except the kids are suffering from seasickness, but they'll be alright soon. Señora Arnaud is on the verge of hysteria. I've given her something to help her sleep." Ross hesitated, then went on. "The oldest girl, her name is Rosalía, has been tortured."

Perrill's head shot up. "What?"

"She's been tortured, Captain. Her nipples have been burned off."

"Jesus Christ," moaned Perrill, sagging back into his seat.

"There's very good healing, but she's in bad shape mentally. She doesn't talk. She just clings to one of the Indian women."

"What the hell went on there, Mister Ross?"

"I've got some of the story, Sir, and their names and ages."

Perrill puffed on his pipe, sending a cloud of smoke to the deckhead. "Don't keep me in suspense."

"Some of them have been on that island since 1908. They're part of a Mexican garrison. It's a guano island. There is a phosphate plant. But the plant closed down years ago. They were serviced by regular supply ships from the mainland. You remember the Nokomis, Sir?"

"Sure. Out of San Francisco. Is that where she was wrecked?"

"Yes, Sir. After the wreck, several of the crew sailed an open boat to Acapulco and the Cleveland went out to take off the other survivors. Señora Arnaud says her husband, the garrison commander, refused the Cleveland commander's offer to take the Mexicans off, thinking the supply ship would arrive any day. It never did. They began to die, one by one, from scurvy. Finally, Captain Arnaud took a boat for help. It capsized in the surf and all the men aboard were drowned or eaten by sharks, leaving only the women and children and Álvarez, the lightkeeper. They're sticking to their story that he died of scurvy."

Perrill re-lit his pipe. "I have to get to the bottom of this. Let me know the minute Señora Arnaud is strong enough to be interviewed."

The day dawned bright and grew increasingly hot and humid. By noon, the sick bay was like an oven and stank of unwashed bodies and vomit. Perrill gave permission for Alicia and the others to be given the quarterdeck for their use in daylight hours. A canvas screen was hoisted to give them some privacy. Ensign Felix Stump leaned against the rail and watched Tirza working at the sewing machine. One of the boatswain's mates had brought up the machine and some cotton duck so she could make clothing for the children. The two Indian boys were scampering around in nothing but Marine jackets that had been unceremoniously shortened with shears.

Stump had a tin of marshmallows in his hand. Smiling at Francisco, he held it out. The boy looked wary but gradually approached Stump and, with a brief smile, took the tin. He sat cross-legged on the deck and wrestled with it. Finally, using his teeth, he was able to lever the lid off and took a marshmallow. He rolled it between his fingers, compressing it and letting it spring back. He stood and walked to the rail and dropped the marshmallow into the sea. He looked back at Stump and smiled then took another and dropped it in the water. Stump stood watching, bemused, not quite understanding, as the boy took each marshmallow in turn and dropped it over the side, watching it disappear in the ship's wake. When the marshmallows were all gone, the boy put the lid back on and lay the tin on the deck. With each roll of the ship, the tin rolled across the deck part way before rolling back again. The boy jumped and laughed with glee each time it came back toward him.

Stump stood watching the boy play the game until Ross came up and stood beside him. The two men turned and leaned over the rail, watching the Yorktown's wake growing astern as straight as an arrow. "Those kids are funny, Stump. I tried to get them to eat some steak this morning. It was good, nice and tender, but they didn't want it. They want 'bobo'. That's what they call seabird. They've eaten so much of it, anything else tastes strange to them. The women say they never want to see 'bobo' again as long as they live. I don't know what's going to happen to these people, Stump, especially the children. That poor girl Rosalía and the two boys are orphans. I doubt that they'll ever find their families."

"I suppose, if worst came to worst, one of the convents or monasteries would look after them."

"Not any more. All the Church property in México has been confiscated. There are no convents or monasteries."

Stump turned around and looked at Francisco playing his game with the marshmallow tin. "You know, if there weren't a war on, I'd adopt that kid myself. He's special. I heard about him carrying the Arnaud baby two miles to the boat landing. Look at the size of him. How the heck did he do that?"

Ross turned to look at Francisco still playing with the tin. "I don't know, but he's a good kid. They all are. I hope to God they'll be okay."

Ross smiled. "Captain, they've all had baths."

"Thank God. It was getting to be bit much. How did you do it?"

"I just took a few dozen towels and some bars of soap down to the wardroom shower bath, then invited them down and left them alone for a while. No embarrassment, no problem. Nothing to it."

"Very good, Mister Ross. We're in your debt."

"They had one bar of Ivory left; they've been hoarding it for years, for the day they were rescued. They had been using sand on pieces of canvas to clean themselves. It's not the most effective way to wash."

Perrill smiled and nodded. "I want to interview Señora Arnaud. Is she well enough?"

"I think so Captain. She's calmed down and they're all over their seasickness and looking a lot better. The only one I'm really worried about is the baby with rickets. That kid is going to go through my entire stock of cod liver oil before I'm finished with him. The funny thing is he really likes it. He'd drink the whole bottle if I let him. It probably tastes like 'bobo'."

"Okay. Bring Señora Arnaud to me tomorrow after breakfast. We've got to get this business with the body straightened out before we reach Salina Cruz. I don't want any trouble with the Mexicans."

It was Perrill's habit in fine weather at sea to stroll the deck before turning in. He stopped a few paces from the canvas screen on the quarterdeck and leaned on the railing, watching the phosphorescence stirred up by the ship's screws glowing in the wake. He turned away from the wind to light his corncob pipe and heard low voices behind the canvas. The Mexicans must be still on deck. It was probably too hot down in the sick bay. Anywhere below decks would be sweltering after today's heat. Two small brown faces peered at Perrill around the screen. Perrill smiled and they promptly vanished. Very slowly and cautiously, they peeked around the edge. Perrill smiled again. Both of their faces came into view, both were smiling.

"Entertaining the children, Captain?" Ensign Stump had come up beside Perrill at the railing.

"Uh, oh yes, Stump." Perrill looked embarrassed.

"I tell you Captain, half of the crew are in love with these kids."

"Judging by the amount of candy they've been given, I'd say that was an underestimate. It's funny that they don't have any idea what to do with it."

"I guess they just never acquired a taste for sweet things, Sir."

Antonio Irra's sparkling brown eyes appeared again. "Hola," Stump spoke hesitantly in Spanish.

Francisco paused for a moment and smiled

CHAPTER 37

There was a knock at the door. Captain Perrill called out and the door opened. Alicia stood in the dress in which she had come aboard. It was long out of fashion and hung slackly on her body but, in spite of her gaunt appearance, she was still a beautiful woman. At her throat, a strand of pearls glittered.

Perrill sat speechless for a moment and then struggled to his feet. "Uh, welcome, Señora Arnaud. Please, sit down." Perrill couldn't believe the change in her. The marks of suffering were still clear in her face but she had transformed herself from a half-savage to a dignified, aristocratic woman.

Perrill looked at the pearls around her neck; they looked real. He smiled inwardly, remembering the wheelbarrow of tattered belongings the survivors had brought to the Yorktown. Somewhere in it had been these pearls and who knew what else. Alicia sat across from Perrill, her hands folded in her lap, her eyes averted.

"Señora Arnaud, I know you have been through a great deal, but I must ask you certain questions. Lieutenant Kerr has told me that there was a dead man by the cabin at the light. Doctor Ross says the man died only a very short time before he found the body. Who was he and how did he come to die?"

Alicia looked Perrill squarely in the eyes. "He was Victoriano Álvarez, the lightkeeper, Capitán. He died just before your ship arrived." Still Alicia did not look at him.

"How did he die, Señora?"

Alicia looked at her hands in her lap for a moment then raised her eyes to Perrill. "Of scurvy, Capitán Perrill. He died of scurvy, like the others."

"Señora, Lieutenant Kerr has told me that the man's skull had been crushed. Doctor Ross confirmed that the man died of massive injuries to the head. What happened?"

"Capitán... I....I.." Alicia faltered. "I cannot....."

Perrill folded his arms across his chest and leaned back. "Señora Arnaud, you must tell me what happened."

Alicia wiped her eyes and looked searchingly at Perrill. "Capitán Perrill, what has happened is too terrible to tell. God has taken his vengeance and the matter is closed. It is better for everyone that it is forgotten."

"Señora Arnaud, this is a ship of the United States Navy. I am required to make a full report to my government. I have entered foreign waters, my executive officer has found the body of a murdered foreign national and we have taken aboard survivors of a foreign garrison, one of whom has obviously been tortured. You must understand that there is no choice in this matter for either of us."

"I am very sorry Capitán. I am grateful to you for everything you have done but I have nothing to say."

"Señora Arnaud, you must understand. An American warship lands an armed party on an island claimed by México. A Mexican citizen, a member of the garrison on the island, is found dead, beaten to death. Do you have any idea what an ill-intentioned person could make of those facts? The world is at war. Do you know how much damage this could cause to relations between México and the United States? I must know what happened on that island before we enter Mexican waters. If you do not tell me, I will be forced to steam directly to the United States and have the matter thoroughly investigated by our authorities."

Alicia reached into the embroidered purse laying on her lap and took out a thick roll of banknotes bound with string. She undid the string and laid the pile of notes on the table in front of her. "I am prepared to pay for our passage, Capitán. I ask charity of no one."

Perrill took one of the notes and examined it curiously. It

had been issued many years and many governments ago. At one time, the pile of notes lying on the table would have bought half of the Yorktown. "I am afraid this money is worthless, Señora Arnaud. In any case, it is not a question of money, my only concern is the safety of my ship and crew. I have no intention of taking the Yorktown into Mexican waters unless I know the circumstances of that man's death."

Alicia sat still for a few moments then sighed quietly and nodded her head. "Very well, Capitán Perrill. I understand your position. You are a gentlemen. I will trust you to use great discretion with what I am about to tell you."

"You have my word, Señora. I will do my best to see that you are not inconvenienced or embarrassed in any way."

It took Alicia almost two hours to tell the story; of their abandonment, the hunger, the deaths, the terrible moment when Ramón and the others died, the storms, the madness of Álvarez, the beatings, the murder of Doña Juana and María, the rapes, the torture, the dread of what he might do to the children, the terror of waking to find Álvarez over her with his knife at her throat. She came to their last day on the island and stopped, her eyes red with crying, her breath catching in her throat. Perrill said nothing, listening appalled. "Señora Arnaud, please take a moment to compose yourself."

Alicia took a lace handkerchief from her sleeve and wiped her eyes. It was the monogrammed handkerchief from Ramón. "I am sorry, Capitán, I have cried too much," she said in halting English.

"No, Señora. You've shown more courage than I would have imagined possible." Even if she hadn't completely understood his words, she understood the look in his eyes. Alicia smiled through her tears and Perrill looked away, embarrassed.

"At our present speed, we'll be in Salina Cruz at noon tomorrow, Captain," Kerr said as he straightened up from the chart table.

"Very good, Mister Kerr." Perrill walked past him onto the bridge to stand at the rail, watching the seas over the Yorktown's bows. Perrill turned and called, "Mister Kerr, did that message go out?"

Kerr joined Perrill at the rail. "Yes, Sir. Sparks just finished sending it. Should get routed to Salina Cruz in a few hours, if the telegraph system is working."

"Good. I hope the British Consul can smooth our way a bit. The U.S. isn't too popular in México these days."

"Yes, Sir." Kerr moved toward Perrill and said, "Captain?"

"Yes, Mister Kerr, what is it?"

"What really happened, Sir? Why did they kill him?"

Perrill continued to stare at the seas ahead and said, "When you've lived a little longer, Mister Kerr, you'll realize that some things in this world are best left alone. Complete your report to me on your landing on the island. Make no mention of the body. Keep it simple. And I want you to tell the officers and men to keep their mouths shut when we're in Salina Cruz and back in the States. We rescued these people, that's all there is to it. Anybody who says different answers to me. Goodnight, Mister Kerr."

Perrill left Kerr standing alone at the rail. Sixteen hours ahead lay Salina Cruz.

Alicia stood on the quarterdeck near the port rail. Behind her, she could hear the shouts and laughter of the children as they climbed and slid down the massive bronze blades of the spare propeller lashed to the fantail. Tirza and Altagracia stood talking quietly. Rosalía sat on the deck beside Tirza. Yorktown's bows swung to port to line up with the entrance to the harbor at Salina Cruz and Alicia saw the low, white buildings along the waterfront. It had been so long since she had seen Salina Cruz. So much had happened but it seemed that nothing here had changed. It looked exactly the same as it had the last time she and Ramón and the children had sailed from here, a lifetime ago.

The weather was fine and her seasickness had long since passed but Alicia felt queasy. All night, she had tossed and turned, waking every few minutes, wondering what lay ahead. Was her father still alive? Where was he? Would she have to speak of what Álvarez had done to them and, ultimately, of what they had done to him? What would become of them in this strange new México?

The deck shuddered as the screws churned astern, sending discolored water streaming along the ship's sides. Alicia could hear the anchor cable rumbling out. She looked again toward the buildings of Salina Cruz. A launch was cutting through the slight chop of the harbor toward them, foam streaming from its bows

CHAPTER 38

Perrill reached the head of the gangway just as the Captain of the Port, in his elaborate uniform, reached Yorktown's deck. As Perrill welcomed him aboard, two men, both with iron-gray hair, both immaculately dressed, started up the gangway. The first to reach the ship's deck ignored Perrill and stood looking about anxiously. The younger man extended his hand to Perrill and smiled warmly. "Welcome to Salina Cruz, Captain. William Wiseman, British Consul. This is Señor Félix Rovira, Captain. He is the father of Alicia Arnaud."

Perrill took Rovira's hand, "Your daughter is on board, Señor, safe and sound."

Wiseman translated Perrill's words into Spanish and Rovira nodded and spoke quickly in Spanish. "He gives you his eternal gratitude Captain. He is very anxious to see his daughter."

"She's back aft, Mr. Wiseman, I'll take him to her." Perrill guided the two men along the Yorktown's deck. "How on earth did you get Señora Arnaud's father here so quickly?" he asked Wiseman.

"Very simple, Captain. Señor Rovira is my next-door neighbor."

Alicia saw the two men being ushered by the Captain toward her. One she recognized as the British Consul. The other was slightly stooped, his face more lined, his step slower, but it was her father. She ran, blinded by her tears, burying herself in his arms crying, "Papá! Papá!

He crushed Alicia to him, his shoulders shaking, tears streaming down his face. "Licha, my Licha. They told me you were dead. They told me you were dead. My darling, all these years, they told me you were dead. You are alive. You have come back. My little Licha," he sobbed uncontrollably and leaned heavily against her.

Alicia pulled back for a moment and looked into his eyes and said, "Yes, Papá, I have come back."

Father and daughter stood, their arms locked around each other, tears of joy and relief mingling. A small group of sailors stood nearby, looking sheepishly down at the deck. One raised a hand to wipe his eye, then quickly looked away to the horizon. The children had stopped playing. Tirza stood with Lupita on her hip, holding Rosalía's hand. Altagracia sniffed and grinned at Tirza.

Perrill, his eyes glistening, smiled at Wiseman. "An extraordinary moment, Mr. Wiseman."

"Indeed, Captain. On the way out in the launch, Señor Rovira told me that he has never regretted his inability to speak English as much as he does today. His gratitude to you and your crew is boundless and it pains him that he cannot express it to you himself. In his mind, you have brought his daughter back from the dead. He tried for years to get one Mexican government after another to go out to Clipperton but he was always told that everyone on the island had died. For the past while, he has lived like a hermit. I think I was his only friend. He was a broken man."

"We'll have to get everyone ashore. Will they be taken care of?"

"Of course. When Señor Rovira had gotten over the shock of learning that his daughter was alive, he made arrangements for all the survivors. He will ensure that they are taken care of."

"By the way, the officers and crew have put together a fund to help the children. There's more than two hundred dollars. Perhaps you could take care of the money and use it as necessary."

Wiseman nodded. "Of course, Captain. Your crew is very generous."

Kerr stood at the head of the gangway, smartly dressed in his best whites. He said, "Ready to go, Captain."

"All right, Mister Kerr. I hope you've picked the men carefully. We don't want any incidents."

"No, Sir. They'll behave themselves."

Perrill watched as Kerr climbed into the starboard launch. The port launch was already half way across the harbor filled with Yorktown sailors and officers. On the municipal quay, the mayor of Salina Cruz stood in full finery, talking with Wiseman and Félix Rovira. The dock area and the main street were a riot of colored banners.

As the first launch reached the quay, a band struck up an American anthem. The mayor stepped forward to greet the crew. They milled around looking bewildered and embarrassed by their reception. The mayor spread his arms towards the crew as the band ended the anthem and said, in Spanish, "México will never forget the Yorktown for bringing our loved ones back to us. A million thanks. The City of Salina Cruz welcomes you with open arms. Anything we have is yours." Most of the sailors had no idea of the words he was speaking but they understood the meaning well enough

The two stokers stood side by side in the middle of the crowd. Although the temperature was over a hundred degrees, they scarcely felt it. They were used to the unrelenting heat of the Yorktown's boiler room. A Mexican afternoon was nothing to them. Both men were slightly built but with a wiry strength. Murphy's forearms were a tapestry of tattoos. He patted each of his pockets in turn. "Hey, no cigarettes. Got any?"

Anderson shook his head. "Not me. Smoked the last one on the way over."

"Okay, let's go buy some. There's some kind of store over there."

The two turned to make their way out of the crowd but were stopped time and again by Mexicans who patted them on the back, shook their hands and smiled and laughed while speaking rapidly in Spanish. Murphy and Anderson couldn't understand a word, but smiled and nodded as they headed for the north end of the square. They finally broke clear and walked towards the store. Inside, it was dark and much cooler. An old white-haired woman sat dozing in a wooden chair just inside the door, her hands folded in her lap.

When the two sailors entered, she opened her eyes slowly. Her heavily lined face broke into a smile and she rose, crying greetings in Spanish. The sailors shuffled and smiled as the woman continued to speak excitedly in Spanish. When the torrent of words slowed, Murphy said, "Cigarettes?" The woman held out her hand palms upward and shook her head. Murphy repeated and mimed taking a cigarette from his mouth and blowing the smoke toward the dark ceiling.

"*Cigarillos!*" The old woman smiled even more, her face like a grinning walnut. She scooped up half a dozen packages from the shelf behind her and thrust them toward Murphy.

Murphy held out two American dollars to the old woman, but she waved them away, then held her hands behind her back, refusing to take the money. Murphy shrugged, smiled and half-bowed. "Thank you, Señora, thank you."

It was long after midnight. The air was motionless and still carried the heat of the day. The lights of USS Yorktown winked across the waters of the harbor. In the hotel dining room, Perrill, Ross and Kerr sat at the head table with Alicia and her father and Wiseman and the mayor and their wives. Behind them, the Mexican and American flags hung side-by-side on the wall. The other tables were empty now. The food had been plentiful, the speeches lengthy and extravagant in their praise of the men of the Yorktown, the toasts too numerous to count. Outside, there was music. The Yorktown's crew were on the street, dancing and celebrating with the townspeople.

Alicia and her father sat at the table holding hands and exchanging smiles. Kerr was deep in conversation with the mayor with Wiseman acting as interpreter. Perrill looked across at Alicia. Despite the joy of the occasion, there was an intense sadness in her eyes. Perrill turned quickly away and saw Ross watching him. He gave Ross a brief, embarrassed smile and bent to fumble with his pipe.

Yorktown shuddered again as she slammed into the seas. Standing at the head of the wardroom table, Perrill could feel the deck trembling beneath his feet as the ship's screws thrashed the sea at full revolutions. Spray flew past the scuttles in torrents. The men would be glad of some leave back in San Diego. Perhaps he'd get the rose arbor built at last. Kerr was on the bridge, but the rest of the Yorktown's officers sat around the table as instructed. Their eyes were on Perrill. He looked at them for a moment and then said, "I have sent my report to the Bureau of Navigation. I reported that we landed a party on Clipperton Island and found the survivors of the Mexican garrison. I reported that the commander of the garrison and all of the men on the island had taken a small boat in an attempt to secure help and had been lost at sea. I reported that we took on board all of the survivors and landed them in Salina Cruz. I also commended the generosity of the officers and crew in collecting money for the children." He looked around the table. "Are there any questions, gentlemen?"

Ensign Stump asked, "What about the rest of it, Sir?"

Perrill folded his arms and looked directly at Stump. "What about the rest of what, Mister Stump? I think the Bureau of Navigation has all the information it needs. Don't you?"

Stump returned the captain's gaze for a moment and then said, quietly, "Yes, Sir."

Perrill smiled and stood. "Very well gentlemen, that's the end of it. Let's get back to work. San Diego and shore leave in four days."

THE END

EPILOGUE

One out of every eight Mexicans, about two million people, died during the Revolution.

Porfirio Díaz shared luxurious exile in Paris with his finance minister, José Limantour and the murderous Ramón Corral. Corral died in 1912, officially of cancer but almost certainly of syphilis. Díaz died in 1915. His last sight of México had been of the grim fort San Juan de Ulúa in Veracruz, to which he had condemned so many thousands of his fellow citizens to end their lives in torment

Victoriano Huerta moved to the U.S. and plotted to install himself as head of a pro-German government in México during World War I. The plot was discovered and he died in an American jail in 1916.

The plentiful arms and ammunition provided by the U.S. to Carranza ensured that he prevailed over Zapata and Villa and so the land and wealth of México remained in the hands of a few families and of the foreign business interests that had profited from the invasion of Veracruz and the murder of Francisco Madero. México remained, throughout almost all of the twentieth century, an oligarchy with rule orchestrated through a single political party, a dictatorship in all but name.

Emiliano Zapata refused repeated bribes of *haciendas* and state governorships from Carranza and would not abandon his fight for the restoration of the *peones'* land. He was lured to a meeting and murdered by Carranza's henchmen in 1919.

Pancho Villa was bought off by Carranza with a twenty-five thousand acre *hacienda* in Durango and a government pension of five hundred thousand gold *pesos* a year. He was murdered in 1923.

Unwilling to initiate meaningful reform and unable to stem the ongoing tide of revolt led by Álvaro Obregón, Carranza attempted to escape to Veracruz and then Europe with a hundred and fifty million *pesos* in silver and gold stolen from the Treasury. He was double-crossed by one of his own generals and murdered in his sleep.

Álvaro Obregón became President of México and began a modest process of reform. He was assassinated in 1928.

In 1931, King Victor Emmanuel of Italy, who had agreed in 1909 to arbitrate the disputed sovereignty of Clipperton Island, belatedly announced his decision, awarding it to France. The King, who had become a puppet of Italy's Fascist dictator, Benito Mussolini, is widely believed to have awarded the island to the French in return for allowing Mussolini to use French Mediterranean ports for his warships.

In order to protect those he had rescued, Captain Perrill took the grave risk of court-martial during wartime, filing grossly incomplete and misleading logs and reports about the events on Clipperton Island including the false report made on his instructions by Lieutenant Kerr. In the ship's log, in Perrill's own report and in Kerr's report of the landing, there is no mention whatsoever of the finding of Álvarez's body. Two months later, rumors about the killing reached the Navy Department in Washington which became concerned that it might be blamed on one of the Yorktown's crew. Admiral Fullam was instructed to get answers from Perrill. In September 1917, Perrill sent an additional report to Fullam in which he reported the finding of Álvarez's body. But this report, like the others, was deceptive and designed to justify his original false reports while still protecting Alicia and Tirza

Perrill died in the San Diego Naval Hospital in 1962 at the age of eighty-seven. Among his effects was the photograph of Alicia Arnaud that appears on the cover of this book. The photograph was taken in Córdoba on January 9, 1918, six months after the rescue. She is wearing the pearl necklace Ramón brought back from Japan for her. The back of the portrait is inscribed, "Harlan Page Perrill, Gratitude and things remembered, Alicia R. de Arnaud."

Ángel Arnaud died shortly after being rescued; he never recovered from the malnutrition he had suffered on the island and was never able to walk.

Alicia Arnaud, her health permanently impaired, died of pneumonia in Jalapa, México on January 20, 1924, at the age of thirty-four. Félix Rovira died shortly after his daughter.

The surviving Arnaud children, Ramón, Alicia and Olga, were taken in and raised by Adela Reyes, Ramón's sister.

There is no known record of the fate of Rosalía Nava, Francisco and Antonio Irra or of Tirza Randon and Guadalupe Cardona.

Two survivors of the tragedy of Clipperton Island were known to be alive in the 1980s. Altagracia Quiroz, by then over eighty, had married the manager of the guano mining operation, Gustav Schultz, and was living in Acapulco. She had spent a lifetime haunted by the memory of what Victoriano Álvarez had done to her.

Ramón Arnaud Jr, still dapper in his seventies, vividly remembered his beautiful mother and his father, the immaculately uniformed man with the Kaiser mustaches. In March of 1980, he returned to Clipperton Island, taking a bottle of holy water with him to sprinkle over the island where his father and so many others had suffered and died.

The story of Clipperton Island is little known in modern-day México but in Orizaba, nestled in its fertile green valley beneath Pico de Orizaba not far from the lovely colonial church where they were married, a modest monument celebrates the lives of Capitán Ramón Arnaud and *"la heroína"*, Alicia Arnaud.

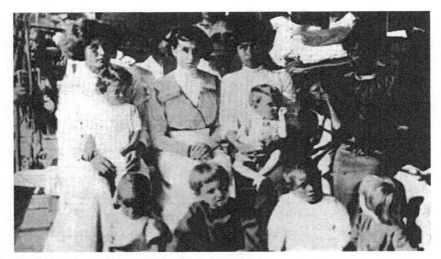

Survivors on board USS Yorktown. Back row left to right: Tirza Randon, Alicia Rovira de Arnaud, Altagracia (Alta) Quiroz, Antonio Irra, Rosalía Nava. On laps left to right: Guadalupe (Lupita) Cardona (Tirza's daughter), Ángel Arnaud. Bottom row left to right: Alicia (Ali) Arnaud, Ramón (Ramoncito) Arnaud, Francisco Irra, Lydia (Olga) Arnaud.

THE LOCKET

In 1944, a British Royal Air Force Catalina flying boat landed on Clipperton's lagoon. The plane had been sent to determine if the island would make a suitable stop for flying boats on a wartime route between Australia and the United States. One night, after dinner around the camp fire, the expedition leader, a World War I fighter pilot, went for a stroll through the nearby coconut grove. He saw something metallic twinkling in the light from his flashlight. It was a woman's locket. In his book about the expedition he led to Clipperton Island, Captain P.G. Taylor described his experience.

He pried open the locket and "found the miniatures of a man and a young woman looking out to me with frank eyes from a beautiful and intelligent face." He held the locket in his hand and described an almost mystical experience of hearing music playing and then seeing a couple strolling together, the young woman singing in a high clear voice. He walked back to where he had found the locket, scooped a hole in the sand and buried it.

Excerpt from Forgotten Island, P.G. Taylor, The Shakespeare Head, Sydney 1948.

ABOUT THE AUTHOR

John Watts

John Watts was a magazine writer, columnist and editor for thirty years before building a schooner and sailing away. His travels took him to Mexico where he researched the true events upon which Abandoned is based.

Printed in Great Britain
by Amazon

17351214R00200